Praise for the works of Kat Jackson

In Bloom

In Bloom delves into profound themes with a level of artistry that deserves commendation. Jackson's narrative skillfully unravels the intricacies of the heart, emphasizing its enduring capacity for hope and resilience. The thoughtful construction of this narrative is marked by compassionate grace. It is raw, tender and remarkable in every way.

-Women Using Words

All the emotions the author explores are very powerful, full of grief and regret, but I never felt overwhelmed. The author gives a reader two women who are finally beginning to feel a need for some kind of relationship after years of emotional pain, making the story about that and not the falling happily into bed as the end goal. There is understated complexity in the plot and an often gorgeously crafted prose that drew me in.

-The Lesbian Review

The Missing Piece

…What I enjoy most about Kat Jackson's writing is she doesn't feel the need to follow the formula. Her characters are just as unconventional as their creator. Her writing is intelligent, and her characters show tremendous growth as the novel progresses. Jackson is a unique voice in the sapphic community and one who seems to improve with every book.

-Laura G., *NetGalley*

Another good read by Kat Jackson! She's becoming one of my favourite authors and I certainly look forward to future releases. I love her writing style, her enjoyable characters that always have that chemistry needed from the onset and her great storylines that capture you from the start.

-Jo R., *NetGalley*

Golden Hour

Kat Jackson has written another excellent book! If you've not already, check some of her other books out. *Golden Hour* is no exception, I love her writing style and her books have "drawn" me in.

-Jo R., NetGalley

Rapidly becoming one of my favourite lesbian authors, she writes intelligent books that explore more than just a romance.

-Claire E., NetGalley

I am coming to find that I really love books by Kat Jackson, she manages to pull me in on an emotional level and I enjoyed the pairing between Lina and Regan very much. The way Lina's PTSD was handled and described gave the book more depth than the average romance novel and when it's done in the way Jackson does it, it's very much lifting the book to a next level. *Golden Hour* can be read as a standalone, yet Lina was first introduced in an earlier book (*Across the Hall*) and that couple has a role in this one as Lina's best friends. Highly recommended!

-Dominique V., NetGalley

The Roads Left Behind Us

5 star, 5 star, 5 star...did I like this story...yes! The writing is beautifully filled with so much emotion and intelligent dialogue, I was sad when it ended. The environment is academia which makes the content of many conversations slightly elevated over other romance novels. Yet very understandable and warm. The characters are real, interesting, and distinct. I liked all of them. I highly recommend this story.

-Cheryl S., NetGalley

That was some marvelous writing; the vocabulary alone was spellbinding. The two MCs and every single supporting character are so well fleshed out that you feel as if you stepped into a room full of your friends and are catching up on all the gossip. The "will they, won't they" makes quite a pull at your heartstrings, but the end result makes the shipwreck all the more survivable. Their love story is charming, it's refreshing, it's as stormy as it is placid, and you will find yourself smiling hard at the MCs' antics throughout. A play at the Student/Professor fantasy, but you'll find these two are on equal footing in the PhD program where a delicious age-gap and big, beautiful brains war to find shelter.

-Alice G., *NetGalley*

Across the Hall

I loved Kat Jackson's first book, *Begin Again*, and I've been not-very-patiently awaiting the release of her second. I was not in any way disappointed! If you're looking for a layered tale of wonderfully flawed people, look no further. What enchanted me so much about *Begin Again*, and what runs through *Across the Hall* is one of the things that makes humans so interesting is that we are not perfect.

Mallory and Caitlin are complex characters with great depth, who I alternately wanted to hug and shake. Their stories are carefully crafted, and I am so thrilled to hear that Lina is getting her own book!

-Orlando J., *NetGalley*

Kat Jackson's *Begin Again* was an incredible debut and she became my favorite new author of 2020. Needless to say I was really looking forward to this sophomore effort. It didn't disappoint.

It's a workplace romance featuring two mains with a lot of baggage to bring to a fledging relationship. This story is really told in third person from Caitlin's POV, so we don't really know what's going on in Mallory's head. I really enjoyed following the ups and downs of the relationship and it was hard to tell where it was going. I started reading and next thing I knew, I was finished. That's what I love about a book.

-Karen R., *NetGalley*

Begin Again

Begin Again is one of the most beautiful, heartrending, and thought-provoking books I've read. Kat Jackson manages the rare feat of making a lesfic novel that toys with infidelity meaningful and elegant. While this all might sound a bit grim, it does have plenty of lighthearted moments too.

-Orlando J., *NetGalley*

Begin Again is one of the most thought-provoking, honest, emotional and heartrending books I've ever read. How the author managed to get the real, raw emotions (that I could believe and feel) down on paper and into words is amazing. If you read the blurb you will know, sort of what this story is about. But it's much more than that. As other reviewers have stated, it's not a comfy read but was totally riveting. I read it in a day, I just couldn't put it down. Definitely one of the best books I've read and if I could give it more stars I would for sure! Superbly written. Totally recommend.

-Anja S., *NetGalley*

Pages from the Book of Broken Dreams

KAT JACKSON

Other Bella Books by Kat Jackson

Begin Again
Across the Hall
The Roads Left Behind Us
Golden Hour
In Bloom
The Missing Piece

About the Author

Kat Jackson is a collector of feelings, words, and typewriters. She works in education and lives in Pennsylvania, where she enjoys all four seasons in the span of a single week. Kat's been consumed with words and language for essentially her whole life, and continues to spend entirely too much time overthinking anything that's ever been said to her (this is a joke, kind of, but not completely). Running is her #1 coping mechanism followed closely by sitting in the sun with a good book and/or losing herself in a true crime podcast. Contrary to popular belief, Kat does (somewhat) believe in the potential of happily ever after. Most days, anyway.

Pages from the Book of Broken Dreams

KAT JACKSON

BELLA
BOOKS

2024

Bella Books, Inc.
P.O. Box 10543
Tallahassee, FL 32302

First Edition - 2024

Editor: Alissa McGowan
Cover Designer: Melodie Pond

ISBN: 978-1-64247-534-0

PUBLISHER'S NOTE

Acknowledgements

First and foremost, thank you to everyone at Bella for providing the space and opportunity for writers like me to bring their dream stories to life. I am forever grateful to be in the ranks of and supported by such incredible women.

Alissa: Thank you for keeping me, a former English teacher, humble (I'm laughing as I type that). I feel like my commas were better this time around, yeah? Next time, I promise I'll use more pronouns. (Truly, thank you for all the time and clean-up you give me and my rambling words.)

My darling Hot Cheetos. Where do I even begin? Your love, support, and incomparable humor keeps me afloat, anchoring me to our incredible (and deeply funny) friendship. I love you so, so much, even when I go hide in my hotel room for an hour or execute a flawless Irish Goodbye.

KV: Your thoughtful feedback and spot-on commentary combined with your love for Emma & Aubrey kept me going while writing this book. I'm very sorry I was rude to Aubrey, but it was all for the sake of plot, and I think we can agree I gave her a happy ending.

And to Borders Bookstores, now defunct but once my primary partner in a love-hate relationship. Thanks for the memories and the experiences, and an extra thanks for how I'll never forget the way a lack of caffeine can bring out the worst in customers. As a coffee-hating college student who was studying to be an English teacher but hired to be a barista, your hiring practices still confound me. Anyway, this book couldn't exist without you.

Dedication

For those of us who have worked in bookstores and cursed every moment of it, then found ourselves working elsewhere…only to wish, nearly every day, that we could go work in the bookstore again.

And for young love and all that comes with it: questions, surprise, intensity, and the way it consumes us. There's simply nothing like it.

CHAPTER ONE

A warm cloud of sugary air poofed against Emma's face as she pushed into the bakery. Despite the fully blasting heat inside the small but cozy space, she pulled her jacket tighter around her, shivering from the chill that lingered from her walk downtown. January in New England was never shy, but she couldn't remember ever feeling quite this cold before.

With a shiver—both from the lingering cold and the mix of emotions running through her—Emma took a few tentative steps toward the display case. Her mouth watered instinctively as she inhaled. The scent in the air promised something doughy and heavy on cinnamon coming from an oven tucked out of sight. She tracked her eyes over the colorful items in the case, certain that none of them could provide such an intense aroma. She cocked her head, surprised to see what looked like individual strawberry cobblers. That, she knew for certain, wasn't your average winter sweet treat. As she calculated the expenses of importing fresh strawberries—because any good baker in their right mind would always prefer to use fresh fruits—she missed the door opening and closing behind her.

"You in line, hun?"

Emma jumped back, startled by the gruff voice that held a rasp of Massachusetts. "No, no," she said quickly, gesturing toward the case. "Not really, I mean. I'm just looking. For now."

The elderly man, clearly unfazed by her unclear response, shrugged as he moved past her and rapped the handle of his cane on the counter. "Ya gotta make a little noise around here or ya never get served."

"Coming!" a voice called from the back. "One minute, sorry!"

Emma grinned at the man, who looked at her with an expression that said "Told ya so." She appreciated his silence as she resumed her perusal of the display case. She wasn't feeling up to small talk, nor was she in a rush. In fact, Emma had no concept of "rush" at present. She was far more into the dilly-dally stage of life, loath as she was to admit it. At times like this, however, it paid off. She surreptitiously eyed the man, who was growing more and more annoyed with the lack of prompt service.

He muttered something under his breath just as the vibrant aqua-colored door swung open. A woman in her early thirties, if Emma had to guess (and she didn't like guessing women's ages but usually couldn't help herself), wiped her hands on the front of her apron as she approached the counter.

"Sam!" The woman beamed at the elderly man, who rapped his cane once more then broke into a grin. "I thought you and Mary had already left for Florida."

In a blink, the annoyance vanished from the man's face, replaced by a genuine smile. "Nah, got a few more days before we get outta here. The grandkids have all their big sports events and…"

Emma let the conversation dissolve into the background as she focused her attention on a single chocolate cupcake sitting in the case. The sign declared it to be "Devilishly Dark and Dreamy," which sounded appetizing but gave little information about what the consumer would actually be biting into. She scrunched her nose as she peered closer. Probably a dark chocolate cake, which was one of Emma's top five favorite flavors, and while the icing was almost equally as dark as the cake, it also had little white flecks interspersed throughout its luscious swirls. Buttercream, most likely, exposing itself with the tell-tale sign of the butter having been too cold when it was mixed with the powdered sugar.

"Rookie mistake," Emma said under her breath. She straightened and sucked her gasp in when she came face-to-face with the baker.

"Welcome to Dough Mama," the woman said. She smiled easily as she rested her forearms on the top of the case. "First time here?"

Dough Mama. Emma loved it and hated it—only because she hadn't come up with it herself. Not that that mattered anymore.

"Yup!" She swallowed hard, urging the gasp-turned-spiky-air-bubble down instead of out. "Everything looks great."

"Thanks." This time, a tone of weariness crept into the woman's voice. "We're a little shorthanded. I know some steps are getting missed and I hate to see it, but…" She shrugged. "Any chance you came in to see about the job?"

Consumed with fireworks of embarrassment, Emma could only shake her head. The gesture was a lie, of course. The bright yellow "HELP WANTED" sign *had* beckoned her in, but only because she'd somehow missed any clues about Dough Mama being a bakery. She'd assumed it was a pizza place…Well, assumed or convinced herself, she wasn't sure.

And while she did need a job, working here would only remind her of all the failures she was trying to run from. Emma shook her head again as she fumbled for the right words. "I—I'm not the right person."

A silence hung over the two women. After several thick seconds of Emma's burning discomfort, the baker spoke.

"That's not the response I was expecting," she said, each word slow and purposeful, as though she knew anything less measured and gentle would send Emma scampering out the door. "Especially since you outed yourself with that comment about the icing, which is obviously correct. So I'm thinking maybe you *are* the right person."

"I'm not!" Emma tried to grin after the words sprung from her mouth. "But could I please have that devilish cupcake and one of the strawberry cobblers? To go? Please?" Her eyes swept over the case once more because there was no way she was going to make eye contact with the woman standing across from her. "Oh, and one of the Earl Gray scones. Please."

"Of course." The baker busied herself with gathering the items and packing them carefully—lovingly, if Emma were being honest—into a pale purple box.

The two met again at the register and the silence was torture. Emma didn't do well with silence in general but this? This would not do.

"I'm sorry," she said, the words a tumbling rush. "I feel like I was rude and trust me, I am not a rude person. I—"

"The butter was too cold."

Emma felt her shoulders drop an inch from their clenched, heightened state. "The butter was too cold," she echoed.

The woman pressed her palms against the counter and studied Emma. "I have a feeling you *are* the right person for the job, but maybe now isn't the right time. I'm Viv," she said, holding out a hand that was still covered with a film of powdered sugar. "Don't be a stranger."

Emma shook Viv's hand, then looked down at the sparkle of sugar that had transferred to her own hand. She smiled despite herself, despite the growing bundle of sadness twining in the pit of her belly.

"Emma," she said, picking up the box and giving Viv her first real smile. "And thank you."

Viv only nodded as Emma turned and walked toward the door. She stepped outside and let the cold seep into her bones, shivering as it effortlessly iced over any lingering warmth from the bakery, the baker, and the baked goods.

Oh, but the baked goods. Ten minutes later, Emma was wiping crumbs from the corners of her mouth. That strawberry cobbler had lured her in with a siren's song not twenty paces from the bakery's door. After giving it an inspection only a practiced eye could deliver, Emma slid the pastry out of the box and took a bite. She'd nearly moaned into the perfect ratio of fruit and dough. Just from one bite, she could tell there was something unique about the flavor profile, but she wasn't going to figure it out while standing on the corner of Main and Ivy in downtown Chestnut Hill, New Hampshire—especially when the winter clouds were slowly converging in a way that threatened some kind of frigid precipitation.

So, though it pained her to do so, Emma gently placed the cobbler back in the box. As she removed her hand, the side of her pinkie finger grazed the crumbly scone and, well, who was she to deny lust at first touch? A couple minutes later, more bites than steps taken, the scone had vanished. It wasn't the best she'd ever had—an execution problem, one she thought could be easily solved by adjusting the temperature of the butter—but that flavor profile was tugging at her, making her question everything she knew about combining ingredients.

A smile lifted and fell on Emma's face as she continued walking. She didn't want to think about Dough Mama, and she really didn't want to think about throwing ingredients together and watching them rise into beautiful, dare she say supple, baked goods. Nope, she would not be returning to Dough Mama anytime soon.

"That part of your life is over," she said under her breath as she continued down Main Street. She tried to push thoughts of baking out of her head, focusing instead on the cobbled sidewalks under her feet. She had no real destination in mind, but the whole "get a job" thing hung over her head, a thicker cloud than the real ones overhead, which were suddenly looking a lot heavier.

Emma scanned the storefronts as she walked, hoping a sign would jump out into her path. She passed a bar and hesitated, wondering if she could pull off being a bartender. More likely than not, she wouldn't even be allowed to enter the building: Though she had turned twenty-one right before Thanksgiving, she hadn't grown past the 5'2" of her high school growth spurt. Add that to what her mom referred to as her "eternal youthful glow," which was weird because as far as Emma was concerned, she was still a youth—anyway, she knew the explosion of freckles across her face didn't add any mature years to whatever people first assumed her age to be when they met her.

So, okay. No bartending for the time being. A single icy drop hit her square on top of the head and she picked up the pace as she crossed Finch Avenue. She tried to resist the urge to look down Finch to where it intersected with Penn Street. There, Pennbrook University began its sprawl over numerous blocks, its old brick buildings stoic and grand. Just before she stepped onto the curb, Emma stole a glance down the street and blinked in the face of her future. Viv's words echoed in her head: "Maybe now isn't the right time."

Just as the chilly drops picked up speed, Emma found herself standing in front of a bold red sign that spelled out Cornerstone

Books in black font, all caps. She tilted her head, appreciating, as always, the literal use of the location to name the store. If she walked inside and discovered that old, faithful Cornerstone, a Chestnut Hill staple, had lost its charm in order to appeal to the modern masses, Emma was going to be sorely disappointed...Even if she didn't exactly enjoy reading. Or books in general.

Emma squealed as a rogue pellet of sleet dropped right down the back of her neck. Not exactly the sign she was looking for, but a moment later, she was standing in the entryway of Cornerstone Books, inhaling that unmistakable, soothing scent of paper, coffee, and an ever-present hint of vanilla.

Not daring to move further into the store, she turned her head to take in the familiar surroundings. Relief swept through her. It didn't look like anything had changed since she'd last set foot in Cornerstone (she wasn't sure when that was, but estimated it was before graduating from high school).

From where she stood, Emma could see the extensive and precisely organized section of magazines. It was Cornerstone's feature, the part of the store that always had at least six people browsing about. Emma smirked, remembering a very specific section that featured "art" magazines. In reality, they were lightly pornographic, which was why that area often collected adolescent boys.

Just beyond the magazine section, the modest café was still tucked neatly into the corner and commandeering the best windows in the store. Emma felt a flutter in her chest as she gazed over the lovingly worn tables and chairs, none of which matched, holding cups of coffee and piles of books. She'd spent countless hours doing homework at those tables, scrunching her nose at whatever elaborate caffeinated drink her friends bought and then barely drank because, well, teenagers.

Emma tilted her head as she swept her gaze past the café and toward the back of the store. Okay, *that* was different. It seemed longer, somehow. Definitely more bookshelves, but it didn't look crowded or tightly smashed together. She looked to her left, then, and appraised the front end of the store: the greeting card section, the pens and journals section, and the random small gift section, all butting up against the register area.

Assured that the world inside Cornerstone Books hadn't changed too much, Emma stepped forward and made her way through the store. With no particular destination in mind, she was free to walk slowly, and as she did, her guard dropped lower and lower. There was a wholesomeness to Cornerstone, a comfort that Emma didn't remember feeling on her previous visits. Maybe it was nostalgia creeping in, but the non-book-lover in her was suddenly feeling very Belle. She giggled to herself, imagining breaking into song and twirling from the finance section to the self-help section, a yellow dress hugging her body, the skirt swirling with each spin of her hips. Her giggle was cut short at the unpleasant thought of a beastly human being holding her captive between the stacks.

Emma cleared her throat and walked with more of a purpose. She was quite aware that life was not a Disney movie. Besides, she was far more Merida than Belle. Emma brushed her hair from her face. Okay, maybe just in the looks department. And in resourcefulness, but that was mostly due to Emma's Scorpio nature. They were also both a bit stubborn, at least in the sense that Emma *really* loved being right, and—

"No, sorry, but I'm out."

"Wait! We can work something out. I know we can."

Lured by the tiny explosion of drama, Emma took tentative steps toward the bulging shelf in front of her. She made sure to stay out of sight as she settled in to eavesdrop.

"There's nothing to work out." The person—a woman, Emma thought—sighed heavily. "It's too much with school. I have to prioritize."

"Okay, I understand that." Another woman, with a voice that was both scratchy and sweet. A little nasally, too, like she was battling a cold. "How about we cut your hours? We can do that. Just give me a number you're comfortable working."

"Zero."

The answer came without hesitation or pause, and Emma fought back a laugh.

"Oh. Okay. Um—"

"Sadie, I'm sorry." There was a rustling noise. "Here. Tell Genesis I'm sorry, too."

Footsteps moved away from the other side of the shelf. A little sigh that sounded more like an exasperated, and very tired, growl crawled through the sudden silence. Emma didn't dare move. She stood there for what felt like ten minutes but couldn't have been more than two. Just as she was summoning up the nerve to walk away, she caught, out of the corner of her eye, rapid movement in the form of a very tall person speeding in her direction.

"Don't even tell me," the person said as they sped past Emma and stopped on the other side of the shelf. The young adult section, if Emma remembered correctly. "She quit."

"I tried to get her to cut her hours instead."

"Great. Fucking great." A thud.

"Hey! Don't kick my books."

"I'll stop kicking your books when you stop hiring people who don't stay for more than a month."

"I thought she had potential," the woman said, her voice slightly muffled. Emma pictured her squatting down to console the book the other person had kicked.

"She didn't, Sadie. I knew that on day two. So can I *please* do the hiring next time?"

"You act like there's a pile of applications and résumés waiting for us to go through," Sadie said. She sounded tired but not unhappy. "And no, but you can be a part of the interview."

"Finally," her coworker grumbled. "There's gotta be at least one or two apps we haven't—"

With a terrible punch of inspiration and a misdirected need to make others happy, Emma flew around the corner of the shelf, coming face-to-face with a tall Latinx woman and a—whoa.

"The fuck?" the Latinx woman said, looking from Emma to Sadie. "Have you been hiding your child in the general fiction section?"

The other woman was holding her hand over her mouth, dark-green eyes wide with surprise. Or shock. Or something in between.

Emma felt her mouth open and close. She had no idea what to say; it wasn't every day you came face-to-face with your doppelganger.

Finally, words popped out: "You could hire me."

"Yes!" Sadie said, her tone joyful. She clapped a few times and Emma got a good look at the freckles scattered across her nose and cheeks, darker than the ones on Emma's face but nearly exact in their placement. "And also, oh my God. Are we related?"

"She literally looks like your child."

Sadie gazed at Emma in wonder. "She really does. And yes! Of course, yes. You're hired."

The other woman groaned. "Sadie, you cannot hire someone on the spot." She turned to Emma. "We'll take you up front and you can fill out an application."

It was then that Emma registered the apron the Latinx woman was wearing. Confusion nudged her, but she ignored it.

"Great," she said. "I can start whenever you need me."

"Tomorrow!" Sadie exclaimed.

"No, not tomorrow. But soon. After we interview you," the other woman said sternly, shooting eye daggers at Sadie. "I'm Genesis, by the way. The café manager."

"Oh," Emma said, but it came out like a squeak. The apron suddenly made a lot more sense. The café? Coffee? She'd never drank a sip in her life.

"Come on," Sadie said, taking Emma by the arm. "Let's go find an application for you."

And that was how, not fifteen minutes later, Emma found herself walking back to her car through sleet and snow, her mind in knots over the interview she would attend in two days. An interview for a position in the café at Cornerstone, despite the fact that she knew even less about coffee than she knew about books.

CHAPTER TWO

The paper cut on Aubrey Glass's right middle finger was throbbing. It was the result of talking to a coworker while unpacking a box of "randoms," the kind of box that should have been dumped directly at the front of the store for a cashier to empty out and place during a lull in customers. Had that happened, Aubrey wouldn't have missed the packing slip and its unnaturally sharp edges. Edges that wasted no time in slicing the tender skin butting up beneath Aubrey's very short nails.

She pressed her pulsing finger against her leg, hoping that would ease the annoying pain. Aubrey was proud of the fact that she rarely suffered from paper cuts; working with books all day had a way of subjecting even the most careful hands to tiny wounds. But Aubrey wasn't careful, per se—no, that wasn't a word on her personality chart, nor was it a term anyone in her life would use to describe her. Especially lately. But careful or not, Aubrey wasn't clumsy, and she prided herself on her deft hands.

A lump rose unexpectedly in her throat. Aubrey pressed her cut finger against it. Wound to wound, the pressure eased, and while she knew the lump would bob around all day, it wasn't something she could deal with until much later.

Right. Aubrey nodded. Time to focus on things she could control, such as the soundtrack for the day.

It was a perilous task, one Sadie had entrusted her with a few months ago. She'd had to earn her way to the honor, and once achieved, she took it very seriously. Every morning, because Aubrey was The Opening Bookseller, she mounted the Hub, which was just a slightly raised desk area in the middle of the store, and pulled out the old iPhone that held a variety of music streaming apps *and* Sadie's top-secret collection in the app that used to be something called iTunes. Now it was just "Music," and although Sadie had explained the progression of the app countless times, Aubrey still didn't understand. MP3s? LimeWire? Uploading music? Burning discs? So much effort just to listen to the songs you wanted to hear. Once, Sadie had given her a fifteen-minute introductory course to the ancient CD player that still sat, dusty and stoic, on a shelf under the counter. Aubrey was fascinated by the mechanics of it but horrified when Sadie went on and on about the timing and how—insert gasp—sometimes the music would just *stop*.

There was no stopping in Aubrey's playlists. The peril entered when she began to understand the way music affects moods—and not those of the customers, but rather those of the employees. Managing a store full of working emotions that could be triggered or glimmered by any unsuspecting chorus or guitar riff was a mighty task. Aubrey wasn't sure she was built for such a feat, but she persevered.

"I can't believe how cold it is out there." Sadie, hands tucked deep in the pockets of her jeans, approached the Hub. She wasn't normally in so early, but since she'd shifted from manager to co-owner who still acted as manager, her presence at the store was nearly constant.

So much for Aubrey's alone time. She side-eyed Sadie, pausing before she stated the obvious. "It's January, you know."

"Believe me, I know." Sadie leaned against the counter. Her gaze roamed around the store, never settling anywhere for more than a blink. "I've never been so happy for a holiday season to end."

Aubrey had to agree. Though her experience working retail during the holiday season was limited to the season that had just ended and the one the year prior, the past two months had felt like the longest of her life. Her days were a steady beat of: get up, go to work, come home, go to bed. She'd worked ridiculously long hours, never complaining about it because it kept her mind off all the things her mind was trying like crazy to focus on. The cramp in her social life wasn't a big deal either, since she didn't exactly *have* a social life at home here in Chestnut Hill. Not like the one she used to have in high school, anyway.

Aubrey tuned back in to hear Sadie going on and on about the store's finances, something Aubrey had nothing to do with and no interest in—aside from the whole needing the store to be successful so she would continue to get paid thing. She let Sadie chatter on as she scrolled through the old phone, searching for the playlist that would best match her own mood: a little bit despondent, and a little bit ready for a fight. Theoretically, of course.

"Bet you're happy to be done with the holiday playlists. What's on the menu for today?" Sadie nudged her elbow into Aubrey's side then glanced down at the phone and groaned. "Again?"

"Again," Aubrey said, hitting play on Volcano Girls, the playlist she'd spent a concerning amount of time creating. It was packed with '90s alt-rock music, all featuring female singers.

"Isn't this a little intense for seven a.m.?" Sadie said, raising her voice over the opening bars of Björk's "Army of Me."

It was, but Aubrey wasn't about to let Sadie know that. "It's just the first song," she said instead. "A little something to wake you up."

"I'm plenty awake!" Sadie yelled as she walked away from the Hub, off to do some managing or owning stuff.

Alone again, or at least kind of, Aubrey closed her eyes briefly as she mentally ran down her morning must-dos. She had a little under two hours before the store opened, which meant the opening barista would show up in about an hour. She couldn't remember who was opening; it seemed like it was someone different every other week. Not her problem. Then she realized what day it was and her eyes popped open.

"How the hell did you forget that?" she mumbled to herself, rushing off the Hub and toward the stock room. Thursday was magazine day, Aubrey's favorite day.

Sure enough, six boxes sat waiting for her. The bottoms of her Birkenstock clogs scuffed the cement floor as she moved the boxes onto a dolly. As Aubrey wheeled the dolly into the store, she paused in the self-help section (an area Sadie was working on rebranding) to pull the bottom of her jeans out from between her heel and her shoe. The battle between jeans and footwear would wage all day long—the consequence of Aubrey wearing midrise baggy jeans with her favorite delicately beat-up, dark-brown Boston clogs.

The magazine section was a feature of Cornerstone. It was, in a word, huge. The magazines that Sadie tracked down and ordered... Aubrey had no idea how she even knew such magazines existed. Want to read all about private islands? There's a magazine for that. Interested in nothing but sheep? Yup, got that too. Fascinated by fashion dolls? Cornerstone is prepared to meet your creepy doll needs. Love potatoes? Not just one, but *three* magazines were wholly devoted to spud farming and the overall industry.

Aside from the quirkier options, there were plenty of magazines for standard interests, like health and wellness, architecture, music, and so on. Aubrey had spent an impressive amount of time learning and memorizing the section, so while a six-box task of removing and replacing looked daunting, she knew she'd have it done in less than an hour.

A whoosh of frigid air accompanied by a growled "Don't talk to me yet" swept past Aubrey while she was elbow-deep in the pottery magazines. She looked up in time to see Genesis, dark hair wild but somehow flawless, stomping past the magazines. Well, that answered her question about the opening barista. Looked like another one had quit, leaving Genesis—a dedicated night owl who probably had slept from three a.m. to six a.m.—to pick up the morning slack.

Just thinking about Genesis's sleep schedule made Aubrey yawn. She didn't love getting up early, but she did love having the store to herself (most of the time) for a little while each morning. There was a healing silence among the stacks of books—unspoken stories and hushed tales—that permeated the store first thing in the morning. And Aubrey, a book lover from the time she could read the word "the," loved nothing more than to be surrounded by pages holding others' words.

But only when they were silent.

"Aubrey?"

Aubrey popped her head up and scanned the area. "Over here," she said, spotting Sadie near the registers.

"Oh right, magazine day." Sadie walked over and picked up a shiny new issue from the box. "Ooh, the winter edition of the miniature toys magazine is out!"

See? Something for everyone.

"I hate to ask you this," Sadie said, her voice lovely and sweet. That same voice had hired Aubrey, had snuck into her dreams and encouraged a tiny little crush that Aubrey had eventually talked herself out of. But there would always be something about Sadie that made her swoon a little, especially when she turned on her "I'm going to ask you to do something and I know you're going to hate it, but you love me, so…" voice.

"The café," Aubrey stated, refusing to make it into a question. At Sadie's confused expression, she added, "I saw Genesis come in a couple minutes ago. And I know what that means."

"We're interviewing someone tomorrow," Sadie said hurriedly. "But we get that weird Thursday morning rush sometimes."

"I'll stay close by."

Sadie grinned, tossing her copper hair over her shoulder. A wave of citrusy perfume flew from the action, hitting Aubrey square in the face. She held her breath. Better to kill off a few brain cells than fall back down the unrequited wishing well of harboring feelings for Sadie.

"You're the absolute best, Aubrey Glass." Sadie winked before walking away, a pep in her step that wasn't there when she'd approached.

Once she was gone, Aubrey breathed slowly, hoping the effervescent scent was gone. Nope. Her shallow inhale filled her senses with Sadie. Aubrey shook her head, reminding herself of all the reasons it would never, *could* never, happen.

Never mind the whole boss-employee thing, nor the fact that Sadie was very close-mouthed about dating: It was the fact that Aubrey was twenty-four and Sadie was at least thirteen years her senior that was the ultimate nail in the coffin.

But, Aubrey reminded herself as she resumed her magazine task, a little daydreaming never hurt anyone.

CHAPTER THREE

As yet another strand of hair escaped her haphazard ponytail and grazed her cheek, creating that uncomfortable almost-tickling sensation, Emma grimaced and tilted her head back, shaking with the fury of a dog with rain on its coat. The strands bounced joyfully, flying away only to swing back and stick firmly to her cheeks. She regretted—again—not taking the time to make a cleaner, tighter ponytail. Or put on a hat. Or even tie on a bandana.

There was also the fact that she'd let her hair grow so long that it seemed to have developed a mind of its own. A mind that refused to be contained by any hair elastic.

She gazed down at her hands, fingers coated in flour and butter that hadn't yet combined the way she wanted it to. The dough was sticky and she needed more flour, which was a slightly more pressing task than corralling the hair that kept slipping against her cheeks.

A quick survey of the counter confirmed that she had already put the flour away (a rookie mistake; she was more out of practice than she'd realized) and she hadn't remembered to pull off a single emergency paper towel, meant to save her face and hair in a moment just like this. Emma shrugged. Ambivalence wasn't something she'd ever excelled at, and as her phone transitioned from early Dave Matthews Band into earlier Tori Amos, any lingering sense of carefree attitude evanesced from Emma's entire being.

"Not now," she whispered into the empty kitchen.

It turned out the music was the most pressing issue. Not removing her hands from the dough, Emma contorted her body until she was face-to-face with her phone screen. In an act honed through rounds of trial and error, Emma touched the tip of her nose to the screen, lighting it up. A short, steadying inhale later, she tapped again, breathing a sigh of relief when Tori was cut off midlyric and replaced with the opening notes of a song she couldn't place. But it definitely wasn't Tori singing about breaking silver linings.

Content with the unidentifiable music, Emma got lost in the art of perfecting little piles of dough into neat, straight-lined triangles. Her mind cleared, something she'd been yearning for, for weeks if not months, and she focused on the precise movements of her fingertips. Using a knife had always felt like a copout to her. Sure, it was faster and mostly guaranteed to make nice lines, but Emma preferred the hands-on shape-making process…even if it meant her hair remained plastered to her cheeks and forehead.

As she moved to the second-to-last blob of scone dough, she was snapped from her reverie by the abrupt return of silence, which was quickly interrupted by the most familiar voice in Emma's world.

"Stress baking already? You couldn't even unpack first?"

"No," Emma said. "And no."

Liam jerked a thumb over his shoulder to the perfectly stacked pile of moving boxes in the corner of the dining room. "Shouldn't those at least be in your room?"

"They will be." She avoided his eyes, looking from the nearly formed scones on the counter to the clock over the stove. "Shouldn't you be at work?" she countered weakly.

"Emma." Liam leaned his elbows on the counter, making sure to avoid the errant piles and streaks of flour. "It's been a week. No, more than a week." He looked confused as he mentally added the days. "Wait, when did you come home?"

"For someone who works with numbers all day, you kinda suck with basic math."

"Well, little sister, at least *I* have a job and can contribute to this household, the very household that you unceremoniously crashed."

Emma held up a single flour-covered finger. "After today, I shall have a job."

"Something more legit than selling these scones on the street, I hope."

"First of all," Emma said, glaring at her brother, "I've never done that. Secondly, no. It has nothing to do with scones." The image of Dough Mama's display case pressed into her mind, uninvited, tempting her to come back and apply for the job she couldn't take because she'd sworn off baking.

She looked back at the line of scones in front of her and cringed. So much for that.

"Again, why are you home in the middle of the day?" she asked, hoping to pull the attention off herself. "Did you get fired?"

Liam's finger came a little too close to the dough and Emma slapped it away. "I came home for lunch, if you must know. What's all the weird flecks in there?"

"Earl Grey tea," Emma said. "I know, it looks kinda gross. I'm hoping it's less obvious once they're baked."

When Liam didn't come back with a trademark retort, Emma looked up at him. She took a step back when she registered the look of concern on his face. That look was definitely not a trademark expression, especially when he aimed it at her.

"What?" she asked, aghast and suddenly filled with a worry that had nothing true to cling to. "What's wrong?"

"Look, Em, if you're not happy staying with me, I get it. I'm sure Mom and Dad wouldn't mind—"

"That's not it," she said, interrupting before he could finish presenting that terrible idea. "It's just…I'm just adjusting. It's a lot, you know? Coming home, getting settled." She shook her head. As much as they needed to have this conversation, she couldn't start it now—not with her interview hanging on the horizon, a mere hour away. "And I do not want to live—*stay* with Mom and Dad. I'm twenty-one. I can't go back under their roof."

Liam cocked a bushy eyebrow at her. In the wild ways of DNA, brother and sister looked almost nothing alike; Liam favored their mom's not-so-Irish looks, with rich brown hair that he kept meticulously cut in a very metrosexual way, and blue-green eyes rimmed with long, fluttery lashes Emma herself would kill for. But he'd also inherited their grandfather's super thick eyebrows, one thing Emma would certainly not kill for.

Standing side by side, Liam towering over Emma by a solid ten inches, it was difficult to find any similarities between the two. Until they smiled, that is, and the way their eyes scrunched just so as the corners of their mouths lifted—it was the Gallagher special, according to their dad, who had the same exact smile.

"Am I missing something here?" Liam asked, his brow still arched—a trick he'd mastered as a kid and refused to teach her. "Are you sneaking out after you go to bed at, like, nine o'clock and hitting the bars and getting wild? Coming home at four a.m. missing a shoe and your dignity?"

The thought amused them both, and Emma shook her head through her laughter. "Hardly. I just need a little independence. Staying with them would make me feel like a kid again." She nudged the last of the scones onto the baking sheet. "These need to chill in the fridge. Don't touch them."

"Wouldn't dream of it. So where's this mysterious interview?"

With her back to Liam, she slid the scones into the refrigerator. "Cornerstone."

Liam coughed out a laugh. "Seriously?"

"Seriously. They have an opening."

"They always do." Liam shrugged when Emma shot him a look over her shoulder. "A bookstore in a college town, Em. Constant turnover."

"I guess." She closed the refrigerator door and turned to her brother, crossing her arms over her chest. "Whatever, it works to my advantage."

"Okay, but a bookstore? When was the last time you read a book? Wait, do you even know what a book looks like?"

Emma mustered her best haughty expression. "I *did* attend college, Liam."

The siblings stared each other down. Emma knew exactly what her brother was dying to say, and she gave him credit for keeping his mouth shut. She watched as his mouth contorted, undoubtedly struggling against the urge to call her out about her college experience.

"Right!" Liam finally said, the word thrust into the world in a bubble of tortured enthusiasm that covered his underlying desire to be a snarky asshole. "Okay! When's your interview?"

Emma risked another look at the clock and gasped. Without a word, she sprinted out of the kitchen, leaving a trail of flour in her wake.

She wasn't late, somehow, which was a godsend. And luck was on Emma's side, as she landed a parking space for her beloved Mini Cooper right down the street from Cornerstone. She held her breath as she parallel parked but didn't need to worry; she'd honed that skill while living in Philadelphia. A couple horn beeps later, she cast a long look at her beautiful island-blue car and went into Cornerstone.

She refused to view her purchase of Selena, said Mini Cooper, as reckless. But considering it was the catalyst to the avalanche that Emma's life had become in Philadelphia…No, nope. Selena was hers, and everything that had come along with her was simply part of Emma's journey.

Cornerstone was surprisingly busy for early afternoon on a Friday. Granted, Emma had never worked in a bookstore so she had no idea what kinds of rushes and lulls to expect. But still, she assumed most people would be at work, not meandering around a bookstore in the middle of a weekday.

As she glanced around, unsure of where to go, she made note of several people who appeared to be working. It was a little hard to tell because they weren't dressed in a particular way that made them stand out, but their mannerisms and interactions with others made it clear they weren't simply hanging out in a cool bookstore. That, and one college-aged-looking guy was carrying a stack of easily twenty copies of the same book, which would be a weird purchase.

Two women in particular caught Emma's eye. One was dressed all in black and moved between the shelves like she was invisible. The only person she seemed aware of was the young woman wearing baggy corduroy pants, Birkenstock clogs, and a navy-blue crewneck sweater. Dark-blond hair hung around her shoulders, and despite the fact that she spoke to the woman in all black, it seemed like all her attention was on one of her fingers.

There was something naggingly familiar about the way the blond woman stood, even as she endlessly inspected her finger, but Emma couldn't place it. She probably would have spent fifteen minutes staring and trying to figure it out had Genesis not swooped in and whisked her away, back to the employee area where a small office was ready for the interview.

"So," Genesis began, eyeing Emma curiously, "what's your favorite caffeinated beverage?"

"Soda," Emma blurted. Any hopes she'd had of covering her non-coffee-drinking ass went out the window.

A heavy sigh came from Genesis, who leaned forward and rested her elbows on her knees. "You don't drink coffee, do you?"

"It tastes like dirt."

"Wow, okay, excellent. Yeah. Dirt, nice. Real nice." Genesis knocked her fists on her knees and leaned back in her chair. "Is this a joke? Did someone put you up to this?"

"No," Emma said, smiling. "I need a job. You have an opening. Sounds like a win-win to me."

Genesis gaped, which Emma had a feeling she didn't often do. There was an imposing nature about the young woman, a thrumming energy that Emma felt from across the table between them. She clearly liked to be in charge.

"Tell me," Genesis said slowly, "why I should hire you to work in the café where you will be making coffee drinks when you believe coffee tastes like dirt."

Emma took a breath. She hadn't prepared for this interview; the arrogant part of her had been banking on walking in and getting hired simply because she was able-bodied and had said she'd take the job that everyone kept quitting.

"I'm really good with flavors," she said, her words picking up speed as they tumbled out. "I know how to mix in a way that makes something come alive and taste really, really good. I understand the mechanics of ingredients. I can follow a recipe word for word, and I can improvise when I need to. I like to create things people will like, but I also know when to give someone exactly what they asked for."

Genesis stared at her. Emma could generally read people well, but this woman was a mystery.

"Have you worked as a bartender?" she asked.

"No, I just turned twenty-one. Well, almost two months ago. I, uh…" Emma hesitated. Despite the scones currently chilling in her brother's refrigerator, she hadn't wanted to bring her baking identity back home with her. She'd meant to leave it in Philadelphia, to waste away with the rest of her failures. She bit her lower lip, trying to think of a way to give more information without delivering the truth.

"Never mind." Genesis tapped a pen on the table. "That's not important. What I need to know is if you're going to be reliable."

"Absolutely." Emma nodded. "I'm a Scorpio."

There, a break in the facade. "Me too."

"Then you know I'm loyal—to people, and to tasks."

"Are you a quick learner?"

"Yes."

"Do you need to be the loudest voice in the room?"

"Only when I'm passionate about something."

Finally, a smile. Emma mentally applauded herself.

"I gotta be honest, it's against my nature to hire someone who doesn't even like coffee."

"I'm not going anywhere," Emma said, and she was struck by the truth of her words. "I, um, I'm here. I won't quit."

Genesis scanned her then, looking for a crack. Emma would have done the same had the roles been reversed. But she was in no mood to give more information than needed, except for one piece that she maybe should have started with.

"I mean, I'm going to be taking classes at Pennbrook. And I'm not going to kill myself with my class schedule because I need to work while I'm in school." She straightened her posture. "So as long as you can work around my classes, I'll be here."

Before Genesis could respond, the door opened and in walked Sadie. Her brow wrinkled as she took in the scene before her, then she leveled her glare at Genesis.

"We talked about this," she said in a tone that wanted to be threatening but was far from it.

"I was just getting the basics out of the way." Genesis glanced at Emma, then looked back at Sadie. "I think she can do the opening shift."

Sadie's body language shifted as she sat down and looked Emma over. "Really? That would be amazing."

Emma wasn't sure she could actually pull off whatever they were talking about, but if it got her the job, she would make it happen. "I meet with my advisor next week. It's late, I know, but—"

"That's perfect!" Genesis pumped a fist in the air. "The morning shift starts at eight o'clock and we can be flexible about when you'd leave."

"Wait," Sadie said, holding up a hand. "If she's registering this late, she might get stuck with early morning classes."

"Or evening classes." Genesis grinned. "See? Perfect."

As Emma listened to their back-and-forth, it was not lost on her that two strangers were discussing how *she* should best plan her class schedule. She let them go on. Judging from the way they fired back and forth, Emma could tell this sort of interaction between them was common.

"Anyway," Sadie finally said, shooting final eye-daggers at Genesis before turning to Emma with a genuine smile, "it sounds like you're going to be a great addition to Cornerstone."

"That's it?" Emma said, then mentally kicked herself.

"Oh, right. I should probably give you some scenarios to see how you'd respond to difficult customer interactions."

"But all our customers are pretty nice," Genesis pointed out. "And when they're not, I deal with it."

"The professors can be challenging," Sadie said knowingly.

"Nothing I can't handle. Especially the ones wearing sky-high heels." Genesis jerked her thumb at Emma. "She's tougher than she looks. Scorpio blood."

Sadie groaned. "Another one?"

"Okay and," Emma interjected, "I've worked this kind of job before. With customers, I mean. Filling their orders and making suggestions of what they might like in addition to what they ordered."

"Right." Genesis pushed her application toward Sadie. "I've gotta know more about this vegan butcher job."

"Vegan butcher?" Sadie echoed. "How...What?"

"I'll gladly tell you all about it after my first shift."

Genesis laughed, then looked at Sadie's expression and laughed harder. "You two may look alike but holy shit are you nowhere near the same person."

Sadie was looking at Emma with an expression of something like awe, and maybe a little fear. Emma grinned. She'd come in here to win Sadie and Genesis over, and if she had to use a little of her emergency arrogance, then so be it.

"Come with me," Sadie said, standing and gesturing toward Emma. "You may be working in the café, but you still need to know the lay of the land."

Emma waved to Genesis as she followed Sadie out of the office. As they stepped into the store, Emma allowed herself a deep breath of relief.

CHAPTER FOUR

She wasn't counting the minutes ticking by, but Aubrey knew her perception of what time it was in relation to how much she'd done throughout her shift did not match the actual time of day. By her calculations, loath as she was to do any kind of math, it had to be at least six p.m. But if it *were* six p.m., then Aubrey would be home. Not *home*, home, but in the place that she was currently living. While she loved the attic studio apartment and was always happy to land there at the end of her day, something was missing. And that something kept it from feeling like "home."

Alas, home or not, it wasn't six p.m. Aubrey had a sinking feeling that it wasn't even two p.m., which meant the amount of time remaining in her shift had hit that point where it felt interminable.

That last hour in a retail job—the silent killer, the destroyer of all positivity and energy.

"Excuse me?"

Aubrey pasted on a smile before she turned from the pile of books she was labeling with clearance prices. She'd tried to bargain with Sadie to be permitted to do this labeling in the stock room, but Sadie had an interview scheduled and needed Aubrey out on the floor. For a situation just like this, in fact: a lost-looking college student in need of bookstore directions. Aubrey could smell that specific aroma of confusion from a mile away.

"How can I help you?"

The young woman—if she had to estimate, Aubrey would guess she was right around her own age, maybe a graduate student, then—held out a slip of paper. "Do you have any of these books?"

Aubrey skimmed the list. Her heart picked up speed when she saw Virginia Woolf's name on the list. A real smile morphed from the fake one she'd thrown on for the sake of customer service. This list was *awesome*.

"Let me guess," Aubrey said, gesturing for the woman to follow her. "Modern Women Writers, 400-level course?"

"Yes!" The woman's cheeks flushed. "Have you taken it?"

The excitement nudging itself into Aubrey's heart quickly departed, leaving that forever empty ache in its midst. "No. I studied something else in college."

"At Pennbrook?"

Aubrey shook her head as they reached their destination: the literary criticism section, which butted up against the biography and history section and combined neatly with a few rows of shelves Sadie had dubbed the "Snob Section." Most of the books in that section were classics, typical texts a student studying literature would be assigned to read. But as the years had gone by, Sadie had had to expand. She still deemed it snobby, even when Aubrey presented informed arguments against that label, but the classics were now nestled amongst "modern classics," otherwise known as books that were contemporary and getting good air time in the progressive literature courses at Pennbrook University.

In other words, it was the section the English department fantasized about. And, actually, spent quite a lot of time in.

And because they were in love with these books, the professors deemed their students also had to develop mad, if not passionate, crushes on them.

Aubrey was simply the keeper.

She crouched down and ran her fingers over the delicate spines until she located Woolf's lesser-known experimental text, *The Waves*. She hadn't read it but was curious about it.

"Oh, this is amazing," the woman said, looking around the section. "I didn't know you guys had this area specifically for these kinds of books."

"Yeah, the owner is really good friends with one of the English professors at Pennbrook." Aubrey stood up and brushed her hands against her cords. "She's friends with a few of them, actually," Aubrey amended. "Anyway, they put the pressure on my boss to keep getting these random old books, so she caved and gave them a whole section. But she still has to special order stuff for them." She inspected her paper cut, which had begun to throb yet again. She was so focused on the pathetic, minuscule rip of skin that she missed what the customer said next.

"Sorry?"

The young woman was holding Woolf's text to her chest as though it was a prize she'd longed for her entire life. "Is it Professor Lewes?"

Aubrey thought for a moment. That could be Callie's last name; she couldn't remember if she'd ever been told. She knew Callie in that oblique way one does when their boss has a friend who comes into the store often. She did know Callie was still working on her PhD, so she wasn't a Dr. yet. But other than that, Aubrey couldn't say for sure. So she shrugged.

"She's gorgeous," the woman went on, undeterred by Aubrey's ambivalence. "She has these incredible dark-blue eyes that get so bright when she talks about literature that she loves. She's just—" The woman cut herself off. "I mean, everyone knows she's taken, of course. It's not like that." She laughed, but Aubrey wasn't convinced. She knew an idol worship-crush when she saw one.

After all, she'd faced herself in the mirror for years.

"And her partner is equally amazing," the woman continued. Aubrey settled in for the duration of the impassioned monologue. "She's wicked smart. So intimidating! Seeing Professor Lewes and Dr. Jory together is—"

"Oh, Kate?" Aubrey interrupted. That name she knew for sure. It was a bit legendary around these parts. Plus, Callie was so deeply enamored with her partner that she never missed a chance to name drop.

The abrupt statement seemed to knock the woman off-kilter. "Kate," she repeated, then nodded, looking a bit starstruck. "You're…on a first-name basis?"

Aubrey shrugged. "Sure." She looked back at the slip of paper still in her hand. "Do you want these other two books?"

"Yes," she said, recovering quickly—faster than Aubrey had expected. "I'm Gretchen, by the way."

"Cool," Aubrey said, now focused on locating the other books so she could politely escape this bizarro conversation.

"So, Aubrey…" It never ceased to send shivers down Aubrey's spine, the way customers took advantage of her damn name tag. "Do the professors come in here often?"

She almost laughed in Gretchen's face. She'd expected a different "come here often" line to slide out of Gretchen's mouth. Used to being hit on in the way that she knew women found her attractive, Aubrey hadn't yet developed the ego that came along with knowing exactly how attractive she was. Then again, that was the only thing anyone had seemed to care about in high school— hot, untouchable Aubrey Glass—and she'd tried like hell to shed that skin and reputation since graduating.

So it was honestly a relief that Gretchen wasn't hitting on her.

"Yeah, they do." Aubrey handed over the other two books. "Come in again and I'm sure you'll run into Professor Lewes at some point."

A sly grin slid over Gretchen's mouth, which was, admittedly, a very pretty mouth. Aubrey, despite her self-imposed moratorium on flirting and dating and women in general, couldn't ignore that fact. She saw the flicker in Gretchen's eyes and groaned inwardly. She'd thought for sure that tacking on the bit about running into Professor Lewes would prevent her words from being flirty, but it seemed she was wrong.

"You know," Gretchen said, cocking her hip in a way that was meant to draw attention to it, but Aubrey, yes indeed, Aubrey ignored the movement. "You kinda look like Professor Lewes."

She nearly scoffed in the poor woman's face but thankfully remembered she was at work and still bound by the laws of customer service. "I don't think that's true."

"Maybe not your eyes, but your hair is almost the same color." Gretchen reached out and trailed her pointer finger against the tips of Aubrey's hair, which was brushing her shoulder. It was a bold move. They'd just met, for Christ's sake.

She dodged out of Gretchen's reach. "I guess so. Anything else I can help you with?" The phrase, one she uttered countless times throughout a workday, had barely left her lips before she cringed, hoping Gretchen would recognize her all-business tone and not turn the words into something she did not intend for them to be.

"I think—oh, oh my God." Gretchen's cheeks reached a new height of blush as her eyes tracked movement behind Aubrey. "That's Professor Lewes. How do I look?" She hitched her shoulders to her ears and bleated a nervous laugh. "I don't mean it like that. I know she's with someone. I—you know what, never mind. Thanks for your help!"

And with that decidedly perplexing parting paragraph, Gretchen was off and nearly jogging to catch up with Professor Callie Lewes, famed gorgeous professor of literature at Pennbrook, who looked like she was on a mission herself. A mission aside from her reputed accidental habit of having students fall madly in love with her, that is.

Aubrey blew out a breath. She barely had time to collect herself before Genesis appeared before her.

"Did you seriously not get her number?"

"Why would I?"

Genesis rolled her eyes. "Glass, we've got to get you back on your game. She was majorly hitting on you."

"And I don't care that she was," Aubrey said pointedly as they walked over to the café. "I'm not doing"—she gestured helplessly—"any of that."

Genesis grabbed Aubrey's hand and pressed her fingers to the inside of her wrist.

"Not necessary," Aubrey said tightly.

"Oh, it is. Because after that hot woman nearly tore your shirt off in the Snob Section and you didn't even *get a phone number*, I'm convinced you're the walking dead."

Aubrey yanked her arm back. As Genesis laughed in the devious way she was notorious for, Sadie's voice floated over the stacks. Aubrey registered the directional speech she was giving. Must be the new hire.

Sure enough, moments later, Sadie and a younger version of Sadie rounded the corner about fifteen feet from where Aubrey stood, suddenly glued to the ground. Normally she avoided new hires—they didn't often last long enough to invest in them personally—and she was sure this one would be no exception.

However, it was always good to scope them out so that she'd recognize them as an employee and not a customer. (Not that that had happened more than three times in the time Aubrey had been working at Cornerstone.)

"New hire," Genesis said, though it was pointless because Aubrey had gathered that. "No barista experience, but her attitude is way better than the last four we hired."

"What's her name?" Aubrey asked.

"Gallagher." Genesis shrugged when Aubrey side-eyed her. "You know I suck with first names. Chronic flaw."

The last name was familiar, ringing a forgotten chord in the soundtrack of Aubrey's mind. But the person standing with Sadie looked nothing like the Gallagher—Liam, her buddy from high school—Aubrey knew. Or, had known. She and Liam hadn't talked in…well, a while. A long while. But she remembered Liam's classic brown hair-bluish eyes combination, which couldn't be further from the literal mini-Sadie standing with regular-Sadie.

This Gallagher had long auburn hair, a shade or two lighter than Sadie's, framing a freckle-splattered jawline. There was another trail of freckles hiking over her small nose. Round honey-brown eyes were framed with thick lashes that looked free of makeup, making Aubrey quite jealous. And not that this was particularly relevant to connecting the possible genealogical dots, but this Gallagher was dressed to the nines, whereas Aubrey remembered Liam being the type of guy to live in joggers and hoodies. *This* Gallagher was wearing black pants with a thin brown plaid print, topped with a rich brown turtleneck that set her eyes aglow.

She looked way too put-together to be working in the café with Genesis, who didn't own a pair of jeans without rips. No, that kind of ensemble would be much better for the book floor. It practically screamed, "This person enjoys enchanted fall afternoons spent next to piles of books and a chai-scented candle."

Aubrey glanced down at her own outfit. She didn't know what it screamed, other than "This person is very likely a member of the queer community."

As Sadie and mini-Sadie disappeared into the back of the store, Aubrey turned back to Genesis, who had been talking the entire time she was caught up in assessing mini-Sadie's outfit. She had no idea what Genesis had been going on about, but it didn't seem to matter. More likely than not, it had been hot topics on Reddit, which was always a one-sided conversation between them.

"So," Genesis said, coming to a conclusion that seemed to make sense to her, "you up for the bar this weekend? Tomorrow, I mean. Not tonight."

There was no excuse banked in Aubrey's mind. Plus, she had to admit she generally had fun when they went out. "Okay," she said. "But I want to get there before ten p.m."

"Fine. Talk later. Gotta go finish orienting."

Aubrey went through the motions of the complex and ridiculous handshake Genesis had created for them one very intoxicated, postbar night out at the diner. It was a miracle either one of them was able to remember it.

Another perk of working the opening shift at Cornerstone was that the sun was still out when Aubrey left work for the day. More and more, she struggled with the idea of working until five o'clock or later, when, during the winter, it was flat-out dark when people left work.

Winter had its grip on New England, but at least the sun was trying to warm spots on the sidewalk as Aubrey walked down Finch Avenue. She needed to go grocery shopping but didn't feel like it, so she'd decided to stop at the nearby pizza place and grab a salad and a calzone to go.

Further down Finch, Pennbrook's campus loomed. It was traditionally beautiful. The buildings were brick and stately, but old and creaky. Haunting, some might say; haunted, others might claim. Nearly everyone, however, was enchanted by the timeless charm the campus offered.

Aubrey was mostly neutral. She had no real feelings attached to Pennbrook. It was simply part of the town she'd grown up in, the town she'd returned to after going to college in upstate New York. Pennbrook was, however, the actual cornerstone of Chestnut Hill.

After securing her dinner, Aubrey traveled back up Finch, passing Cornerstone Books on her way home. She glanced into the café through the large, very old windows that held together the entire side of the store. It was more crowded than when she'd left. Probably the professorial crowd. Sadie was a damn magnet for them.

Aubrey had nothing against professors. In her world, they existed in the way that milk did. Present and available for those who were interested, whether that be for practical reasons or for something more exciting, like ice cream (listen, it wasn't her best analogy but she liked it). The amount of professorial gossip that she overheard in Cornerstone was enough to assure that Aubrey would never date someone who aspired to become a professor.

Cornerstone faded into the distance as she crossed Main Street and headed down Lilac Avenue. She'd grown to love this street, one she'd probably never set foot on prior to returning from college. Huge, ancient trees lined the sidewalks, providing shade and a great cover for getting caught in the rain. The houses were larger in this area of Chestnut Hill, and also very old. On this block were mostly Victorians sprawled across plots of land that could barely contain the houses. Very few were single-family homes anymore; typical for a college town, they'd mostly been cut up into apartments for students and visiting professors.

It wasn't long before Aubrey was climbing the stairs to the Victorian that housed her attic apartment. It was one of the smaller homes on the block, but still crazy spacious. The bottom floor had been chopped up into two separate apartments, while the second floor had been renovated into one very large one. Sadie lived there now with a roommate.

At the top of the second flight of stairs was Sadie's old studio apartment, now Aubrey's place. She unlocked the door and breathed deeply as she walked into what had become a sacred space. Her collection of hanging plants swung gently as she passed them on her way to the small but efficient kitchen. She put her food down then immediately headed for the shower. There was something about rinsing off the day that Aubrey felt very strongly about. She wouldn't be able to unwind and enjoy her evening until she was clean, in baggy sweats and an equally baggy hoodie.

Later, in said comfy clothing with a belly full of salad and calzone, Aubrey stretched out on her sofa and stared up at the ceiling. It was only six p.m. She had hours until she could reasonably go to sleep.

But there was nothing she wanted to do, no one she wanted to talk to. After a lifetime of never having it, silence was the only companion Aubrey needed.

CHAPTER FIVE

Emma stepped back from the enormous hunk of steel that Genesis kept referring to as "Bernard." For the past hour and a half, Genesis had spouted term after term—words like boiler, gauge, grouphead, knock-box. The woman hadn't stopped talking since Emma had walked into the café, nor had she let Emma actually touch the machine. No, apparently Emma's sole job today, her very first working day at Cornerstone, was to watch Genesis and listen to her impassioned lectures about the sophisticated skill of making espresso shots.

"See this?" Genesis gestured to the miniature white ceramic cup of dark brown liquid. "That's beautiful. That's what we want every time."

"I see," Emma said. And she did. But she was tired of watching, so with the caution one might reserve for approaching a hissing cat in a dim, garbage-filled alley, she tentatively reached her hand toward the machine.

"Not yet." The words came with what was probably meant to be a friendly slap on the wrist, but landed with more bite than Emma was prepared for.

"Is workplace abuse part of what I can expect working here?" she asked, rubbing her wrist.

"Sorry." Genesis dumped the shot of espresso into a cup and went about her seven-step process of cleaning and prepping for the next one. "Perfect shots get me too excited. I'll chill once you start pulling them."

"Because mine won't be perfect?"

"That's not exactly what I meant but yeah, kind of."

Emma rolled her eyes at Genesis's back. It hadn't taken her long to adjust to the woman's vibrant, if vaguely offensive nature. Emma knew the type well—she'd had a couple of friends over the years with similar personalities. She was beginning to wonder if there was something about her that attracted, well, assholes.

As Genesis began a new lecture, this one about steaming milk—which couldn't possibly be as difficult as she was making it out to be—a movement at the edge of the café caught Emma's eyes. She tried to focus on Genesis, but she was so tired of listening to the woman perform soliloquies about her beloved espresso machine that she allowed herself a moment of distraction.

It was the shoes that Emma couldn't stop staring at. The idea of working in Birkenstock clogs seemed deeply...not inappropriate, but just wrong, somehow. She couldn't explain it. Anyone working on the book floor was bound to be moving around a lot, never mind the fact that they also had to stock books, which meant lugging boxes and carts from the back room. Even though the young woman's Bostons looked perfectly worn in and were probably extremely comfortable, Emma just could not get past the impracticality of the footwear.

She tore her eyes from the clogs and glanced down at her own feet, securely protected in a pair of surprisingly comfortable black combat boots. Paired with jeans and a plain black T-shirt as requested by Genesis, the look was not something Emma would have voluntarily chosen for herself. She leaned toward slightly dressier attire that she hoped projected an image of "this girl has her life together."

Because she absolutely did not have her life together, but dammit, she wanted people to think she did.

A wild sucking noise erupted from the espresso machine, jolting Emma back to her training. Genesis wasn't rattling off instructions, though. She was gleefully staring into the metal milk pitcher, watching the froth get bigger and bigger. Emma took the opportunity to sneak another look at the wearer of the inappropriate shoes.

Emma still couldn't place what was familiar about her. It was like a memory had resurfaced and hovered just beyond her grasp. Not figuring it out was driving her crazy.

It was in the slouch. The woman—and if Emma had to guess, she'd say she was a couple years older than herself—had this way of standing that looked like she was slouching but she wasn't. It was the weirdest thing, the way her shoulders hung from her body. The "I don't care" attitude shot like firecrackers from her posture. It was both intimidating and welcoming, a duality Emma couldn't figure out.

But there was something naggingly familiar about that slouch. Something that raised the hairs on the back of Emma's neck.

"And that," Genesis exclaimed, jerking Emma's attention back, "is how you froth milk for a cappuccino."

She held out the pitcher and Emma peered inside, then frowned. "It's all foam."

"No," Genesis said petulantly, dragging out the o. "Just on the top. There's steamed milk below." She poured the entirety of the pitcher into the cup and held it out for Emma to inspect.

She sniffed the cup and instinctively wrinkled her nose.

"Yeah, we have to work on your face," Genesis grumbled.

"You mean my expressions."

"Sure, that too." She stepped back from the counter, though it looked like the two steps pained her deep into her bones. "Your turn."

Emma shook out her hands and stepped up to the machine. "A cappuccino?"

"Genesis." The tone was filled with warning and a touch of friendly disdain. Sadie stepped up to the opposite side of the counter and crossed her arms over her chest. "You cannot have her first drink be a cappuccino."

"Sure I can. I have a whole theory of why you have to start with the hardest."

"I'm sure you do, but—"

"Let me go over it with you real quick."

As they bickered, Emma got to work. She measured out the espresso and tamped it down until it was firm in the portafilter. After a brief hesitation, she raised the portafilter to the grouphead and cautiously locked it in. She resisted a small celebratory dance, but was over the moon with having gotten it in on the first try. After studying the buttons for a moment, she pressed the one Genesis had used—for one shot of espresso—and positioned the funny little shot glass under the grouphead. Emma bit the inside of her cheek and released it when brown liquid began streaming through the portafilter.

She glanced at Genesis, who was still animatedly explaining to Sadie the many, many reasons she was right to start Emma on cappuccinos. The truth was, Emma didn't care which drink Genesis started her on. She was determined to make a good impression, and would do whatever it took to make that happen.

As she steamed the milk, the Boston clogs caught her eye again. She tried like hell to keep her eyes glued to the pitcher and the insanely hot steam wand, but couldn't help but sneak another look at the sloucher. She was with a customer now and had perked up a bit, but Emma knew a dark cloud when she saw one, and that woman was pretty much shadowed in gray.

A little tug in Emma's heart yanked her attention away from the human-sized storm cloud. The *last* thing she needed was to get involved with someone else's problems. Not that she was getting any kind of involved with the sloucher, because she didn't even know her name, and she wasn't on the market for new friends, even though she probably should be, but it didn't matter and—

A tell-tale whistling let Emma know her frothing time had come to an end. She felt Genesis's eyes on her, but she and Sadie had gone silent. Emma ignored them as she dumped the espresso shot into a cup, then picked up a serving spoon and held it against the top of the pitcher, making a nice little barrier so the steamed milk could slide through first. Once the stream slowed, Emma lifted the spoon and watched the foam tumble on top of the milk and espresso. She gave the cup an appreciative tap before handing it to Genesis.

Sadie caught Emma's eye and grinned as Genesis took a sip. Neither of them said a word, anxiously awaiting Genesis's critiques.

"Okay," she finally said, putting the cup back on the counter and narrowing her eyes at Emma. "Why did you feel the need to lie about your work experience?"

Emma put her hands on her hips. "I didn't."

Sadie lifted the cup and took a sip, careful to use the opposite side, mumbling something about germs. "Oh," she said softly after she swallowed. "Wow."

"That is a cappuccino made by someone who has absolutely made cappuccinos in their past." Genesis squinted harder. "You even knew to hold the foam back. Just own it, Gallagher. You've done this before."

"But I haven't. I swear."

"I'm taking this," Sadie said as she walked away, cup in hand. "Thanks, Emma! You're still hired!"

Genesis, meanwhile, looked perplexed and frustrated. Emma had a hunch that she'd accidentally bested the drink master at her own game.

"Oh, I get it." Genesis leaned against the counter, eyes still locked on Emma. "You're one of those people who can do anything right the first time they try it."

"I'm not—" Emma cut herself off. There might be some truth to those words, but it wasn't something she'd ever given much thought. But now she wanted to. "Maybe?"

"Fine. So you're a natural. That makes my life a hell of a lot easier." Genesis turned back to the machine and patted it. "Bernard, let's teach her the art of latte making."

Though Emma was accustomed to working—she'd never been one of those privileged kids whose parents said, "Oh, don't work, just focus on school!" plus she'd spent the last year working full time at the vegan butcher shop—she was still somehow surprised to realize how exhausted she was at the end of her shift. Must have been the whole "learning an entire menu of drinks, even the ones that aren't on the menu" training she was subjected to for six hours. Once she'd proven herself to Genesis with that cappuccino, she'd been given drink after drink to make. Both the staff and the customers had been handed free treat after free treat, especially since Emma refused to taste more than two of her own creations.

But she had to summon up some energy, because she was doing the unthinkable: having dinner with a high school friend she hadn't seen in three years.

Emma knew it would be fine. Why wouldn't it be? Surely they still had things in common, and if she was asked about college, she would immediately change the subject. As often as required. Forever and always.

She sighed as she sat in the driver's seat of Selena. This wasn't how her life was supposed to be going right now. Emma had carefully mapped out her life before she graduated high school. She loved a good plan, typically thrived in executing them, but she'd hit an endless amount of roadblocks with this, her master plan for success. It had been shredded and thrown out with the majority of her dreams, and since then, she'd been languishing.

Fortunately, she thought as she exited her car and walked toward the restaurant on the outskirts of Chestnut Hill, college students were still home on winter break, so there was a high possibility that Collins, someone Emma had once considered her absolute best friend, wouldn't even figure out that she was back for good.

The vestibule was thrumming with activity, complete with a wave of canned heat that blasted as soon as Emma walked through the front doors. She ducked her head and moved through the bodies, making her way to the hostess stand. She was just about to give her name when she heard it yelled from the cacophony of the bar.

"Emmalynn! Get over here!"

The sound of Collins's voice cheered her immediately. Maybe they could pick up where they'd left off so many years ago. Maybe things were exactly as they'd left—

Emma covered her mouth to hide her gasp as she approached. Well, so much for that theory.

Gone was her roughly athletic friend, the queen of sweats and T-shirts no matter the time of year. Gone, too, was Collins's trademark shoulder-length hair that never saw life outside of her hair elastic.

Standing by the bar was a shockingly mature-looking, beautifully styled young woman. Her blue-black hair was long and free, punctuated by shaggy bangs that swooped over one side of her face. This Collins didn't look like she even *owned* a pair of sweatpants. In their place were tight black jeans that hit right above her ankles, leather ankle boots, a white shirt with a deep V-neck, and a vibrant green blazer. The shirt and blazer had the dizzying effect of drawing Emma's eyes right to Collins's chest, which now boasted very noticeable breasts that *definitely* had not been there at graduation.

Emma blinked, wondering when and how Collins had sped up her age and raced past their mutual twenty-one years.

"C-Collins?" she managed, still blinking to try to right the image before her.

"Yes, you weirdo. Why do you look so shocked? You still follow me on Instagram!"

While that was factually true, social media was yet another piece of Emma's life that had faced a forced death when she'd had to abandon her college goals. She couldn't stand to see her friends trucking along, hitting milestone after milestone, while she idly sat by. She'd kept the apps on her phone but logged out and moved them into a folder she never opened, eventually forgetting they were there.

"The last time I saw you," Emma said, still shocked but feeling less blindsided, "you didn't have *those*."

Collins glanced down then laughed. She threw her arms around Emma and squeezed her. She smelled the same, at least: that unmistakable mixture of sandalwood and men's soap, something that was probably called Deep Blue Mountain Springs or Rustic Hiking Trail Leaves.

"I look more like my mom now, right?" Collins grinned as she sat down and patted the barstool next to her. "Totally thought I was going to look like my dad's side of the family for my entire life, but then, outta nowhere, my mom's curvy goddess genes woke up and took over."

Emma relaxed. So Collins was still Collins, even if her appearance was no longer narrow-hipped and flat-chested. With an Asian dad and a Black mom, Collins had prided herself on being their high school's only student of that particular racial mixing. Aside from her older brother, that is, whom she deemed didn't count because he was a male clone of their mother.

"So!" Yup, typical Collins: Emma never had to say much when they were together. "Since you apparently don't look at my Instagram, you're obviously totally out of the loop. Lemme fill you in."

Emma spent the next fifteen minutes—interrupted only by the bartender taking her order—listening to the long list of Collins's life updates. In short: She was excited to see the light at the end of the college tunnel; she'd cycled through seven boyfriends and two girlfriends since starting college; she was living her Best Single Bisexual Life at the moment but had a big crush on an "androgynous girl with killer swagger" in one of her classes; and despite pressure from her parents, who both worked in the homeopathic medical field, she was holding strong to her decision to major in digital arts.

"I haven't decided what I want to do when I graduate," Collins went on, stirring her drink. "I might do the whole backpacking-in-Europe thing before I find a job. Or is that too cliché? Ugh. Who cares. You should come with me!"

"What's Marcus doing?" Emma blurted, figuring it was a safe way to keep the conversation off herself.

Collins rolled her dark-brown eyes, still makeup-free like they were in high school. "Studying medicine. Shocking, I know." Her smile widened mischievously as she leaned closer to Emma. "Speaking of brothers, how's my boy Liam?"

Emma groaned. Truly, some things never changed. Collins had fostered an enormous crush on Liam throughout high school. Fortunately for everyone, Liam had not reciprocated the interest.

"He's good. He has a great job and bought a house, which is awesome because now I have somewhere to stay."

The words were out before Emma even realized what she'd said. When she did, she felt heat rising from her chest, building its way up her neck. She stole an angry glance at the empty glass on the bar top. That blurt was definitely the alcohol's fault.

"Stay? Like during breaks?" Collins looked confused. "Did your parents move?"

Emma weighed her options. She could lie. Though it wasn't her favorite pastime, she could do it well enough. But this was Collins, and Emma suddenly felt very aware of the fact that she needed someone in her corner, someone who'd known her through one of the hardest times in her life.

"No, they're still here. It's, um..." She nodded when the bartender stopped in front of them. She'd definitely need another drink to get through this. "I'm staying here for now."

Collins sat silently, eyes focused on Emma. She waited, and when Emma didn't give any more information, she asked, "Did you transfer?"

She could work with that. "Basically, yeah. I'm starting at Pennbrook in a couple of weeks."

"Emmalynn!" Collins gaped at her. "We promised we'd never do that!"

It was the curse of growing up in Chestnut Hill: While Pennbrook was an incredible university, it felt too much like thirteenth grade to the kids who lived in its shadow their entire public school lives.

"I know," she said, then took a long sip of her fresh drink, savoring the taste of vodka that cost more than ten bucks a bottle. "It just kinda happened. It'll be fine."

"It's crazy how we all wanted to get out of this town, and soooo many of us have already ended up right back here."

Crisis of having to explain everything averted, Emma breathed a sigh of relief and eased into the conversation. "Oh yeah? Like who?"

Collins rattled off several of their classmates' names, giving the abbreviated versions of their stories. As she went on, Emma felt less and less like an incompetent freak who had monumentally screwed up her life and more like a regular brand-new adult who was still trying to figure her shit out.

"Oh!" Collins gripped Emma's arm. "And Aubrey Glass."

Emma's hand stilled on its way to her drink. Aubrey Glass. The name preluded a ping of memory, followed by a thread unspooling itself, a curved line leading to a blank space in Emma's mind.

"That one really surprised me," Collins continued, oblivious to Emma's brain freeze. "I mean, I thought she couldn't wait to get out of this town and stay away. After all that craziness with her family, you know? And then, bam, she graduates from college and comes home. I heard she's working at a bookstore or something. A bar? No, definitely the bookstore."

It was a good thing Emma's hand had never reached her glass because she definitely would have dropped it after hearing that.

"The sloucher," Emma whispered, recognition dawning and spreading through her.

"The what?"

"Nothing." She shook her head. The thread that connected Emma to Aubrey was thin and snagged with one giant knot, a knot Emma still hadn't unsnarled—and it had nothing to do with Aubrey. She was just, unfortunately, attached to the string on the other side of the knot.

The very knot Emma would much prefer to leave tangled, dusty, and crammed in the darkest corner of her memories.

CHAPTER SIX

In Aubrey's history of homes—hers, those of her friends, and so on—she'd never encountered a doorbell that rang quite as obnoxiously as the one in her mother's house. It was ear-piercing, condescending somehow despite being a mere four-chime tone. It intended to be sophisticated but instead came across as a fraud. At its base level, it demanded attention. It was, regrettably, an inanimate incarnation of Corrine Thompson, who at that very moment was "tied up in the kitchen and couldn't possibly answer the door."

So Aubrey was the one who trudged to the front door of the sprawling McMansion where her mother lived with her third husband, Trent Thompson. Yes, *that* Trent Thompson—the local politician whose entire platform was dedicated to being "approachably conservative." Though she tended to avoid him as much as possible, Aubrey had yet to find anything remotely approachable about Trent. For his part, he ignored her, which she chalked up to not hiding or lying about her sexuality. Because of that, her mother had politely asked that Aubrey make herself scarce anytime Trent might have his picture taken.

Aubrey could admit that, in his own aggressively metrosexual way, Trent was handsome. But she knew the real reason her mother had even entertained the idea of him was because of his money.

She flung the door open and was greeted by five faces, four of which stretched the limits of the melancholic scale. The fifth looked tired and a cross between relieved and sad.

"Hey, Aub." Penelope, Trent's ex-wife, gave her a weary smile. "I didn't know you'd be here."

"Mother's orders," she responded. "Hi, small people."

Not a single child replied as they stalked past Aubrey and disappeared into the depths of the house. Even little CeCe, just five years old and not old enough to have been tainted by her father's twisted opinions, was mute as she followed her siblings inside.

Aubrey raised her eyebrows. Pen sighed, then gestured for her to come out and close the door.

"They're mad," she said, her voice quiet and mouth barely moving, lest someone (i.e. Corrine) was watching the front door camera. "It's hard on them when their dad changes the visitation schedule."

Aubrey tried to stay away from the McMansion as much as possible, so she didn't have much firsthand experience with Trent and Penelope's four kids, but she had seen enough tears and immediate changes in attitude to know that they preferred to be with their mom. Trent didn't make time for them, didn't treat them as much more than props. And Corrine...Aubrey could vouch for the fact that her maternal instincts were lacking. They were nearly extinct when it came to helping raise "that awful woman's offspring," which, yes, was a direct quote from Aubrey's loving mother.

"So this time," Pen continued, "they decided to give *me* the silent treatment." Her eyes sparkled with unshed tears, which she quickly blinked away. "They'll be fine, I know, it's just hard on all of us."

"I'm so sorry." And she was. Aubrey genuinely liked Pen, and had a bit of a soft spot for her. Despite the friendship they'd formed (initially based on their mutual dislike of Corrine), Aubrey didn't know the specifics of the divorce and everything that had happened since. She did, however, know enough about the timeline to know that her mother was a homewrecker.

Not that Aubrey was altogether surprised about that.

"It's okay!" Pen smiled and it just barely reached her eyes, which were still swimming with exhaustion and disappointment. "I heard tonight's a big deal, huh?"

Aubrey groaned and leaned against one of the columns on the front porch. Her mother would rip her a new asshole if her outfit came away stained or dusty, but after twenty-four years, Aubrey knew how to handle that.

"The biggest, if you believe anything Corrine says."

Pen laughed. "You know she hates when you call her that."

"She hates everything I do."

"Aub, that's not true." Pen laid a gentle hand on Aubrey's shoulder. "She's proud of you."

"For what?" Aubrey shifted so Pen's hand fell away. She wasn't in the mood for pity, even from someone who knew most of her secrets.

"Don't do this to yourself," Pen said, her voice stern. "You never give yourself enough credit."

It was true, and they both knew it, so Aubrey didn't bother to argue. After all, she had made her way through college and emerged with a degree. And while it maybe wasn't ideal, or the career of her dreams—never mind whatever Corrine had dreamed up for her—she did have a job.

But that other truth, the one that stuck to every edge of Aubrey's existence, the one Corrine dangled over Aubrey's head every chance she got, went unspoken.

Pen reached out again and squeezed Aubrey's shoulder. "I should go. Try to have some fun tonight. We'll talk soon, okay?"

Aubrey watched her walk to her shiny silver Lincoln Navigator, one of many divorce perks. Pen waved as she circled around the driveway and drove off toward the quiet part of her life.

Not for the first time, Aubrey found herself wishing she could have hopped in the passenger seat and driven off with her, far away from the unappealing scene behind the dramatically oversized front doors.

Much like she did at work, Aubrey spent the majority of the evening moving like an eel between the endless sea of bodies that paraded in and out of the McMansion. Trent loved to host Tea

Parties, a title that Aubrey found ridiculous because they were simply excuses for making people dress up in clothing that cost way too much to wear just one time and herding them into the ornate home to consume an inordinate amount of champagne and bourbon. Then, Trent could take full advantage of having trapped people in the house so that he could do the only thing he was halfway skilled at: schmooze.

Corrine was no better. Aubrey watched from a safe distance as her mother threw her head back in laughter, the fakest gesture Aubrey had ever witnessed. Her hands, fingertips glistening with a fresh manicure and bulbous diamond engagement ring secured atop a shockingly modest wedding band, fluttered from guest to guest, patting arms and holding shoulders with fingers like clothespins as she kissed once, twice.

It had only been an hour of this torture, and Aubrey was already crawling out of her skin.

She hated the fact that she had to be there. She'd had to wear a Trent-approved outfit (wide-legged black pants and a pale pink top she'd throw into the Goodwill donation bin after the evening ended; at least Trent had gotten the message early on that there would be no skirts or dresses) and had sworn to do little more than smile and nod. Not exactly Star of the Show preparation.

The truth of this matter was simple. Corrine had raised Aubrey in Chestnut Hill, and Aubrey's dad had been well-known around town. His funeral, though Aubrey didn't remember much of it since she'd been in fourth grade at the time, had drawn a crowd that hadn't fit inside the funeral home. In short, everyone around town knew Aubrey existed, and if she didn't make an every-so-often appearance at family events, rumors would start, and Corrine wanted nothing to do with rumors.

So there Aubrey was, slipping between conversations in order to avoid small talk. She kept her eyes on the kids, all of whom had positioned themselves in the corner of the library on the sofa. They sat in a row from oldest to youngest: Lyla, thirteen; Trent Jr., ten, who looked like a copy-paste version of his mother which made Aubrey secretly love the Jr. tag; Trevor, eight; and Aubrey's favorite, CeCe, five. Because Aubrey wasn't around much, she didn't even have semisibling relationships with any of the kids. They were okay, for the most part, if a little too like Trent at times.

Aubrey continued to hold out hope that Pen's influence would end up having a stronger influence.

"Darling," Corrine said, suddenly appearing at Aubrey's elbow. "Could you at least *try* to smile?"

"Relax. No one's even looking at me."

Corrine steered her away from the kids, which is where she'd been unconsciously heading. "Au contraire. There are eyes everywhere, and they are bound to land on you."

This was nothing new. Corrine, though she had been slightly more down to earth when Aubrey's dad was alive, had always had a preoccupation with image. It was actually what had driven them into debt following Aubrey's dad's death, and why Corrine had rushed to marry her second husband. All that marriage did was level them out financially, but Corrine continued to live outside of her means. She claimed it was for Aubrey's sake, but Aubrey had never asked for anything she'd been given.

She'd settled for the materialism because it was the only indication that her mother cared about her.

"I was going to make sure the kids are doing okay," Aubrey said, looking over her shoulder. Her view was blocked by a circle of men in flashy suits that looked iridescent beneath the lights.

"They're fine. I need you to do me a favor."

The words stung like daggers piercing Aubrey's softest flesh. Like that spot right above her armpit. Corinne didn't ask for favors, especially not from her own daughter.

Wincing, she asked, "What?"

Corrine had led them to the kitchen, where a few caterers were busy preparing fresh trays of hors d'oeuvres. Aubrey wondered when she'd last eaten. She tended to lose her appetite when she was around her mother and Trent, but now that she was thinking about it, she wasn't sure she'd eaten at all that day.

After scanning the area to make sure they were alone aside from the caterers, Corrine leaned in close and said in a whisper outlined with bullets, "You will no longer speak to Penelope."

Stunned, Aubrey took a step back and her lower back collided with the corner of the massive kitchen island. "What are you— what? That's ridiculous."

"I mean it, Aubrey." Corrine straightened up, brushing her fake blond curls off her shoulders. (Extensions, Aubrey knew. At fifty-one, Corinne's hair was still blond enough not to need much dye other than at the roots, but the length was entirely a removable mirage.) "We do not need another scandal in this family."

Aubrey rolled her eyes, then felt a cascade of ice settle over her shoulders. She didn't want to ask, but she had a good idea what her mother was referring to, and that—

"You've made that grievous error once in your life, young lady. Don't think we would be so forgiving a second time."

There were many, many things Aubrey yearned to say in that moment, but her tongue was a frozen slab in her arctic cave of a mouth. She knew precisely what her mother was inferring, and while it was completely stupid and on the far end of the "never gonna happen" scale, Aubrey couldn't find an argument to lob back.

And so she stood, mute, chilled to the bones that barely kept her body upright.

"Now that that's settled, your father and I—" Beneath the mask of a woman who refused to show emotion, a tremor of pain swept across Corrine's heavily made-up features. Aubrey didn't miss it, but she was too stricken by her mother's "favor" to summon up empathy. "Trent and I—" Corrine hastened to correct herself, but it was too late.

Years of hurt swarmed up like furious bees and buzzed angrily from Aubrey's mouth. "Fuck Trent," she spat. "And fuck you too, mother."

Aubrey spun on her heel, grateful that she'd rebelled and worn black Vans instead of the hideous heels Trent had supplied. She stormed out of the kitchen, sleeting shards of ice as she fled the house, stopping only when she hit the brisk February air and froze anew.

Back in the sanctity of her attic apartment, Aubrey shed her clothes and took a steaming shower, trying to thaw herself back to normal. It wasn't even eight p.m. She didn't want to spend the rest of her night boiling over with anger toward her mother.

It wasn't the first time Corrine had pulled some shit like that, and it wouldn't be the last. But her statement about Pen and the implications surrounding it…That was a new low for her.

After her shower, Aubrey sat on the edge of her bed. From the drawer in her bedside table, she took out her favorite yellow bowl, the one she'd gotten in college. She carefully packed it then cracked the window next to her bed. The first inhale hit hard, like it always did, but the second was smoother. By the third, she was starting to feel the sweet trickle of release and relaxation.

After setting the bowl on the bedside table, Aubrey dropped back against her pillows and stared at the ceiling. She loved the ceiling of her apartment. It was wooden and knotty and rustic. For such a little space, her apartment always felt like a warm hug at the end of the day, no matter how cold the day was. Like hot chocolate. Or a heated blanket.

Oh. A heated blanket sounded *amazing*.

Aubrey shivered, thinking of her mom. She swept the image of her and her ratty fake hair out of her mind. Now was not the time.

The pot—some of the best Chestnut Hill had to offer, thanks to a couple guys Aubrey had gone to high school with—worked its mellowing energy through her body. It rubbed up against sore spots and jagged wounds, areas she tried to tend to but had never managed to heal. Sometimes she wrote about them, tapping away at her typewriter (okay, laptop, but for the sake of ambience…) in the haze of evening sun through the windows of her attic apartment. She never did like writing with pen and paper—

Pen. Aubrey sat up. She had to contact her. There was no way her mother could force them not to communicate, especially since Pen was a literal adult and owed Corrine nothing. Aubrey had gone around her mother's wishes countless times before; she saw no reason to stop now. But the mere idea of not being able to talk to one of the few people who was unconditionally kind to her…It felt horrible, like a life raft tipping over the edge of a bottomless waterfall.

Aubrey's head swam, her thoughts, too, sweeping over the edge of a waterfall. She couldn't believe her mother had dared to bring up the thing they never talked about. And to make it seem like Pen…like Pen and Aubrey…as if Aubrey…She shook her head, trying to move out of the angry haze and back into the chill fog.

Fuck Corinne. Fuck family obligations. Fuck bullshit Tea Parties and fuck everything Trent stood for. Fuck image and policy and rumor and stupid fucking parents who didn't know how to love their kids.

But most of all, fuck the day Jamie Morrison was born.

CHAPTER SEVEN

As Emma rounded the corner of Penn Street, the edge of Pennbrook University's campus came into view. Her breath caught in her throat. It's not that the view was new—she'd grown up here, after all, and had lived within walking distance of the campus throughout her childhood. It's that Pennbrook, with its sprawling, Old World, brick-and-mortar charm, always inspired a gasp or two. Especially in the dead of winter, when the trees were shrouded in ice; somehow, the campus was even prettier when barren.

Emma walked carefully, doing her best to avoid the invisible icy patches on the sidewalk. She could have driven, and had considered doing so, but the anxiety rattling her body propelled her to walk. She'd hoped she'd feel calmer after the fifteen-minute trek. So far, as she circled the front of the campus and headed toward Chasten Hall, home of the business department, the anxiety hadn't shifted. It may have even gotten worse.

She stuffed her hands in the pockets of her coat and trudged along. The battle continued to rage inside her: to college, or not to college. Emma liked learning. She was a good student, always had been. But school life post high school had not been kind to her. Or meaningful. Or, frankly, worth it.

However, she was determined to attach a college degree to her name, and this time, she was dropping the whimsical side of her career aspirations and focusing on the grit, the baseline, the "know how."

"Gross," she muttered as she gazed up at the towering brick walls of Chasten Hall. "I can't believe I'm doing this."

Inside, the chill persisted, but there was a draft of warm air coming from somewhere. Emma strode down the hall, hoping she was going in the right direction. Her advisor's office was room 114, hopefully logically meaning it was on the first floor. She counted along as she passed 108, then 110. All too soon, she was faced with the doorway of 114.

The door was ajar, so Emma knocked before nudging it further open. As the door slowly creaked wider with an ancient sigh, Emma peered inside. Her stomach both deflated and whooshed with relief when she realized that, aside from standard office furniture, the room was empty.

Taking that as the sign she'd secretly been waiting for, Emma took a step back and turned to leave the way she'd just arrived. She'd taken no more than two steps before she heard someone call her name, which was a shock to the system since she'd convinced herself she was an utter unknown on this campus.

"Emmalynn?" Her name again, this time as a question.

She slowly turned on her heel, coming face-to-face with a man and his legendary beard. It was thick and curly, but neatly trimmed and showed dedicated maintenance. It was *shiny*. Really, Emma had never seen such lustrous facial hair.

When she took her eyes off the magnificent bristles, she realized with a start that the beholder of the whiskers was waiting for her to admit she was, in fact, Emmalynn.

"Hi!" She waved, then quickly dropped her hand. "Yes, I'm Emmalynn. Or Emma. Hi. That's me."

He gestured toward the door. "I'm Greg Felk, your advisor who thought he had time to grab another cup of coffee before you arrived and was evidently wrong about his time management skills. Come on in."

Once they were situated in the small space, Greg filled the air with chatter about his day (as if Emma needed to know the daily events of a professor; on the flip side, she was thrilled that she didn't have to tell her college sob story to this stranger). As he talked, he tapped away at his computer until he exclaimed, "Here we go!" and spun around to face her.

"So, Emma, what brings you to Pennbrook?"

She wanted to groan out loud but remembered it was very likely she'd end up in Greg's class one day, and dammit, she needed to maintain some kind of positive first impression.

"Well," she started, mentally bartering with herself, "I needed a fresh start. For school, I mean. Chestnut Hill isn't a fresh start because I, like, grew up here?" She cringed, hearing herself uptalk. "Um, yeah, so. I decided to major in business because it seems, uh, reasonable. It's the smart choice for me."

Greg studied her, seeming nonplussed by her sideways rambling. "Do you *want* to major in business?"

Emma crumbled internally. No. Not one bit of her. Or, maybe, a very small part of her that was clinging to a logical decision amidst an overgrown field of decisions she'd made with the most vibrant beats of her heart.

"Yes," she said, but it was quiet. She cleared her throat. Tried again. "Yes."

"Forgive me, Emma, but I'm not convinced." Greg nodded toward the papers on his desk. "And judging by your previous college experiences, I'm guessing you're not sure what you want to do."

"I do." And she did. Or, she had. "Okay, maybe not completely? But I did a lot of research and I figured out that a business degree is the best option for me." She hesitated. "I think that I'm going to end up doing what I want to do, and in order to get there, I need this degree."

"That's a much more convincing response." Greg grinned at her before turning back to face his computer. "Let's get this schedule in order."

It took longer than Emma had anticipated, but Greg seemed unfazed by the hour and ten minutes they spent puzzling together her schedule. By the time she left his office and made her way back into the chilled air, she was actually feeling a little better about the whole "trying college yet again" thing.

She didn't love her schedule, though. She'd known it would be a challenge to get the courses she needed and wanted because she was registering so close to the beginning of the semester. But that was her own fault for dragging her feet prior to moving home. What was good was that Genesis's theory had proven true: There were tons of evening classes open, and despite the fact that they were longer, Emma had scooped them up. The end result was a schedule that put her on campus just three days a week, and left her mornings available for that opening café shift.

But the classes. The anxiety she'd felt while approaching campus was nothing compared to the feeling that accompanied knowing she had to take not one but two literature classes. And in true Emma fashion, her "let's get it over with" attitude had convinced her to take both this semester. Why not? Better to suffer all at once than prolong the misery, right?

As she trudged home and began mentally planning the rest of her month, she wondered if, perhaps, her idea of suffering was quite, and problematically so, wrong.

Later that day, Emma found herself lying on the bed in Liam's spare room (when exactly had her brother become so adult that he owned a home that had a *spare room?*)—ostensibly now her room, but that just didn't feel real—staring at the ceiling. It was rare that she found herself in such a position. She kind of hated downtime; she functioned much better when she had a list to complete, an agenda to attack. That precise part of her personality was kindling for the fire she intended to build over however long it took to earn the degree in business. She would burn the candle at all ends until she got where she needed to be, and apparently she was going to do that while working *and* attending college full-time.

There would be flames and bombastic booms of fiery explosions, Emma had no doubt. History showed she didn't have a knack for taking the easy path toward anything. But at least this time, she felt more in control and slightly more confident.

She picked up her phone, wanting a distraction, and held her finger just above the screen before finally pushing down on the Instagram icon. After cursing and racking her brain for her login information, she was greeted with the social world of her friends. After one scroll that slid her past four different people living their best college lives, Emma nearly tossed her phone to the ground. Instead, she toggled over to search for Collins's profile.

For a moment, she simply stared. Collins had the most aesthetically pleasing Instagram she'd ever seen—especially considering she was a person, not a business. And she didn't have tons of followers, so Emma was pretty sure her old friend hadn't morphed into an influencer, but when considering Collins's personality, she wouldn't be surprised if that did happen at some point. She just had that thing about her, that je ne sais quoi so many other people in their early twenties seemed to have. Emma was aware that she did not have that special but undefinable characteristic, nor did she want it. It seemed like it came with a lot of pressure and demand from the outside world, something she preferred to leave out of her life.

Collins's account was curated now, that was for certain, but it still stretched back to high school, and that's where the curation stopped. Emma smiled. It was a little detail, one easily dismissed by someone who hadn't known Collins for as long as she had, but Emma recognized it for what it was. For as much as Collins had changed and matured and grown into the young adult who'd stopped her in her tracks earlier that week, she was still the same person. Otherwise, she would have deleted those old pictures. Emma was sure of that.

She bypassed the past, not wanting to get bogged down with a lifetime that no longer existed. Instead, she started her careful upward scrolling at the point of Collins arriving at college. The pictures created a visual path of evolution. There she was as a freshman at Keene University, the liberal arts school about an hour from Chestnut Hill that catered to privileged students. She still had the ponytail there, but within six pictures, it faded away. From that point, her hair slowly grew until it reached the length it was now, complete with those trendy bangs.

The fashion changed too, a bit slower than the hair. And then the people started changing. There were a lot of pictures during freshman year with one girl, presumably Collins's roommate. She was still there the summer after freshman year, which Emma remembered Collins had spent in Maine, working at a seafood restaurant. She squinted, trying to put the pieces together. It looked like this particular girl was also connected to the restaurant, but once sophomore year began, the girl disappeared. Collins's words echoed in Emma's brain—maybe that was the first girlfriend.

From that point on, Emma could only gaze at the pictures and wonder about their meaning. Collins wasn't big on captions. It looked like a fairly normal college experience: parties, candids of friends, artistic shots of campus and classes. But each year showed a maturation. Collins looked different each time a new semester started, older and more secure in her skin.

Emma dropped her phone on the bed and crossed the room to stare herself down in the mirror. Yeah, just like she thought. She looked exactly the same as in high school. Her hair might have been a little longer, but she'd had it long since middle school so no earth-shattering difference there. She didn't even look older, which was something she was sure she'd appreciate when she was old, like in her forties or whatever, but she'd been carded enough times in the last couple of months to know she still looked seventeen.

She perched on the edge of the bed and resumed scrolling through Collins's life, spending a little more time on the detailed photo journals of the trips she took over breaks with her family. Combined with her jet-setting off to a new state every summer to work some random job that inevitably fell into her lap because that was simply Collins's life, Emma hadn't seen her friend since the summer before their freshman year in college. Now that they'd reconnected, she wished the last couple of years had been different.

And not because she wished she'd been able to tag along on all of Collins's exotic and national trips. Sure, that would have been a perk, but she felt an acute sense of loss at having so easily detached herself from the friendship that had been a mainstay throughout high school. Both girls had wanted fresh starts in college, and while they hadn't ended their friendship, neither had done much to maintain it. And so it had slipped to the edges of their vision, best left undisturbed as they cruised along, making mistakes and unearthing new versions of themselves.

Speaking of…Emma turned a careful eye to Collins's pictures from last semester. She was curious about that specific new side of Collins, the bisexual one she'd so casually dropped into conversation. *That* hadn't been a thing in high school. Well, okay, it had been—but not for Collins, who was steadfastly boy-crazy all four years. They'd had friends who were bi, some who were gay. It wasn't a big deal in their school and Emma had never given it much thought; she really didn't care who people dated, slept with, or loved.

She couldn't find any pictures of the girl Collins had described so thoroughly that Emma knew she'd know her when she saw her. She did, however, linger on a picture of a young woman with dark-blond hair and an easy, friendly smile. Emma knew it wasn't Aubrey Glass—Aubrey didn't smile like that—but it looked a hell of a lot like her.

Since Collins had mentioned Aubrey, Emma hadn't been able to get her out of her head. And it was annoying. She hadn't known Aubrey well, or much at all, but there was something she didn't like about her. She always seemed so…so above everyone else. A bit of a snob, really. Just thinking about her made Emma's right ankle twinge angrily, which didn't make logical sense because that whole incident wasn't Aubrey's fault.

But Aubrey Glass had run over from the opposite side of the field and stood over Emma as she laid silent and deathly still on the ground, knowing the collision she'd just suffered with that brute of a girl from their rival high school was the end of her freshman-playing-varsity field hockey career.

And Aubrey Glass's face was the last face Emma saw before her body decided it'd had enough pain and knocked her out cold, right there on the field.

CHAPTER EIGHT

"Excuse me, miss."

Aubrey's shoulders shot up, her neck muscles constricting and hardening into stone. She was not in the mood to be called "miss." She was not in the mood for anything or anyone, and an hour into her workday, was woefully aware of her grievous error in even leaving her bed.

Slowly, so as not to give any indication that she was at a customer's beck and call, she set down the pile of books she'd been reshelving and turned to face the voice that had summoned her.

"Hello," she said, trying to inject kindness into her tone. It was a failed attempt, but she applauded herself for the effort. She couldn't muster up the "how can I help you" and hoped she hadn't accidentally implied the phrase in her emotionless greeting.

A sheet of paper was thrust into her personal bubble. She stumbled backward a step, hackles raising with alarming speed. Man, either her energy was super off, or there was a vibe coming from this customer that was going to hit every item on her long list of customer annoyances.

"Do you even have these books here? I tried to find them but this store has zero organization."

Well, that was a lie. Sure, Sadie was known to move sections around on a whim, but after a few interventions with Aubrey and a couple of other booksellers, she hadn't moved a single section in two whole months. She still hadn't renamed or rebranded the self-help section, but Aubrey knew she was working hard on it. In her head, anyway.

Aubrey looked at the list instead of firing back a snarky response. "Sure," she said after scanning the titles. "We should have all of them."

When she looked back up at the customer, he shot her an exasperated look, as though she should have been able to snap her fingers and bring forth his required texts.

"Would you like me to show you where you can find them?" She bit the inside of her cheek after forcing the words out.

"No," he said, his voice the exclamation point of his facial expression. "I want you to get them for me."

Aubrey watched him scan her chest. Instinctually, she took another step backward and had just begun to raise her arms to cover her chest when she realized he was looking for her nametag. Which she had forgotten. Purposely.

Sure enough, the next sentence out of his mouth included the word "miss" yet again, which sent ants crawling over Aubrey's skin. The presumption of her gender identity—he was correct, but still—was something that always shocked her.

She held the list out in front of her. He stared at it. She stared at him.

"The horror books are in the mystery section," she began. "That's located near the front of the store, next to the area with greeting cards and other small gift items. The two books on the bottom of your list are new releases, so you can find them in general fiction or on the display in front of the registers. As for the Kahneman title, you should be able to find that in self-help. If it's not there, try the business section, which is right behind the self-help section." The Kahneman book was the only indication that this guy wasn't a total asshole; then again, it could have been a gift.

He narrowed his gaze at her. "Don't you think it would be easier if you would just get them for me?"

"I'm not your personal assistant."

He laughed then, a sound that sent a shiver through Aubrey's body. A scarlet cloud of fury and embarrassment began to cloud her vision. She was still thin-skinned and brittle from her conversation with her mother, and this interaction was only compounding her existing feelings.

Belatedly, she realized the man had stopped laughing and was now smiling like they were old friends.

"Trent told me you had some sass, but he didn't mention the vitriol."

Nearly blinded by her emotions, Aubrey spat out, "I am not vitriolic." After sending up a mental high five to her months of SAT Prep, she blinked rapidly, trying to make sense of what he'd said. "Did you say Trent?"

"Sure did." This guy was all glee and joy now, all his former boss-bro attitude blown away like it was a fart in the wind. "You're Aubrey, right?"

This time she did cross her arms over her chest. "And what if I'm not?"

He laughed again. "Good one, kid. We spoke the other night, at your dad's house. And I never forget a pretty face."

Aubrey felt her body shutter up like a home facing a hurricane. She couldn't even begin to feel the wrath of this douchebag referring to her mother's third husband as her "dad." The "pretty face" comment along with the apparently purposeful rude interaction felt disturbingly like some kind of fucked-up middle-aged man flirtation, and if she didn't remove herself from the situation, she was either going to say something highly regrettable or vomit directly on this man's shoes, which looked very expensive.

She wouldn't feel bad about the vomit, for the record.

"I believe you're here to get books," she said, hoping her voice wasn't shaking. She pushed the list back toward him. She didn't know what kind of creepy good-old-boy hijinks Trent and this assclown were up to, but she had no desire to be subjected to any more of them.

"Aw, kid, I was just having some fun. Don't be so serious."

She was going to snap. She felt it rise in her muscles and tendons, the mad rush of untethered feelings. She had to get away, immediately.

"Here," she said. Her voice barely registered as a whisper as she forced the paper into his hand.

"You know," he said, looking around as if Cornerstone was a foreign fantasy land he wasn't sure he wanted to explore. "Corrine doesn't give this place enough credit. It's nothing like she described. Much nicer."

A wave of sadness crashed into the boiling anger consuming Aubrey's body. So that's what this was all about. Corrine sending little spies out to scope her out at work. It was a new low for her.

"It *is* nice," Aubrey said defensively. "It's a great place to work."

"Great for now. I know your parents would like to see you—"

There. *There.* Aubrey felt the latch lift and a swoop of new emotion charged through her body, cresting in the words that spewed from her mouth. "He is not my father," Aubrey spat, each word loaded with as much ire as she could muster. "And what I do with my life is no more your concern than it is Trent's."

If the man was shocked, Aubrey wouldn't have known, because she stalked away before the period attached itself to Trent's name. She tried to keep her head up but the effort proved too much and with each step she took, her shoulders slouched further and further until she was certain her elbows were scraping the hardwood floor of the bookstore.

"Are you okay?"

She wanted to snap her head up because that was the last question she wanted to answer but her body was made of pudding. Slowly, Aubrey looked up. Her first thought was, *who the fuck are you?* And the second thought, tumbling recklessly after the first, reminded her: *oh fuck, the new hire. Sadie Jr.*

She just stared at the girl in front of her. She didn't know her name, but she felt like she should. Even if she did, she didn't know her any better than she knew the assbag she'd just interacted with, so to even answer that question—

"Do you, um, need a minute?" The young woman looked deeply concerned. "I overheard most of that," she added, her voice quiet enough that only the two of them could hear. "Do you know him?"

"No," Aubrey said, the word a sledgehammer. "And I'm fine."

Honey-brown eyes stared at her. The girl was unconvinced, and Aubrey couldn't blame her. "Do you want me to find Sadie?"

"I do not want you to do that." Aubrey glanced over her shoulder. She needed to know where that asshole was. She scanned until she found him at the front of the store, laughing heartily with his phone pressed against his ear. Probably telling Trent how he'd just gotten a rise out of her. She shivered. She'd rather pretend the last four minutes of her life hadn't happened than figure out what any of that meant, or was supposed to be.

She'd never trusted Trent, and Mr. Assman with the Shiny Shoes had only made that worse.

Aubrey winced, her whole body flinching, remembering the comment he'd made about her mother.

"He's checking out," Sadie Jr. said softly. "Oh, wow, he has like eight books."

"Great, a star customer." Aubrey moved behind the Hub, pretending she had something magnificently important to do.

"I mean, it's the least he could do after being such a dick to you."

"Mmhmm."

"Does that happen often? I feel like it wouldn't, right? Chestnut Hill is, like, chill, you know? All the professors and stuff. I guess maybe they can be intense? I don't know, it just felt super wrong—"

"Do you need something?" Aubrey said acidly.

"What? Me? No." Sadie Jr. shook her head, sending her thick red hair into rolling waves about her shoulders. Her hair, Aubrey realized, was *long*.

"Shouldn't your hair be pulled back?"

If Sadie Jr. was affected by Aubrey's less than friendly tone and words, she didn't show it. "Ugh, yeah. I just wait until the last minute." She gestured toward her body, which was covered by the shapeless black apron donned by all baristas. "But I probably already got hair on my apron."

Now that Aubrey's attention had been drawn to said apron, she noticed the nametag secured at the top of the black sack. "Just Emma," she said aloud.

Sadie Jr., or Just Emma, sighed dramatically. "Yeah, I made the critical error of correcting Genesis."

Aubrey blinked. She felt like she should know the punch line here, but her brain was still tied up in trying to manage her red-hot emotions and how to, or if she should even, approach Trent about what had happened and what he was trying to do.

"Oh," Just Emma said, nodding once. "Yeah, okay, I'll explain. Genesis kept calling me by my last name, so I reminded her that I have a first name. Then she wouldn't stop calling me Emmalynn, which is obviously fine because it's my *name*, but I said, 'Just Emma,' and she made my nametag with Just Emma on it. I don't know if she thought I was serious? And that my name is Just Emma?" She shook her head and rolled her eyes, not missing a beat in her explanation. "I guess she might have been kidding, but then she gave me this, and…Yeah, I guess I'm Just Emma now."

"Emmalynn," Aubrey repeated.

"Emma," Just Emma said. "Or Emmalynn. That's fine. Sure."

Aubrey pressed her palms against the edge of the Hub's counter. "Emma Gallagher?"

Just Emma turned paler than her already pale-ish skin, her freckles popping in alarming hues. Then, just as quickly, a blush started at her jawline and crept forward, spreading across her cheeks until the two waves met at her nose. Aubrey's gaze slid to a patch of freckles on the right side of Emma's jaw, which seemed to get darker instead of disappearing into the blush like the rest.

"Yes," Emma said. "I'm Emma Gallagher."

And Aubrey should have known that, because the young woman standing in front of her, who—if she was guessing correctly—was probably twenty-one now, looked exactly like the fourteen-year-old super hyped-up freshman field hockey player who'd hopped right on the varsity team as if she belonged there.

But just as quickly as she'd joined the team, she was gone.

The why was escaping Aubrey, probably because her neurons were still firing toward her preoccupation with that asswipe and Trent. She tried like hell to reroute her thinking, but there was a massive blank space where the memory of Emma should be.

"You don't remember me," Emma said plainly. Then she laughed. "I wouldn't either, honestly."

"No," Aubrey said quickly. "I do. Kind of."

"We didn't know each other." Emma shrugged, visibly uncomfortable. She tugged at the apron string around her neck. "It's okay, really. We can just pretend we never knew each other."

Guilt snagged around Aubrey's heart. She blamed all the pot she'd smoked in college for the empty ditch of Emma memories. But she knew, she *knew*, she had one.

"Just Emma! Move it!"

Both women turned to the cackling sound of Genesis yell-whispering on the walkie from the café, where she had a line of exactly two people. Emma cast a sidelong glance at Aubrey before waving and walking toward the café.

And as Aubrey watched her go, she noticed the nearly imperceptible limp, the way Emma just barely favored her right leg. She wouldn't have noticed it if something in her foggy mind hadn't told her to watch for it, it was that minute.

"Number Twenty-two," Aubrey said to the empty space around her. Emma Gallagher, the field hockey star. Number 22. The one whose high school career ended during the first game of the season.

Aubrey could have kicked herself. She was mortified that she hadn't remembered Emma, because she *had*, she just couldn't piece it all together fast enough. And if she were in a better mental space, she would have rushed over to apologize, or make a stupid joke, or something—anything—to clear the air.

Instead, her feet stayed glued to the floor behind the Hub, holding her steady to keep her safe.

CHAPTER NINE

"Oh good, freshly baked breakfast is on its way. Almost makes up for the fact that you're not paying me rent."

Liam's voice cut through the thoughts that were hyperactively breakdancing in Emma's head. She didn't look up, though, because despite the pounding footwork ricocheting through her brain, her focus was (mostly) on the dough that she was patiently rolling across the kitchen counter. That, and she didn't feel like engaging in his annoying banter.

"Em-ma," he repeated, drawing out the word. "Hey. Sis. Snap out of it."

Emma wordlessly raised the rolling pin. Liam, ever the obnoxious older brother, grabbed the other end and yanked it cleanly from her hand.

"You might have baking muscles or whatever, but these"—he gestured to his biceps—"are gym muscles. Big difference."

"Such a male thing to say, but also weird, considering you don't go to the gym." Emma put out her hand. "Give it back."

He held on, but only by his fingertips, knowing from past experience that if he dared touch the section that was dough-only, he wouldn't even get to look at the finished baking product. And tasting it? Not a chance.

"I'll give it back when you tell me what your problem is."

Emma stood up straighter. She didn't have a *problem*. She was just annoyed. Frustrated. Pissed off. Lots of negative emotions, apparently, but she didn't have a problem. She was just feeling shit she didn't want to feel because she'd buried it almost seven years ago and—

"Aubrey Glass," she blurted, then immediately clapped her hand over her mouth.

Liam just looked at her. Emma knew she didn't need to explain who Aubrey was, because everyone knew Aubrey Glass. If "iconic" had been a word they'd used in high school, it would have been typed in boldface beneath Aubrey Glass's senior picture in the yearbook.

"What about her?" Liam finally said. He looked unimpressed, but also overly nonchalant.

"I work with her," Emma said, her tone dull. "Or, she works at Cornerstone and so do I. We don't really work together. More like coexist in the same store."

"Wait, wait. Aubrey Glass? Is here? Working at Cornerstone?"

Emma took advantage of her brother's break in nonchalance and grabbed the rolling pin back as he stood there, clearly surprised.

"That's what I said."

"Huh."

She didn't like the sound of that "huh." Liam wasn't a "huh" kind of guy. An uncomfortable and unidentifiable emotion spun through Emma's stomach. "'Huh'? What does that mean? Nobody says 'huh' about Aubrey Glass, Liam."

He recovered from his surprise, hopping up to sit on the part of the counter Emma hadn't commandeered for her Saturday morning anxiety bake-off. She glared at him anyway, because why shouldn't she?

"I'm just surprised," he said. It was unfair, Emma thought, how effortlessly handsome her brother was. He'd just rolled out of bed and he looked like he could strut down the sidewalk and have his damn picture taken by local paparazzi. She, on the other hand, had woken up looking like she'd spent the night in an overcrowded bird's nest.

"She's one of those people who wanted to get out of here so bad," Liam went on. "She left for college and disappeared. Never showed up at parties over breaks. And she definitely wasn't here over the summers. Weird." He said the last word to himself, as though he'd forgotten Emma was in the room.

"Well," Emma said loudly, "she's very much here now."

Liam grinned. "And that's driving you crazy."

"It is not." Her voice was far louder than she'd intended. "I could care less where Aubrey Glass is or what she's doing."

"What's your problem with her, Em? Did you guys even know each other? She was in my class, and it's not like you ever hung out with upperclassmen."

Emma didn't say anything. She answered by attacking the already overrolled dough. Her brother was smart, had a memory like a lockbox, and he'd put the pieces together on his own, eliminating the need for her to spell it out for him.

Liam scrubbed his hand over his hair, leaving it sticking up in a way he would never allow in public. "I'm missing something," he said. "C'mon, Em. Spill it."

"No." She gave up her one-sided fight with the dough and began spreading the filling, a classic and irresistible combination of brown sugar and butter, over it. If she got to the raspberries before Liam put it together, she'd be forced to pelt—

"Ohh," he finally said, sliding off the counter and moving toward the coffee maker. He pressed a few buttons and stepped back, regarding Emma. "Field hockey."

The two words used to send a knife slicing through her from head to toe. Now, they induced a dull ache of memory and discarded dreams. *Fractured* dreams was the more appropriate descriptor, but Emma tried to avoid using that word.

"Yep," she said. "Field hockey."

"Look at you!" Emma looked up at her brother, who was grinning like she'd won the fifth-grade spelling bee. "You can say the words without passing out!"

"Very funny," she muttered. She didn't expect him to understand. While Liam had the genetic blessing of being fit and muscular without doing more than the occasional pushup, he'd never been a serious athlete. He had no idea what it was like to watch your dream of playing collegiate—maybe even professional—sports vanish in one awful stick-to-ankle collision during the very first game of your high school career.

Emma felt her shoulders move closer to her ears. She'd had enough conversations with athletes and trainers over the years to know several things:

1)   She needed to stop dramatically describing the event. (But, you know, teenagers—it *was* dramatic.)

2)   She needed to move past it as much as she could, which touched back to the first item on the list.

3)   She could have played again.

Truthfully, Emma still hadn't resolved that last entry. Her injury had been brutal, yes, and the recovery had felt endless (it wasn't, obviously, but again—teenage brain). Her shattered ankle had to be fused back together, requiring multiple surgeries and some strategically placed pins. But she could walk, run, sprint, jog, dash. She could mostly turn on a dime, though she felt like her ankle didn't love that, so she tried to avoid doing it. When she was tired, she felt a little limp take over her stride, but when she'd had it checked out by her orthopedist, Dr. McKinnon had explained it was a somatic response to the trauma. Emma had a hard time choking down that explanation. No one had used the word "trauma" with her in relation to her injury before. She considered seeking out therapy but, being more of a task-oriented person than a deeply thinking one, Emma did her own "therapy" by researching ways to move past traumatic experiences.

The end result wasn't what she'd hoped for. All she emerged with was new terminology to describe the incident and the feelings within her related to it. She wasn't over it. She couldn't seem to shake the injustice of it, the way one moment on a field had completely altered her planned course of life. Her dream, cracked through and destroyed in an instant.

She looked down at the pastries forming beneath her fingers. It was only the first of several dreams to shatter, as it turned out.

"So have you talked to her?"

Stuck in her memories, Emma's mind swam with wavy images of the girl who'd collided with her. She glared at Liam. "Are you serious?"

"Why wouldn't I be?" He was sitting at the counter now, sipping his coffee, which he took black. Now that Emma had a little barista experience under her belt, she found his preferred coffee style appalling.

"Liam," she said, more exasperated than angry because her body had a way of dispelling big red emotions before she could hold on to them. "I don't even know her." *She doesn't know you*, her subconscious whispered.

"You work with her, Em. Just say hi."

Emma's mind cleared and Aubrey filtered in, replacing the blurry image of the field hockey player from their rival high school team, a girl whose name she'd never learned. Aubrey, standing in the shadows of bookshelves. Aubrey, slouching in that effortless way. Aubrey, looking at Emma yesterday while they stood at the Hub, peering at her as though she was a ghost from a story of her past that was better left unread.

Funny, because Emma felt the same way.

"Maybe you two have more in common than you think," Liam went on.

His words snuck in and layered in Emma's brain like a cake stacked to the ceiling, ready to topple over if someone so much as looked at the table upon which it sat. Aubrey Glass? And Emma? Have something in common? Unfathomable.

And yet...

"I mean, you're both back home under mysterious circumstances."

Oh, Liam. Just shut up.

"I get it," Emma said. "Besides, I have talked to her. Yesterday. A little."

"And?"

She scrunched up her nose and looked at her brother. He was way too curious about this. "Why do you care so much about her?"

He rolled his eyes. "Relax. It's not about her. I'm looking out for you."

She scoffed as she went about rolling the dough, prepping it to be sliced into buns. "I don't need to be looked out for." She held her knife up as an exclamation point before carefully pushing it through the dough.

"That's where you're wrong, little sis." He folded his arms over his chest and watched as she placed the buns on a baking sheet and covered them with a tea towel. "You show up back home without an explanation and expect me to just be cool about it and not ask questions, which makes me think you're hiding something crazy, which makes me think I need to make sure you don't do something else crazy. And that, dear sister, is why I'm looking out for you."

Emma used the noise of the mixer to drown out anything else he might say. Surely that would be a clear sign, an evident end to the conversation. But when she turned around with a bowl of whisked egg yolks, sugar, and cornstarch, Liam was waiting patiently for the story she dreaded telling.

She opened her mouth but he spoke before she could fire off a distraction. "I get that you don't want Mom and Dad to know. But since you're crashing with me indefinitely, I think it would be nice for me to know if you're on the run from drug dealers or human traffickers."

"Jesus, Liam."

"Hey, that's what happens when you shroud yourself in mystery."

"I didn't do anything crazy," Emma began. "Let's get that out of the way, okay?"

He smiled beatifically, an expression that should have been reserved for his former days as an altar boy. He then spread his arms out as if to say, "Bring it on, my child."

And so, Emma brought it. She kept her hands busy with making the custard, knowing she could only tell this tale if she distracted herself.

It wasn't sordid or jaw-dropping. The truth was that Emma had simply failed. As she measured out the rest of the ingredients for the custard, she told Liam about lasting a full year in Drexel's Culinary Arts and Sciences program before deciding not to return the following year. Her grades weren't cutting it because she hated everything about the program. She knew it was a bad fit after the first week, but felt like she had to stick it out because she'd made the decision to move to Philadelphia and Dream Big.

When she was home that summer after freshman year, Emma confessed to her parents that she wouldn't be returning to Drexel. They urged her to find a program that felt like a better fit (and promised not to tell Liam, which was silly, but Emma hated the idea of her brother knowing she couldn't hack it at Drexel). She spent a lot of time that summer doing what she did best—researching— and found the culinary arts program at the Community College of

Philadelphia. In August, she returned to Philadelphia, moved into a remodeled apartment in a questionable area of the city with three roommates, and started fresh at the community college.

A semester later, she felt utterly defeated. All she wanted was to get an education that would help her be a better baker. Nothing about the classes she was taking seemed applicable to what she felt she needed to learn. Call it naivety or overblown young adult confidence, but she decided right then and there, moments before heading home for Christmas break, to end her college journey for good.

As she spooned the custard into the buns, Emma admitted to Liam that part of her knew dropping out wasn't the answer. But she was at a loss and hadn't had the courage or the wherewithal to seek out advice from any of her professors. She avoided owning up to her struggles while home for break, and when she returned to the city, she called her parents and said she needed a break from school. They didn't love that little info bomb, not that she'd thought they would. Emma was given strict instructions to find a job because, surprise, her parents weren't willing to pay her rent—which had just jumped $300 due to a roommate moving out—if she wasn't actively taking classes.

Emma's first thought was to find a job at a bakery. It was the obvious choice, one that might even help her figure out how to make a career out of her one true love. But the moment she walked into one, her stomach cramped and her lungs decided to stop working. She barely made it out before she had a full-blown panic attack in front of the perfectly frosted cupcakes.

Baking tossed to the side, Emma sought out new ventures. A girl she knew from the community college had talked endlessly about her amazing job at a vegan butcher shop. The mere idea of such a thing confounded her, but she was also intrigued enough by it to apply when she heard there was an opening.

"A what?" Liam interrupted. "You said vegan butcher? How do those two words even go together?"

"It's actually amazing. They make so many things, all plant-based," Emma said. She finished brushing the buns with egg wash and slid the baking tray into the preheated oven. "And I learned a lot."

She detailed the various offerings of the shop: vegan ribs, pork chops, jerky, salami, meatloaf. She ignored Liam's look of disgust—he was a carnivore, through and through—and focused instead on how that job had taught her more than she'd bargained for. So much so that she'd stayed up until just a couple of months ago.

Emma wasn't sure if she would have completely abandoned the idea of finishing college if she'd stayed at the vegan butcher. It was a possibility, but the overachiever inside her knew there wasn't a chance in hell that she'd continue on in life without a college degree. After a year and a half of working nonstop at a small business, Emma came away with skills and know-how that no degree could provide. But she still wanted one, even if it was in something—business, for example—she'd never dreamed it would be.

As it was, another roommate left, bringing the rent to an amount Emma couldn't afford...Especially considering she'd bought that new car. So, tail tucked between her legs, Emma quit her job, packed up her belongings, and headed home to Chestnut Hill.

What she hadn't told anyone was how she'd applied to Pennbrook on a whim back in September. Call it a gut instinct or fate, she'd done it, and now she was on the brink of starting college for the third time.

Emma glanced at the oven timer. In just five minutes, she'd have a full tray of raspberry custard buns. Her mouth watered, but her stomach flip-flopped like a fish in shallow water.

"I'm not disappointed in you, Em."

She jerked her head up and looked at her brother. He seemed sincere enough.

"You could have just been honest with me from the start," he continued, shrugging. "You're young. You're figuring everything out. That's basically life in your early twenties."

"It's not what I wanted my early twenties to be," she huffed. "This isn't—no offense—where I'm supposed to be right now."

"Okay, but it's where you are." Liam raised an eyebrow at her. "What I don't understand is why you're working at Cornerstone, making coffee, which you hate, instead of working in a bakery or something. Doing what you love." He nodded in the direction of the oven, in case Emma had somehow missed the implication.

The fish flipped right out of the water. Emma pressed her hands against her stomach. "I just can't right now, okay?"

Her tone must have said more than she could hear because Liam instantly backed off. "Okay. I guess it works out for me, since you keep baking like a maniac whenever you're upset about something."

"Oh my God, Liam." Emma stalked over to the oven and peered through the door. "I'm not upset! I have a job. I'm starting classes next week. Everything is fine."

"Sure it is," he drawled. "But the mere mention of Aubrey Glass still gets you all flustered."

Flustered? Is that what happened? And "still"? What the hell was Liam talking about? "Why are you so obsessed with her?" Emma shot back, deflecting as best she could.

He stood up and twisted, cracking his back. "I'm not. She's a cool girl, Em. You should learn something about that from her."

"You're an asshole."

"Takes one to know one, shit brick."

Emma threw the oven mitt at her brother's retreating form. He was right, of course. Aubrey was effortlessly cool, always had been—that much Emma remembered. Some people just had that gift.

The oven timer dinged, and she wasted no time in taking her buns out. She stared at them. They were beautiful, definitely one of the most appetizing pastries she'd ever made. She might not be cool, but at least she could bake.

"Oh my God," Emma mumbled, pressing her face into her hands. "You're hopeless."

CHAPTER TEN

Aubrey rubbed her arms as she walked through Cornerstone. She had a chill she couldn't shake. It had crept up on her the previous night, sinking low into her bones as she stared blankly at the movie playing on her laptop. It wasn't a sick kind of chill; she knew those well from bouts of chronic strep throat when she was younger. No, this was a chill that settled and lingered, pressing icy fingertips into each inhale and squeezing on the exhale.

It was possible Aubrey had smoked too much last night. It was the only coping mechanism she used lately. It helped her sleep, sure, but she'd started smoking earlier and earlier in the evening. Since Aubrey lived by herself and didn't glorify smoking on her social media, no one but the guys she bought it from knew how much she was using. She didn't have a problem, and she wasn't high all day long. But she didn't want to get to a place where she felt like she *had* to smoke in order to function.

She scrolled through her playlists, searching for the perfect early morning Monday mood. It would have to be something chill with an energetic undertone. Definitely not the right time for Volcano Girls, even though Aubrey could write a dissertation on how it was the perfect playlist for literally any time. She did try to take other people's Monday morning moods into consideration, so she hit play on Brighter Light, a playlist filled with indie artists from the early 2000s.

The music worked—of course, Aubrey could only speak for herself—and tasks that had felt impossible when she arrived quickly became routine and simple. She spent extra time in the newest part of the store, the dedicated Pennbrook zone. After the owners had purchased the small storefront next door, they'd merged the buildings, and suddenly Cornerstone had gained much-needed extra space. Sadie had planned carefully, and when Aubrey started working at the store, the additional space had just been unveiled. (Yes, Sadie had a ribbon-cutting ceremony.) The young adult and kids sections had grown and expanded. Poetry and drama got their own space, nestled next to the revamped photography, art, and travel section.

And at the head of the addition was the Pennbrook zone, unofficially named. Since Cornerstone was technically a college bookstore because it was located a mere block from campus, Sadie had decided they should ramp up the college aspect—but only in that one corner. There were standard texts along with the usual college supplies. Sadie had even sprung for a small selection of apparel. It was obvious to Aubrey that Sadie didn't love this addition, but it did bring in a nice profit, so everyone in the store tolerated it.

With the beginning of the spring semester right around the corner, the Pennbrook zone would take a beating. Aubrey lugged over several boxes and spent the majority of her preopening shift rearranging and organizing as she replenished the stock. When she finished, she realized she hadn't been blessed with Genesis's cranky morning attitude.

Broken-down boxes shoved under her arm, Aubrey took the long way back to the stock room so she could check in on Genesis. When she reached the edge of the café, she stopped. No Genesis, unless she was in the back, but the coffee was brewing and the pastry case was stocked. Aubrey moved behind the counter, careful not to knock into anything with the boxes beneath her arm, and stuck her head in the back area of the café. Again, no Genesis, just the industrial sink and refrigerator, plus all the café stock.

"What the hell," Aubrey mumbled as she left the café. Her friend—a term she used loosely with Genesis, as they did socialize outside of work, but didn't often have conversations that stretched beyond the superficial and mundane—had a mighty presence, and a loud one. She couldn't have slipped past Aubrey, especially since her passionate distaste for mornings announced itself the moment Genesis stepped inside the store.

She nudged the boxes higher then came to an abrupt stop a few feet away from the Hub. Apparently she hadn't missed Genesis, but she had somehow missed Emma.

There she was, standing at the Hub, slowly scrolling the old iPhone, a.k.a the store DJ. She was wearing that horrible black apron and her hair was neatly pulled back into a ponytail. Emma was so focused on—

The playlists.

Aubrey froze. The cardboard slid from her grasp and tumbled to the floor. Cardboard hitting a hardwood floor didn't make a commotion, but it was enough surprise movement to make Emma look up.

And the moment she turned those warm brown eyes on Aubrey, the floor tilted. Aubrey stepped to the side, trying to find stable ground. She stumbled slightly. Right. The floor hadn't tilted. She had tilted.

The only thing Aubrey could do to combat the sudden instability inside of her was to fire off a barrage of questions. "What are you doing? Why are you looking at my playlists? Who let you in? Where's Genesis?"

Emma widened her eyes and stepped back. She gestured to the phone. "I—I'm sorry. I didn't realize that was yours."

"Of course it's mine," Aubrey grumbled. It wasn't, but Emma didn't need to know that.

"I thought it was the store's," Emma continued, either truly not hearing Aubrey or giving her the grace of pretending that she hadn't. "I really like this song and I was surprised to hear it so I came over to see what else was on the playlist."

Aubrey took an involuntary step closer to the Hub. Emma liked Arcade Fire? That fact didn't fit with her internal list of Emma facts, of which, honestly, there were very few. (Namely: she used to play field hockey, she had great hair, she probably had terrible taste in music.)

Emma aimed a cautious smile toward Aubrey. "And to answer your other questions, Sadie let me in, and Genesis is off duty for morning shifts." She pointed to herself with her thumb. "Meet your new opening barista."

"You," Aubrey said.

"Me."

As they stared at each other, "In the Backseat" continued playing in the background. Aubrey cursed it for being such a long, but beautiful song—one she and Emma both apparently liked. Since their conversation last week, Aubrey had been trying to piece together other memories of Emma from high school, but she came up empty. If her recollection was correct, they hadn't had any interactions after Emma's short stint on the team—not that they'd had much to say to each other then, either. It wasn't unusual, considering Aubrey had been a senior when Emma was a freshman, and high school politics influenced the boundary between them.

But Aubrey hadn't forgotten about her. She simply hadn't remembered Emma being this...magnetic. Yeah, that was it. And Aubrey held the other magnet in her hand, which was super disconcerting. She had no idea how it had gotten there, let alone what she was meant to do with it.

"It's a good playlist," Emma said, breaking the silence between them. "And I promise I didn't look at anything else on your phone."

Aubrey sighed, feeling her towering defenses droop. "It's not my phone. Sorry. I overreacted."

"Yeah, you did."

Oh, and she had spunk. Aubrey bit the inside of her lip to avoid smiling. When she looked up, she expected to see a confident young woman glaring at her, but instead Emma looked like she wanted to run as far away as possible.

Before Aubrey could get a word out, Emma had turned and started toward the café.

Oh well. Aubrey gathered up the cardboard she'd dropped. *There's always tomorrow.*

On Tuesday morning, Aubrey paid a little more attention to the preopening playlist. She wanted something invigorating, but nothing that would be hard on still-sleepy ear drums. After scrolling for over ten minutes, she settled on This Is Not Your

Wedding Day, a title that had absolutely no relevance to the songs lumped beneath it.

After she pressed play, Maggie Rogers's voice accompanied her as she began setting up a display of new releases. She was acutely aware of Emma's presence over in the café, but the history and biography section provided a thick barrier between them. It was best that way, Aubrey thought. There was something about Emma that made her feel very slippery, like she couldn't hold a grip on the bricks she'd surrounded herself with. But while she was slip-sliding around, she was dodging bullets of her own curiosity. She didn't know why Emma was here, in Chestnut Hill, and working at Cornerstone. And she kind of wanted to know the answer.

It was in the middle of Hozier's "Almost" that Aubrey stood up and peered over at the café. She'd heard a little crash. She had no intention of saving Emma or even asking if she was okay, but again, that curiosity.

Emma's red hair popped up from behind the counter. Her face was flushed and she was holding something in her hands.

"You good?" Aubrey called.

Judging by the speed with which she turned her head to look in Aubrey's direction, her neck should have snapped. "All good," she said.

"You sure?"

Emma made a face, but it wasn't the "get me the fuck out of here" expression she'd worn the day before, so Aubrey took that as a win. This was more of a "of course I'm okay, didn't you hear me the first time?" look.

"Yes, I'm sure." She paused as she looked back at her hands. Slowly, Emma lifted up a piece of ceramic. "I may have broken a mug."

Aubrey shrugged. "Happens all the time. Toss it and let Genesis know."

"Okay." After another hesitation, Emma nodded. "Thanks."

"No problem."

Aubrey waited a beat, selfishly hoping for a comment about the playlist, but Emma went about the business of tossing the broken mug and sweeping up the remnants on the floor.

Wednesday morning brought a storm of flurries that looked like they might add up to something shovelable. Aubrey was moving as slowly as the clouds. She'd slept like shit. Getting out of bed at six a.m. had been a monumental feat. She was wishing she could have stayed in bed, but if she didn't go to work, she didn't get paid.

So there she was, yawning mightily while she stood at the Hub. One part of her brain wished for hard, full-volume indie-rock, while the other part wanted nothing more than to envelop itself in the falling snow. The soft side won out, and Aubrey started up Cold Dream, her standard winter weather playlist. This one was filled with lo-fi ambient tunes, a veritable marshmallow for the ears.

Another yawn stretched the limits of Aubrey's jaw. She rubbed her eyes and groaned, knowing what she had to do. With the speed of a sloth heading toward a meal, she made her way to the empty café.

Once there, she hesitated. She and Genesis had an agreement that Aubrey could make herself a drink before the store opened. But now that Emma had replaced Genesis, she wasn't sure what move to make.

Fortunately, Emma bustled out from the back room before she had to decide. She glanced at Aubrey as she slid croissants into the pastry case. "The music fits the mood," she said by way of greeting. "Nice job."

"It's a talent," Aubrey said, then winced. "I mean, it's something I like doing."

Emma grinned, and it was the most genuine expression Aubrey had seen yet. "You can be cocky about it. You're good."

Aubrey fought back a blush. This girl, Emma Gallagher, had no reason to make Aubrey blush. It wasn't the person, Aubrey assured herself. It was what she'd said. Yes. Right.

With that in mind, she snuck another glance at Emma, who was filling the espresso grinder. Okay. Fine. Aubrey could admit to herself that Emma was attractive. It didn't mean a damn thing, it was simply science.

"So," Aubrey said, focusing on the counter instead of Emma's pretty face. "I—"

"Need a drink?"

She sagged in relief. "Yes. Badly."

"Genesis said you sometimes come over in the morning. I've kinda been waiting for you."

Those words, innocent and honest, perfectly in tune to the conversation and definitely not holding any extraneous meaning, should not have fizzled in Aubrey's stomach the way they did. She shooed them away.

"Do you want to make it?" She purposely left off "for me," knowing that could sound unintentionally flirty. *Stick to the facts, Glass.* "Or, uh, I could."

Emma stuck her hands on her hips and eyed Aubrey. "She left out the part about you making your own drinks."

Aubrey leaned against the counter. "I pretty much only do that when she's busy. So you can make it. Totally fine."

With a nod, Emma moved toward Bernard. Aubrey watched as she prepped a shot of espresso, then bent over to pull milk from the fridge. Aubrey opened her mouth then closed it when she saw the skim milk container in Emma's hand.

"She left me instructions," Emma explained as she added one pump of vanilla syrup and two of caramel into a large cup. She set the cup down and prepped a second shot of espresso.

Emma gave Aubrey a pointed look as she poured exactly one and a half shots into the cup, then topped them with hot skim milk. She snapped a lid on and placed the cup on the counter, gently pushing it toward Aubrey.

"It's lukewarm, just like you like it."

Aubrey, shocked by both Genesis's thoughtfulness and Emma's seamless movement around the art of drink making, mumbled a thank-you. She tested the drink, wanting to make sure Emma was right about the temperature, then took a long, full swig.

"It's perfect," she said after swallowing. "Maybe even better than Genesis's."

Emma's eyes glittered beneath the dim café lights. "I won't tell her if you won't."

"Wouldn't dream of it."

Sadie rested her chin in her hand. Her eyes glazed over as they always did when she gazed around her beloved store. "I'm glad you're becoming friends with Emma."

Aubrey coughed, nearly choking on the iced tea she'd tried to swallow. "What? No. That's not a thing."

"I saw you two talking yesterday morning." Sadie smiled. "I'm pretty sure that constitutes the beginning of a friendship."

Aubrey flashed back to the previous morning, when Emma had made her the best caramel vanilla latte she'd ever had. She hadn't lingered, since they both had work to do, but she could have easily stayed longer and asked Emma something, anything, about her life. "Uh, no? People can just talk."

"Well, sure. But sometimes people talk and they both look happy while they're talking." Sadie ruffled Aubrey's hair. "Why shouldn't you be friends? Don't fight it, Aub."

She wasn't fighting it. She just wasn't sure it was a good idea.

Later that day, Aubrey was in the magazine section. Their Thursday shipment had come late, so she was spending the end of her shift elbow-deep in *Croquet Gazette* and *Water Polo World*. It was a reasonably busy day, which made up for Wednesday's lackluster sales. It hadn't snowed much, just enough to encourage people to stay home.

Aubrey had just slid last month's remaining issues of *Mini Extravaganza* (usually a big seller; lots of people were interested in all things miniature) into the recycle box when she heard Emma's voice much closer than it should be.

"Oh. Hi. I mean—hello."

A group of laughing teenage boys hovered behind Aubrey just long enough for her to miss what came next. When the hyenas moved along, an unfamiliar voice had taken over the conversation.

"...I was hoping you'd come by again."

Aubrey straightened up, immediately spotting Emma about five feet away. Standing with her was a woman who looked a little younger than Sadie. She was probably around Penelope's age. At the thought of Pen, Aubrey sighed. They hadn't talked since her mother's house, and Aubrey didn't know if that was just circumstance, or if her damn mother had said something out of line to Pen.

Lost in her own thoughts, Aubrey missed what Emma said back to the woman. Not immune to the beauty of any woman, Aubrey took quick notice of how attractive this particular woman was. Her body was all curves, all feminine warmth. She had dark, curly hair piled on top of her head. But there was something about the way she moved that was especially sexy.

Aubrey shook her head and bent down to pick up the recycle box. She didn't need to know anything more about the random woman Emma apparently knew well enough to prompt her to ask why Emma hadn't been by—where, Aubrey didn't know—recently. For so many reasons, Aubrey needed not to care one bit about that woman.

But as she began the slow walk back to the stockroom, she thought it would be a good idea to walk past Emma and the woman, just to make sure everything was copacetic. She didn't know Emma well enough to read her body language, but there was definitely a sign of unease in the way she was standing with her arms folded behind her back, fingers clenched around her elbows.

The two women were speaking quietly. That's all Aubrey could discern. It didn't seem intimate—not that it mattered! In any way at all!—but it also didn't seem contentious. Maybe a little awkward?

Aubrey didn't love the weird feeling that settled in the pit of her stomach as she kicked open the door to the stockroom. Nothing about Emma's life was any of her business.

"Stop it," she muttered as she left the stockroom and walked into the break room. She really did not need to care about Emma Gallagher. And she didn't. Did she? No. How could she? She didn't even know her.

But she did—a little, anyway. Throughout the week, they'd made comments back and forth about the playlists and the songs. Aubrey learned enough to delete "probably has terrible taste in music" from her bank of Emma knowledge. It turned out Emma had great taste in music. She also knew Emma was a really, really good barista, which was weird because Genesis had told her Emma didn't have any coffee-making experience prior to coming to Cornerstone.

Aubrey also knew that Emma had a way of making her feel like she could talk to her. She didn't, of course, because that was out of bounds for Aubrey. But she had a feeling that she could. If she wanted to. And if she did, Emma would listen.

And finally, there was that unavoidable truth that Emma had fully grown out of the awkward, very young-looking ninth-grader Aubrey remembered. This Emma seemed to have no idea how pretty she was, and Aubrey very much liked that about her.

As Aubrey tugged on her coat, she heard the door open and close behind her. Emma, flushed but not in an angry way, stood there, holding her balled up apron in her hands.

"Oh," she said, seeming surprised to see Aubrey. "Hi."

"Hey." So much for that feeling that she could talk to Emma; Aubrey was struck mute.

"What a day," Emma said, graciously filling in Aubrey's silence. "It was so busy. Is that a Thursday thing?"

"It was probably because of the snow yesterday."

Emma stuffed her apron into her locker. "Oh, right. That makes sense." She pulled on her coat, then pulled out her hair tie and shook out her hair. Aubrey was momentarily mesmerized by the auburn strands that flew about Emma's head before settling perfectly down her back. "I always reek like coffee when I leave here. I swear the espresso attaches itself to my hair."

"Kinda sucks for someone who doesn't even like coffee."

Aubrey was gifted with a wide smile. "Yeah, honestly. But this job isn't going to break me. I shall emerge a noncoffee drinker, just as I entered."

Something clenched in Aubrey's gut. "Are you quitting?"

"Oh, no. I can't." Emma laughed. "I mean, I need a job. And my schedule here works perfectly with my class schedule."

That was news to Aubrey. "Class?"

"Pennbrook," Emma said. "I...I have to finish my degree." She looked like she wanted to say more, but also like doing so would be physically painful.

Aubrey knew enough about that dueling feeling to let it go. "Well, at least you can save money by living at home while you finish up." She cringed. She had no idea what she was talking about, but it seemed a safe enough assumption.

"I'm not living at home," Emma rushed to say. "Not exactly, I mean. I'm staying with my brother." She sighed heavily. "It's a long story, sorry. I don't want to bore you to death with it."

Aubrey doubted Emma could bore her, but there was a more pressing matter. "Your brother? Not Liam."

"Uh, yes Liam?"

"Liam Gallagher is your brother?" Aubrey felt like a total shit for not knowing this. In her defense, they really looked nothing alike, and she'd never been to Liam's house when they were in high school. He also, typical high school boy that he'd been, never bothered to mention he had a younger sister.

Okay, actually, it was entirely possible that he had, and Aubrey hadn't paid attention to that announcement because *at the time*, it hadn't meant anything to her.

"Yes," Emma said, suddenly looking annoyed. "Liam is my brother. Did you guys, like, date or something?"

Aubrey laughed so suddenly and so hard that she actually doubled over. "No! Holy shit, no. We definitely did not date."

"I almost believe you."

Between laughs, Aubrey managed to say, "Emma, trust me. Never happened. Never will."

Something about the words must have settled Emma because her annoyance disappeared. "Okay. I'll trust you. This time."

The two walked out of the break room and made their way through the store, which was still bustling with activity. Sadie, parked at the registers, waved as they left. She also held eye contact with Aubrey and gave her a knowing smile, to which Aubrey rolled her eyes.

The snow from Wednesday had mostly melted away, but the wind was charging in, bringing dropping temperatures. Both Emma and Aubrey stuffed their hands in the pockets of their coats.

"See you tom—"

"Who was that woman?"

Emma, effectively cut off from her departing words, shot a look at Aubrey. "What woman?"

"The one you were having that top-secret conversation with." *None of your business, Glass.* But she couldn't help herself.

"It wasn't—were you spying on me?" But there was a playful lilt in Emma's voice.

"Uh, no, it can't be considered spying when you're having a conversation in the middle of the book floor where your coworkers are working."

Emma gave a little laugh. "Okay, fair. That was Viv. She's the owner of Dough Mama."

"Which is literally the best bakery in the state," Aubrey stated. The pieces clicked into place and she realized she did know Viv—at least the vision of her standing behind the counter at Dough Mama.

"Is it?"

"Yeah. I feel like you should know that."

Something shifted in Emma's expression, a sweep of emotion that flew in as quickly as it left. "And why should I know that?"

Aubrey raised her eyebrows. "Because you know Viv?"

After a beat, Emma nodded. "Right. Yeah."

Aubrey got the sense their suddenly awkward conversation needed to end. "I gotta go."

"Me too."

They stood for another moment, the sound of the wind whirling around them. Finally, Emma shot Aubrey a smile, then disappeared into the darkness down the street.

CHAPTER ELEVEN

Emma threw another pair of jeans across the bedroom. She'd finally unpacked and settled into Liam's guest room, but couldn't bring herself to call it "her room." At least not yet. Maybe when she got some decorations up; for now, it still felt like a space she was existing in instead of living in.

One could argue that, however, since approximately twenty percent of her wardrobe was strewn across the room, making it look very lived-in. She didn't normally stress so much about getting dressed, but it was a big night: Emma was going out.

She still wasn't sure if she was technically invited, but she was going. Genesis had casually mentioned that a group was going out to a local bar—one Emma had never been to, mostly because she'd just turned twenty-one—and that if she felt like stopping by, that would be "chill." So, not a real invitation. But Emma, tired of sitting in Liam's living room every night, was taking it. She'd even taken a nap when she got home from work, because Genesis had said no one would be there until around ten p.m., which sounded insane, but, alas, when in Rome.

There was a quick knock on the door before Collins's head poked in.

"I'm so glad you called!" she squealed, hurrying into the room. She stopped a few feet in and looked around. "Wow, Emmalynn. Where do we even begin?"

Emma threw another cardigan into the "nope" pile. "I have no idea. I've never felt so clueless in my short life." She eyed Collins's outfit, which was more casual than the one she'd worn last week, but still tipping the scales of classy. Emma groaned, slammed with hopelessness. "How do you manage to look so good all the time?"

"Oh, please. I don't. And besides, our styles are totally different." Collins went about picking through the clothing lying around the room. "What kind of look are you going for?"

"Casual," Emma said quickly. "But fun? I don't know, I feel like my usual outfits aren't the kind of thing I should wear to a bar."

"And what bar are you going to?"

"Lotus."

Collins paused, a pair of black pants dangling from her fingertips. "Never heard of it. It's here? In town?"

"Yeah, it's down on Main, a couple blocks off campus."

"What do we think the vibe is?"

Emma shrugged. "Cool? Genesis said it's got, like, a club situation downstairs. I have no idea what happens upstairs."

Collins wiggled her eyebrows. "But your sweet little innocent ass is gonna find out." She handed Emma a pair of jeans. "Put these on."

She kept her grumble to herself, trusting the Collins outfit-selecting process. Emma hated jeans and only wore them to work. But this was exactly why she'd panic-called Collins: If left to her own devices, Emma would have rolled up to Lotus wearing her usual dark-academia-inspired clothing. She saw nothing wrong with that, and actually did not care one bit if anyone else saw something wrong with it, but she wanted to fit in tonight. Not stand out.

The next item Collins passed over, however, required a bit of a fight.

"Absolutely not." Emma pushed the shirt back.

"Emmalynn. Put it on. Honestly," Collins said, grinning, "I'm surprised you even own a shirt like this."

"Can't remember why I do," Emma mumbled, the words muffled as she took off her crewneck sweatshirt—a relic from her days at the vegan butcher, with smiling cartoon animals printed on the front—and flung it on the bed.

"Who are we trying to impress, by the way?"

Emma balked. She held the stupid white crop top over her face for a moment. "No one," she finally said, tugging the shirt down.

Collins gave her a look of disbelief, then gestured toward Emma's chest. "Bra off."

"What? No! Not happening."

"Listen, Gallagher. One of us has been blessed with the ability to go out without wearing a bra, so please, for my sake, take advantage of it."

Emma shivered. "It's February."

"Your nipples will be fine," she said dismissively. "And—aha, here we go." With a triumphant smile, Collins handed Emma a black motorcycle jacket, made of the finest pleather Target had to offer. "This'll keep 'em toasty."

"I can't believe I'm doing this," Emma said as she smoothly removed her bra without fully taking off her shirt. Not that she cared if Collins saw her topless, because she already had, many times. It was just the reality of being an athlete.

Emma slipped into the jacket, half-listening as Collins rambled about her imminent return to school. Now was the perfect time for Emma to ask the little question poking at the recesses of her brain, but she couldn't think of a neat segue and was worried she'd blurt, "How'd you figure out you're bi?"

She was curious, that's all. And the curiosity was borne from Collins's all-boys-all-the-time approach to high school. She'd never given an inkling of being anything but straight, so to casually announce she now also dated girls…It was a surprise.

"So are these work people you're going with?"

"Not going with," Emma said, turning so Collins could assess the outfit. "I'm meeting them there."

"Same difference." Collins nodded her approval. "You look hot, Emmalynn. You should ditch the cardigans more often. Wait a minute," she said, dropping onto the bed, eyes bright. "Is Aubrey Glass gonna be there?"

Ever since Emma had told her that yes, Aubrey was working at a bookstore, and yes, it happened to be the bookstore where Emma was also working, Collins had been on an Aubrey Glass bender. From a gossip perspective, Collins was dying to know why and how Aubrey had ended up back in Chestnut Hill. She'd been encouraging Emma all week to talk to Aubrey, which, in combination with Liam's little nudge, had helped her put aside her irrational negative feelings so she could actually do so. And she had, here and there.

But honestly, Emma was so tired of everyone being obsessed with Aubrey Glass. Liam had asked about her multiple times. At work, someone mentioned Aubrey's name at least five times per day. Emma couldn't escape the damn girl.

"I don't know." And she didn't. She suspected Aubrey might be there, but it hadn't come up in their mini conversations all week, and she hadn't seen Aubrey when she left work earlier.

Collins swung her legs back and forth, looking very proud of herself. "I hope she is, because I bet she'll *love* your outfit."

Emma suddenly felt very hot. "Okay," she said, totally unsure how to navigate this new path of conversation. Why would Aubrey even look twice at her outfit?

"Wait wait wait. You don't know?"

"Don't know what?"

"Aubrey Glass is a lesbian." Collins's voice barely contained her excitement.

Emma swallowed, refusing to look at Collins. This news didn't matter at all. It was entirely inconsequential to Emma. Good for Aubrey, for living her truth. Sure, it was kind of unexpected, because Emma definitely wouldn't have guessed that about her in high school. But if Emma *had* to be judgmental, she'd agree that Aubrey's outfits—and yes, she noticed them every day which did not mean anything at all—basically yelled "gay woman!"

"There's some wild backstory," Collins continued. "But no one knows the details. It's very weird, very secretive. But she's totally out now."

"Are you going to date her?" Emma blurted. Great, yes, there was that excellent segue she'd been searching for.

Collins's eyes damn near glittered. "Oh, I definitely would. Do you think she'd date me?"

That damn hot sensation crashed through Emma once again. "Probably," she said. "So she's your type?"

"Not really," Collins admitted. "But it's Aubrey Glass, Emma. *Aubrey. Glass.*"

Yeah, yeah. Aubrey Glass. Emma knew who she was, what she looked like, how she carried herself, what music she listened to when she was tired, what music she listened to when she looked like she wanted to disappear into thin air. She knew the way the bottom of Aubrey's pants constantly got caught between her heel and her Birkenstock clogs, the way she often smelled like smoky vanilla. And she knew that Aubrey Glass had eyes the color of pine trees that held steady when she looked at Emma, even when they flickered with darkness around the edges.

Yes. Emma knew a little bit about Aubrey Glass.

"If she's out tonight, you have to get a pic with her." Collins bounced off the bed. "You look amazing, Emmalynn. Go have some fun, okay? You deserve it."

With a kiss on the cheek, Collins said her goodbyes and moments later, Emma heard her feet pounding down the stairs.

Emma caught her reflection in the mirror and stood for a moment, gazing at the young woman she was just getting to know. The outfit made her look different. Older, maybe. A touch more sophisticated but also way more fun. No, not fun—like someone who would make risky decisions. How very un-Emma. She would probably never wear an outfit like this again, but she could do it for one night.

Putting Aubrey Glass and the entire world's preoccupation with her out of her mind, Emma grabbed her black mini backpack (Collins probably wouldn't approve, but it was the only option at the moment) and made her way downstairs.

Lotus was unlike any bar or club Emma had ever been in, which wasn't saying much since she'd been in, like, three. From the moment she passed through the entryway and handed over her ID, she was consumed with the steady *thump thump thump* booming from the DJ booth. She peered through the foggy darkness of the club, trying to locate the dance floor. There, toward the back of the room, briefly illuminated by passing strobe lights. It gave major den of iniquity vibes, and Emma felt strangely drawn to it.

Before she could take four steps toward the dance pit, Emma heard Genesis's voice filter into the intense crescendo of the music.

Squinting, her eyes not yet adjusted to the indecent lack of lighting, she caught sight of Genesis's hair and made her way through the crowd.

"Just Emma!" Genesis grinned. "You made it!"

"Hey," Emma said. She'd never been so thankful for Genesis's height and her larger-than-life energy; she was certain she'd be stumbling around like a lost child in a crowded mall if Genesis wasn't so…so obvious.

"Drink?"

"Sure, yeah." Emma leaned against the bar, wincing when her hand met something sticky. She waited an eternity before the bartender, a supremely handsome guy who was wearing…*Wait. What the fuck is that guy wearing?*

Incredibly short and obscenely tight neon-blue spandex shorts, apparently. And not much else.

Emma refrained from gawking as she ordered a vodka soda with lime. He was very nice, Tiny Shorts Man, and clearly very well…endowed. Emma looked away as quickly as possible without being rude and came face-to-face with Genesis's gleeful expression.

"It's her first time," Genesis said to the handful of people around her, none of whom looked familiar.

Emma smiled, hoping she didn't look as awkward as she suddenly felt, and took a moment to really scope her surroundings now that her eyes had adjusted. Thankfully, the bartender was the only person lacking clothing. Everyone else was dressed, and in a wide range of styles. There was a lot of hair color that defied nature, and a lot of piercings. And right there behind Genesis were two men, thoroughly making out.

Emma felt her pulse jump. Hold on.

She looked around again as the things she'd missed became clearer. There, a giant rainbow flag hanging behind the bar. How had she missed that? Right next to it was the blue and pink trans flag. Lots of male couples dotted the seats at the bar, laughing and swilling drinks. In fact, there were hardly any women at all.

When Emma's drink arrived, she graciously accepted it and downed half as soon as she got her hands on it. Her nerves were swimming upstream and she really wished she'd taken a minute to Google Lotus before hopping in her car and driving here.

She didn't care that it was a gay bar. She just wished she would have known what she was walking into.

On the plus side, Emma thought as she drained her glass in another big swallow, none of these men would look twice at her nipples.

She waited for the bartender to come back, and was pleased when he came quickly. She ordered another drink and he winked at her, as though they were conspirators. On second thought—Emma looked down, and sure enough, her nipples were front and center.

All she could do was laugh. Collins was right—of the two of them, Emma could get away with going braless. She was small breasted and perky, the combined blessings of her genetics and being in her early twenties. She would have never made the decision to wear this slightly cropped white T-shirt without a bra, but now that she was here, in the comfort of a bar where the majority of the patrons had zero interest in her, she was going to enjoy the little display of her features.

New drink secured, Emma swung back around and nearly lost her footing.

Aubrey. In front of her. Staring right at her.

Instead of a hello, Aubrey's eyes traveled from Emma's face down to her chest. Had Emma not already thrown back a menacingly heavily poured vodka soda, she might have hurried to pull her jacket over her two protruding friends. Alas, the drink had been drunk.

Aubrey's eyes snapped back up to Emma's face. It was possible she hadn't even noticed. Emma dared a look down. Oh, yeah, no, she couldn't have not noticed.

"Hi," Emma said, breaking the sudden silence they found themselves in despite the crunch and crash of the techno song encasing the room. "I didn't know you were coming."

"I didn't know *you* were coming," Aubrey retorted. She crossed her arms across her chest. Emma didn't mimic the movement. She may have even accidentally pushed her own chest out instead.

"Well we're all here now, so deal with it," Genesis interrupted, throwing an arm around Aubrey.

Emma took a drink while Aubrey stared her down. She didn't look mad, but she didn't look happy, either. The expression on Aubrey's face was as confusing as she was. Emma, a lightweight who should never have more than two drinks, was already feeling the vodka and decided it would be a great time to start talking.

"There's a really sick gay bar in Philly," she began, totally unsure of where she was going but, sans seatbelt, had her foot slammed on the gas. "One of my roommates used to go every week, and she said they had the best shots. I never actually went, wasn't old enough or whatever, but I just, like, lived vicariously through her. She wasn't gay, though. She just loved hanging out with gay people." Emma tilted her head. "She might be gay now. Not sure. We haven't talked for a while. You never know, right?"

Aubrey had moved next to Emma. She was half-sitting, half-standing, one leg cemented to the floor and the other dangling, aimlessly kicking the footrest on the stool.

"She went for Halloween last year and the pictures were insane," Emma continued. "I mean, most of the costumes didn't involve a lot of actual, uh, costuming. More like a ton of body paint. I saw some things." Emma giggled then hiccupped. She looked at her glass, surprised to see it was almost empty.

"Just Emma! Drink?"

Emma hesitated. Then, very slowly, she nodded at Genesis. She glanced at Aubrey, expecting to see her placing an order. But she was sitting like a stone in a river, stubbornly immobile as the waters rushed around her.

"You're not drinking?"

"Not at the moment." Her voice was different, scratchier maybe.

"Do you like beer or liquor?"

Aubrey shrugged. "Neither."

Emma waited until Aubrey turned to look at her. It was then that she noticed the redness in Aubrey's eyes. For a split second, her heart thumped sideways, thinking Aubrey had been crying. Her heart righted itself when she realized, no, Aubrey was just high.

She was a little surprised about that. It certainly didn't fit with high school Aubrey Glass. Then again, Emma was on the fast track to learning that the Aubrey everyone thought they knew in high school had very little in common with the Aubrey sitting next to her at a gay bar called Lotus in their hometown, where neither of them expected Emma to be.

"I'm not friends with her anymore," Emma said, needing something to keep her brain moving.

"Who?"

"My roommate. The one who went to the gay bar all the time." She waited for Aubrey to ask for details, but she didn't, so Emma plowed on as soon as Genesis handed her a fresh drink—which would absolutely be Emma's last.

"I was dating someone." She could have sworn Aubrey perked up at that statement. "Obviously my roommate knew because we would hang out at the apartment. So we would all hang out and eventually I noticed my roommate was always home when we were there. It felt weird but I ignored it because, I don't know, I didn't want to make a big deal out of nothing. But they would find reasons to talk and go into the kitchen together. Sometimes they'd been in there for a really, really long time and then they'd come back like nothing was weird about it. I'm not stupid," Emma said plainly. "I saw it. It was so obvious. So one morning we were out at brunch because it became a thing where, like, the three of us would hang out." She shook her head. "Don't know what the fuck I was doing. Anyway, I watched how they talked to each other while I was sitting right there at the fucking table with them and I finally said, 'Why don't you two just fuck and get it over with?'"

Aubrey laughed, her first sign of life since Emma had started talking. "No you didn't."

"Oh, I very much did. Right there over pancakes and bacon." Emma straightened up and angled her body toward Aubrey. "And they looked at me like I was insane. But guess what?"

"What?"

"They hooked up that very day."

Aubrey's eyes, though a bit droopy, widened. "Shut up."

"Not kidding."

"Emma, that's…That's colossally fucked."

"I know. Hence, the end of that bullshit relationship and the end of that equally bullshit friendship."

"Have you dated anyone since then?" Aubrey kind of mumbled that, but Emma heard it.

"No," she said. "You?"

Aubrey side-eyed her. "That was your story."

Emma flushed. "I mean, are you dating anyone now?"

"No." And that was it. Emma had been hoping for more, but Aubrey gave no indication that she was going to provide it.

Before Emma could poke and prod a little, just for curiosity's sake, Genesis grabbed her arm and pulled her away.

"Dance time," was all she said, loud and clear above the music. Emma glanced back at Aubrey, who hadn't moved from her lopsided perch on the barstool. She was watching Emma, though, with a concentration that Emma felt in every nerve ending.

Genesis gave a hearty yank and there she was, in the middle of the den of iniquity. It wasn't nearly as sordid as she'd secretly hoped it would be, but there were a lot of bodies making moves that couldn't qualify as dancing. Thankful for the drinks because without them, Emma would not be caught dead on a dance floor, she shimmied her shoulders and let the music settle into her bones.

Song after song passed. Almost drunk and swept up in the haze around her, Emma was only mildly aware of the bodies that pressed up against hers. She stopped thinking about her nipples and let loose in a way that only Crop Top Braless Emma could do. And it was freeing—not something she wanted or needed to do regularly, but the freedom of the dance floor was a kind of intoxication she understood could be addictive.

The haze lifted enough for her to realize she had to pee, and she had to pee immediately. She wiggled her away around the gyrating bodies and got to the edge of the dance floor before she remembered she had never been there before. Genesis was still fully enveloped in the sea of writhing human forms, so Emma walked until she found a very nice-looking man who kindly pointed her in the direction of the bathrooms.

It was much quieter in the bathroom, also empty, thanks to the extremely low female population of the bar. Emma banged out of the stall, wincing at her own loudness. She spent a long time at the sink, running her hands under tepid water and gazing at herself in the mirror. She certainly looked like she'd spent an hour dancing. She also looked like she needed sleep.

She splashed her face with cold water, then dried her hands, flung open the bathroom door, and walked into the dark hallway. She'd noticed a flight of stairs at the end of the hallway, which must lead to the upper floor, a.k.a, the non-dance floor. She considered going up then realized what she really wanted to do was go home and go to bed.

As she walked down the hall toward the front of the bar, someone rounded the corner and began walking toward her. Emma pressed closer to the wall to let the person pass, but they didn't pass. They stopped right as Emma approached them.

Emma cursed the horrible lighting of the building. It had taken her a moment too long to realize her hallway companion was Aubrey.

"It's so dark," Emma said, half-laughing.

"Thought you left," she said, not quite meeting Emma's eyes.

"Bathroom." She jerked her thumb over her shoulder. "And I had to sober up, but I'm gonna head out now."

"You're okay to drive?"

Emma nodded. "Yeah. I feel okay. Are you…What are you doing?"

Aubrey opened and closed her mouth, shook her head slightly as though to throw away the thought that wanted to become words. "Heading out. I'll walk with you."

Emma let Aubrey take the lead and followed her out of the club, away from the music that would likely keep stomping its beat in her head throughout the night. Speaking of, Emma had no idea what time it was. She felt like she'd just spent an entire day in an underground room.

"Where'd you park?" Aubrey asked.

"Just down the block."

Wordlessly, Aubrey began walking in the direction she'd pointed. Emma rushed to catch up. Aubrey had a solid six inches on her and she was all legs. Even without the head start, Emma would have to kick up her normal walking tempo to stay in stride.

The night was cold, dark, and quiet around them. Emma wanted to say something but was reminded of Aubrey's playlist from the day it snowed. She knew Aubrey could melt into the quiet, and while it was truly difficult to keep her mouth shut, Emma wanted to give her that peace.

"This is me," Emma said quietly as they reached Selena.

"Nice car."

"Yeah, she's great—"

Aubrey's lips swiftly cut off Emma's praise of her car. There they were, pressed against Emma's in a way that both possessed and questioned. Emma couldn't move her body. Her lips, on a plan of their own devising, moved against Aubrey's. But the rest of her was numb, barely registering the way Aubrey cupped her face in both hands. Had she been able to feel it, she would have been struck by the tenderness, the delicate and cautious softness of the gesture.

Again, time fell to the irrelevant and indescribable. By the time Emma's body woke up, she could feel the cold seeping through her cheap jacket. She gasped, certain other parts of her body were wildly jutting out, and it was that thought that brought her back to Earth and away from Aubrey Glass's mouth.

Emma took a sudden step back, tipping against the side of her car. Aubrey, silent and still, stood across from her. She looked lost, like she was cracking open and didn't want to but couldn't stop. So many words ricocheted between them, lost in the winter wind and abrupt awakening.

All Emma could do was shake her head, and it was disbelief, not a "no," but she couldn't articulate that. The only thing she could do that made any sense at all was to hurry around to the driver's side of her car, get in, and flee.

CHAPTER TWELVE

Thwack.

Aubrey stood, one hand on her hip and the other wrapped around her field hockey stick, watching the beat-up but still brightly colored orange ball skim over the frost-tipped grass. It wasn't field hockey season, so the field she stood on wasn't prepped for the sport. More specifically, considering it was the dead of winter and she was in New England where winter sports were played indoors, the field wasn't prepared for anything other than snow.

But the grass had been shorn before the first frost, and Aubrey liked the way her hits soared over the icy filaments. The balls weren't deterred by the early morning frozen dew. In fact, they seemed to pick up speed as they rolled over the cold fingers of the grass.

Aubrey dropped another ball onto the ground and toed it until she liked where it was. She took a deep breath in then blew out, watching the tendrils of her exhale cloud the air. Cold didn't quite capture the way the morning felt. The air teemed with the thickness of it, like a wall of algidity pressing in from all sides. The sun had risen not long after she'd stepped onto the field, but it was hidden behind clumps of gray clouds.

The cold didn't bother her. She'd grabbed her equipment bag and left her apartment as soon as she'd deemed it a reasonable time to venture outside.

To be clear: Aubrey hadn't slept.

She reached up and tugged her beanie down, then took a few practice swings. The movements were a constant, a familiar that felt and looked like it was scripted into her muscles. Aubrey had always had a little bit of a weird swing. Coaches over the years had critiqued it and tried to fix it, but no matter the level of influence, Aubrey never stopped jerking her right shoulder up just before her stick connected with the ball. At some point it stopped mattering. She was the top scorer in high school and earned a full ride to play at a great college in upstate New York.

To be clear: She wasn't just the top scorer in her high school. No, Aubrey was the top scorer of all the high schools in the entire state. Massachusetts, too, which was a bigger claim to fame than New Hampshire.

To be even more clear: She didn't *want* any claim to fame. They just sort of arrived over the years.

And her slightly unconventional swing, which she executed now, connecting the blade with that sweet spot on the ball, had its own fame. It became her trademark, the thing scouts looked for during her junior and senior years of high school. Her college coaches hadn't tried to change it. Well, one had. In her own way. But she hadn't been successful.

Aubrey gripped her black and neon green Osaka and, in a move that had been banned from all practices and games, twirled it like a baton as she strode across the grass to retrieve the balls. She would have never made it as a majorette, but there was something about playing a sport with a stick that made it impossible not to occasionally attempt a sloppy wrist twirl or the nearly impossible fishtails.

If she'd slept, she might have run across the grass. But at her last estimation, Aubrey had been awake for twenty-seven hours. Despite the fact that she couldn't sleep, she was exhausted.

It wasn't all Emma's fault. Actually, fine, none of it was Emma's fault because Aubrey was the one who had—

She growled, a low noise that ached when it vibrated against her vocal cords, and chopped at two of the balls. Her angles were off and the balls bobbed away from her, sad and uninspired. The third ball received a royal whacking that sent it winging over the field in the direction she'd come from. Those kinds of hits were the most satisfying for Aubrey since she'd spent her playing time as a forward and never had the need to crack enormous shots down the field.

The thrill of the forbidden hit swiftly deleted her remaining manic energy. She dropped onto the frozen ground and hugged her knees to her chest. She rested her forehead against her knees for a moment as thoughts swam in and out of her brain. Nothing latched on, nothing stuck. Her mind was a busy aquarium, overstocked and in need of a scrubbing.

When she looked up, her vision focused on the rectangular buildings of Franklin Prescott High School. They'd added a new wing since she graduated, but, strangely, the school seemed smaller to her. It was as though she was looking at it from a long distance away. And yet she was close enough to see the exact path she'd traveled from the parking lot to the main building, and the gym to the field she currently sat on. She could picture herself walking the halls, not having to push through bodies because it seemed a clear path always opened for her, even when the halls were the most clogged with teenagers. She could even call up a clear image of her lockers—both the one in the senior hallway and the one in the girls' locker room.

Aubrey squinted against the sudden sunshine. Though she sat right there on campus, high school felt incredibly far away. Like another life. And she wasn't that old, didn't have that much actual distance from it.

It was because of everything between graduation and the present moment, she decided. Her choices and mistakes, piled up like dirty laundry on the floor of an apartment she'd long ago grown out of. They made her past seem like a vision best seen through...whatever was the opposite of binoculars.

As she pushed herself off the ground, Aubrey took a final look at the school that had turned her into Aubrey Glass, Golden Girl. She'd never wanted the title, hadn't even known what to do with it. For years, she'd let everyone else dictate its meaning and its power.

It was so much easier to go along with it than try to fight it. And truthfully, Aubrey knew it had protected her.

To be clear: She'd realized that a bit too late.

After collecting her equipment and stuffing everything into her bag, Aubrey realized she was hungry. Lately her appetite had been doing this thing where it came and went, fluctuating with a tempo she couldn't keep in step with. But she knew enough to take advantage of actually feeling hungry, so she hiked her bag high on her shoulder and made her way over the field, which was slowly losing its icy glow as the sun stretched further across the sky.

Once in her car, Aubrey gave a loving pat to the dashboard. There was always a chance the ancient Honda Accord wouldn't start, especially in the depth of winter. The car had been with her since high school, when it had been regularly stuffed with peers (she couldn't use the term "friends," because Aubrey was pretty sure friends stayed, even when life got weird and rough). Cigarette burns and unknown stains painted the back seat. Aubrey winced, remembering that terrible fall when, for some crazy reason, she and two of her "friends" had decided it was time to start smoking. Fortunately, she'd realized she hated nicotine within the first few puffs. That had been the last of that particular smoking experiment.

The streets of Chestnut Hill were quiet. It was still early, after all, and a Sunday. Aubrey glanced nervously at the half-lit clock on her dash. Seeing it was early enough to avoid the postchurch crowd, which included her mother and her mother's husband (neither of whom Aubrey had made any attempt to communicate with since the party), she relaxed and drove toward The Greek.

Situated just a block off campus from Franklin Prescott, The Greek was a hot spot for the before and after school crowd. It was a deli cum convenience store, offering a little bit of everything a teenager might need. Most importantly, however, it had the best bagels in town. Everyone swore the owners imported water from another state, and that had to be the secret to the doughy, chewy, perfectly baked ovals.

Aubrey parked and stuffed her hands in her jacket pockets as she walked toward the deli. The windows were foggy and when she stepped inside, a cocoon of warmth enveloped her. It was stifling but welcome after an hour on the field.

She approached the counter and waited, then ordered her usual: a toasted everything bagel with olive cream cheese and crispy bacon. It was a salt attack of the finest variety.

Aubrey shifted from foot to foot as she waited for her food. The lack of sleep was beginning to creep into her bones, and while she consciously understood she was tired, her brain was still banging around like a madwoman surrounded by yellow wallpaper. If she smoked when she got home, she could maybe keep the exhaustion from melting into anxiety. If that didn't work, she worried she'd be knocked off-kilter for the rest of the day—and end up with another sleepless night.

"Aubrey," the man behind the counter called, holding up her wrapped bagel. She thanked him as she took it and moved toward the register.

"Aubrey?"

Confused, because she saw the bagel in her hand and knew she hadn't ordered more than one thing, Aubrey looked back up at the counter. But no one there was paying her any attention.

Great, she thought. *Now I'm hearing things. Thanks a lot, Charlotte Perkins Gilman.*

"Glass, that you?"

Maybe not. She turned to her right and came face-to-face with a familiar smile. She was, to her massive embarrassment, momentarily starstruck. So Emma didn't hate her after all. She'd tracked Aubrey down, and now—

Wait a minute. Aubrey squinted. She'd kissed Emma last night, and while the lips in front of her bore a smile that was a copy-paste of Emma's, there definitely hadn't been a scattering of facial hair rubbing against her mouth. Never mind the fact that Emma wasn't tall enough for Aubrey to be eye-to-mouth with.

Aubrey shook her head slightly. She did know this person, and that smile.

"Liam?"

He grinned, seeming relieved. Instead of hugging her, he reached out and clapped her on the shoulder. "Thought that was you."

"It's me." She shrugged, at a loss for how to talk to someone she hadn't seen since the summer before she left for college.

Thankfully, Liam picked up as though they'd never left off. "Remember when we used to come here for lunch? Every time, I was convinced we'd get caught coming back to campus, but we never were."

Aubrey smiled at the memory. She and Liam hadn't hidden their friendship, but it always felt like no one knew they were friends. He was on the outskirts of her crowd, showing up here and there at parties but never fully indoctrinated because he wasn't involved in sports. Liam was super likable and also very hot, so Aubrey's female peers wanted him around even if he wasn't an all-star athlete. And that was exactly why Aubrey was drawn to him—he wasn't anything like the rest of the guys she hung out with. That, and he never hit on her. It was an immediate unspoken rule between them that they would only ever be friends. Aubrey could not have loved Liam more for giving her that space and safety, especially when it felt like all anyone wanted from her was romantic or sexual attention. She wasn't even out in high school, to herself or anyone else, but that attention had still come from all angles and peers.

And yet, despite her friendship with Liam, she hadn't remembered the enormous fact that he had a sister. On cue, Emma's face swam in her mind.

She swallowed as she looked at Liam. The phrase *I kissed your sister* ran through her mind like an overplayed pop song, an earworm that wouldn't quit until it was sung aloud. Aubrey rolled her lips in. She was not going to sing in The Greek no matter how badly she wanted that refrain to exit her brain.

Liam took her weird silence in stride, just as he always had. "I heard you were back in town," he said. "But to be honest, I didn't believe it."

"Me either," she said, then cracked a half-smile. "It's a long story."

"I bet." Typical Liam, he didn't prod. And he wouldn't.

Aubrey's heart swelled with tentative happiness. Liam was just who she needed. Easy, uncomplicated. They had enough in common—or at least they had. Liam didn't look like he'd changed that much. Okay, yes. Aubrey smiled, a real one. This could work.

Her heart sank as she thought of Emma.

Sure, rekindling her friendship with Liam could be just what she needed—except for the fact that Aubrey had, less than twelve hours ago, kissed his sister.

"So," Liam said, leaning against the shelf behind him, which was filled with Gatorades of every flavor. "Wanna hang out sometime? Not in a date way. Just like old times."

He didn't have to throw in that disclaimer but Aubrey appreciated it, even if it was kinda awkward.

"Yeah, definitely. I'm free most nights."

Liam grinned again, his blue-green eyes scrunching just like Emma's did when she smiled. "Heard you're working with my sister."

By some miracle, Aubrey didn't flinch. "Yeah." She blew out a short breath. "Honestly? I forgot you even had a sister."

Liam shrugged, seemingly nonplussed by that admission. "She didn't hang out with us in high school. And you never came over to my house. So, other than the whole field hockey thing, I guess you wouldn't have really known her."

It was just the forgiveness Aubrey needed to hear. He was right, too.

"Is she being nice to you?"

His tone was playful, but the words still speared her heart. Emma was being perfectly nice. She, Aubrey, was the one who had…What had she done, exactly? Taken advantage of Emma's kindness? Made a move before having all the required information for which to make the move? Doing something uncharacteristically spontaneous?

"She is," Aubrey said. She bit the inside of her cheek. "Yeah, she's cool. I wish I'd known her in high school."

She wasn't sure about the truth level of that statement, but it didn't matter. Liam took up the conversational baton and Aubrey half-listened, half-wondered what Emma was doing right then.

"You'll have to come by sometime," Liam finished, pulling out his phone. "I'll text you my address."

"Oh, wait." Aubrey flushed, hoping she wouldn't have to explain herself. "I have a new number." She rattled it off and Liam typed it in.

"I'll call you," he said. "So you have my number."

"Sounds good."

Liam put his phone back in his pocket and turned that charming smile on her once again. "It was really good to see you, Glass. Don't be a stranger, okay?"

"I won't." She hoped that was the truth.

Aubrey waved as she turned and made her way out of The Greek. It had somehow gotten colder while she was inside, or maybe that was the effect of her sweaty clothes and the overwhelming warmth of the deli.

Either way, she sat in her car while it warmed up. Absently, she reached for her bag and rooted around until her fingers hit the cool surface of her phone. She yanked it out and held it up, examining the handful of notifications.

An unknown 603 number had called and not left a message. She thumbed through the process of entering Liam's contact information into her phone, then sent him a quick text, a casual *Got your number, talk soon.*

As she swiped out of her messages, a little red dot on her voicemail icon caught her attention. She furrowed her brow. Liam hadn't left a voice mail. Her heart did a funny shake in her chest, wondering if Emma had gotten her number and called. Hoping through a veil of nerves, Aubrey pressed on her phone icon, expecting to see another unknown 603 number that she'd somehow missed while looking at Liam's.

Her shaking heart sank with the speed and heft of a boulder. Emma hadn't called; there wasn't another unknown 603 number in her missed calls that was quietly requesting a call back, or at least a text.

It was a 518 number that had called, one that was still saved in Aubrey's phone, one that had been blocked off and on. Aubrey stared at the black lettering on her screen, dumbfounded and heartbroken all over again.

CHAPTER THIRTEEN

Cornerstone was quiet. It was always quiet in the preopening hour that Emma spent preparing the café. Without customers, every clanking and crinkling sound she made echoed off the walls only to bounce back and present itself as though to say, "Hello, yes, it's just us here."

But on this cloudy and blustery Monday morning, forty-eight hours and then some after Aubrey had kissed her (*kissed* her, on the mouth, no warning given, no signs that Emma could remember seeing), there was a much more noticeable silence in the store.

Eerie silence: There was no music.

It wasn't because Aubrey wasn't there. No, Emma had seen her moving like a ghost between the stacks, her dark-blond hair floating behind her she disappeared around the corner of the science fiction section. Every time Emma heard the slightest rustle—and she heard every damn one of them because, duh, no music—her head jerked up on its own volition, eyes scanning her surroundings.

She wasn't *waiting* for Aubrey to come talk to her. That was absolutely not the case. It was just that Emma had made the mistake of getting used to—looking forward to, even—their early morning chats. And on a day like today, when the store was silent and the long-distance air between them was crackling with unasked questions and an entire novel's worth of words unspoken, it seemed like Aubrey really should be standing at the counter, waiting for Emma to come out with an armful of premade croissants that weren't half-bad.

The image of Aubrey standing and waiting made Emma's stomach clench uncomfortably as she slowly kicked open the swinging door and emerged into the café proper. The space on the opposite side of the counter was empty. A trickle of disappointed confusion made its way down her spine.

Confusion had been her overriding emotion since Friday night. And that, for Emma, was a crime against humanity. Emmalynn Gallagher did not experience confusion regarding her thoughts or feelings. She only ever *knew* what she was thinking and how she felt, as well as what she thought about how she felt and how she felt about what she was thinking. There was nothing unanswered in Emma's mind.

That concrete vise grip on her thoughts and feelings had been thrown carelessly out the window the moment Aubrey Glass leaned in and kissed her. And Emma hadn't even been the one to throw it! No, it was ejected from her without warning or permission. Just gone, in a moment of lip-to-lip connection.

Emma's stomach clenched again, but it was a different sensation this time. She leaned against the counter, wishing and pressing the fluttery feeling away. She didn't have time to obsessively circle her thoughts around Aubrey, or the kiss, or the funny tickle in her gut when she thought about Aubrey kissing her. She had a job to do, and then she had a class to attend.

And that class was causing her more anxiety than each flash of Aubrey in her mind or the corner of her vision. Today was the day Emma was officially embarking on what absolutely needed to be the last college adventure of her life. That was leaps and bounds more important than anything that might have transpired between Emma and Aubrey a few nights ago.

Turning her attention away from her futile desire to figure something—anything—out, she eyed Bernard. She had to get him ready for the day.

The early morning sounds of Bernard waking up had, against all odds, become comforting. Two weeks into her job as a barista, Emma still did not like coffee and would not be partaking in any of the drinks she created. What she had opened her heart to was the art of coffee drink making. There was a science to it, for sure, but also a flair. A skill. A talented flick of the wrist...Okay, maybe it was more like hitting the syrup pumps in just the right way and making sure the milk was heated to its optimal temperature, but whatever. Not just any non-coffee drinker could put so much of themselves in the drinks they crafted. Emma was in, heart and soul sans taste buds, totally, full stop.

A murmur of conversation made its way over as she snapped the top on the espresso grinder. Not wanting to appear too obvious or too curious, she slowly moved down the counter, nudging various items along the way to keep up the pretense of doing her job when all she wanted to do was eavesdrop the hell out of whatever Sadie and Aubrey were discussing. When she made it to the edge of the counter, just a few steps from the edge of the café, she craned her neck and saw them.

She smiled despite the torrent of question marks floating and popping in her brain. It was her first full look at Aubrey since that moment by her car, and it was a relief to see her. She was wearing baggy olive-green cargo pants, a striped T-shirt, and a very comfy looking cream cardigan that was just the right kind of oversized and swung as she gestured to the shelves in front of her. Her usual Birkenstock clogs had been replaced by beat-up black high-top Converse.

Sadie was listening intently, sipping a drink that definitely hadn't come from the café. Emma narrowed her eyes. That seemed wrong on several accounts.

Her focus slid back to Aubrey, who had stopped talking and was listening to Sadie. Emma now had a perfect view of Aubrey's profile. She'd never noticed, or maybe she hadn't paid attention to, the lines of Aubrey's jaw. They set her face at an angle that somehow stayed feminine but projected power and confidence. Instinctively, Emma understood this was one of the things about Aubrey that had set her apart from the crowd in high school. She had the look of someone much older than she was, someone who carried herself differently from her peers. There was something about the shape of her face and its features that perfectly combined a masculine and feminine image. It was probably why literally everyone had been in love with her in high school.

Not Emma, though. She straightened, but her eyes refused to leave Aubrey's profile. She most certainly hadn't been in love with Aubrey in high school. She hadn't even known her, and since she was a freshman when Aubrey was a senior, there was no way Aubrey would have paid her any mind anyway. As Emma mulled this over, Aubrey smiled, and Emma blew out a frustrated breath. That smile. It was so beautiful because it was so rare. When Aubrey let it out, the space around her glowed with a warmth that was inviting and intoxicating—almost addictive. The way her lips curved up and parted slightly to reveal perfectly straight, very white teeth that expertly nibbled bottom lips when kissing—

Wait. Wait a damn minute. Forgetting that she was trying to be invisible, Emma whirled around and rushed into the café stock room, not bothering with trying to be quiet. Safely behind the door, she pressed one hand to her mouth, the other against the cool surface of the wall.

She was here to work, not think about that kiss. She'd tried to forget about it, repeatedly telling herself it hadn't been real. Yes, it had happened (her lips still felt it despite the amount of times she'd touched them as though to smear it away) and yes, it had felt better than any kiss Emma had had before it, but it wasn't *real*. That kiss was a one-off, a mistake.

Emma grunted and kicked the wall. Leave it to Aubrey Glass to ruin her master plan of moving home, finishing her degree, and figuring out her next step. All Emma wanted to do was make it through those items on her mental agenda without any drama or bullshit. She didn't have time for anything other than work and school. Add in being forced to make time to face her growing, layered questions about her sexuality? Absolutely not, thank you very much, Aubrey Glass.

"Emma?"

She jumped at the sound of her name. Recognizing the voice and batting down the relief she felt, Emma pushed through the swinging door and fixed a smile on her face.

"Hey, Sadie. I was just—" She turned around, hoping she'd find an excuse written on the door from which she'd just come.

"Looking in the freezer. For lava cakes. Did you know we only have one box left? I should tell Genesis."

Sadie merely smiled, unaffected by Emma's awkward rambling. "Yes, definitely let Genesis know. She has to put in an order tomorrow."

"Great! I'll add it to my list." Right under *Avoid Aubrey Glass for the rest of my life so I don't have to ever be reminded of how that kiss made me feel.*

"You're the best, Emma. I'm so glad you took this job."

That makes one of us, Emma thought. "Me too," she forced out. And it wasn't a complete lie. She did like her job.

A thud sounded from the business section. Emma willed herself not to look in that direction.

Sadie rolled her eyes, but there was genuine affection in her expression. "Aubrey's in a mood this morning." She peered at Emma. "And it sounded like you might be too."

Every one of Emma's nerves stood at attention, sending a wave of anxiety rippling through her. Had Aubrey told Sadie? No. She wouldn't. Right? Oh God, Emma had no idea.

"I thought I heard a little bit of banging around over here," Sadie went on. "Just wanted to check on you."

Emma shrugged, hoping she projected a look of careless ease. "I'm good. Thanks."

"Good! Great. I just want everyone to be happy." Sadie's eyes lit up. "Oh! Today's the first day of the semester! Are you excited?"

Emma swallowed the panic she was dying to expel. "I mean... Kind of? More nervous than excited, I think."

Sadie's eyes glittered. Emma knew her well enough by now to know that was genuine excitement in her expression. "That makes perfect sense. I have no doubt you're going to be amazing. And you have a whole store full of people rooting for you."

The idea of Aubrey cheering for her as she hoisted her backpack on her shoulders and marched off to her first class of the semester made Emma want to laugh. She just couldn't picture it.

"You're sure you're good?"

Emma blinked away the silly visual and nodded. "All good. Thanks, Sadie."

"Anytime. I'm always a couple of steps away if you need anything, even just to talk."

Okay, maybe Aubrey had said something to her. Or maybe she could see the imprint of Aubrey's lips on Emma's, and intrinsically knew that Emma had no idea what to do with that imprint and the looping memory of it.

Not trusting her mouth, Emma simply nodded and watched Sadie walk away. Alone again, she sucked in a deep breath and held it until her jumping nerves stilled.

"Okay, Gallagher," she whispered after she exhaled. "That's enough of Aubrey Glass for one day."

Perhaps Aubrey had heard the whisper as it traveled through the air vents of Cornerstone, or perhaps Emma had just become so busy that it left them no opportunity to cross paths. Either way, she made it through her workday without any more Aubrey sightings.

It was then that she had to face the next installment of her day: class.

Suddenly, the distraction of Aubrey and the tornado of curiosities her lips had inspired didn't seem so awful.

Emma trudged through Pennbrook's campus, heading toward the one building she never imagined she'd spend much time in, but Pennbrook liked "well-rounded scholars," and there Emma was, making her way into Berringer Hall, home of the English department, cesspool of all things reading and writing.

It wasn't that she hated English-y things. Reading was a perfectly fine hobby. Emma had enjoyed a few books over the years, but they'd all been nonfiction, and she hadn't fully read more than three of them. She'd always been an average writer who scored high Bs on essays with little effort. These things—words—simply weren't her passion. She didn't see the need to study them and interrogate their meanings. She was more of the "a person wrote a book, and I can read it without analyzing it to death and still enjoy it" class of reader.

As she stepped into room 303, Emma threw her shoulders back and held her head high. Maybe if she faked confidence she might begin to believe she could glide right through this class. Perfect plan. She nodded, belatedly hoping no one caught it, and settled into a seat in the front row. Satisfied with her choice and hoping it would help keep her focused, she got out her fresh spiral notebook (she thought laptops in class were disrespectful to the professor) and favorite dark-blue gel pen.

Emma's confidence lasted until she looked up from her carefully arranged desktop and focused on the professor she'd somehow missed as she walked into the room. She fought like hell not to gape, but her jaw strained with the effort.

The professor stood behind a long table, slightly bent over as she scribbled on a piece of loose paper. Even bent over, Emma could tell she was tall, not far from six feet. The dark-gray chinos and black V-neck sweater she wore seemed made for her body. Her honey-blond hair had a gentle curl to it and was messily pulled back, as though she couldn't be bothered to spend too much time on something as insignificant as a tight bun. Some strands had escaped and framed her jawline. Emma felt an inexplicable urge to brush the strands away.

When the professor stood to her full height and looked out at the class, she glanced at Emma and smiled before her dark-blue eyes swept the rest of the room.

Emma pressed a hand to her throat. She'd never seen such a beautiful woman. Or maybe she had, but she hadn't realized it because she suddenly felt like she'd never truly *seen* women until right this moment.

"Hi, everyone," the professor said, interrupting Emma's barreling train of thoughts. "I'm Professor Lewes." She stopped and grinned, putting her hands on her hips. "I just realized this is the last semester I'll be able to say that."

The girl sitting next to Emma was practically vibrating in her seat. "I heard you're getting married!" she blurted.

The secondhand embarrassment Emma felt was real. Who in their right mind would have that be the very first statement they made in a college class? Emma crossed her arms and shifted to her right, not wanting Professor Lewes to think she was so much as acquaintances with that idiot.

The smile Professor Lewes bestowed upon the class was nothing short of blinding. Emma blinked furiously, trying not to fall under her spell.

"That's news to me," Professor Lewes said easily. "I was referring to the fact that I'm finally finishing my PhD, so starting in August, I'll get to introduce myself as Dr. Lewes."

Clapping and cheering sounded from every corner of the room. Startled, Emma turned to look at the group behind her. It was a pretty full room, and everyone looked genuinely happy for this professor and her upcoming achievement. Emma, not wanting to look disrespectful, managed to get a few claps in before the noise died down.

As Professor Lewes moved effortlessly into an overview of the course and the syllabus, Emma tried to keep up but was annoyingly distracted by the woman's beauty and charisma. On one hand, she was thankful that she wasn't hanging on every word Professor Lewes said, but on the other, she was so preoccupied with her presence that she knew she was missing critical information.

There was no way around it: Professor Lewes was insanely attractive. She was also very, very smart. As she talked and walked around the room, all eyes followed her. She had a magnetism that no one seemed immune to. Her humor coincided with her obvious knowledge of the subject matter (Emma, frankly, had forgotten what the course was focused on), and she took comments and questions as though she'd been doing this job since the day she was born.

The hour and a half passed in a flash, and soon, everyone was slowly packing up. It was a marked difference from the college courses of Emma's past, where people raced out of the room the moment the professor stopped talking. Here, no one really seemed to want to leave. They were all lingering in their own way, whether it was to talk with peers or stand in line to talk to Professor Lewes. For a moment, Emma wondered if she'd stumbled into a cult.

"She's amazing," the girl next to Emma said, her voice dreamy. She turned her vibrant blue eyes on Emma. "Is this your first time?"

Emma still felt a needling of embarrassment for the blurter, but she had enough manners to be polite. "You mean, is this my first class with her? Yeah, it is."

"You're going to love her." She laughed loudly. "We all do. It's kind of impossible not to. I'm Carly, by the way."

"Emma," she said, not sure if she wanted to become more than distant acquaintances with this person. "So…It's always like this?" She gestured around the room.

"Oh, yeah. Callie—I mean, Professor Lewes—has *waiting lists* for her classes." Carly pushed her thick black hair over her shoulder. "She's definitely the most popular professor in the department."

It must have been a stroke of fate, then, that Emma had been able to get into this class. She made a mental note to ask her advisor how he'd made it happen.

"It helps that she's super hot," Carly said.

Emma dared to look up at Professor Lewes, who was having an animated discussion with three students. She was, indeed, super hot. Strands of hair were still brushing her jawline, and she tucked one behind her ear as she laughed along with the students in front of her. When she crossed her arms over her chest and arched her back just so, Emma was hit square in the stomach with something akin to yearning.

She felt a lick of heat beginning its way up her chest. Soon, her entire face would be red. She had to get out of there.

"Nice meeting you," she said to Carly as she stuffed her belongings into her backpack. "Gotta go—I have, um, another thing. Stuff to do."

But Carly had moved on, edging ever closer to the outskirts of Professor Lewes's magnetic field. Emma was freed from her awkward goodbye, and she hurried to the door, needing major distance from the illustrious professor.

Emma burst through the doors of Berringer Hall, the cold air a welcome smack of reprieve. Her breathing was already unsteady as she practically ran through campus.

Never in her life had Emma been so...so...enamored with someone she didn't even know. She understood that Professor Lewes was objectively attractive. Anyone with eyes could see that. *Fine, fine, makes sense.* Emma tightened her grip on the straps of her backpack. So Professor Lewes was hot. Big fucking deal.

A snowflake landed on the tip of her nose and she blinked, turning her head skyward. Flurries floated onto her face, melting as soon as they made impact with her still flushed cheeks.

"Okay," she said softly, head tilted back as she let her heartbeat slow. "Okay, Emma. You're okay."

But she wasn't. Apparently all it took was one kiss from a woman (*with* a woman, because Emma was well aware that she had kissed back) to blow a hidden internal door straight off its hinges, leaving Emma fumbling in the darkness of a new room, fighting to find a light switch. She couldn't see how big the room was, nor did she know how many secrets hovered in its corners.

She hadn't meant to keep that door hidden, or locked. She truly hadn't realized it was even there.

As the flurries crowded in the corners of her eyes, Emma blinked, feeling a thin stream of melted snow cascade down the sides of her face. She could handle a semester with Professor Lewes. That wouldn't be a problem, regardless of how attractive she was. Emma was certain she was a great professor and that's what she would focus on for the next four months.

She would find something else to look at during class, like the whiteboard or the window. Even the door. Because Emma recognized that spending too much time looking at Professor Lewes could be distracting. It was more than her impossible beauty, however.

Emma shut her eyes against the snow. Looking at Professor Lewes was, in a way, like looking at a future vision of Aubrey: the height, the incredible jawline, the mouth—oh, the mouth.

Emma pressed her fingertips against her lips.

"Damn you, Aubrey Glass," she breathed, the words disappearing in a breath of fog.

CHAPTER FOURTEEN

If Aubrey did one thing right that Thursday, it was going to be setting up the new display at the front of the store and filling it with romantasy books that were trending but also categorically good. Sadie had recently become fixated on BookTok. If she had it her way, a.k.a if Aubrey didn't rein her in, the display would be filled with all the overly hyped books being lauded by BookTokers. Alas, Aubrey had put her foot down and given Sadie a list entitled "These are actually good." She knew as well as anyone that taste in literature was completely subjective, but she refused to advertise books that simply were not well written.

It had taken a while, and a few impassioned arguments on both sides, but Sadie had eventually relented.

And now Aubrey was faced with the task of display creation. When she was hired, Sadie had overseen the displays and was quick to offer the assignment to Aubrey. She'd gladly taken it, as she liked losing herself in arranging books in such a way that pleased both the eye and the brain.

This particular display demanded a lot of attention to detail. Since romantasy was all the rage, Sadie and Aubrey both wanted it front and center. It would be the first thing a customer saw when walking into the store. Because of that, Aubrey wanted to be certain the display showcased the super popular books as well as lesser-known titles that were equally incredible.

Aubrey was standing a foot away from the table, one arm wrapped around her torso and the other cupping her chin, when someone nudged her from behind.

When she turned, her body sagged with relief, letting loose a tension she hadn't even realized she'd been carrying. "Pen. Hey."

Penelope grinned. She had snowflakes in her white-blond hair (it had snowed every day that week, much to the entire city's dismay) and her cheeks were rosy from the cold and her natural vivacity.

"Aub. Hey yourself." She brushed a gloved hand over her hair. "Oh, it's so warm in here. Whatcha working on?"

"Sadie's breaking into trendy territory," Aubrey began, then went on to explain the display and her heavy hand in selecting the titles for it. She didn't mince words or hurry through; Pen shared her love of reading and, as she'd said multiple times, was "infinitely jealous" that the majority of Aubrey's coworkers were books. It was one of several things the two had in common, their mutual dislike of Corrine notwithstanding.

Pen, however, wrinkled her nose as Aubrey completed her explanation. "Romantasy? Not my favorite."

"Mine either, but this one"—Aubrey picked up a book with a solid black cover decorated with vibrant pink flowers—"is deceptively incredible."

"Sold," Pen said. She took the book and skimmed the blurb on the back cover. "Oh, this is dark. But also light? Interesting."

"I promise you'll like it."

"You've yet to be wrong." Pen glanced over her shoulder toward the café, which was sparsely populated. "Can I steal you away for a coffee?"

Aubrey assessed the display—mostly complete, just in need of finetuning but that would be best if she walked away for a while and returned with a fresh perspective. She nodded and walked to the café with Pen.

It wasn't until they were standing behind the one person in line, a young mother juggling a toddler and an infant, that

Aubrey realized she hadn't spoken to Emma all week. She wasn't consciously avoiding her, which meant, yes, she was unconsciously maintaining space between them. She didn't know what to say, or how to say it, or if anything needed to be said at all.

Besides, when she had seen Emma (because of course she checked every morning to see if she was there), she'd seemed more and more frazzled by the day. Aubrey couldn't talk herself out of the idea that whatever she would say to Emma would just make her more frazzled, or something worse. And despite the nagging feeling that repeatedly whispered, "Talk to her," Aubrey chose not to.

She was a coward, and she knew it.

Her heart thudded anxiously in her chest as she watched Emma hand the young mother a to-go cup and smile. Aubrey wouldn't make the claim that she knew Emma well, but she could tell that smile was tired and maybe a little forced. Aubrey stuffed her hands in her pockets as she waited for Emma to see her. She was only slightly terrified of how Emma's smile would shift when their eyes met.

As it turned out, the smile disappeared entirely, replaced by a look of sheer surprise. Nothing but professional, she immediately greeted Pen. Aubrey scanned Emma's face as Pen ordered her drink. Emma didn't seem angry, which was a relief. But her expression wasn't giving any clear emotion away.

"And for you?" Emma asked, turning to Aubrey.

"Hi," Aubrey blurted.

Emma blinked twice. "Hi, Aubrey."

"Hey." She really wanted Emma to smile at her, but Aubrey could tell she wasn't going to have that wish granted. Not today, anyway. "May I please have my usual?"

Emma nodded and Pen nudged Aubrey. "Look at those manners. Your mother would be so proud."

Aubrey scoffed, forgetting about Emma at the mention of her mother, which reminded her of their last conversation. "Has she called you?"

Pen laughed, a hearty sound that was at odds with her lithe, socialite appearance. It was what Aubrey liked most about her, the way her personality absolutely did not match the image she presented to the world. It was her little secret, how incredibly cool and down to earth she actually was.

"No, Aubrey, she hasn't blessed me with contact. Why? Should she?"

Aubrey shook her head. She was relieved, but not convinced Corrine wasn't waiting in the background, leveraging her little asinine request for a time when it would have maximum impact.

"No reason. How are the kids?"

The glow returned to Pen's face before she even answered Aubrey's question. Her detailing of Lyla, Trent Jr., Trevor, and CeCe's lives carried them through their wait for their drinks (and provided a pleasant buffer to the game of keep-away Emma and Aubrey played with their eye contact), through the short journey to a table by the windows, and into the first fifteen minutes of the time they spent sitting in the understuffed armchairs.

By the time Pen finished, Aubrey had counted seven instances of catching Emma looking her way. She still couldn't discern the expression on her face, or the feel of the air between them.

"So," Pen said, leaning forward and knuckling Aubrey's knee, "what's got you so distracted today?"

Aubrey took a time-killing sip of her drink and smiled despite herself, because Emma had yet again absolutely nailed it. She must have killed a little too much time because Pen gave her an appraising look before tilting her head toward the café counter.

"Tell me about the barista."

"There's nothing to tell," Aubrey said quickly.

"Really? Because it certainly feels like there is." Pen grinned. "You could cut the tension in here with a knife."

"Come on, it's not that bad."

"So you admit there's tension." Pen was practically bouncing in her seat. For a moment, Aubrey forgot there were any years between them; the eight that were there sometimes seemed to disappear, bringing Pen back down her twenties and allowing her to enjoy silly shit like bookstore gossip.

"There might be," Aubrey all but grumbled, making sure to avert her eyes, lest Emma telepathically discern what she and Pen were almost discussing.

"She's cute," Pen remarked. "But a little young for you."

At that, Aubrey sat up straight. "She's twenty-one. That's not young. Perfectly legal."

"Relax," Pen said, tapping her nails on the lid of her coffee cup. "I just meant that you've always seemed more interested in women your age or, well, older."

Aubrey sank back into the chair and slid down until she was comfortably slouching. "Let's not, okay?"

Pen kicked Aubrey's foot. "Hey, I'm not being hard on you. You know I'm the last person who would ever judge you, Aubrey." She laughed, an empty sound that still managed to sound amused. "Let's not forget that I married someone thirteen years older than I am when I was just eighteen." She shook her head. "I still can't believe I did that."

Aubrey also couldn't believe young, gorgeous, free-spirited Penelope had latched onto someone like Trent. But Pen was right—she hadn't ever judged. When everything had gone down, Pen had been the only person Aubrey confided in. She knew truths that no one else would ever know, and she still hadn't judged Aubrey or made her feel even worse than she already did. Pen had just listened and empathized. She'd also repeatedly pointed out exactly where Aubrey had gone wrong, which wasn't Aubrey's favorite part of their discussions, but whatever. It was necessary. Apparently.

It was those memories that compelled her to quietly say, "She called me."

Pen's eyes widened. "No. No she did not. Did she? Aubrey!"

"Relax," she said, glancing around them. They were, somehow, blissfully alone aside from Emma moving behind the counter. "I didn't answer. I mean, I didn't have my phone on me when she called."

"Mmhmm, now that part I don't love. Are you implying you would have answered if you had had your phone?"

Aubrey shrugged. She couldn't answer because she honestly didn't know.

"She left a voice mail." This she nearly whispered.

"And?" Pen was nearly vibrating with excitement tinged with terror. "What did she say?"

"I haven't listened."

The thrill left Penelope in a whoosh of an exasperated sigh. "Get out your phone. Now."

Aubrey did, smiling a little. It was moments just like this that she forgot Pen was the mother of her step-siblings. Sometimes, it just didn't add up.

She unlocked her phone and motioned for Pen to lean in. Once they were situated in a way that would allow both of them to hear the message, Aubrey took a breath and hit play.

They were greeted with an abundance of background noise. Shuffling sounds, maybe other voices, it was hard to tell. Could have been a TV, or people sitting at a bar.

Pen pointed at the phone. The message was two minutes long. "This is weird," she whispered. "Do you think—"

Aubrey shushed her and they listened to the full two minutes, but at no point was anything said directly to Aubrey. It was one hundred-twenty seconds of noise with no meaning.

"Well that was anticlimactic," Pen said, crossing one leg over the other. "Side bar, do you like my leggings? They're Lululemon dupes." She shook her crossed leg in Aubrey's direction.

Aubrey rolled her eyes. What her mother would never be willing to understand was that Pen existed solidly in the "older sister" role for her, and could never move out of that space. Hence her little threat being not only absurd, but also hurtful. Aubrey genuinely liked Pen, even when she talked about shit that made no sense, e.g.: leggings and dupes.

"Yeah, they're great. Should I call her back?"

"What? No! No, Aubrey. Why would you even suggest such a thing?"

Because it had been years (two and a half, if she were counting) since she'd heard Jamie Morrison's voice. Because despite everything she'd done to set fire to that part of her life and move on, she still felt the shiver of closeness and the stark reminders of what she'd thought was love.

For as honest as Aubrey was with Pen, she couldn't bring herself to admit that the words "what if?" were still taped to the interior walls of her heart.

"Aub?"

"I'm not going to call her," she said. "It's okay. You don't have to worry."

"I'm choosing to believe you." Pen grinned wickedly. "You know what would be a great distraction? The barista," she finished, not waiting for Aubrey to attempt to answer her question.

"She's not—it's not like that." What she couldn't say was that Emma was a distraction unto herself, regardless of Aubrey's emotional baggage.

"I still think you should talk to her."

How Pen knew there was a conversation to be had, Aubrey would never know. But she nodded, knowing Pen was right.

"Yeah. I will."

"And delete that voice mail, right along with the number, which I thought you had blocked, by the way." Pen stood up, brushing off her precious leggings. "I've got to run if I'm going to make my Pilates class."

"Oh, heaven forbid you be late for that and all your snobby political friends talk shit behind your back about your fake-ass leggings."

Pen punched Aubrey in the shoulder, then pulled her tight for a quick hug. "You're lucky I like you. See ya later, Aub."

"See ya." Aubrey stood and watched her weave through the magazine section before exiting Cornerstone. "And yeah," she said softly as the door closed behind Pen. "I really am."

"Don't you have books to shelve? Trinkets to stock? Boxes to break down? Something other than standing in my café, taking up space?"

Aubrey instinctually shot up her middle finger behind her back, then whirled around, having forgotten there could be customers around. Meanwhile, Genesis cackled.

"I hate you," Aubrey said, making her way toward the counter.

"Far from the truth, Glass. Did you have a nice little heart to heart with Pretty Miss Penelope?"

"Actually, yes, I did. Not that you'd know the feeling since you don't have a heart." Aubrey tapped her finger on her chin. "Or a soul, for that matter."

Before Genesis could retaliate, the swinging door bounced open and Emma emerged, face flushed. Both Genesis and Aubrey turned their focus on her.

"What?" Emma asked immediately, patting her face, then her apron. "Do I have whipped cream all over me again?"

Aubrey's urge to laugh was tempered by the image of Emma with—wow, no, not going there. She cleared her throat and stared at the countertop.

"Nah, you're good. Thanks for restocking the milks."

Aubrey's head snapped up. Genesis? Handing out a thank-you? Well, this was new.

"No problem." Emma looked between Aubrey and Genesis. "Okay. So. Bye."

"Later, Just Emma. Oh, wait!" Genesis held up a hand, which stopped Emma in her tracks. "You're coming out Saturday night, right?"

A look passed over Emma's face, and again, Aubrey couldn't place it. Either she was woefully out of practice with reading people's expressions, or Emma felt things too quickly and the emotions didn't linger on her features.

"To, um, Lotus?"

"The one and only." Genesis held up her hand for Aubrey to high-five, and Aubrey, amused at this odd behavior, gleefully slapped it.

This time, Emma squared her shoulders and turned a completely emotionless expression toward Aubrey. It was so intense that she actually gulped.

"I can't," Emma said, still looking at Aubrey. She bit the corner of her lower lip as she dropped her eyes to the floor. "I'm kinda overwhelmed with classwork."

"Already? It's only the first week of classes." Genesis sounded as incredulous as she looked.

"It's a lot," Emma said, her tone steady. "I have to take these lit courses and books—reading—it's not my thing. I feel insanely stupid when I sit in those classes, and I hate that feeling. Like, really hate it." As her words gathered speed, so too did a deep pink flush as it crept up from her collarbones. "It's my Achilles heel or whatever. Feeling stupid. Not knowing what I'm doing." She laughed. "Yeah, okay, major weakness. Anyway, I have work to do this weekend. And I can't come out." The blush was flaming her cheeks now, and Aubrey couldn't help but notice how its arrival was paired with that last sentence. "To the bar," Emma hurriedly added. "This weekend. Okay. Good talk. Bye."

With that, she charged past Genesis and disappeared around the corner. Aubrey wanted to jog after her but no part of her wanted to explain that to Genesis, so she waited until she and Genesis had exchanged looks and a few words (nothing mean; in fact, Aubrey could tell Genesis had a real soft spot for Emma, which made her smile) before she made her exit.

Aubrey slipped into the employee's lounge and spotted Emma immediately. She was standing in front of her locker, fanning her face with what appeared to be a beanie. Not the best cooling device, but it looked like a desperate maneuver.

"Emma," Aubrey said softly, not wanting to startle her.

"Yup."

Aubrey shifted from one foot to the other. She'd come in here with no planned speech and now she couldn't find the necessary words to repair what she feared she'd broken.

"What, Aubrey?" Emma had turned to face her. The beanie, in a death grip with her fingers, hung by her side.

"I want to apologize to you," she said quickly, trying to avoid second-guessing herself. "About last week."

Emma didn't make a move or a sound. Finally, her lips moved and all that came out was, "Apologize?"

"Yes," Aubrey said. "I'm sorry."

"For kissing me?"

Well, *that* was unexpected. Aubrey took a step back, thrown by Emma's blunt question. She shrugged. "Yeah? I mean, yeah."

"Okay, sorry, wait." Emma took a breath and lost some of her bravado. "That was aggressive."

"The kiss?"

"No! Me. What I said." She tilted her head to the side and her ponytail followed the motion. "I guess the kiss was a little aggressive."

"Was it? I—shit, Emma. That's not me. I'm sorry it—"

Emma shook her head, cutting Aubrey off. "No, it wasn't the kiss that was aggressive. It was...I don't know how to explain it. Okay. Can we start over?"

"Sure," Aubrey said slowly.

"Great. Let's start over." Emma stared at her, waiting.

Aubrey huffed. She was getting lost in everything that wasn't being said. "With the apology? Or, like, in general?"

"Oh," Emma said. "That's a good question."

They stood in silence for a matter of seconds, the kind that felt like weeks stacked upon months. Just as Aubrey was gearing up to try a different route, Emma spoke up.

"I don't want to start completely over. Maybe...Maybe we start from right before the kiss?"

Aubrey could have screamed at her body for betraying her with the way it lit up, responding to the idea of reliving that kiss. Because it had been a really, really good one—especially considering it was a first kiss.

She couldn't help herself. With a shadow of the Aubrey Glass smile she'd become famous for in college, she asked, "So, should I kiss you right now?"

"Oh my God," Emma blurted. "No! I mean, no." She was wringing her beanie toward its slow, yarn-filled death.

"Then…" As much as Aubrey had intended to apologize and move on, she was having too much fun with this side of Emma—someone who obviously wasn't mad about the kiss having happened, but also wasn't sure if she wanted it to happen again.

Or she did, but she couldn't face it yet. Aubrey knew that feeling well, so she told herself to back off.

"It's not a big deal," Emma said. "Right? Kisses happen."

"They do."

"Yeah, they do." Emma looked everywhere but at Aubrey, which only stoked Aubrey's desire to mess with her a little bit more.

"And they can happen more than once, Emma."

"Shut up!" Emma clapped her hand over her mouth. "I'm so sorry. That was rude. And I don't want you to shut up."

Aubrey bit back a bout of laughter. "Okay, okay. I'm sorry."

"Because you were high, right?"

Her words were a solid punch in the gut. Of all the things Emma could have said in that moment, *that* wasn't even on Aubrey's list.

"Excuse me?"

"You were high," Emma repeated, sounding more confident as she gathered steam. "So it doesn't really count. The kiss. Because you, I don't know, probably didn't even realize what you were doing."

The words were eerily familiar, stirring up memories and emotions Aubrey didn't care to revisit. She shuffled her feet, shoved her hands deep in her pockets. She had just about had enough of this day.

Emma was still talking, belaboring her own (incorrect) point about how kisses don't count when one or both people are under the influence. She was nearing a lecture about roofies when Aubrey swiftly cut her off with, "You're right. It's not a big deal. We can forget about it."

Emma, mouth still open after being cut off, gave her head the slightest shake. "No, I didn't say that. I didn't say we should forget about it."

"We should." Aubrey avoided Emma's eyes as she turned and headed for the door. "Have a good rest of your day, Emma."

CHAPTER FIFTEEN

Emma hadn't forgotten about the kiss. She still thought about it at least four times a day, more often when she was at work and saw Aubrey. And when they resumed their early morning, pre-store-opening chats? Forget about it. The memory of the kiss flashed in Emma's mind after every fucking sentence Aubrey spoke.

And yet, in the fourteen days that had passed since Emma ruined her opportunity to have Aubrey Glass kiss her again, right there in the employee lounge, neither one of them had so much as uttered the word "kiss" in their conversations.

Any kind of clarity Emma had hoped to gain had been shoved aside—both by that volleyball match of a conversation they'd tried to have, and by the intensity of balancing work and school. Her classes were no joke. Even the business class felt like it was over her head, but she'd proactively joined a study group and was starting to feel better about the course material.

Those literature classes, though...Just the thought of them made Emma tamp the ground espresso with more gusto than was warranted. She gripped the metal apparatus, which looked like something a person might find in a sex toy shop, and pressed as hard as she could. Genesis had told her early on that there was no such thing as tamping too hard, and Emma was taking full advantage of that piece of advice.

She wanted to like the course material. She really did. She just didn't. She understood it on a basic, "I attended four years of public high school English classes" level, but while her professors and peers cliff dived into the abyss of literary analysis, Emma lingered at the edge of the precipice. It wasn't the height that scared her. It was the fall itself—the cascade of symbolism and imagery that paved the drop right into the ocean of full understanding.

Emma took a step back from Bernard, impressed with herself. Maybe she wasn't as far off the literary analysis path as she'd thought.

"Here you go," she said, sliding the extra dry cappuccino to the elderly man. He was a Thursday morning staple, but despite Emma's attempts at drawing him into conversation, he preferred to order, receive, and settle into a chair with a couple of magazines.

He thanked her and walked away, choosing the chair that, at this point, likely had melded to fit his body.

"How's Dr. VanKirk today?"

Emma, surprised to hear Aubrey's voice at this time of day, composed herself before turning to see her leaning against the counter. "Who's that?"

Aubrey jerked her head toward the elderly man in the chair. "The guy who orders an extra dry cappuccino every Thursday at eleven a.m. and enjoys it while flipping through three different magazines, all about tattoos."

Emma gawked at her. "Tattoos? Him?"

"You'd never guess it." Aubrey smiled and tucked her hair behind her ears, a gesture Emma watched from beginning to end. "He used to be in the Art department at Pennbrook. But legend has it, he never shared anything he created."

"So...He's an undercover tattoo artist?"

"Key word is artist. Some people think he's behind some of the best designs in those magazines he's reading."

Emma snuck a look at Dr. VanKirk. He did seem awfully pleased with whatever he was looking at in the tattoo magazines.

"How do you know all this?"

Aubrey hadn't moved from her leaning position, and Emma was entirely distracted by the way her hip pressed against the edge of the counter. She'd never met someone who could slouch and lean so effortlessly.

"Sadie," Aubrey said, making it sound like quite the obvious answer. Because it was. Sadie was very connected to the Pennbrook professors and knew things most non-Pennbrook employees wouldn't.

"Right." Emma nodded. She looked back at Bernard, who was in need of some serious TLC. She'd gotten through the Thursday morning rush as well as she ever had, but left a trail of coffee destruction in her wake.

"I should let—"

"Slow day?" Emma said quickly, interrupting Aubrey's prelude to leaving.

"Kind of." She looked back toward the book floor, where customers were wandering around. "I slept really well last night so I had energy this morning. I—" She stopped, as though realizing she'd said something she hadn't meant to. "Um, I got through my to-do list quickly today."

Emma felt her face light up. "You make to-do lists?" She tried to tamp down the excitement in her voice but heard it edge its way out despite her efforts.

"Only when I have to," Aubrey said, looking unimpressed.

"I love lists." Emma was nearly bubbling over with said love. "They're so helpful! I swear, I'm so much more productive when I'm crossing things off a to-do list."

Aubrey cringed. She actually *cringed*. "Wow, okay, that's…That's really great for you."

"Aubrey," Emma said seriously. She pressed her palms onto the counter and leaned toward her, still maintaining an appropriate no-kiss distance. "How do you get things done if you're not working off of a list?"

"Persistence," she said, as though it was the most natural answer in the world.

Emma took a step back, feeling her heart race up a small hill. "Oh," she nearly whispered. "Are you a Taurus?" She pressed her hand to her lips, mumbling the next words through her fingers. "Oh my God, that makes so much sense."

"What? Why?" Aubrey looked clueless and adorable. No, no. Just clueless. Definitely not adorable.

Emma cleared her throat. "Just, you know, your entire personality."

Aubrey gaped at her. The cluelessness had been ushered out by something that looked like indignance. Emma tried not to smile. It was exhausting, really, trying to avoid admitting to herself how every damn expression that flashed across Aubrey's face was charming, if not captivating.

"What's with your face, Glass?"

Both Emma and Aubrey turned to see Genesis standing there, watching them curiously.

Aubrey recovered first, pointing accusingly at Emma. "She was making accusations about my personality."

"I what? I just told you it makes sense that you're a Taurus."

"Total cop-out," Aubrey said. "You didn't even explain what you meant."

Emma pointed at Genesis. "Because she came over and interrupted."

"And if she hadn't?" That was a damn near devious glimmer in Aubrey's eyes. The sight of it made Emma gulp.

"If she hadn't," she said, pretending she didn't have a bubble of nerves in her throat, "I would have dazzled you with an explanation of why you, Aubrey, are such a Taurus."

"Dazzled?" Oh, that glimmer.

"Dazzled," Emma repeated.

"Here's an idea. You two stop flirting and get back to work. Yeah? Sound good? Stellar."

"No," Aubrey said immediately. "No one was flirting."

"If you say so, Glass."

"We weren't," Emma protested. "Not even close. Since when is talking flirting?"

"Denial is a river in Egypt and your boats are sinking." Genesis paused, then cackled. "Shit, wait, I gotta write that one down."

As Genesis rooted around for paper, Aubrey took the opportunity to shoot Emma a look before leaving the café. The look was indecipherable, and Emma knew she'd be thinking about it for the rest of the day.

"What did I say, Just Emma? Something about a boat?"

"We were *not* flirting," Emma said emphatically, though she couldn't bring herself to meet Genesis's eyes.

"Yeah, sure, whatever. Keep telling yourself that." She tapped the pen against the counter. "It was a boat, right? Or was it a raft?"

Not willing to dignify Genesis with a response, Emma busied herself with the cleaning and restocking she'd intended to start after making Dr. VanKirk's cappuccino. She was in the middle of wiping down Bernard when a hot blush made its way up her neck.

Genesis thinking they were flirting had to come from somewhere, because while Emma didn't have legions of experience with flirting, she was pretty sure what she and Aubrey had been doing was *not* flirting.

Of course, she thought, cheeks heating. It wasn't Sadie Aubrey had told about their kiss outside Lotus. It was Genesis. They were friends, or at least friendly. Come to think of it, Aubrey didn't seem to have friends. She never mentioned anyone when they were casually chatting, and Emma had mentioned Collins numerous times.

A faint ache pulsed at the base of her throat. As much as she hated that Aubrey's mere existence (fine, yes, and her mouth) had stirred up flurries of questions within her, the thought of Aubrey being alone—lonely—nearly broke her heart.

The only thing to do was distract herself, and so, with the lull in customers and the added bonus of Genesis being on hand to help out, Emma swept through the cleaning and restocking. She had to pause only twice to take care of customers. When she finished, she looked around her sparkling domain and decided, yes, it was time.

Though she was loath to do so, Emma pulled out her notebook from beneath the counter. She tucked herself into a corner, in clear sight of the register and any approaching customers, and opened to the section she'd labored over for two hours the previous night.

The photocopy of H.D.'s poem "At Ithaca" was decorated with annotations Emma had jotted down during class. None of them had made sense at the time, but she heard the importance of them. Now, as she ran her finger over her notes, she tried to see them in a different light. A light of yearning, of loss, of fear and hope.

It was a beautiful poem, Emma realized that much. Plus, she'd read *The Odyssey* in high school and remembered enough of it to know the poem's speaker (Penelope) and the man she was yearning for (Odysseus). She'd had to read a quick summary to remind herself exactly what the problem was in their relationship (simply put: The

Trojan War coupled with Odysseus's arrogance, plus a shit-ton of suitors). The summary had also provided the helpful reminder of Athena (Athene in the poem), and her role in Odysseus's life, which also affected Penelope.

But the imagery. The symbolism. The inferences and personification. Even some of the words—the third stanza had "woof" in it, which Emma only knew as a sound a dog made. She couldn't get her brain to let loose and take it all in.

She kept getting stuck, too, on one line: "My weary thoughts / play traitor to my soul." Emma was pretty sure Penelope didn't have a blooming crush on one of her maids, but every time she read that line, all she could picture was a maid slouch-leaning against a wall in Penelope's bedroom, watching her weave and unweave, waiting for the perfect moment to make her forget all about Odysseus.

"What's that?"

Emma squeaked, hurrying to cover up the poem as though her own traitorous thoughts were typed in bold font on the paper. "Nothing. A poem. It's nothing."

Genesis rolled her eyes and held out her hand. Emma double-checked to make sure she hadn't somehow spilled her soul onto the paper then handed it over.

"Oh, H.D., nice. Lemme guess. Professor Lewes?"

"Yeah," Emma breathed. "I mean, yes. It's her class."

"Oh come on, Just Emma. Not you, too."

"Not me what?"

"'Yeah,'" Genesis said, mimicking Emma's breathy tone. "You sound like every other starstruck ingenue who takes one of her classes and falls madly in love."

"I am not in love!" Emma said, much louder than she'd intended. "God, Genesis," she hissed. "It's not like that."

"Yeah okay. Damn, you're full of little lies today." She whistled, slightly off-key, but Emma still recognized the opening synthesizer chords to a Fleetwood Mac song.

Emma grabbed the paper and yanked it away from Genesis, who stopped whistling to laugh.

"Relax, Just Emma. It's not a crime to have a crush on a professor."

She weighed her options for responses, settling on, "It's a little hard to concentrate in her class," which was true and didn't fully indicate that she maybe did have a crush on Professor Lewes. A purely academic crush, that is.

Genesis shot out a laugh that sounded like a firework. "For you and everyone else. Wait," she said, suddenly sounding much more serious. "Who's your other lit class with?"

"Professor Frances. I mean, Imani. She's big on us using her first name."

Genesis looked disappointed. "No Renee Lawler?"

Emma shrugged. "Never heard of her."

Genesis outright gasped, a sound Emma had yet to hear her make. "That's a crime, Just Emma. Don't ever say that to me again."

"Okay, I won't. Who is she?"

"Only the singular most gorgeous woman who has ever walked the cobblestones of Pennbrook's campus," Genesis said, awe vibrating in every word.

"And I'm the one with a crush."

Genesis pointed directly at Emma, glee on her face. "You said it, I didn't. And also, get your shit together because your crush is about to walk over here and order a coffee."

Emma's heart stampeded in her chest. She opened her mouth to ask the incriminating question, "Which one?" but didn't get it out before Genesis continued with, "And she's with her slightly intimidating girlfriend, so please, Just Emma, for the love of God, be cool." She then disappeared into the café stock room.

A fleeting image of Aubrey with a faceless girlfriend blew through Emma's mind and when it exited, she found herself looking directly at Professor Callie Lewes.

"Emma, hey," Callie said easily, as though they frequently ran into each other outside of the classroom. "I didn't know you worked here."

"Hi," Emma said, eyes darting to the beautiful and incredibly well put-together woman standing next to Callie. "Yeah, yes, I work here. In the café."

"It's a great place to work," she said, glossing right over Emma's awkwardness. Emma imagined she had an absurd amount of practice with that. "I miss it sometimes."

"I'm sure Sadie would let you come back whenever you wanted," the woman with Callie said, and Emma belly flopped directly into the smooth, soothing waters of her voice.

"I think I have enough to keep me busy." Callie gave her companion a look that melted Emma. She didn't understand how the other woman was still standing after having that look directed right at her.

"What's up, Cal-Lew?" Genesis reappeared, deftly stepping over the puddle of Emma on the floor.

Callie grinned and high-fived Genesis. "My dude. How's things?"

Emma, irritated by how easily Genesis interacted with *the* Callie Lewes and that she even had a *nickname* for her, turned her eyes to the other woman. Just as she was about to ask if she wanted to order something, Callie interjected.

"Emma, have you met my partner?" She looked between them. "I don't think you're taking any of her classes."

"We haven't met," the woman said, reaching her hand across the counter. "I'm Kate Jory. It's lovely to meet you."

"You too," Emma said. "Can I make something for you two?"

Callie ordered for both of them, and Emma set off to make the drinks, leaving Genesis to socialize. As she steamed the milk, Emma stole glances at the couple. They had an air about them that calmly stated how in love and how in sync they were. They made a striking couple, too. Kate looked a bit older than her partner and carried herself in a way that made her seem almost regal. It was an interesting and, yes, sexy contrast to Callie's tomboyish demeanor.

Emma hadn't known until that moment that she could have a singular crush on a couple, but, well, there it was.

She brought the drinks over to Callie and Kate, who had been joined by Sadie. Emma didn't dare ask them to pay, knowing without being told that these two had a permanent free drink card. She'd heard through the book floor grapevine that they were responsible for a huge chunk of the store's sales because they purposely had Sadie stock rare texts that their students needed to buy.

"Enjoying 'At Ithaca'?" Callie asked, breaking away as Sadie and Kate wandered off to another part of the store.

Emma winced as she glanced down at the counter and saw the poem and her scattered notes lying bare for her professor to see. "It's…coming along."

"I know literature isn't really your thing, Emma, but I hope you know that your discussion points in class have been right on target."

Huh. Callie must have actually read the info sheets she'd had her students fill out on the first day of class.

"I'm trying," Emma said. "I want to do well."

"Then you're on the right track. If there's anything I can help you with, swing by during my office hours." Callie smiled, and Emma could see how easy it was to read the wrong thing into her kindness and easygoing nature.

"Thank you. Maybe I will."

"See you next week." She waved then left.

"Not bad," Genesis said from behind Emma. "I was convinced you'd be way messier when you talked to her."

"It's not like that," Emma said firmly. "She's—I don't know, she's just…"

"Ridiculously attractive and smart? And really fucking nice?"

"All of the above." Emma sighed. "Which is why I'm going crazy trying to get everything right in her class."

Genesis clapped Emma on the back, sending her stumbling forward. "That's impossible, Just Emma. It's literature. There's never a black-and-white meaning. Anyway, you obviously need help." She side-eyed Emma. "With your poems and shit, I mean. Leave it up to me."

Later, as Emma was stuffing her apron into her locker, she heard Aubrey and Sadie walk into the employee lounge. For once, they weren't arguing—it seemed like that was all they did lately. Emma couldn't quite figure out how their employee-boss relationship worked, but it was clear that Sadie respected Aubrey's opinions, even if she put up a fight about them.

Emma slowed her movements. She was fighting a weird urge to apologize to Aubrey about earlier, even though she knew she hadn't done anything warranting an apology. Emma sighed. It seemed this was their thing: miscommunicate, apologize, lather, rinse, repeat.

"Heading out?" Aubrey asked.

Emma nodded, then turned around while she finished buttoning her peacoat. "Yeah, I have class in an hour."

"With Callie?" There was that devious glimmer again. It made her dark-green eyes sparkle.

"No," Emma huffed. "That's on Mondays and Wednesdays. And I don't call her Callie."

"Of course not." Aubrey shrugged. "But she wouldn't mind if you did. In the store, anyway."

"I won't."

Aubrey grinned. "You're so proper."

"That," Emma said, crossing her arms across her chest, "is mostly true."

At that, Aubrey laughed. She seemed looser than she had in weeks. It was a lovely change and Emma was curious what had precipitated it. Maybe it was just the sleep she'd mentioned she finally got.

"It's okay to have a crush on her," Aubrey said. "Literally everyone does, whether or not they're gay, straight, bisexual, whatever."

Emma stiffened. Why was everyone obsessed with her noncrush (fine, mini-crush) on Professor Lewes? "Do *you* have a crush on her?"

"Nope." Aubrey gestured toward herself. "That'd kinda be like crushing on myself."

So she saw it too. Emma had been trying to talk herself out of the comparison, but the more she watched Professor Lewes in class, the more she saw Aubrey, slingshot into the future.

At a loss for a good response, Emma simply nodded.

"I should let you go," Aubrey said. "Have a good class."

"Thanks. You too." Emma rolled her eyes and jammed her hands in her coat pockets. "I mean at work. Have a good day at work."

"I know what you meant," Aubrey said, a gentle lilt in her voice.

It wasn't until hours later, when Emma was in the silence of her borrowed bedroom in her brother's house, that she slapped her hand to her forehead, realizing that Aubrey had given her the perfect opening to establish her sexuality.

Then again, Emma couldn't provide an answer for something she was still questioning.

CHAPTER SIXTEEN

If a bookstore brought Aubrey comfort and happiness, libraries took it all to the next level. Less populated (except around midterms and finals), quieter, overwhelmingly stocked with pages to flip through, and a scent that was the same in every library she'd ever stepped into.

The library on Pennbrook's campus was no different. It was a model of what university libraries should aspire to be: lofty with shelves arching toward the ceilings, just spacious enough while also maintaining those tight aisles of tomes that the rare student explored. It was a great library, but the area Aubrey had staked out on the second floor was too brightly lit for her liking. She had a soft spot for dim, moody spaces lined with books. Not the most conducive for studying or learning, but atmosphere mattered. And this atmosphere wasn't giving her the cozy, slightly melancholic feel she was craving.

As she waited, she tapped out a beat on the table in front of her. On her walk from home, she'd listened to one of her newer playlists, I'm Only Playing. Speaking of moody—oh, yes, it was. It was a wild roller coaster of a mood ride, stocked with Billie Eilish,

Lorde, Hozier, Lord Huron, Halsey…all the moodiest of the moods. The name of the playlist came right from a Halsey song she hadn't been able to stop listening to, "Finally // beautiful stranger." It was as much stuck in her head as it was in her heart, and she let it sit there, taking up space, unwilling to read into it.

A song could be just a song. She'd told herself that countless times. But for Aubrey, songs were never just songs. They were maps, signs, detours from heavily traveled paths.

She looked up and stopped her drumming as a few people entered the back area where she sat. Their voices rang somewhere above the preferred library level and Aubrey couldn't help but to glare at them. They carried on through the stacks, not paying her any attention. She wiggled her fingers, ready to resume her nearly silent table drumming.

"What are you doing here?"

Aubrey looked up, surprised to hear Emma's voice. And there she was, standing with a backpack slung over one shoulder, coat buttoned to her chin. Her long red hair was pulled back tightly, no strands framing her face. The look could have been severe, but on Emma, it only served to turn the spotlight onto every freckle, which was…something Aubrey wasn't ready to admit.

"Waiting," Aubrey said. Her quick-thinking rational voice was rapidly putting the pieces together—Genesis, Pennbrook, "just show up, you owe me"—but her denial was swinging down in full force. There was no way Genesis had sent her here to tutor Emma.

"For what?" Emma looked flustered, but also very tired.

"For someone?" Aubrey shrugged. "Genesis gave me—"

"A piece of paper with instructions, directions, and a time," Emma finished, her shoulders slumping. Her backpack slid with the movement, and she didn't bother to hoist it back up.

"So…it's you I've been waiting for?"

Emma blinked, then let her bag slide fully to the ground. "Waiting? No, I was told to be here"—she glanced at her watch—"exactly right now."

"Oh." Aubrey fished in her pocket for her slip of paper, certain she hadn't misread it but also wanting to be sure. "Okay. She gave me an arrival time of ten minutes ago. And I was early."

"Well that part's on you."

Aubrey held up both hands. "Whoa, easy. What's with the hostility?"

"I'm not *hostile*." But the way the word slithered from her barely moving lips generated its own kind of hostility.

"Emma," Aubrey said quietly, gesturing to the chair across from her. "Please sit down."

"No." The word fell like the stomp of a two-year-old approaching a full-blown tantrum.

Aubrey bit back a grin. "Why not?"

"Because! This is—this is absurd." She tried to cross her arms, but the strap of her backpack was tangled around her wrist, plus her coat was extremely puffy and wasn't the type that allowed for an effective arm-crossing. "You're not—this isn't—why are you here?"

"You already asked me that," Aubrey said patiently.

"And *you* didn't give me a clear answer." Emma's eyes were blazing but she was losing some of her fight.

Aubrey sighed. She could pack it in and head out, chalk this up to a disaster she hadn't seen coming. But the way Emma's shoulders slumped and the memory of her frustration a couple of weeks ago when venting about her coursework pinged Aubrey's heart. She could sit through Emma's anxiety riddled anger until she calmed down. But first, answering the damn question.

"Genesis asked me to do her a favor. I agreed. She gave me this paper"—Aubrey pushed it across the table—"and told me the woman of my dreams would show up at exactly the time written on the paper."

Emma, who had been studying the piece of paper, snapped her head up. "She said—what?"

Aubrey shrugged, the picture of nonchalance. "Don't worry. Your assigned time was ten minutes later."

Emma gaped at her, an expression that should have been some level of unattractive, but all it did was draw attention to her mouth, which Aubrey now couldn't stop staring at. Her eyes remained locked there even as Emma fumbled in the oversized pocket of her coat until she pulled out a paper that looked like (and Aubrey wasn't going to say it out loud, not wanting to give Emma more to freak out over) the other half of Aubrey's ripped loose-leaf.

Several charged beats of silence passed before Emma slid the paper back into her pocket. "Just wanted to make sure," she mumbled.

"Will you please sit down?" When Emma hesitated, Aubrey went on, keeping her tone purposely gentle. "Look, Emma, we're both here. If you haven't noticed, Genesis is maybe a little crazy but also annoyingly smart about things." She waited to see if Emma would smile. Nope. "For example," Aubrey went on, "she knows I really enjoy old American literature. It's kind of my weirdo party trick, but no one ever gets it."

That got a sliver of a smile. "What, do you sit there and rattle off quotes from all your favorite nineteenth-century poets?"

"Um." Aubrey laughed nervously. "I can't say that hasn't happened."

"Wow," Emma said, sounding more like herself. "You're a nerd."

Aubrey shrugged. "Yeah, kind of. Always have been."

"That doesn't—" Emma cut herself off and broke eye contact again.

"Doesn't what?" When Emma remained silent, Aubrey kicked the chair across from her. "Sit down and finish your fucking sentence."

Emma raised her eyebrows as she followed half of Aubrey's command. "Bossy."

"When I have to be."

Aubrey did not miss the blush that threatened Emma's cheeks. Nor did she miss the way Emma suddenly unbuttoned her coat in a flurry of motion and pushed it off her shoulders. She flattened her hands as though to fan herself, but instead tugged down the turtleneck of her dark brown sweater and pressed her fingertips to the base of her throat, which was quite flushed.

"Hot?" Aubrey said, amused.

"When I have to be."

Aubrey grinned. "Well played. Now finish your sentence."

Emma heaved a sigh that told the tales of years at sea. Appropriate, as Aubrey knew she'd recently been working on "At Ithaca" in Professor Lewes's class.

"Okay, I'm just going to say it."

"Like I've asked you to, you mean?"

Emma shot her a glare. "Fine. Yeah. Okay." She took a deep breath and dropped her hands to the table. "You being a nerd doesn't fit with the image of you I have from high school."

Aubrey waited to feel some sharp internal sensation, like she always did when someone made a comment like that. Her body was calm, though. Oddly so.

"You didn't know me in high school," she said, choosing her words carefully.

"I know, which is why I used the word image."

Haughty. That was how Emma sounded. Aubrey brushed it off, knowing she was fending off her own vulnerability.

She wasn't sure what to say, though. They could spend hours dissecting High School Golden Girl Aubrey Glass vs. Post-College Bookseller Aubrey Glass. But that wasn't why they were here.

"To be clear," Emma said, swooping in to redirect them, "you're here to tutor me?"

"If you want to call it that, yeah."

"What the hell else would I call it?"

Aubrey tilted her head to the side as she conducted a lengthy mental search for phrasing that wouldn't make Emma feel less-than. "A study group?" she settled on.

"Pretty sure both people in the study group—which isn't even a group because it's only two people—have to be enrolled in college in order to use that name."

Okay. Aubrey was just about hitting her "that's enough" threshold. She had compassion for Emma, but the constant rebuttals weren't sitting well.

"Maybe I should go," she said, moving to grab her bag.

"No, Aubrey, don't." Emma interlocked her fingers in front of her. The expression she wore was pained but there was a softness beneath it. "I'm not—I'm not good at asking for help," she said in a rush. "And I hate feeling like I don't know what I'm doing, and holy shit, Professor Lewes's class makes me feel like I have absolutely no idea what I'm doing. And I hate that feeling. Did I say that already? Sorry. This is all a lot for me. And I just want to be successful. Apparently I need help to be the kind of successful I want to be, especially since I'm totally in over my head with these lit classes, so if you can help me—if you're willing to help me—I'd really appreciate it."

Aubrey took a moment to let the hailstorm of Emma's words settle around them. When she was certain Emma was still breathing and wasn't preparing another verbal avalanche, Aubrey nodded.

"I'll help you. On one condition."

Emma winced. "One condition. Go ahead."

"Stop fighting me."

The quiet of the library shifted around them, seeming to recognize the weight of the statement she'd push-passed over to Emma—a move she never got to execute during the brief time they played field hockey together. It wasn't long before Emma nodded, apparently unable to agree with more than a silent gesture.

"Great. Let's get started."

An hour and a half later, Emma leaned back in her chair and dropped her pen on the table. "So my biggest takeaway is that Whitman is super full of himself."

"Well, he was a fabulous gay man, so I feel like he had the right to be full of himself."

"Wait, Walt Whitman was gay?" Emma's cheeks flushed with the wideness of her grin and she laughed. "Okay, hold on, this poem makes a lot more sense now."

Aubrey shook her head. "The poem isn't about him being gay."

"No, I know, but that one section…Hang on." Emma flipped through the pages of her textbook, jabbing her finger at the section she'd been looking for. "Section eleven. Come on, Aubrey. The way he describes that group of men bathing by the shore?"

"It is pretty detailed," Aubrey agreed. "And the unseen hand passing over their bodies."

"'It descended tremblingly from their temples and ribs,'" Emma quoted. She shook her head. "You gotta admit, that's sensual."

"Does he describe any women like that in the poem?"

Emma looked up, then narrowed her eyes. "Are you quizzing me?" Her tone was playful, a far cry from how she'd sounded upon arriving at the library. So far, she'd kept up her agreement to stop fighting.

"Not at all, just wondering what else you've picked up on."

"I don't remember anything about him describing women. But, like you said, the poem is about how the self is everywhere and everything, so—" She stopped and twirled her pen between her fingers. "Never mind."

"No, keep going."

Emma looked away, and when she settled her gaze on Aubrey again, the look in her eyes gave Aubrey pause. She filed it away to analyze later, in the privacy of her apartment.

"How did you describe it? The individual and…?" Emma asked.

"The individual and the universal."

"Yeah," Emma said, nodding. "That. If you look at it that way, when the speaker's describing himself, he's, like, describing everyone. Man, woman, all of us. So I guess some of those descriptions could be about women. Maybe?"

"Maybe."

Emma pointed at Aubrey. "See! This is why I don't like poetry! There's no black and white. It's all gray."

"And that's exactly what I love about poetry."

The two smirked at each other across the table. Aubrey would have preferred sitting side by side—for nothing more than it being easier to look at the same part of the poem together, of course.

"Agree to disagree," Emma said.

"I have a feeling we're going to be disagreeing a lot." Aubrey held up her hand when Emma tried to interject. "Which is totally fine. You just can't fight me on it."

"I won't," Emma said, doing her best to sound dejected. "But you're no fun, for the record."

"Not the first time I've heard that."

Emma raised her eyebrows. "Are we still talking about poetry?"

"Clearly not," Aubrey said through a short laugh. "We should wrap up, though." She nodded toward the window. "It's getting late."

"And dark," Emma added. "And probably even colder. But before we go, I have one question."

Aubrey's nerves, those traitorous bitches, fluttered with anticipation. "Shoot."

"How are you so good at this?" She pointed at her textbook, an unnecessary move since Aubrey knew what she was asking. "Did you study literature in college? Wait." Emma shook her head. "I don't even know what you majored in. Oh my God, hang on. Did you even graduate?" She clapped her hand over her mouth. "Rude, sorry," she said from behind her fingers.

"That was way more than one question. I feel like you might need a math tutor, too."

"Absolutely not." Emma slapped her notebook shut. "I'm a numbers girl. I just have an unfortunate habit of asking questions that lead to more questions because I can't wait for the answers."

Emma's awkward rambling had definitely grown on Aubrey, but what she liked the most was when Emma suddenly snapped out of her unraveling speeches and became incredibly articulate. It was fascinating. Intriguing, even.

"I didn't study literature in college. I was a philosophy major. And yes, I graduated, thank you very much."

"But you love this. And you're so good at it. Why didn't you study literature?"

"And do what? Teach?" Aubrey coughed out a laugh. "No thank you." She cringed as the truth of the matter unwrapped itself. "I guess I can't do much other than teach with a philosophy degree, either."

"Or write," Emma suggested.

It was the most innocent of suggestions, but it still managed to slice right through Aubrey and flay her out right there on the table, spilling her organs and secrets for everyone to see. She grabbed her coat and yanked it on, holding it tightly to her body.

Emma, somehow oblivious to the blood, guts, and tiny typewritten words decorating the table between them, went on. "Or maybe you could be some master literary analysis person. Yeah, I could see you doing that."

"A professional literary critic?" Funny, Aubrey hadn't realized a person could speak while their insides were flooding out of their body.

"Yes! You'd be awesome at that."

Aubrey smiled, feeling her skin begin to zip itself up again. "Because I'm so judgmental?"

If she'd expected Emma to get all awkward and shy, she would have been dead wrong. In a move she would have never predicted, Emma leaned in, dropped her elbows on the table, rested her chin in her hands, and served Aubrey a smile that was teasing, too smart, and a little nasty. Good nasty.

"Aubrey," she said sweetly. "I think it's time to let go of your high school baggage. Don't you?"

Aubrey leaned forward, coming dangerously close to Emma's waiting mouth. "You're the one who brought it up, Emma. So maybe you're the one who needs to let go of who you think I am."

"Maybe."

"Maybe," Aubrey echoed.

"Aubrey," Emma whispered.

"What?"

Emma leaned in just a tad closer. "You're just as bad as the fucking poetry."

"And you're not?"

Emma's lips split into a toothy grin. "Never said I wasn't." She pushed back from the table, stood, and pulled on her thick coat. Aubrey watched as Emma packed up her bag and threw it over her shoulder. She pulled ChapStick from her pocket, applied it, and adjusted her long ponytail before finally looking back at Aubrey.

"You comin' or what?"

CHAPTER SEVENTEEN

Emma, surprised by her surge of confidence and assertiveness, couldn't wrap her head around the fact that Aubrey had actually gotten up and walked out of the library with her. She was well aware of the attitude problem that had blown from her like a stiff wind when she'd arrived at Aubrey's table. While they'd managed to move past it, and Emma felt she'd really given her all in not being a little shit for the duration of their study session, she'd convinced herself that Aubrey would bolt the moment they finished working on Whitman.

She hadn't yet figured out how wrong she was.

Ten minutes after walking out the doors of Pennbrook's library, they were still strolling side by side at a pace that wouldn't have edged out a snail in a foot race. They'd cruised the front half of campus and were slowly making their way to the stone arch that sat on one side of Penn Street. When she was in elementary school, Emma and her family used to camp out near the arch to watch the annual holiday parade. She'd fantasized that the arch was a portal to a secret, magical world. Little did she know then that the sprawling brick building yards from the arch wasn't a home for young witches. It was just Old Main, though with its ancient grandeur both inside and out, it still managed to hold a certain magic.

Passing through the arch, Emma held her breath, hoping to hold on to some of the mysticism sparking between her and Aubrey. They were quiet, maybe both caught up in their own whirling thoughts—or perhaps that was just Emma. She snuck a glance over at Aubrey. Her eyes were cast down toward the ground, hands stuffed deep in her pockets. Tiny puffs of breath floated in front of her face, cheeks red with the cold. She seemed lost in her thoughts.

Emma was about ready to admit that she was kinda dying to know some of those thoughts. Before she could summon up the courage to ask a casual, "Hey, what are you thinking about?" or a less casual "Tell me all your deepest secrets," Aubrey broke their silence.

"There's just something about this campus. You know?"

"I do," Emma said, cringing when she heard the awe in her voice. "You'd think because it's so old, it would be boring or downtrodden. SAT word," she added with a grin. "But it's—"

"You didn't use it correctly," Aubrey interrupted.

"What? Use what?"

"Downtrodden." She was laughing as she said the word, so hard that it sounded more like "dow-rod-un."

"Seriously?" Emma huffed, the action sending a cloud of fog into the air. "So I didn't get smarter during our study session?"

"Not that I can tell." The words were bookended by laughs.

Emma elbowed Aubrey but couldn't feel anything through the puffiness of her coat, so she might have elbowed the air for all she knew. "Guess you'll have to work harder next time."

"I'm pretty sure *you* have to work harder next time."

She didn't feel like justifying that with a response, mostly because it was true. Emma trailed her fingertips over the stone in the arch as they passed through. Everyone walked through it, despite never having to—it's not like there was a towering wall or fence securing the campus and spreading out from each side of the arch. It was completely open to the street it sat on. It didn't seem to matter, though. The arch held that kind of power.

"I used to sit here with my family for the holiday parade," Emma said. "They always strung the arch with those glowy lights. They're not really yellow or white. It made the campus seem so magical, like it wasn't just a university." She laughed nervously. "That sounds dumb."

"No, it doesn't. I get it."

"Did you come to the holiday parade with your family?" She winced as soon as the word escaped her mouth. Emma had never been privy to the details, but everyone in Chestnut Hill knew Aubrey's biological dad had died when she was young. "Your mom, I mean," she hurried to say.

Aubrey walked them a few steps before she answered, her voice quiet but calm. "Only in elementary school. Before my dad died. After that..." She trailed off, leaving the thought unvoiced.

"We made a huge deal out of it," Emma said, the words rolling out of her at top speed. "My dad makes this incredible hot chocolate from scratch—it's thick and literally luxurious. So he makes a huge batch and puts it in a couple of thermoses and we get all bundled up." She laughed, shaking her head. "I don't know why I'm telling this in present tense. We don't do it anymore. I mean, we could. Maybe next year? If I'm still here. Wow, okay, getting off track. So! Yeah, the hot chocolate." Emma darted a look at Aubrey, who was gazing at the sidewalk as though it held all the mysteries of the universe. "Um, my mom was hellbent on making sure we were all warm enough, so by the time we left the house, my brother and I—you know my brother, Liam, right—we were waddling around like Oompa Loompas. But we were definitely warm, never complained." She paused only to take a breath. "We'd park it right around here, my brother and I would sit on the curb and never froze our asses off because we had so much padding on. Liam loved all the floats, especially the ones that had kids riding on them. He was so jealous. Every year, crazy jealous, but he never bothered to join one of the organizations that had the floats, so, sucks to suck." Emma laughed, quite aware of her exuberant rambling, but she could not stop her mouth from moving. "I liked the marching bands. Especially the one that dressed up as elves. Definitely my favorite." Her brain and tongue finally began to slow. "My mom brought homemade Christmas cookies, too, so Liam and I were absolute sugared-up maniacs by the end of the parade. When we got home, my parents would cue up a bunch of Christmas movies in the basement and leave us down there until someone passed out from pure sugar-fueled exhaustion. It was usually me."

Emma sucked in a mouthful of cold air. She'd run out of words, finally.

"It sounds like you have a really great family." Aubrey's voice, desolate, scratched the inside of Emma's heart.

"I do," she said. "I do."

They lapsed into silence again. Emma silently cursed herself for accidentally—and also somewhat knowingly—scratching open that wound for Aubrey. Then again, she couldn't help but to think, if Aubrey would just open the hell up and share something about her life, maybe Emma wouldn't keep stepping on the tiny landmines of her past. She vacillated between her own embarrassment and splintery anger at Aubrey as they walked.

As they turned onto Ivy Avenue, Aubrey spoke, yet again gently cracking the silence that had settled between them.

"Did you ever wonder what it's like to not grow up in a college town?"

Emma rubbed her hands over her ears, wishing she had a beanie. "Not really. Did you?"

"All the time," Aubrey said, glancing over at Emma before returning her gaze to the path in front of her. "I felt so much pressure to be *Pennbrook proud*." The words were inflated with forced enthusiasm. "There are perks, I guess. We have a lot of cool small businesses. But, I don't know, Pennbrook always felt like it was looming in the distance, and if I didn't end up there, I was going to be a massive disappointment."

Emma was holding her breath as Aubrey spoke. It was the most she'd said, the most she'd revealed about herself since they'd ended up working in the same locally owned bookstore after facing—Emma assumed, anyway; she still didn't know the details of Aubrey's recent past—disappointments and failures alike. She waited to see if Aubrey would go on. After sixteen steps, she hadn't spoken again, so Emma cleared her throat.

"Is that why you left the state? For college, I mean."

Aubrey laughed, a dark, mirthless sound that raised the hairs on the back of Emma's neck. "One of many reasons."

"Pennbrook isn't known for its world class philosophy department," Emma ventured.

"There's that." Aubrey ran her hand through her hair. The movement wafted her ever present scent of smoky vanilla over to Emma's nose.

"Or field hockey, I guess," Emma tried, pressing as gently as she could. She surreptitiously took a deep inhale, hoping to catch more of that scent.

"They have an okay team."

"Sure, but everyone knows your scoring abilities were way above the caliber of Pennbrook."

Emma didn't miss the look Aubrey shot her. She also had no idea what was behind it.

"Yeah," was all Aubrey said.

Oh, Emma's desire to rip off the duct tape covering Aubrey's mouth was *strong*. However, she'd learned enough to know doing so would backfire so powerfully that Emma herself could be launched as far as Cornerstone, a full block and a half away. And so, though it was physically painful to do so, she kindly and compassionately rerouted the conversation to a safer topic: her own failings.

Convenient timing, too, as they were passing Dough Mama, dark and quiet for the night.

"I wanted to get out of here, too," she said, wading slowly into the daunting waters of her collegiate missteps. "I thought leaving was going to be the key to my success. And I didn't even need a fresh start." She threw that out there even though it was a half-truth, hoping Aubrey would tuck it in her pocket to use later. "I wanted something different. And, lol, I got it."

"Did you just—Emma, what the fuck." Aubrey stopped them and gave her a look filled with disbelief, edged with disgusted concern. "Did you seriously just say 'lol' like a word?"

"Oh shit," Emma said. "Did I? Shit. Okay. I thought I'd stopped doing that." She felt her face heat with embarrassment.

Aubrey was shaking her head. "I don't even know what to say to you right now." But there was a shadow of a smile on her face.

"One of my former roommates used to say that, literally all the time. It was impossible not to start saying it, too." Emma kicked the toe of her boot at the sidewalk. "Hard habit to kick."

Aubrey started walking again. Without saying anything, her implication was clear: Walk and keep talking, Gallagher.

"Pennbrook is the third school I've attended." The truth, unavoidable, still chafed Emma's throat and pride. "Obviously not what I intended my college career to look like," she muttered. "I just couldn't...I couldn't find my way."

"What were you majoring in?"

"Culinary." The word whooshed from Emma's mouth, free from the ropes she tried to keep tied around it.

"You cook?"

"Bake."

They were turning onto Main Street, Dough Mama hovering in the background. Emma could practically smell it, wafts of cinnamon and clouds of caramel beckoning her back.

Aubrey took the opportunity to state the obvious. "Pennbrook doesn't have a culinary program."

"Right. That's why I'm here."

"To...what? Avoid what you really want to do?"

The short but mighty wall around Emma's heart cracked. Not enough to crumble, but enough for a shard of pain to wiggle free and splinter right through her.

She fought the sudden urge to cry. There was absolutely no way, in any circumstance, that Emma was willing to cry in front of Aubrey Glass. Instead, she forced a laugh, but it sounded like a jammed shotgun.

"I'm trying a different angle," Emma said, hoping her words weren't tinged with the sadness free-flowing through her body. "The business angle. It's more, um, responsible."

Aubrey turned so she was fully facing Emma. "Is that why you're working at Cornerstone and not Dough Mama? For business reasons?"

Emma wrinkled her nose. She knew it didn't make sense, and the way Aubrey said it made it clear she also knew that. "No. Or maybe? I can't work there."

"At Dough Mama?" Aubrey looked thoroughly confused. "Didn't the owner come into Cornerstone and, correct me if I'm wrong, look happy to see you?"

A buzzing sensation slithered through that damn crack in Emma's wall. She shouldn't care about Aubrey remembering that, but she did. Too much.

"I just can't work there. Okay?" Emma felt herself getting sucked into a confusing swarm of emotions. "Let it go, Aubrey. Please."

For once in their unhurried journey, Emma was the one to lift her finger from the pause button and begin walking again. She registered that they were, and had been, walking in the opposite direction of Liam's house. She had been hoping Aubrey had a destination in mind, one for both of them, but as they continued down Main and Cornerstone came into view, Emma was beginning to doubt it.

"When I came back here," Aubrey said suddenly, "the first place I went was Cornerstone. It was that place for me. The place where I could go and feel like I belonged. I spent more time there in high school than anyone knew." She side-eyed Emma. "Except for your brother. Anyway, I needed to be somewhere that felt familiar. Where I felt safe, I guess." Aubrey hunched her shoulders for a moment, breathing deeply before dropping them again. "Sadie offered me a job and a place to live. No questions asked. It was like she just knew what I needed."

A delicate punch of jealousy caught Emma right below her ribs. She wasn't convinced Aubrey and Sadie hadn't been more than coworkers at some point, and this bit of information wasn't persuading her otherwise.

Before Emma could blurt out that inappropriate and inconsequential question, Aubrey went on, her words hushed in the night air. It sounded like she was talking herself through the history, not explaining it to Emma. "She remembered me from when I used to hang out there in high school. Said I still had that lost look. I never asked what she meant by that, mostly because I don't think I want to know. But it was all good timing. She'd just moved out of her apartment and no one had moved in yet. She lives right downstairs, and I…" Aubrey shook her head. "She was really good to me. More so than I deserved."

They'd stopped walking again and were standing at the entrance to the park. Sprawling, old, expensive homes butted up against it on both sides on the side streets, but the view from Main was always beautiful, filled with trees and a large pond. Emma stared into the leaves set aglow by the lantern lights in the park, watching them shake each time the wind jostled the tree limbs.

"I wasn't in a good place when I moved back here." Aubrey gave a short laugh. "I had some serious fuck-ups during my junior year, and I took all online courses for my senior year. I pretty much didn't leave my apartment." She paused then. Emma watched her carefully, sensing that Aubrey was leaving something significant out of her story.

She tried, she really did, to wait for Aubrey to pick up her story, but she couldn't. "Not even for field hockey?" Emma asked.

Aubrey hesitated before answering. She avoided Emma's eyes as she said, "I didn't play my senior year."

Well, that was news—shocking news. Emma was dying to know more.

"Coming back to Chestnut Hill was never my goal," Aubrey said, cleanly steering them away from a topic she obviously wanted to avoid. "It stopped feeling like home after my dad died. And I...I left thinking I would find a new home. I thought that's what I had to do."

"Did you? Find a new home?"

"No, Emma. I didn't. I don't even know what home is anymore."

Emma shivered, but not from the cold. Aubrey's tone was far chillier than the New England February air.

"I guess what I'm trying to say is that sometimes we have to come back to the things that have broken us, because they're part of what puts us back together." Aubrey nodded once, her hair shielding her profile as her chin dipped down.

"I don't love that theory," Emma mumbled, and Aubrey laughed, a real one this time.

"You don't have to love something in order for it to be true."

"Wow, yeah, I don't love that either, Aubrey."

Aubrey leaned in, close enough to bump their shoulders together. She moved away before Emma could slip her arm through Aubrey's, just to keep her close. "You don't have to," Aubrey said. "It's almost eight. You need a ride home?"

"Oh, no." Emma's head spun as she tried to keep up with the topic hopping. "That's okay. I don't want to keep you, um, from your night."

Aubrey leaned her head back and gazed up at the clear night sky. "You're not keeping me from anything."

An annoying little voice in the back of Emma's brain disagreed, certain Aubrey was dying to get home to she could meet up with Sadie, who conveniently lived just one floor below and was older, smarter, wiser, certainly more experienced—

"I guess I could go out," Aubrey said, still looking up at the sky. "Genesis is going to Lotus later."

The mention of Lotus sent a wild shiver through Emma's entire body. She fumbled for a response, coming up silent.

"Did you have fun that night?"

Emma narrowed her eyes. That felt like a trick question. She wasn't in the mood to play games, so she gave a simple "Yes," and left it at that.

"You seemed pretty comfortable for it being your first time there."

Emma may not have been a master of language or literature, but she knew subliminal messages when she heard them. It took her a moment, but eventually she said, "I was very comfortable."

Aubrey finally moved her stare from the sky directly to Emma. The intensity in her deep green eyes—dark and endless like a forest of treasures undiscovered—was palpable, and Emma swallowed hard. Those untamed shivers settled in a place low in her belly, sparking south in a way she'd never felt before.

"I'm glad," Aubrey said softly, and at once, Emma knew for certain that brief exchange had nothing to do with the bar itself, and everything to do with what had happened after.

And now, Emma was at a loss. She was fighting a desperate urge to kiss Aubrey the exact way Aubrey had kissed her all those weeks ago, the longing rubbing against a thick ribbon of confusion about the desire itself.

Had she really never *wanted* like this before? Emma blinked, hoping she'd clear her vision and her mind all at once. How had she kept this part of herself tucked deep in slumber, silent for all these years?

She shook her head, registering Aubrey's voice but not grabbing on to any of the words. "Sorry. I spaced out."

"I noticed." Aubrey was smiling. "I said, if you want to get together to work on more of your classwork again, we should exchange numbers."

Right. Tutoring. The real reason they were standing here beneath a vast, star-filled night sky, each silently warring over the space Emma kept between them.

"That sounds good," Emma said. She pulled her phone out and recorded Aubrey's number as she recited it, then sent a text with a smiley face. "Kinda funny we've smashed our mouths together but didn't even have each other's numbers until right now." Her eyes flew up to Aubrey's face. "I didn't mean to say that out loud."

But Aubrey, thankfully, was laughing. She covered her mouth and shook her head, eyes bright with amusement. "Emma," was all she said.

"I know, I'm sorry."

"Don't apologize," Aubrey said, all laughter gone from her voice. "But about that."

Those shivery sparks lit up again, responding to the low tone of Aubrey's words, the way she looked at Emma with such startling sincerity.

"We said we wouldn't speak of it," Emma blurted. Immediate regret.

"Right." Aubrey's voice was so quiet, it nearly disappeared in the crisp air. "But do you want to talk about it?"

"No." A whisper, one of truth, because Emma didn't want to talk. She wanted to act.

Aubrey stared into her eyes, seeming to search them for the truth that was wavering right there on the surface. Emma knew without a doubt that Aubrey absolutely saw the truth. She saw Emma's desire. And she didn't make a single move to act on it.

Breathless, Emma waited for her body to take over, to break through the flimsy chains she'd wrapped around her mind. She hadn't even padlocked them. But nothing happened. She stood still, lips parted, willing Aubrey to make the move.

Just as keenly as Emma knew Aubrey saw right through her, she also knew Aubrey wasn't going to make that move until Emma gave her something solid to go on. And right then, she had nothing solid outside of the ground beneath her feet, and even that felt wavy and uncertain when she stood this close to Aubrey.

"I should—" Emma cut herself off, overwhelmed by the ache rising within her. She took one last look at Aubrey, memorizing the heated intensity in her gaze, before turning and hurrying down the sidewalk.

She made it as far as the corner of Ivy and Main on the opposite side of the street from where they'd stood before she stopped and turned around. But Aubrey was gone, cut from the scene as though she'd never been there.

CHAPTER EIGHTEEN

"Hang on, let me switch up my weapon."

Aubrey sat back and watched as Liam scrolled through various options. She didn't have to look at him to know he was biting the side of his lower lip in concentration. The scene was familiar, comfortingly nostalgic. In fact, if one deleted the bottle of beer on the coffee table (Liam's; Aubrey hated the taste and, with Liam's blessing, had smoked in the backyard when she arrived) and changed some of the decor, it was a snapshot of seven years ago. Both of them clad in sweats, feet propped on the coffee table, game controllers in hand.

In high school, Liam used to bring his console to Aubrey's house and they'd hole up in the basement for hours as they moved through a few different RPGs. Those were the golden years when Aubrey's mom was too consumed with finding her next husband to pay attention to what her teenage daughter was doing. In retrospect, Aubrey could have done a hell of a lot worse things than hiding out and playing video games until her eyes were bleary, or sitting in the bookstore for hours. Missed opportunities. Oh well. She smiled to herself, thinking of the weed she'd purchased that morning. She was making up for lost time now.

"Okay, let's head down toward the water." Liam, now appropriately armed, directed his character toward the coastline.

"This gameplay is seamless," Aubrey murmured, watching her character hop over a log and simultaneously emerge from a cloud of fog that had swept in from the water.

"Right? I can't believe you haven't played this before."

Aubrey shrugged. "I stopped playing in college. Had too much else going on."

Liam shot her a quick glance before focusing back on the game. "Hockey?"

"Yep." Aubrey wanted to leave it at that, because it was true—in more ways than Liam could know.

"I guess that would take up a lot of your time."

"It did." She navigated her character, a tall, striking redhead named Lohse, nearer to Liam's character. He'd chosen Fane, a far less attractive choice, but the two worked well together.

Liam, laid-back as ever, dropped the subject and kept his chatter connected to the game. Aubrey lost herself for a while, a combination of the remaining threads of marijuana in her system and the slightly hypnotic gameplay. She felt relaxed, a word she hadn't been able to use for quite some time. Being around Liam had always brought up that feeling, but she'd been worried time had changed their connection.

When he'd texted that morning, Aubrey had stared at the utterly nonchalant message for ten minutes: *Gonna spend the afternoon with my Xbox. Wanna join?*

It was so Liam, so reminiscent of their old friendship, that Aubrey—despite her surprised staring—didn't even consider saying no. It wasn't until she was on her way that, with a not entirely unpleasant jolt, she remembered Emma was living with him.

Alas, when Aubrey pulled up to the curb, Emma's beloved car was nowhere in sight. That didn't mean she couldn't appear at any time, but Aubrey was ready to indulge in old pastimes with an old friend for the afternoon. If Emma showed up, fine. That would be completely fine.

After all, they'd managed yet again to avoid kissing the previous night. They were getting very, very good at not kissing. So it's not like Emma would throw herself into Aubrey's lap if she came home and found Aubrey sitting on the sofa with her brother.

See? No risk. Everything was under control.

"I gotta say, your whole pot thing surprises me." Liam grunted as a tree crashed down right behind his character. "Don't get me wrong, I don't have a problem with it. Plenty of my friends smoke. It just doesn't fit with what I thought I knew about you."

Okay, maybe Liam wasn't quite as laid-back as he'd once been.

"It's—" Aubrey stopped her automatic response of "it's not a big deal." It wasn't—the smoking itself, that is. Everything that had brought her to it? Sure, that was a much, much bigger deal.

She leaned into the pillow next to her. She was so tired of holding back. And it was *Liam*. Yes, Liam was Emma's brother, a speed bump that was causing a bit of a slowed pace in Aubrey's navigation of what to do with Emma, but this was the one guy in Aubrey's life she'd always felt comfortable with.

She curled her socked toes over the edge of the coffee table. What she really wanted was another hit, but considering the topic at hand, she figured that wasn't a stellar idea.

"I started smoking in college," she said quietly, keeping her eyes on Lohse and the giant slug-type creature that was trailing her up the sand. "It just sort of happened. It's not like I went looking for it." She rubbed her hand over her forehead. "A lot of girls on my team smoked, and at first I was shocked. I know the athletes at Prescott drank and smoked and who knows what else," she said, laughing a little. "But you know that wasn't my thing in high school."

"Exactly. Because you were so focused on your sport."

"I was." It felt so far away, her high school dedication to field hockey. She'd always imagined it would stay that way in college. Maybe it had, just in a different way. "College was different. Those girls were high all the time. I swear some of them even smoked before games." She shook her head. "I hated that."

The next part was hard. Aubrey hadn't gone into it for a couple years, and the last person who'd gotten the whole story, every last gritty piece, was Pen. She hadn't judged Aubrey (well, aside from the parts that deserved a little judgment) and Aubrey felt safe enough being honest with Liam.

But Emma. The thought of her, the image of her, sent a thick, warm rush through Aubrey's body. She chilled immediately, imagining Emma hearing this from Liam and not directly from her.

Aubrey cleared her throat, as much to push Emma out as to prepare herself for telling the sordid tale of her Introduction to Marijuana.

"I eventually found out that one of my coaches was selling to the players." She felt Liam shift on the sofa but knew if she looked at him, she'd stop the story right there. So, eyes on the TV and Lohse's fiery hair, Aubrey continued, "Yeah, it was fucked up. It took me a while to find out because everyone had this perception of me as the golden girl. They thought if I knew, I'd sell them all out."

"So your high school image *did* follow you to college," Liam said.

"Briefly. I'd say I smashed it to shit when I started buying from that coach, though."

"Oh, shit."

"Yeah, I know, there are other ways to shed images." Aubrey smiled despite the acid in the back of her throat. "But I was stressed. College hockey is way more intense than high school hockey, plus the whole attending classes, writing papers, studying thing. It was a lot. And yeah, I know there are way better ways to cope with stress, but I—it was like, I saw all my teammates doing it and they were absolutely fine. So why wouldn't I do it, too?"

"Because you're not a follower?"

Aubrey bit the inside of her cheek. "I'm not. But it turns out that I really, really like smoking pot. I never smoked before games, though. Or practice. It was strictly something I did after hours, so to speak."

"And you got hooked."

"I'm not addicted." She shot him a glare, which he deflected with a crooked grin.

"Not saying you are. I told you, I have friends who smoke. And they're perfectly functioning people."

"I may have started selling," she mumbled, half-hoping the words would get lost in the sounds from the video game.

"I heard that."

"Let's pretend you didn't."

"Fine by me."

Aubrey angled Lohse so she was facing Fane. "To be clear, I don't sell anymore. It was a brief, stupid stint."

Fane stared Lohse down. He dodged from left to right before finally darting past her, leaving her to chase after him. "Good."

Okay, one hurdle cleared. The *next* next part was much harder.

As Aubrey geared herself up for treading a path she genuinely preferred to forget she'd ever forged, Liam's phone rang, breaking through her "should I, shouldn't I" mental tango.

Barely breaking his screen stare, Liam picked up his phone and answered it.

"What's up, shitbrain?" He narrowed his eyes as he continued to maneuver Fane through the underbrush where Lohse already was, searching for items. "Yeah. Okay. No, I didn't forget. Fine. Bye." He put his phone down and immediately navigated to the save menu. "You hungry?"

Aubrey set her controller on the coffee table and stretched her arms over her head, feeling her back release crackly pops from sitting too long in one position. "Starved, actually." She looked to her right and gasped at the darkness hovering outside the window. "Holy shit. What time is it?"

"I don't know, six or something?" Liam got up and put the controllers away. "I always lose track of time when I'm playing. Come on, let's go."

Aubrey stood and sat right back down. "What? Where?"

"My parents'. Put your shoes on. We're late."

She was definitely no longer high, but the confusion she felt at Liam's words made her feel like she was. "Your parents'? Why?"

Liam threw one of Aubrey's dark-gray Converse at her. "Dinner, Glass. And don't argue with me. They love extra guests."

Wordlessly, because even if she'd wanted to say something, she had nothing, Aubrey put on her shoes. It wasn't until they were in her car (Liam's suggestion, since he'd had a couple of beers and Aubrey was beyond sober at that point) that she pointedly asked, "Do you call one of your parents 'shitbrain'?"

Liam laughed as he gestured for Aubrey to turn the car on and get moving. "No. Only Emma."

She gulped then, an actual gulp that she'd swear Liam could hear.

"Hang a right at the end of the block," he said.

Not seven minutes later, Aubrey was trailing Liam as he walked up the stone steps toward the front door of his childhood home. She hadn't had time to reconcile her mixed emotions about showing up unannounced at the Gallaghers' home, expecting a meal, and having to face Emma without giving her some kind of warning. For as frustrated as Aubrey was with their slow, back and forth, will-they-won't-they, she also genuinely liked Emma and didn't want to upset her by nudging right into their Sunday family dinner.

"We're here!" Liam called out as they walked through the front door, both kicking off their shoes and pulling off their coats.

"In the kitchen!" came the reply, a woman's voice that sounded nothing like Emma.

Still a little stunned at the fact that she was in the Gallaghers' home, Aubrey diligently followed Liam down the hallway. Her nose picked up a delicious scent and she was salivating by the time they walked into the brightly lit kitchen where an older woman stood at the stove and an older man sat at the counter with a glass of very dark beer. Next to Emma.

"I brought a lost girl I passed on the street," Liam announced, heading right for the fridge and taking out a beer. "She said she was starving so I figured it was the right thing to do."

Emma, who had been looking at a magazine with her dad, glanced up with annoyance. "You're such an idiot," she said. "Why would—" The rest of the sentence disappeared the moment she set eyes on Aubrey, who was standing in the doorway.

Aubrey waved. Emma's face mirrored the movie reel of emotions taking place somewhere deep within her. She settled on a subdued kind of shock.

"Mom, Dad, you remember Aubrey Glass, right?"

"Oh, sure, honey." Liam's mom turned from the stove and greeted Aubrey with a wide, genuine smile. "It's so good to see you, Aubrey. Did Liam really pick you up on the side of the road?"

"No," she said, hoping her ability to win parents over was a skill she could still access. "We were playing video games and lost track of time." Aubrey darted a look at Emma, who was still gaping at her. "I'm sorry to crash your family dinner, Mr. and Mrs. Gallagher."

The Gallagher kids' dad stood up and walked to Aubrey with his hand extended. "Liam's friends are always welcome for dinner. And call me Jack. I don't think we've met," he said, shaking Aubrey's hand.

"That's because Liam used to hide away at Aubrey's house when they were in high school," Mrs. Gallagher said.

"And that's because I had an annoying little sister." Liam slid his arm around Emma's neck in a headlock, which jolted her out of her shock.

"Get off me," she growl-mumbled, throwing an elbow into his ribs. Liam did as requested and gestured for Aubrey to sit with him at the table toward the back of the kitchen.

For the next ten minutes, it was as if Aubrey wasn't even there, and she was completely okay with that. The Gallagher family lapsed into what could only be described as the routine of a lifetime of family dinners. Their conversations overlapped, sometimes spinning off into asides that one person would find incredibly funny. Inside jokes were made, barbs were exchanged, drinks were poured. They moved around the kitchen effortlessly (except for Liam, who continued holding court at the table with Aubrey). By the time everyone sat down at the table, an incredible homemade spread laid out before them, Aubrey had come to understand that this was precisely what she'd been missing all her life.

The recognition left a soft, heavy pit in her stomach. She willed herself not to have a visible emotional reaction, but one of the unfortunate side effects of getting high midday was an inability to shield herself from her own feelings. The rawness was usually handled in the privacy of her apartment, but here she was, swallowing repeatedly and hoping she could avoid crying while sitting at the dinner table with Emma Gallagher and the rest of her family.

Looking up from her plate and directly into Emma's honey-brown eyes, which were brimming with curiosity and kindness, nearly knocked Aubrey right over the emotional edge. Just as Emma opened her mouth to say something, her mother's voice carried down the table.

"Aubrey, please, help yourself. Don't be shy. I always make too much."

With a nod, the only communication Aubrey trusted herself with, she reached for the nearest bowl and began piling food onto her plate. For a few minutes, the only sound at the table was the repeated clink of serving spoons in bowls.

"So good," Liam said around a mouthful of roast beef. "Did you marinate this in something?"

"Just the onions and carrots it roasted with," Mrs. Gallagher—Diane, if Aubrey remembered correctly—said happily. "There's nothing like a good old-fashioned roast."

Aubrey was busy falling in love with the mashed potatoes when she registered someone saying her name. She looked up, sad to part ways temporarily with the potatoes, and realized Jack was looking at her, waiting for her response. "I'm sorry, I was so focused on these potatoes."

He laughed heartily. "Incredible, aren't they?"

"Seriously," Aubrey said. "But I missed what you asked me."

"Oh, just your basic postcollege questions. How are you liking your freedom from academics, where are you working, what are your new goals, so on and so forth."

"Nothing intrusive at all," Liam interjected with a roll of his eyes.

Aubrey lifted one corner of her mouth in a half-smile. "I'm happy to be done with college, but I do think about going back for a masters." She caught Emma's head jerk up. "As for now, though, I'm working at Cornerstone and enjoying that."

Diane tipped her wineglass in Emma's direction. "Emma? When were you going to tell us that you two are coworkers?"

"When it came up in conversation, like it just did," Emma said with a bright smile.

"Aubrey works on the book floor," Liam said. "She knows that store inside and out. She can find any book within minutes."

It was true, and it had taken time for Aubrey to learn the store that well. And she was proud of it, even if she was surprised to hear Liam singing her book slinging praises.

"She's also in charge of the soundtrack of the day." Emma was speaking to her mom but looking at Aubrey. "She's really, really good at fitting music to a mood."

"I just love Cornerstone," Diane said, sounding a bit dreamy. "They have a little bit of everything, don't they?"

"It's a great place to work," Aubrey said, nodding. "It's not forever for me, but it's a very good right now."

She directed that at Emma, who gave her a small smile before turning her attention to her dinner plate.

"It sounds like you and Emma have some things in common," Jack said as he wiped his mouth with his napkin. "Aside from working in the same store, that is."

Liam pointed the mouth of his beer bottle at Emma. It seemed the Gallaghers had a predilection for using drinking vessels to punctuate their points. "Didn't I tell you that?"

Aubrey looked between Liam, who was smiling as though he'd won the lottery (which was likely enhanced by the amount of beer he'd had over the last five-plus hours), and Emma, who wore a look of vague chagrin and something else, something Aubrey couldn't place.

"I didn't think we did," Aubrey said, saving Emma and plowing ahead into a snowdrift she was certain was way over her head. "But as Emma and I get to know each other better, yeah, I do see that we have a lot in common. Probably more than either of us realized a month ago."

"That's wonderful." Diane gave Aubrey a dazzling smile. She and Liam looked nearly identical, but Aubrey couldn't find much of their mother in Emma. Their dad, on the other hand—he seemed to be the captain of Emma's DNA. "And you two didn't know each other in high school?"

"We did," Emma said quickly. "Briefly. Field hockey. Not so much after that."

"Oh, that's right! Aubrey, you played in college, didn't you?"

Aubrey saw the look of panic stripe across Emma's face, but in comparison to her conversation with Liam earlier, this was nothing. She gave Emma a reassuring smile before saying, "I did. Things didn't end up working out the way I'd hoped they would, but that's okay."

"Sometimes that happens," Diane said easily, reaching over to squeeze her forearm. "Better things always come along, Aubrey, usually when you least expect them. At any rate, I'm glad you're here with us."

The words hit Aubrey in a way they wouldn't strike someone who had a positive, healthy relationship with their parents. She could only smile and nod before shoveling more mashed potatoes into her mouth, hoping to end the conversation. Fortunately, the spotlight slid off her as Jack steered the conversation toward Liam's job. Diane hopped in as well, leaving Emma and Aubrey to trade looks across the table as they ate their dinner.

As the plates and meager leftovers were cleared, Aubrey offered to help with the dishes. Both Jack and Diane assured her she didn't have to help, but she insisted, leaning into the manners she'd been brought up with, along with wanting to make a good impression on Emma's parents. As Jack washed, Aubrey dried, and Liam put away, the three chatted about the video game she and Liam had been playing. Jack seemed genuinely interested, to the point of suggesting Liam bring over his console sometime so he could watch. The image brought a smile to Aubrey's face even as her stomach dropped yet again, missing her own father in a way she always tried to avoid.

The family plus Aubrey reconvened at the table. This time, there was only one item waiting for them: a pie. Diane tried to give Emma the honors of slicing and serving, but she handed the knife back, claiming she could never get the slices even.

It was Emma, however, who handed Aubrey a plate with a slice on it. Their fingers brushed beneath the plate and Emma nearly yanked hers away. Aubrey couldn't resist shooting her a look that clearly stated, "are you serious right now?" and Emma defiantly looked away in response, flicking her hair over her shoulder as an annoyed exclamation point.

The moment Aubrey put a bite of the pie in her mouth, however, all thoughts of playfully torturing Emma came to a halt. That pie was *insane*. It was creamy and firm, melt in your mouth delicious.

"Damn, sis," Liam said, yet again speaking despite having a mouthful of food. "Knocked this one out of the park."

"Mmmm," was all Diane could offer.

"You made this?" Aubrey asked quietly, hoping everyone else was distracted by their piegasms.

"Every bit of it," Emma replied.

"Emma...This is..." Aubrey shook her head. "Unreal."

"Thank you." The pride was evident in her voice, and it was the first time Aubrey had felt a sense of true accomplishment and confidence from her.

In short, PG terms: It was a massive turn-on, and Aubrey had to remind herself that they were sitting at Emma's family's kitchen table, and she absolutely could not, under any circumstances, lunge across the table and press her lips to that beautiful, assured, sexy smile on Emma's face.

"It's a salted maple pie," Emma said, not just to Aubrey but to everyone at the table. "Not terribly hard to make, but it's pretty good, huh?"

"It's one of your best," Jack said, sounding as proud as he looked. "It's a keeper, Emma."

Liam shoved another forkful into his mouth. "I'm taking leftovers."

"Liam, for the love of God, where are your manners?" Diane looked at her son with loving despair. "Is it impossible for you to swallow before you speak?"

"He's essentially a caveman," Emma said.

Banter and loving sarcasm overtook the table once more. Aubrey ate slowly, savoring both the pie and the feeling of completion.

Once dessert had been cleared away, Aubrey began saying her goodbyes. She fully expected the family to hang out for a bit before Liam and Emma headed back to Liam's house, and while it pained her to leave the sanctity of that kitchen, she wanted to give them time to themselves.

"Please, Aubrey, come back anytime." Diane leaned in and gave her a quick hug. "And I'm not just saying that because you helped with the dishes."

"Thank you, I'd be happy to come back." Aubrey looked to Emma, who was hovering at the entryway leading to the hall. She waved to Jack and Liam, having already promised Liam they'd get together soon, and followed Emma to the front door.

"So," Emma said quietly, though judging from the noise coming from the kitchen, no one could hear them. "This was a surprise."

"Sorry about that." Aubrey pulled on her coat. "I should have texted you a heads-up."

"No, no, it's okay. I mean, yeah, that would have been fine, but it all worked out." She eyed Aubrey. "You were with Liam all afternoon?"

"Yes, but don't worry, I stayed downstairs." She grinned wickedly. "I didn't dare snoop in your bedroom."

The idea of being in that room, however, made Aubrey subconsciously drop her gaze to Emma's lips. She had no desire to be in that bedroom without Emma there as well.

"Aubrey," Emma said, her voice nearly just a breath. "About last night."

She looked at Emma curiously.

"I shouldn't have run away like that." Emma crossed and uncrossed her arms. "You just…No, not you. Me." She shook her head. "I don't know how to explain it."

"You don't have to." True, but Aubrey wouldn't mind if she did, because Emma was becoming more confusing by the day.

"I get nervous around you," she blurted. "Oh, God, okay. I said it."

"Emma, it's okay."

"It's not, though." Emma crossed her arms again, this time holding them protectively against her chest. "And I'm not nervous around you all the time. Only when…when…"

"When we get too close?"

Emma's shoulders dropped. "Kind of."

Aubrey wished she could push her hand right past her ribs and stop her heart from sinking. "It's okay," she repeated, though she felt anything but.

When Emma met her eyes again, Aubrey was startled to see a shining clarity in them, which stopped her heart's slow descent.

"I'm trying to figure it out," Emma said, her words sounding less confident than she looked.

"You will." Aubrey wanted to touch her, and badly. A hug, an arm around her shoulders, a stroke of her fingers across Emma's cheek. Anything.

The clarity in Emma's eyes gave way to a different look, one that pushed the boundaries of Aubrey's already shaky self-control. She watched as Emma drew her bottom lip into her mouth, popping it out after running her tongue over it. Aubrey's hands twitched at her sides. Emma took a step closer, arching her neck just so. Their height difference caused Aubrey to have to look down when Emma was that close, and as she did so, she brought one hand up to stroke the back of her head.

A loud laugh from the kitchen broke the spell. Aubrey, her fingers still tangled in Emma's thick hair, took a quick step back. Emma tried to step away as well, but was held still by Aubrey's fingers.

"Sorry," Aubrey said, running her fingers all the way through Emma's hair before removing them. "Your hair is so soft."

Emma nodded, then reached up and pulled it over one shoulder. "I'm working on it. Not my hair," she amended as her cheeks flushed. "This. Figuring it out."

Aubrey was dying to tell her to fuck the figuring out process, and just run with the feelings. But Emma wasn't like her. She was a planner, a thinker. She was calculated.

Respecting Emma's process was part of being in her life, but Aubrey wasn't loving it. Especially considering she wasn't sure what the damn process was all about.

Another time, she thought. Her fingers were itching to get back in that soft hair, so she said, "How's Tuesday?"

"For what?"

Us. "A study session."

"Oh." There, a film of disappointment layered over the single word. *Oh.* "Yeah, actually. That would be great."

Aubrey, on a wave of courage, stepped closer once more and wrapped her arms around Emma's shoulders. A moment of hesitation later, she felt Emma's arms encircle her. Friends hugged, after all. And they were, against all odds, friends.

"See you tomorrow," Aubrey said as she begrudgingly released Emma.

"Tomorrow? I thought we said Tuesday?"

Aubrey grinned. "I meant at work."

"Oh, right." Emma looked a bit dazed. "Work. Of course."

"Good night, Emma." Aubrey opened the front door of the Gallaghers' home and stepped into the cold night. As she walked toward her car, she heard "Good night, Aubrey," follow her down the path.

CHAPTER NINETEEN

Emma pushed the little white cardboard container back and forth on the café counter. Inside, a very fresh cocoa buttermilk breakfast biscuit sat waiting to be delivered. Emma had included a small container of homemade brown sugar cinnamon butter. She thought the whole thing would be a sugar overload, but Liam had assured her earlier that morning that sure, it was sweet, but it was the kind of sweet that made you want more, not the kind of sweet that made you think your teeth were falling out with each bite.

It was unclear as to who was benefiting the most from Emma's week of baking insanity. Possibly Liam, who was the crowned taste tester. Maybe Liam's coworkers, who were gifted the leftovers each morning. It could also be Aubrey, who had graciously accepted a baked good every morning that week. Or potentially it was Emma herself, emerging from her floured-over fears.

She wasn't completely out of the woods yet. She felt close, almost close enough to return to Dough Mama and at least have a conversation with Viv about possibly going to work there at some point (not right now, but later, maybe). But Emma knew her week of intense baking wasn't because she had a renewed love for the craft.

It was because of Aubrey.

Something had happened to her the moment she watched Aubrey take her first bite of that salted maple pie. Maybe it was because she hadn't watched someone new taste her creations in a long time, or maybe it was because it was Aubrey. Emma wasn't sure. What she did know was that a trapdoor deep inside of her, one that had been bolted for several years, creaked open when she realized Aubrey wasn't bullshitting her—that she truly did love what Emma had made.

But more than that, their moments together in the foyer of Emma's childhood home had initiated a new war within her. She knew, without a doubt, that she was wildly attracted to Aubrey. She did want her, in all the ways.

And that's where Emma halted. Because she'd never felt *that* way about a woman. She'd found other women attractive, sure. And she'd maybe harbored a little crush here and there, but had chalked it up to boredom or dissatisfaction with the guys she was dating.

But this...Aubrey...It was new. It was chaotic within her, spinning and swirling and taking her along for the ride. It was dangerous and sticky and overwhelmingly alluring.

It was lust. It was desire. It was primal sexual attraction, a need to kiss Aubrey and feel her fingertips slide up and under the bottom of Emma's shirt and—

And that's where the baking storm had come in. Because Emma, for some absurd, unknown reason, could not simply accept the fact that she wanted to have all the sex with Aubrey Glass. Instead of facing it and working her way through it, she threw herself into the kitchen every evening and every early morning, whipping up a bakery's worth of confections. There were cinnamon rolls and chocolate chip cookies, mixed-berry scones and pound cake layered with chocolate ganache. Mini apple pies. Cranberry almond shortbread cookies. Brown butter honey and pistachio cookie bars (Liam did not like those, Aubrey did). She'd even tried her hand at Swiss gingerbread even though she didn't like gingerbread-flavored things (Liam loved that, Aubrey did too).

Bleary-eyed and nervous, Emma went to work each morning that week armed with a treat specifically for Aubrey. They'd reverted back to the friend zone again, which Emma was semirelieved about, but also moderately crushed by. Aubrey was her usual moody self but always had a smile ready for Emma, especially when presented with that little white cardboard box each morning. Their chats were short but comfortable while Aubrey dug into whatever Emma had brought her. She was complimentary and sometimes asked questions, like how had Emma found a certain recipe, or what were her favorite flavors to work with. Emma's disdain for gingerbread had caused Aubrey to literally gape at her.

They were so firmly bound by their silently agreed upon friend zone that even their Tuesday tutoring session went off without a hitch. Emma had brought an extra treat, too, happy to watch Aubrey's eyes light up when she opened the box to find an assortment of cookies. Her uncontained delight over something so simple—cookies and muffins and miniature cakes—made the exhaustion worth it.

Emma gave the box with the biscuit another nudge before looking up and scanning the part of the book floor she could see from her position. Her shift was almost over, and Aubrey still hadn't come over. Emma furrowed her brow, racking her brain over their interactions the previous day. Nothing was said or done that would have caused Aubrey to avoid her. And Liam had eaten three of the miniature apple pies—Thursday's treat—without collapsing from food poisoning, so that couldn't be the problem.

With a sigh, Emma picked up the box and made her way to the Hub. Music had been playing steadily before the store opened and since it had, and Emma had been tricked into believing Aubrey was there because everyone knew music was Aubrey's job. The particular playlist that began as Emma walked was one that she knew Aubrey had made, so either Aubrey was there and avoiding her, or she'd been super busy all morning and was now standing at the Hub, waiting for Emma to deliver her treat.

But it wasn't Aubrey standing at the Hub. It was Lissa, she of the all-black wardrobe who barely spoke to anyone aside from Aubrey and occasionally Sadie. Word around the store, however, was that Lissa was great with customers. Quiet, but extremely helpful.

"Hey," Emma said anyway, figuring she could at least try to get some words out of Lissa. "Have you seen Aubrey?"

Lissa shook her head.

"She's out today, Emma."

Emma turned to the sound of Sadie's voice and saw her walking in their direction. A zing of jealousy shot its way through Emma's gut, reminding her of her belief that Aubrey and Sadie had once been involved.

"Out?" Emma said in disbelief. Aubrey never missed work.

Sadie just nodded. Emma blinked twice. Lissa had evaporated.

"She needed a day," Sadie said, her voice quieter now. "She's okay. No need to worry."

Emma shook her head. "I wasn't—I'm not worried. Just surprised. It seems like she's always here."

Sadie smiled and Emma recognized the threads of sadness that held it up. "Right? Our girl Aubrey, the mainstay of Cornerstone." She leaned her elbows on the counter and studied Emma. "You two have gotten pretty close."

There was no use in denying it, especially since it was an innocent statement. "Yeah. Kind of. We're getting there, I think." Emma shrugged. "She's not the easiest person to get close to."

Sadie continued studying Emma, seeming to weigh her options on how to respond. Emma appreciated that, knowing how much Aubrey respected Sadie. She still felt that flicker of unfounded jealousy, though.

"It's not always worth it," Sadie began, "sticking around to see if someone will lower their walls for you. I've been there and have the scars to prove it." She shook her head. "Not actual scars. Heart scars. Anyway. Sometimes, someone comes into your life when you're already lowering your walls, and they make it easier to bring them down."

Emma nodded once, wondering how much of this was about Aubrey and how much was about Sadie. There were rumors in the store that Sadie had long been in love with her best friend, none other than Professor Callie Lewes. Genesis swore up and down that nothing had ever happened between the two, and considering how close she was with Sadie, Emma believed her. But there was definitely something Sadie was talking around, and as Emma was very aware of the magnetism that Callie Lewes held in her palm, she couldn't help but wonder if the rumors were true.

"Aubrey has a good heart," Sadie said. "A really good heart."

It was the sweetest, least confrontational warning that could ever be delivered. Emma nodded, having no idea how to respond.

When Sadie didn't go on, Emma placed the box on the counter and pushed it toward her. "Can you drop this off for her?"

"Absolutely. Oh! Are you heading to campus?"

"Yeah, I have a meeting with Callie." Emma's cheeks flamed. "I mean, Professor Lewes."

Sadie giggled. "Oh, please. Call her Callie while you can because once she finishes her PhD, she's going to be insufferable about making people call her Dr. Lewes." Sadie bent down and came back up with three books. "Can you do me a huge favor and deliver these? The top one is for Renee, and the bottom two are for Kate." Her smile was mischievous. "Or, if you're feeling fancy, Dr. Lawler and Dr. Jory."

At the mention of Renee Lawler, Emma grinned. "Isn't Dr. Lawler the one Genesis is obsessed with?"

"Oh my God, yes! It's *so* funny. Genesis can't function when Renee is around." Sadie threw her head back and laughed. "Please tell her you're going to see Renee today. Oh, wait, let me watch!"

After Emma had sufficiently tormented Genesis, and Sadie had gleefully witnessed, she headed toward campus. Because she had a little extra time, and perhaps also because she was riding the moderate high of her bake-a-thon, Emma took the long way, past Dough Mama.

Purely for curiosity's sake, she slowed as she approached the bakery. Through the windows, she could see a handful of customers waiting in line. Emma slowed to a stop, shifting from foot to foot. She wasn't hungry. She had no reason to go into the bakery. None at all.

When she pushed open the door, she was met with the familiar haze of sugary warmth, reminiscent of what had floated over Liam's kitchen throughout the week. There were two people in line, the rest having sat down with their food. Emma peered first at the case. It was well stocked with standard items. Nothing remarkable jumped out at her. But it all looked very good, and she didn't see any icing mishaps like the first time she'd come in.

Next, she dared to look at the person manning the counter and was both relieved and disappointed when it wasn't Viv but a woman with golden-brown skin and a wide, friendly smile. She talked and laughed easily with the customers, but she wasn't wearing an apron, which made Emma believe she wasn't there to help with the baking.

Just as the door to the back room began to swing open, Emma snapped back to her senses and turned, bolting from the bakery.

She didn't dare look back as she speed-walked away from Dough Mama and toward Pennbrook.

"Okay," she said through deep breaths as she walked through the arch and turned toward Berringer Hall. "You're not ready. And that's okay. Totally okay."

They were words she wanted to believe, and maybe someday would. Beneath them was a boiling frustration that Emma worried would soon spill over, dousing her path and burning her dreams yet again.

By the time she reached Berringer, she was mildly out of breath and reaching a point of complete exhaustion. The late nights and early mornings had caught up with her, and she felt sensitive in a way she wasn't comfortable with. Maybe it was best she hadn't seen Aubrey today after all.

Still, Emma thought as she climbed the stairs to the second floor, she had to admit she didn't like not seeing Aubrey at work. It felt wrong and uncomfortable.

Also uncomfortable was the blast of air befitting a sauna that gagged her as she approached the door to the English department. She found the door wide open and sucked in a breath, hoping it was at least a tiny bit cooler inside, but no. Not at all. It was a literal sweat box.

The secretary was just hanging up the phone as Emma approached her desk. Delicate beads of sweat clung to her hairline, which was stretched to the max by a severe bun.

"Yes?" Her voice was clipped and Emma regretted having to talk to her.

"Hi, I'm Emma." She winced. "Not that you—um, I have a meeting. With Callie." Another wince, especially when she caught the secretary raising her eyebrows in disbelief. "Professor Lewes," Emma rushed.

"Professor Lewes," the secretary repeated.

Emma would have been sweating even if it didn't feel like August in the Deep South in that office. "Yes," she squeaked.

"I see." The woman lifted the phone from the desk, never taking her eyes from Emma. Just as she was about to press a number, her face lost its shield of intimidation and morphed into something much softer, complete with a smile. Emma gawked at the transition.

"Professor Lewes," the secretary called, her eyes on someone behind Emma. "I believe you have a meeting with this young lady."

Emma whirled around and saw Callie walking toward her, an easy smile affixed to her face. "Hey, Emma. Sorry I'm late."

She wasn't alone. Emma, thankful she'd already gone through the motions of meeting this power couple, smiled at Dr. Kate Jory, who had stopped at the wall of mailboxes before joining her partner.

"It's my fault," Kate said. "I needed fresh air and a chat before my next class."

"It's okay," Emma said. "I just got here. Oh, wait, I have something for you." She dropped her bag to the floor and rooted through it, emerging with two books. "From Sadie."

Kate's face lit up as she took them. "Perfect timing. Thank you, Emma."

"I, um—I have something for Dr. Lawler, too." Emma held the third book up. "Where should I put it?"

Kate and Callie exchanged a look. Emma, having nearly recovered, began to sweat again. Or sweat heavier, since she hadn't actually stopped sweating since stepping into the steamy office.

"I'll take that."

The crisp voice from behind Emma made her jump a bit. Slowly, she turned back around to face the secretary. Who apparently wasn't the secretary at all.

The woman stood up, her height matching her intense authoritative air. She was dressed in an immaculate outfit, a black pencil skirt topped by a blinding white single-button blouse with a deep V-neck and a black blazer. When she came around the desk, Emma's eyes immediately went to her shoes—candy apple red stilettos. That explained the height, *and* Genesis's infatuation. Emma's mouth went dry as she forced her gaze back to the woman's face.

"Emma," Callie said, amusement in her voice, "this is Dr. Renee Lawler. She's our department chair."

Emma attempted to smile as she handed Dr. Lawler the book Sadie had sent for her. "Nice to meet you," she managed.

"Likewise." Dr. Lawler took the book and turned her attention to Kate. Again, her expression changed, like cold foam melting into the hot coffee below it. "I just got off the phone with maintenance. As usual, they *swear* there's nothing they can do." She gestured with the book toward the ceiling. "I don't know how anyone expects us to work under these conditions."

Emma felt a light touch on her arm. She peeled her eyes from the intense, intimidating, and illegally attractive Dr. Renee Lawler and met eyes with Callie, who simply angled her head and began walking down the hall. Emma followed, both disappointed and relieved to escape the hot English professor energy that was bringing the temperature to a boiling point.

Callie's office was only a fraction cooler than the rest of the department, but it also carried a laid-back, chill atmosphere that brought immediate relief. Emma dropped into one of the chairs sitting opposite the desk and startled slightly when Callie sat next to her.

"I always find it weird," she said, leaning forward to grab the textbook on the edge of her desk, "to sit behind my big, imposing desk and have conversations with my students. It feels too CEO to me, you know?"

Emma certainly did not know, but she nodded all the same.

"So, Emma, how are you getting along with Emily D? You made some great connections in class this week."

"Thanks." Emma smiled, wishing she could stop sweating for five minutes. Unfortunately, Callie chose that moment to apologize as she whipped off her sweater and then resumed waiting for Emma's answer, now wearing just a plain white T-shirt. There would be no ceasefire for her sweating today. "Um. I think I'm getting it. Kind of." She shook her head. "I'm trying. But honestly, poems are just words to me."

"Well, yeah, they are words. And don't get too hung up on the deeper meaning. Like we discussed in class, every reader brings their own experiences and emotions into whatever they're reading, so interpretation becomes more personal than a matter of right or wrong."

"Emily Dickinson is dead," Emma said bluntly, smiling when Callie laughed. "So she can't, like, tell us whether our analyses are wrong."

"Exactly. And part of being a writer is knowing you're opening your ideas up to anyone's interpretation. It's all a matter of the reader, or the analyst, being able to back up their claims. Which brings us right to your essay."

Emma felt the familiar thump of anxiety, but that's why she was there, so she pulled out her laptop. While she was truly enjoying

Callie's class, she still had a strong and powerful dislike for reading and writing.

The two spent the next twenty minutes going through Emma's notes and the draft of her essay. Thanks to Aubrey, she no longer felt clueless about all this literature shit, but Callie also had a way about her that made Emma feel comfortable. She expertly guided Emma to see a few spots in her essay that were lacking in those dreaded claims, and instead of feeling stupid or incompetent, Emma only felt relief and gratitude for the help.

"This looks good, Emma. I think if you clean up those areas we discussed and tighten up your ending, you'll have a solid essay."

"Thank you so much. I'll keep working on it." Emma slid her laptop back into her bag. She hadn't cooled down one bit and was ready to get the hell out of the interminable heat and back to the frosty outdoors.

A light knock sounded on the open door, and both Emma and Callie swiveled around to see Kate standing in the doorway.

"Don't mind me," she said, walking into Callie's office. "I just need to grab this folder."

Emma watched as Callie tracked every move Kate made, a look of beloved infatuation on her face.

"I thought you grabbed that folder earlier," Callie said, mischief in her voice.

"Funny, I thought I had too." Kate gave her a knowing look before excusing herself and leaving the office. Callie stared after her for a moment, seemingly transfixed.

The brief exchange stirred up a new kind of yearning within Emma. She'd never seen a couple so consumed with each other, and in a healthy way. She didn't know much of the story of Callie and Kate, only little bits from Sadie and Genesis, but it was clear to anyone who saw them that their love was solid and derived from a deep mutual respect.

Callie came back to Earth and gave a crooked smile. "Sorry about that. She still manages to knock me just a little off balance every time I see her."

Emma's heart swelled. If she hadn't been slightly infatuated with Callie Lewes prior to that moment, she certainly was now. And not in a way that she actually wanted her—no, it was more like she was infatuated with the image and idea of Callie, infatuated with the desire to find someone like her.

Those rumors—the ones about Callie having a domino line of female students falling for her—were undoubtedly true. Emma was seeing firsthand how easy it was to stand in that line.

Callie stood and brushed her hands on her khakis. "I'm glad you came in today, Emma. Anything else I can help you with?"

Emma took the cue and stood as well, picking up her jacket instead of putting it on, not willing to die of heatstroke before she got outside. "Nope! I'm good. Thank you for meeting with me."

"Anytime." Callie paired the word with a genuine smile. "Have a good weekend."

"Thanks, you too."

Emma slipped out of the office, Callie leaving immediately after her and disappearing into an office across the hall. Emma smiled to herself as she left the English offices (only slightly disappointed that Dr. Renee Lawler was no longer holding court at the secretary's desk).

Once outside, she breathed deeply and held the cold air in her lungs. Slowly, she pulled on her jacket and began the walk to her car, which was still parked at Cornerstone. She fumbled her phone out of her jacket pocket and glanced at the screen, hoping to find a text from Aubrey. Nothing. Emma nodded, sliding her phone back into her pocket. Sadie hadn't left work yet, probably, meaning Aubrey hadn't yet received the biscuit.

Later, then, Emma thought. Surely Aubrey would text later.

CHAPTER TWENTY

When Aubrey moved into the attic apartment in the old Victorian on Lilac Ave, Sadie had given her a care package. Left more than given—the basket had been on the small, round table right outside the kitchen when Aubrey lugged the first of her suitcases inside. The gesture had hit right in a tender spot she was working on healing, and she'd collapsed into a chair at the table, leaning her forehead against the worn wood and letting the tears fall. It wasn't the last time she'd cried in that space, but it was the last time she'd cried over someone's unexpected kindness.

The package was filled with both household necessities (Clorox wipes, a roll of paper towels, and so on) and self-care items (Aubrey's favorite was the weighted eye mask, which came in clutch when she had a bad headache). Sadie had also included an assortment of candles—a smart move, considering how picky people could be when it came to candle scents. There were two distinct misses in the lineup, and they'd been banished to the back of the linen closet outside the bathroom. One, however, was a home run.

Aubrey loved it so much that she burned it sparingly so she could prolong its life as long as possible. The candle's name, River

Moss, suggested something less aromatic than what filled the room once it was lit. The scent was clean, tinged with mint and salt. It was earthy with just a hint of sweet.

On that particular Tuesday morning, she'd had it burning for close to an hour, and, with a shrug of dismay, pulled it closer and blew it out. She watched the melted wax glisten and sway as it hurried back to its solid form.

Aubrey leaned back in her desk chair, stretching her arms high over her head. She avoided looking to her left or right, not wanting to face the current lived-in state of her apartment. She hadn't left since she'd gotten home from work last Thursday, and considering she'd spent the majority of Friday through Sunday in bed or on the sofa...Suffice it to say, the apartment reflected that.

If she didn't look, she didn't have to face it or fix it, so Aubrey kept her eyes trained forward. She looked at her desk, her open laptop, then out the window in front of her. She gazed at the plants hanging above her. They looked like they needed a good, long drink. That, she could handle. But first, finishing what she'd started.

Aubrey tapped the space bar on her laptop, waking it once again. She would have cracked her knuckles if that was something she did, but some coach along her long line of coaches had warned her against developing that habit, citing it would decrease the strength of her stick grip. She'd never researched it to verify the coach's claim; the warning alone had been enough to scare her out of knuckle cracking.

The open document on her laptop was twenty-eight pages, single spaced. Aubrey wasn't sure what to call it—a short story, a novella, the beginning of a novel. It was a shit-ton of words, some more eloquent than others. It was a festival of feelings, a stream of consciousness poured into three characters whose lives kept intersecting, no matter how physically far apart they managed to get.

She didn't have an outline (Emma would have made one) and she didn't have a goal (Emma would have that, too, and probably a whiteboard dedicated to tracking her progress). Aubrey just had words. Nearly 15,000 of them. And about 2,000 of them were new. Brand new. The others...not so new.

The words traveled back to Aubrey's senior year of college, a.k.a her Year of Hibernation. Like she'd told Emma, she'd taken online courses and not played field hockey. What she hadn't mentioned was that for the majority of that school year, she was rarely alone.

She knew, or suspected, that eventually she would have to tell Emma the piece of the story she'd managed to avoid in her discussion with Liam last weekend. Every time she thought about it, she vacillated between "it's not such a big deal" and "holy fuck, that's a *big* deal." It made sense, considering she'd spent three years of college ping-ponging between those two statements.

Somewhere in the depths of her four days of overthinking, Aubrey had convinced herself the whole situation was a semi-big-deal. Coming to that conclusion had opened the part of her brain that had blocked her from remembering the 13,000 words sitting on her computer. When the unlocked memory surfaced in her murky brain, Aubrey had sat up from her bed-cocoon with a start. The words. The writing—no, *that* writing. The one thing that had kept her afloat when her entire world had crashed down (dramatic then, still painful now) around her.

She hadn't looked at the document since she'd left upstate New York, but it was suddenly imperative that she open it and change the name of one of the characters. Aubrey didn't have any plans for the document—she didn't even know what it was or could be—but she knew for certain that she'd never go back into it if she didn't give Jess Maxwell a name that did not include the initials J.M.

And so, Sam DiCarlo stepped in to take over the character. Once the change was made and she'd reread the entire document twice to make sure J.M. was nowhere to be found, Aubrey's brain kicked into action and produced those 2,000 new words. She went along for the ride, thinking the whole thing wasn't half-bad. Maybe, especially since she was thinking about going back to school at some point for a master's degree, the words deserved another chance.

An idea struck and she draped her fingers over the keyboard, watching the screen as sentences, then paragraphs appeared. It had always been that way, like she wasn't totally present when her writing brain stepped into action. Kinda weird, but she had grown to like the distance.

An hour or so later, she was back to staring out the window. Part of writing was staring, after all, a fact she'd verified via WriterTok. She wasn't sure if her brain was done for the day, but she didn't have more time to give it because her phone pinged with a text.

"Oh, shit," Aubrey said out loud, the first words she'd spoken since the previous night.

It was Emma, texting to confirm they were meeting to work on her essay in…Aubrey looked at the time. Two hours.

She quickly replied and said she'd be there, then sprang from the chair. Oh, God. Her apartment was a wreck. She moved in the direction of the bathroom, then stopped. If she was going to go as far as showering and leaving, she might as well do a little house cleaning before she cleaned herself.

By the time she left to go meet Emma, some order had been restored to the apartment. She'd thrown away all the trash she could find, then taken it out to the giant cans outside. She'd done dishes. She'd put away clean clothing and thrown dirty clothing into the hamper. She'd changed her sheets, a step so huge in the right direction that she'd high-fived herself afterward. There was more to do, but she didn't want to be late to meet Emma.

It wasn't until Aubrey was a block from Pennbrook's campus that she realized how quickly she'd jumped at the chance to leave her apartment, the very place she'd rotted in for four days straight, because she knew she was going to see Emma. Nothing else, not even Pen with a promise of her favorite takeout Indian food or Sadie with an offer of a movie, popcorn, and "zero conversation" had yanked her out. Neither had—

Work.

Aubrey slowed as she approached the library. Emma was going to have questions about Aubrey's mysterious absence from Cornerstone. They'd only texted once, back on Friday when she'd thanked Emma for sending that incredible chocolate biscuit thing. And Emma, sweet Emma, hadn't pressed for any information. Then she'd left Aubrey alone, which was the right thing to do, even if a part of Aubrey very much wanted her to do the opposite.

As it was, Aubrey needed a story, and she needed one fast. The truth wouldn't…No. She couldn't confess the truth. How could she possibly explain that her stupid ass phone had delivered a "photo memory" late Thursday night that happened to be a photo she could have sworn she'd deleted, and just seeing the photographic evidence of 1,095 mistakes she'd made with one very specific person was enough to take her out at the knees and drop her deep into the depression she'd been clawing out of for *years*?

Nope. She'd have to lie.

Bad cold. That would do.

The moment Emma walked up, the lie sitting on the tip of Aubrey's tongue dissolved, leaving a forbidden sweetness in its place.

"Your hair," Aubrey said, standing up. She had no idea why she stood, like she was greeting royalty. But there she was, standing, as Emma came to a stop at the table.

Emma reached up and touched the ends of her hair. "Oh, yeah. I needed a change."

Gone was the long, luxurious mane that tumbled down her back. She'd gotten it cut so it grazed her shoulders and was a little choppy, an intentional look that took away some of the thickness and gave it more movement. She'd been beautiful before, but now…Now she was stunning.

"It looks great," Aubrey said quietly, not wanting to overdo it. "You look older."

Emma rolled her eyes, but it was paired with a playful smile. "That's what my mom said."

"Oh, cool, so I sound like your mom."

"A little bit."

Aubrey sat back down. "Does your mom also tell you that you look hot?"

Emma blushed instantly, freckles popping against the pink flush of her cheeks. "No. Definitely not."

"Okay then." Aubrey narrowed her gaze. "You look very, very hot with your new haircut."

Emma fumbled with her bag. She was having sudden difficulty meeting Aubrey's eyes. Aubrey couldn't blame her—she hadn't been that verbally bold before. Aubrey couldn't tell if she was more surprised by Emma's silent reaction or by her own sudden and charged change in demeanor. The depression that had plagued her seemed to have vanished the moment she laid eyes on Emma.

That realization left her feeling unsettled. It wasn't a connection she wanted to rely on. It was too similar to the disaster from her past.

With a steadying breath, Aubrey patted the chair next to her, willing herself to keep her mouth in check and move on with the task at hand. "It'll be easier if you sit next to me."

Emma raised her eyes and stared right into Aubrey's, issuing a silent, loaded challenge.

"So we can both see your computer," Aubrey said slowly.

"My computer. Right." Emma pulled said computer from her bag and walked around the table, sliding into the seat next to Aubrey.

The severity of the mistake hit like a fist to the mouth. Emma smelled so, so good. Aubrey half-expected her to smell like a bakery, but no, this was so much better. It was a deeply layered scent, floral and spicy with an undertone of sandalwood.

She could have stayed there for hours, inhaling that scent, but Emma turned and Aubrey found her own mouth centimeters from lips that were dusky pink, full, and begging to be kissed.

Maybe it was having been away from people for four days, or maybe it was Emma's haircut. Maybe it was her perfume. Maybe it was a need to feel alive, or maybe it was *just Emma*, but Aubrey could no longer hold herself back, or wait for Emma's word, signal, nod, little breath. She leaned in, hesitating only a moment to see if Emma would pull back. When she didn't, Aubrey closed the minuscule distance between their mouths.

Her body hummed with the contact. She breathed a miniature sigh of relief into the kiss, happy to feel herself in her body once again. She faintly registered Emma's lips pressing into hers before the warmth disappeared, replaced by the temperate air of the library.

Aubrey blinked, pulling back to put a safe distance between them. "Hello," she said, a terribly belated greeting.

"Hi."

"Your perfume," Aubrey said. "It's—"

"Aubrey."

"Yeah?"

Emma's eyes were wide. "You just kissed me."

"Should I not have?" Aubrey was fumbling. She'd never misread someone so badly. Emma's lips, after all, had been *right there*. "Emma, do you not want me to kiss you?" She lowered her voice. "You do realize you kissed me back, right?"

"I know I did!" Emma looked perfectly calm, despite her wide eyes. "But you can't just—you can't almost kiss me in my parents' house then friend zone me at work all week, then disappear for days, not even texting me to say hi. And then you—you do that." She bit her lower lip, which did not help Aubrey quell her desire to kiss Emma again. "It's a lot of mixed messages, Aubrey. A lot."

The irony was not lost on Aubrey. She'd been plodding along, trying to respect Emma's process—a process she had yet to explain, but Aubrey had a feeling it had a little something to do with Emma not being certain of her sexuality, since those classic signs were present and shining in neon red lighting. She couldn't throw that on Emma, though. Aubrey, patient as the day was long, had been waiting for Emma to just *say* it. But here she was, making Aubrey seem like the one who was directing their haywire back and forth.

"I need a minute." Aubrey stood, knocking her kneecap on the table in her haste. "I'll be right back. I promise."

Moments later, Aubrey collected a handful of icy water and lowered her face into it. She held herself there for as long as she could, then dumped the water and repeated the action. When her body settled back into something close to normal, Aubrey straightened and looked at herself in the mirror.

She was only human. A human with a sex drive, an attraction, a growing connection to someone who needed time to figure out who she was, and what she wanted. But that kiss had been a mistake. Aubrey knew it; she didn't need Emma to spell it out for her.

What Emma didn't realize was that Aubrey had needed that kiss. It didn't even have to be with Emma, though there wasn't anyone else Aubrey wanted to kiss. She needed the touch, the contact, the physical connection. After spending so many days feeling untethered, like a balloon bobbing on an impossibly long string, she needed to come back down to Earth.

And Emma…Just seeing Emma had started her descent. She should have stopped it there.

Aubrey gripped the edge of the sink. She lifted one hand and wiped it across her mouth. Enough. She had to stop this before it got out of control.

Before it ended badly.

After splashing another handful of water on her face, Aubrey dried off and made her way back to the table. Emma watched her approach and didn't say anything as she sat down.

Aubrey waited a few seconds, wanting to give Emma the space to speak. When she didn't, Aubrey interlocked her fingers and set them on her lap.

"It won't happen again," she said, doing her best to keep her tone flat. "You have my word."

Emma stared, hard enough that Aubrey felt the heat of her gaze. "Okay," she said eventually.

Aubrey released her fingers, shaking out both hands from her self-imposed death grip. She pointed at Emma's laptop. "Show me what you've got."

CHAPTER TWENTY-ONE

Just like that, Aubrey dropped the metaphorical keys into Emma's lap. She hadn't included a map, which Emma would have appreciated as she still felt she was careening toward a destination and taking the absolute hardest and longest route to get there. And now, Aubrey had set her in the driver's seat. Not ideal. Under normal circumstances (i.e.: when she knew how to get where she wanted to go), Emma was a focused, appropriately cautious driver.

Currently, she seemed only capable of driving off the road at every turn.

Aubrey was quiet, waiting for Emma to pull up her essay, which she should have done during Aubrey's brief absence, but she had been too consumed with memorizing the feeling of that kiss because she knew—or had convinced herself, she wasn't sure—she wasn't ready to experience that feeling on a daily basis. It was treacherous ground; Emma felt like she was straddling a fault line, waiting for a seismic rumble to shift her one way or the other. Truly, she felt as though she'd lost her grip on connecting her thoughts to her feelings and didn't trust herself to make a decision. She still couldn't grasp the root of her curiosity when it came to Aubrey. Maybe it was the fact that she was *Aubrey Glass*, untouchable golden girl (to be fair, Emma realized that "untouchable" label wasn't true, like, at all). Maybe it was because Aubrey was the first woman who'd shown an interest in her. Maybe it was being home and feeling a renewed connection to things Emma thought she'd lost. Maybe it was simply because Aubrey was so, so damn pretty, and so, so incredibly...Aubrey.

She was just Aubrey.

Emma snuck a glance at the cause of all her chaotic and alluring confusion. Aubrey's eyes were locked on the screen. Okay. So she'd decided to avoid eye contact. Emma couldn't blame her.

She'd noticed, of course, the way Aubrey didn't seem quite like herself. Her absence from work had been weird and uncomfortable for Emma, but now that she was in front of Aubrey, Emma couldn't blame her for having disappeared for a while. It was like Aubrey was on a delay, not quite fully present. Her eyes lacked their usual vibrancy, and she looked like she was in dire need of vitamin D. She looked incomplete.

"It's called Beautiful Fool," Emma said.

"What is?" Aubrey looked confused, and Emma couldn't blame her. "The title of your essay?"

Emma gestured toward her neck. (See? Three seconds behind the wheel and she was flooring the engine straight into the trash-scattered brush beside the highway.) She wouldn't be mad if Aubrey leaned in for another sniff, but she felt the walls Aubrey had erected around herself during her escape to the bathroom and knew she wouldn't come closer than she needed to in order to see Emma's laptop screen. "My perfume."

"Huh." Aubrey looked toward the ceiling, then, finally, at Emma. "Like from *The Great Gatsby*?"

"I know you'll be shocked to hear this, but...I never read it."

"'And I hope she'll be a fool—that's the best thing a girl can be in this world, a beautiful little fool.'" Aubrey grinned, pleased with herself and her party trick. "Notice how I'm deliberately not reacting to the fact that you've never read *Gatsby*, which is honestly criminal."

Emma avoided looking at Aubrey as she clicked around on her laptop. What was really criminal about this moment was that they weren't making out, and it was all Emma's fault.

"I'm pretty sure," Aubrey went on, knocking her knuckles on the table, "*Gatsby* was required reading in Honors English at Franklin Prescott, Emmalynn Gallagher."

The little spinning sensation in Emma's low, low belly briefly exploded into horizon-scraping fireworks. She thought for sure she would explode right there at the table in the library.

Stop, she commanded herself. *Stop stop stop stop. You cannot have this kind of reaction to her saying your full name. Get it* together, *Gallagher.*

"How did you know I took Honors English?" Emma asked, grateful her voice didn't give away anything she was feeling.

"Lucky guess." Aubrey shifted, creating an inch more space between them. Loud and clear, Emma thought. "But not because you have a love for literature."

Emma shot her a look as her essay finally loaded and presented itself on her laptop screen. "Why, then? Because I'm an overachiever?"

Aubrey's smile was lazy, directionless. Emma loathed it, and wanted to kiss it off her beautiful damn face.

"You said it, not me."

There was a fight simmering right there, one Emma could ignite with a careless flick of her tongue. And not in a sexy way— no, in a—

"Maybe perfectionist is better," Aubrey went on, oblivious to Emma's growing irritation. "Or a combination of both." She nodded, seeming to come to a conclusion that pleased her analysis of Emma's character. "Yeah, let's go with both."

"And what exactly qualifies you to make those claims?" Emma heard the ice in her tone and felt no desire to melt it.

Aubrey blinked at her, and Emma, borderline furious, watched as a confident smile slowly spread itself across her mouth.

"I know you met with Callie about your essay," Aubrey said quietly, that fucking smile still pinching the corners of her mouth. "And I have no doubt you took everything she said to heart and worked really hard over the weekend to make improvements. And yet, here we are." She pointed at Emma's laptop. "I'm willing to bet this essay is as perfect as it's going to get."

There was a compliment there, Emma was certain of it, but the overriding implication felt more like a sideways stab. Instead of giving Aubrey the satisfaction of asking what the hell she meant, Emma turned the laptop toward her.

"Could you please read this and give me your honest feedback?"

She felt Aubrey's eyes on her, but Emma, really leaning into not giving Aubrey whatever the hell it was that she wanted, did not look at her. She placed her hands on her thighs and focused on them. The silence spun like a web between them, intricate and fragile, but neither spoke to break the delicate tendrils. Aubrey moved the laptop closer to her and leaned forward. She tucked her hair behind her ears and began reading.

Meanwhile, Emma reached up to pull her own hair over her shoulder and froze. The length she'd used as a shield for so many years was gone. She still wasn't sure what had encouraged her to cut off so much of her hair, other than some young-adult-crisis attempt at creating a new image for herself or whatever. She missed her long hair but also loved the new Emma she saw in the mirror. Yet another internal conflict, and holy shit, she was getting really tired of stocking her internal shelves with them.

Aubrey murmured something, a sweet noise that jolted Emma out of her obsessive hair thoughts. This was wrong, all wrong. She wanted to be pulling Aubrey closer, not encouraging her to move further away. She was so tired of telling herself that she didn't know what she was doing, that this was a fluke. There was something between them—something bold and brilliant—and Emma could see it, could touch the edges of it.

It was powerful. Maybe too powerful, she reasoned. Maybe she wasn't meant to feel that kind of power at this—

"This is really good," Aubrey said softly, almost as though she hadn't meant for Emma to hear.

Emma looked over at her. She was still focused on what she was reading, and her mouth moved slightly as she silently read Emma's hard-earned academic words.

"Really?"

Aubrey nodded. "You shouldn't doubt yourself so much." She glanced at Emma before returning to the laptop. "Your analysis of this poem is interesting."

"Interesting." Emma didn't like the taste of that word in her mouth. "Meaning wrong? But artfully wrong?"

"I'm surprised you chose this poem," Aubrey said, cleanly avoiding Emma's interrogation. "It's not one of her more popular ones."

"I liked it, so I picked it." Emma leaned forward and angled her laptop so she could see the screen. She scrolled to the second page and pointed at a section. "I thought her use of capitalization was interesting." There was that word again. "Or, I don't know, unique."

"That's a Dickinson trademark," Aubrey said, sounding like she discussed Emily Dickinson on the daily. "Capitalization, dashes, interrupted thoughts. It's like she thrives on keeping the reader off balance."

Just like you, Emma thought. "Right, Callie talked about that in class. So I didn't spend a ton of time on that stuff, because it's, you know, common." Emma pointed to another section. "How did I do with the colors?"

"Now that was cool." Aubrey hit a few keys and highlighted a section. "I like that you spent time with her obvious uses of color, but also talked about the line 'Without a color, but the Light / Of unanointed Blaze—'" She smiled. "You gave 'blaze' a color."

"Well, yeah. When you picture the word blaze in your head, you see red. Right?"

"I do. And orange."

"Exactly." Emma gestured toward her laptop. "So when Dickinson gives the image of 'without a color,' then follows that up with 'the light of unanointed blaze'—that's the brightest color in the entire poem."

"The contrast. Colorless, but on fire."

Emma swallowed. She reached to pull her turtleneck from her throat but realized she wasn't wearing one. That thick, constraining, but somehow extremely pleasant feeling was coming from somewhere else.

"And," Aubrey continued, highlighting another section of the essay, "I love this."

Emma leaned in, careful to keep a fraction of space between them. "The sound stuff?"

"The sound stuff." Aubrey grinned. "Yeah. I think we can do a little more with it. If you want."

"I want." Oh, God. Emma sat up straight. "To add more. Make it better. Yes."

Typical Aubrey Glass, smooth and unbothered. She didn't react to Emma's stumbling awkwardness. She simply nodded and clicked on another tab, bringing the poem up.

"You're right there," Aubrey said.

Oh, okay. Shit, right, okay. Emma braced herself, fingers gripping the arms of her chair. Aubrey had turned on her hot-for-teacher voice. Emma hadn't even known she had one of those, but oh God, she did. Gentle, direct, and smudged with an air of authority. It was nearly unbearable.

Unaware of the professorial hotness she possessed in that moment, Aubrey went on, undeterred. "You mention the ring and the soundless tugs. They work together, also kind of against each other. What do you think?"

"I—" Emma stopped, cleared her throat. "The anvil ring is loud, but the soundless tugs are—they're silent."

"Yes. Keep going."

"The contrast," Emma said, fumbling. "Something is really loud while something else is very quiet."

Aubrey simply nodded. Her eyes had regained some of the life they'd been missing when Emma first walked up to the table.

"So whatever is quiet is going to be silenced by the really loud thing." Emma scrunched her nose. "The loud thing is blocking out what really needs to be heard."

"Which is…"

"The soundless tug."

Aubrey nodded again. "And the tugs are…"

"Within," Emma said confidently. She looked to Aubrey for approval.

"Keep going, Emma."

Jesus Christ. Thankfully, she had already spent some time daydreaming about Aubrey being a professor, so Emma was just able to keep her shit together. Had she not…

"Okay," Emma said slowly. Anything to get Aubrey to continue telling her to "keep going," which were now the two hottest words Emma had ever heard spoken. "Um. Outside noise, internal silence." She flicked her gaze to the ceiling. "But a tug isn't silent. Right?"

"In this case it is. But just because it's silent, or soundless, doesn't mean it's not felt."

Do not look at her. Emma kept her eyes on the ceiling. "But if something is silent, it's easier to ignore. You can't ignore big, loud things that are happening externally."

"So that big loud thing on the outside is a…"

"Distraction," Emma finished. "Easier to focus on. Probably less scary, I guess, than the silent internal pull."

"Keep going."

Damn you, Aubrey Glass. "The soundless tug within is the thing that we really want. The thing we're lacking, maybe? But we ignore it because it's quiet, and the rest of the world is loud, and if we ignore something long enough—especially something that's soundless—eventually it will go away, kind of disappear into the greater noise outside. But…" Emma finally looked at Aubrey and was rewarded with an expression filled with intrigue. And maybe a little something else. "The tug toward what we truly want never goes away." She bit the inside of her cheek. "Even if it's toward something scary, or new."

"Or something unknown," Aubrey finished, holding eye contact in a way that felt like Emma was sinking into the most delicious fire.

Emma had an entire internal list of things she would like to do while basking in that look. But the moment she gathered the courage to act on the simplest—move closer—Aubrey sat back in her chair, swiping away the closeness that had grown between them.

Point taken. Emma gave herself a mental shift, not really wanting to apply this damn poem to herself even though she'd tripped right into that trap.

"Wait, wait. Is Emily Dickinson fighting something? Like, resisting the urge to go after something she wants? Is she letting the outside noise silence her internal tugs?"

Aubrey had a look of pure pride on her face. "I don't know, Emma. Does that sound right to you?"

Emma leaned in, suddenly gleeful. "Is Emily Dickinson a closeted lesbian?" *Yeah, Emma, way to make it not about you at all.*

"There are rumors," Aubrey said, grinning. "Callie hasn't talked about that?"

It was possible she had, during a time when Emma had spaced out. "She may have. She says a lot, honestly."

Aubrey laughed. "I'm pretty sure this poem is about a blacksmith, not Emily's potential lesbianism."

"Okay," Emma replied. "The blacksmith thing is obvious. But is it—are my thoughts and explanations wrong?"

"I'm not Emily Dickinson, nor am I a blacksmith," Aubrey said. It seemed like she wanted to laugh again but was holding herself back, which Emma, despite still being caught up in a literal tornado of mismatched feelings, appreciated. "So I can't say if it's right or wrong. And I'm sure Callie told you the same thing."

In spite of herself, Emma laughed. "No. Actually, I said that. To Callie," she clarified. "I was defending myself in case she told me my essay was horrible. And wrong."

Aubrey grinned. "I bet she loved that." She shook her head and gazed off into the distance of the library. "She makes me wish I had stayed here for college."

Emma's tireless little math brain was dying to calculate the timing of Aubrey's college years and Callie's beginning of employment, but she put aside her need for math facts and tried to take advantage of the opening Aubrey had slid over to her.

Even though she was still agitated. Because she was.

"Would you have still majored in philosophy if you'd gone to Pennbrook?"

"Loaded question," Aubrey said. She didn't look at Emma as she continued, "I don't think so. But maybe. I think…Yeah, I think I would have started off as a philosophy major, but if I'd started working at Cornerstone and met Sadie, then met Callie…" Aubrey nodded. "I would have changed majors."

"Just because of Callie?" Emma couldn't argue that base logic— she was witnessing firsthand the impressions and impacts Callie Lewes made in the classroom, enough to make a literature-hater want to analyze Emily Dickinson's poems—but she had a feeling there was something Aubrey wasn't telling her.

"No. Don't get me wrong, she's amazing, and I've never even had her as a professor. It's more…" Aubrey sighed. "I didn't think I could major in English. Or literature."

"But you're so good at it. You just—you get it, Aubrey. You make it seem so easy."

Aubrey did look at Emma then, and her smile was cracked around the edges. Emma's heart swooped with the desire to Band-Aid those broken spots.

"We've already gone over this, Emma. Remember?"

She did, but she still had questions.

"Would I have followed my heart if I'd stayed here? Majored in English and soaked up all the literature I could?" Aubrey went on, still looking at Emma. "Yeah. I probably would have. But I don't see how I would have ended up anywhere differently than where I am right now."

"Working at Cornerstone." Emma meant for it to come out as a question, but in her haste to get words out, she missed the question mark.

Aubrey's expression shifted, several layers of emotions slipping over her features. "Do you have a problem with my job?"

There was no way for Emma to backpedal as fast as she wanted to after hearing Aubrey's tone, which was devoid of emotion.

"No—obviously no, I—" But the words tumbled out of her mind, somersaulting and cartwheeling with the integrity of a renowned gymnast. She'd never been that flexible, with her body or her language.

"Work there too," Aubrey finished. "Right. But here you are, finishing your degree. Meanwhile, my degree sits somewhere in an apartment I'm renting from my boss while I go to work and move books around a store for eight hours." There was emotion back in her voice, but it wasn't one Emma loved hearing. "Cornerstone is a stepping stone for you. But it might not be for me."

"It doesn't have to be that way." Emma winced. That wasn't the sentence she'd planned on starting with. "It's a great job, Aubrey. And you're good at what you do. You're passionate about books, so it fits—"

"But it doesn't have to be that way?" A question, yes, but one dripping with sarcasm. "Please, by all means, tell me what else I can do with a degree in philosophy."

"I don't know," Emma blurted. "I think—"

"I don't want to have this conversation with you." Aubrey stood. "I've had it enough times with my mother. I don't have the answers everyone wants me to have, Emma. Do you get that?"

She merely nodded, unnerved and upset by this version of Aubrey.

"And you," Aubrey said, then paused. "I can't believe you're judging me. Of all people."

"Wait." Emma stood too. "I'm not judging you. I'm, I don't know, trying to help you?" It was the wrong thing to say, she knew so immediately, and yet there it was, splattered violently across Aubrey's stricken face.

"I don't need *help*. Especially from you. It's not like you're the beacon of good choices when it comes to college and career."

Perhaps Emma should have expected that knife to be thrown, but it hit her before she could dodge it.

"I've tried," Emma said, equal measures angry and sad. "I've kept trying. You know that." She gestured around them. "You *know* I'm trying."

"But you're not really. You want to be a baker, right? So you, what, went to culinary school? And gave up. Twice. And now you're here."

"I did not," Emma said, sucking in a breath, "*give up*."

Aubrey looked at her, leveling her with an empty stare. She had reverted back to the version of herself Emma had first seen when she arrived at the library. But worse now, somehow, in a way Emma couldn't articulate. The change roused a wave of empathy within her, but it was dappled with shock and anger.

"Well maybe I did."

Before she could respond, Aubrey was gone. The air around Emma chilled in her absence. She pressed her hand to her chest, the ache acute and fierce. She felt as though she'd experienced every emotion available to her in the last two hours. Emma was exhausted and wanted nothing more than to disappear just as Aubrey had.

And yet, in the depth of her subconscious, white heat was ablaze, encircling the soundless tug that pulled relentlessly, silently, within.

As the outside noise of the library—dim but present—rose around her, Emma knew with certainty that the hushed flame within her would not stand much longer for being ignored.

CHAPTER TWENTY-TWO

Aubrey had become comfortable with the numbness that had plagued her during her brief hibernation. It was more pleasant than the usual desolation that accompanied her backslides into memories she wished she could eternal sunshine away. Nevertheless, they persisted. By the time she'd left for the library on Tuesday, she was ready to feel something. She'd assumed that seeing Emma would push her out of the numbness and into something actually pleasant. What that pleasant feeling was, she couldn't say, since Aubrey never quite knew what to expect from the time she spent with Emma.

She was ready for the good, if confusing, feelings. What she hadn't expected or been prepared for was to be slingshot into feelings she rarely dabbled in. Anger, hurt, the heaviness of being misunderstood. Those were things Aubrey didn't associate with Emma—because she didn't want to, and because she didn't recall handing Emma the ability to get so far under her skin that she could cause those feelings to bubble up.

"And you were wrong," Aubrey said to the empty room. She scuffed her shoe—an old Doc Martens boot since it was snowing again—against the concrete floor of Cornerstone's stock room. On the plus side, the kickstart to feeling again had kept her moving. She'd made it to work on Wednesday and was entering the final hour of Thursday's shift. In an effort to pick up some lost hours, she'd persuaded Sadie to let her work fourteen hours on Wednesday. Sadie had flat-out refused a repeat performance on Thursday, and now that four o'clock was rearing its head, Aubrey was beginning to wonder what she could possibly do for so many hours before she could go to bed.

Emma, anything involving Emma, was out of the question. As Aubrey nudged the door open, she scanned the immediate area, worrying about seeing a familiar head of red hair. When she assured herself that the coast was clear (she knew Emma's shift had ended an hour earlier but she hadn't actually seen her leave the building), Aubrey made her way to the children's section with an armful of books.

They hadn't spoken or even looked at each other since Aubrey had left Pennbrook's library two days earlier. Fortunately, avoiding Emma at work wasn't too difficult, considering she was tethered to the café. And if Emma left her area, Aubrey had the advantage of being able to dodge around shelves and stacks. It was childish, absolutely, but until she felt more regulated and found the right words to circle back to the conversation she'd run from, she preferred pretending Emma didn't exist.

Aubrey hated this whole charade of avoidance—not just of the *right now*, but of the entirety of the blooming connection between them. The pretense felt wrong and unfair. But every time she acted on her gut feelings, she felt like she was missing a sign that Emma desperately wanted her to see. She knew now, quite clearly, that Emma was, despite her protests, good with words. So for her to be silently waving a sign with paragraphs written in a language Aubrey wasn't fluent in…Something wasn't adding up.

Aubrey slipped her phone from her pocket and, after scanning the area for Cornerstone's other notorious head of red hair, pressed play. She had one AirPod in and kept her hair hanging over it. The music she needed today, a playlist titled Tourist of the Heart, was not something she could subject the entire store to. She kept it in her own little world as she moved between the sections of the store, feeling the ache of the songs and assuring herself that she wouldn't always feel this way.

Work was good, too, for distracting purposes. Aside from the Emma bullshit (harsh, maybe, but Aubrey was still edgy about their last interaction and felt bullshit was an appropriate descriptor), Aubrey wasn't fully out of the woods from her depressive spell. She was tired of the thoughts and feelings looping on endless repeat. She couldn't go back and change her past, she was well aware of that, but the desire to do so was strong and knifed through her with eerie precision.

It was so painful and tiresomely so that Aubrey was *thisclose* to returning Jamie's call—the very call that wasn't a real call at all. She'd brought herself to the brink of being convinced that Jamie Morrison held the key to her ability to finally move on. Not just in terms of her heart, or her body—Aubrey had already done that, more than once, to varying degrees of success—but in every aspect of her life. In all the places she felt stuck, at least, like her limbs and her brain were encased in Jell-O.

Aubrey shoved a book about the unlikely friendship between a duck and a crocodile onto the shelf. The words she'd spoken to Emma not long ago reverberated through her mind: the need to return to the very things that have broken you, because they're part of what puts you back together.

Was it a need, though? Or just a desire? A point to prove, a reasoning to barter? It was likely none of those, but rather a heart-shaped Band-Aid with cactus spines in place of the absorbent pad.

Aubrey huffed as Rachel Yamagata's voice eased into her ear. Perfect timing, though the opening words of "Elephants" made her reach for her phone and hit skip because she did not want to dissolve into an emotional mess right there in the children's section. She might as well slap that spiky bandage right over her heart. Or maybe her mouth. Yeah, then if she *did* make the mistake of calling the number she'd once had memorized forward and backward, then she wouldn't—

"There you are." Penelope's voice cut through the rainstorm in Aubrey's brain. "Since when do you hide out in the kid's section?"

Aubrey pulled out her phone again, this time cutting the music completely. "When I have work to do here."

"Mmhmm." Pen studied her and Aubrey knew she wouldn't be able to lie if Pen dared ask how she was. Luckily, Pen took a different tack. "You went MIA, Aubrey. I was worried."

The irony of Penelope, the ex-wife of Aubrey's mother's current husband, showing up at Aubrey's place of work to track her down (because she knew without Pen saying so that that's exactly what this was) because Aubrey hadn't responded to her texts her in over a week was not lost on her.

Aubrey hadn't exchanged a single word with her actual mother in over a month, and that woman wasn't trying to find her or talk to her. But here was Pen, looking genuinely concerned, and also annoyed.

"I actually called the store to make sure you were here," Pen continued, crossing her arms over her chest in a huff, "because you weren't when I came in on Friday with the kids, nor were you here when I came in on Monday by myself. Honestly, Aubrey. You can't disappear like that."

"Well, I can," Aubrey countered. "But I shouldn't."

Pen rolled her eyes. "What's going on?"

Aubrey appreciated the direct cut to the chase, but she didn't know where to begin, so she shrugged. "Just a run of bad days."

They'd been down this path a few times before, so Aubrey didn't need to elaborate. Pen simply nodded, then uncrossed her arms and grabbed onto one of Aubrey's.

"You're coming with me."

"I'm—what? Pen, I'm working."

She gave a mighty tug and Aubrey, off balance because of her damn emotions, stumbled into motion. "Yeah, Sadie said you can leave. In fact, she said you need to leave because you worked too much yesterday and were probably going to try to do the same today."

As they approached the Hub, where Sadie was standing, Aubrey narrowed her eyes. "I don't like you two plotting together."

Sadie grinned, and it was just on the edge of maniacal. "Go get your jacket, Aubs. It's time for you to leave."

Even if she'd had the energy, Aubrey knew there was no point in fighting. She looked between Penelope and Sadie then sighed. "Fine. I'll be right back."

She wasn't gone long, but when she returned, she found Sadie and Penelope chatting like the oldest of friends. Aubrey appreciated them getting along—she'd long suspected they would—but did not love the idea of them becoming such friends that they'd frequently gang up on her.

"Okay, fine, you win. Let's go. Now."

Pen raised her eyebrows. "My, what a change in attitude."

"Oh, don't mind her," Sadie said, coming around the Hub to put her arm around Aubrey's shoulders. "She doesn't want us to start exchanging our deep, dark Aubrey secrets."

Aubrey shrugged out from under Sadie's grasp, which only made Sadie laugh.

"There are no secrets," Aubrey said, gesturing to Pen that she needed to start walking.

"Don't worry, Sadie," Pen called over her shoulder. "I'll get all the dirt for you!"

"Thanks, Pen! Text me later!"

"Oh my God," Aubrey grumbled as she and Penelope walked outside. "That's not happening. You two cannot be friends."

"That's not for you to decide, babe." Pen steered Aubrey toward her Navigator. "Hop in."

"This feels like kidnapping."

Pen started the car and adjusted the vents so they weren't all pointing toward her. "Well, when you pull the shit you've been pulling lately, one has to take drastic measures." Satisfied that Aubrey would get some of the heat, Pen turned to face her. "Look, Aubrey. You don't need to explain anything to me, but I need you to not ever drop off the face of the Earth like that again. You're not on your own in this life, even when you pretend you are. I care about you. Sadie cares about you."

"Sadie knew I was alive," Aubrey muttered.

"Yeah, I know." Pen feigned a look of innocence when Aubrey glared at her. "We've been texting since I came into the store on Friday. She wanted me to know that you were okay."

There. A pierce of emotion, one Aubrey hadn't felt in far too long. She closed her eyes against the threat of tears.

"Aubrey, what's going on?" Pen's voice was gentle and layered over Aubrey like a worn-in blanket.

"Everything," she said, not even trying to clear the emotion from her throat. "It's everything." Now she cleared her throat. "I can handle it. I can. I always do. I just let it get the best of me for a while. Past tense."

"I can tell you don't want to talk about it. And I'll respect that. But if you change your mind, Aub, call me. Okay?"

Aubrey nodded, brushing the back of her hand against her cheek. One bold tear had made its way out of her eye. Proof of emotion gone, she touched the door handle. "Did you lock me in?"

"Sure did!" Penelope grinned as she shifted the SUV into drive.

"And you're taking me home. Right?"

She cackled. "Girl, no. We're going to hot yoga!"

The next day, Aubrey was sore in places she didn't know could be sore. She still considered herself an athlete, but attending that hot yoga class with Penelope—someone who did shit like yoga and Pilates multiple times a week—had been humbling. Turns out that strong didn't necessarily equate to flexible, a lesson Aubrey had learned repeatedly during the hour-long sweatbox of a class.

On the plus side, the combination of yoga and time with Penelope had helped clear some of the dust from her mind. Aubrey no longer felt the pressing urge to call Jamie. It was a lingering idea, but it had been pushed to the recesses of her thinking instead of banging around in the front of her brain. In her chat with Penelope over Indian food, Aubrey hadn't even mentioned Jamie's name. She had, however, touched on the topic of Emma but obliquely. It didn't matter. She knew Pen saw right through her.

But to her credit, Pen didn't push her to do anything about Emma. And so, Aubrey decided yet again to stay in her own lane while Emma stayed in hers.

Until one of them crossed the dotted yellow line.

Again.

The driving gods must have been on Aubrey's side, because she made it through work without having an Emma run-in. She wasn't even sure that Emma had been at work. It was possible she had the day off and was working a weekend shift, or maybe she'd called in sick. It was also possible she *was* there and they'd both become experts at avoidance.

Whatever the case, Aubrey left work feeling tense. The magic of yoga had evaporated sometime during the day. She wanted to text Emma—no, she wanted to see Emma—but she held herself back. There was an apology that needed to be made and Aubrey didn't have it fine-tuned quite yet. She was tired of fumbling and stumbling; the next time she and Emma spoke, she was determined to set them squarely in a place of clarity, regardless of the repercussions.

Once home, Aubrey wasted no time in packing her bowl and lighting it up. She'd abstained all week and craved the release. After a few hits, she made her way to the bathroom. There, she turned the shower on as hot as she could stand, stripped, and stepped under the stream.

The combination of the weed and the steamy shower did the trick. By the time the water began to cool, she was ready to dry off and wrap her naked body in as many blankets as she could find. She did just that, falling asleep within moments.

When she woke a few hours later, she had two primary cravings: food and distraction. She handled the first one with ease, pulling out leftovers from last night's dinner with Pen. The second was more challenging. Aubrey's options were limited, a situation of her own creation. She could text Sadie, who was probably one floor below and would happily hang out. But Sadie would make Aubrey talk. On a whim, she sent Genesis a text.

And that was how, not two hours later, Aubrey found herself walking into Lotus.

For as much as Genesis said she loved to stay home and do Internet deep dives, she also loved to be out at the club, watching everyone around her get into fun trouble. She was Aubrey's go-to for going out, and the two had spent many a night at Lotus over the past two years. They'd seen bartenders come and go, petty fights die out before they could escalate, and far too many break up/make up/break up sessions acted out. They had a silent agreement to keep the drama limited to what they could watch, and never let themselves be the ones being watched. So far, they'd held up that agreement.

"Glass!" Genesis held up her hand for a high-five, which Aubrey slapped enthusiastically. "To what do we owe the pleasure of your company this evening?"

Aubrey nodded hellos to the handful of friends surrounding Genesis. She didn't know any of them by name, mostly because Genesis's friends were on a rotation and very few stuck around for more than a month at a time.

"I just needed to go out," Aubrey said.

"You've come to the right place. Drink?"

Aubrey thought for a moment, then shook her head. She'd smoked again before she left the house. She wasn't super high, just enough to feel loose and able to enjoy herself. A drink didn't sound terrible, but she wasn't ready for it yet.

"You feeling better?"

Aubrey shrugged. She and Genesis didn't have what she would consider a close friendship. She hadn't said a word to her about her recent struggles, but of course Genesis knew Aubrey hadn't been at work. Aubrey sometimes confided in her, but she always had the feeling that Genesis never truly listened when she was talking.

"It's Jamie shit," Aubrey said, feeling lighter having said that much, even if Genesis didn't remember who Jamie was. "I don't know, sometimes the old stuff comes back up."

Genesis nodded, sipping her drink. "Like what?"

Okay, so she was listening. Aubrey tilted her head, wondering if she was high enough to talk. "It's like, after her, everything just stopped. I stopped. Everything." Genesis was looking out toward the dance floor, which gave Aubrey the courage to go on. "I stopped playing field hockey because of her. Who knows what would have happened if I'd played my senior year? I could—I could be playing professionally. I could be anywhere but here."

Genesis shouted at one of her friends, then burst into laughter. A moment later, she said, "Yeah, you could."

"And she thought everything I did was pointless. She hated my major, which, okay, maybe she wasn't totally wrong about that. But she knew..." Aubrey trailed off, nervous about the territory ahead. "She knew I wanted to write. Or, she knew I was writing. And she thought that was stupid, too. I gave it all up to be with her. Everything I loved, everything that made me happy. I tossed it away. For her. And she fucking destroyed me."

The music pounded around them, absorbing most of Aubrey's words. She kept talking, though, rattling off all the ways Jamie Morrison had ruined her life. It was a long list, considering the unavoidable truths of how young eighteen-year-old Aubrey was swept up by the bright charisma and irresistible attention and attraction of her twenty-seven-year-old field hockey coach. How she'd sold weed to get in Jamie's good graces, how Jamie had repeatedly kissed her while she was high, claiming it didn't count that way, until Aubrey showed up at her apartment and demanded to kiss sober. How they'd hooked up that night and hadn't stopped until over three years later when another player reported Jamie for supplying the team with weed, effectively ending her coaching career and their semblance of a relationship.

How Aubrey had loved Jamie more than she'd loved herself, and had convinced herself over and over again that Jamie loved her too, even though she never said the words.

Aubrey pressed her hands against her forehead. She needed more. Whether it was weed or a drink, she needed something. After a week in the trenches of her darkest feelings, she was craving anything that would help her feel something different. A drink was probably a bad idea, especially considering she didn't even *like* alcohol, but she didn't have any weed with her.

On second thought…Aubrey's eyes latched on to a woman walking toward the bar with determination. She sidled up a few seats down from where Aubrey stood and leaned her elbows on the bar while she waited for the bartender.

She was tall and dark-haired, wearing ripped jeans and a loose, long-sleeved T-shirt. There was nothing remarkable about her; she was just another woman at the gay bar. But Aubrey, needing to feel something that wasn't real but still felt like *something*, couldn't take her eyes off her.

With a nod at Genesis, Aubrey slipped away and walked down the bar until she was a seat away from the woman. She didn't have to take a step further before the woman turned and looked at her, smiling slowly as she appraised Aubrey.

"Is the service always slow here?"

Aubrey smiled and mirrored the woman's posture. "Unless you have a dick, yeah. It can be pretty slow."

"Ahh, I see." The woman looked around. "There's an upstairs, right?"

Aubrey nodded, clocking that. Either she was new in town or she was on the straighter side of the spectrum. Fine either way for tonight.

"Should we try our luck up there?"

"Might as well," Aubrey said. "Follow me."

For reasons she wasn't willing to explore, Aubrey couldn't bring herself to look at Genesis as she and the dark-haired woman walked past. Once they were safely upstairs in the quieter, more laid-back part of the bar, Aubrey breathed a sigh of relief.

"Female bartender." Aubrey's new friend nodded approvingly.

Up here, with the better lighting, Aubrey realized the woman was quite a bit older, probably in her early thirties. "Surely we'll get faster service."

"Only one way to find out." Aubrey led her to the bar.

Less than three minutes later, both women had a drink and were making their way to the front area. The bar upstairs was always less crowded, and most of the patrons were at the pool tables toward the back. Up front, where Aubrey and the woman settled, were a few couches and chairs, creating a cozier space.

It was also, by default, a more intimate space. The moment Aubrey sat down, she realized this was the last place she wanted to be.

"I'm Heather, by the way," the woman said.

"Aubrey," she replied. "Nice to meet you."

"You as well. Come here often?" Heather laughed, a lyrical sound that didn't match her slightly raspy voice. "Sorry, I don't normally use lame pickup lines."

"Kind of unavoidable, don't you think?" Aubrey, despite desperately wanting to be back downstairs in the chaos of the music and dancing bodies, felt her old self peek around the corner.

"Yeah, it is. Should I ask what you do for a living?"

"Do you really want to know?"

Heather looked at Aubrey intently. There was no mistaking that look, even through her lingering high and the half-drunk drink— something with vodka, she was pretty sure—in her hand. "No."

"Good." Aubrey threw back the rest of her drink. Her entire body winced as the liquid plunged down her throat. "Let's go."

"Whoa," Heather said, but she stood anyway. "Already?"

"I meant downstairs," Aubrey said, and she smiled, knowing she could—if she wanted to.

Heather ran her hand through her hair, then swallowed the last of her drink. "How about a shot first?"

It was a terrible idea, so of course Aubrey agreed. One shot led to two, led to three. Before Heather could suggest a fourth, Aubrey grabbed her hand and led the way back downstairs, right into the sea of moving bodies.

The mixture of substances gave her exactly the release she'd been chasing. She was mildly aware of her body, less so of others'. The music pounded through her bloodstream and she kept her hands locked on Heather's waist as they moved together. It wasn't long before Aubrey leaned in, knowing Heather's mouth was ready and waiting for hers.

The kiss was hard and on the rougher side of passionate. Aubrey felt no desire other than needing to feel a physical connection. Heather could have been any woman in that bar (except for Genesis, of course). Her mouth was solid and Aubrey clung to it with her lips, wanting the buoy in the midst of her raging ocean. She allowed Heather to back them up to the edge of the dance floor, leveraging Aubrey's intoxication to her advantage as she pressed them against the wall.

Aubrey gripped Heather as they continued kissing. She wanted nothing from this woman and knew she could have whatever she wanted. It was that exact power that had enabled her to move on from Jamie, the knowledge of other women wanting her. And she had moved on, if by body only for a long period of time, through woman after woman until she began to feel used.

The moment Heather's fingers crept beneath the hem of Aubrey's shirt, Aubrey snapped back into her body. She stopped their kiss without slowing it, and gently pushed Heather away from her.

"Okay," Heather said immediately, holding up her hands. "I get it."

"No you don't," Aubrey mumbled. "You can't."

"Try me."

Something terrible was building in Aubrey's throat, and that taunt, too similar to things Jamie had said to her over the years, tricked her body into doing something her brain wanted nothing to do with. Aubrey reached out and grabbed Heather by the hips once again, spinning them so Heather was the one pushed up against the wall. Before her mind could catch up with her body, Aubrey reignited their kiss, fueling it with every pent-up feeling she could find. Heather softened beneath her, a sure sign that Aubrey could snap her fingers and find them in her bed. She considered that through the murk in her brain, testing her desires by gliding the back of her hand over Heather's breast. The instant arch into Aubrey's touch verified her suspicions.

And she might have done it, taken Heather home, if Heather hadn't responded by once again touching Aubrey. This time, Aubrey had to step back and when she did, she collided with someone who pushed her right back into Heather.

"No," Aubrey said, steadying herself. The shots had caught up with her. She was pretty certain she was underwater.

"One more time," Heather said, trying to kiss Aubrey. "I promise I'll keep my hands to myself."

"No," Aubrey repeated. God, she wanted to go home.

"I bet you're amazing in bed." Heather's teeth grazed Aubrey's jaw. "God, I want you to fuck me so bad."

Aubrey groaned. She pressed her hand against Heather's stomach, testing her ability to feel. Just as her thumb touched the button of Heather's jeans, Aubrey lost the connection. She was jerked backward by a firm hand and would have fallen had her captor not been both strong and ready for her unsteadiness.

"She's not going to call you." The voice was gruff and forceful and very female.

Aubrey dropped her shoulders. Genesis.

Moments later, Aubrey took huge gulps of the fresh winter air. She leaned forward, her elbows on her knees, and swayed through waves of nausea.

"What the fuck, Glass? What the fuck did you think you were doing?"

"I don't know," she mumbled.

"I'll tell you what you were doing. You were seconds away from fucking some woman you don't even know, Glass. In the middle of the fucking club!" Genesis was yelling and, oh, it hurt.

"I'm sorry."

"Are you? Really? You're going to be fucking sorry in a couple seconds."

On cue, Aubrey threw up. She rode it out, each spasm removing more of the poison from her body. Once she was sure she didn't have anything else to expel, Aubrey slowly stood up. She couldn't bring herself to look at Genesis.

"I'm sorry," she said again.

"Are you done now? Are you done with your fucking bullshit now?"

Aubrey's eyes swam with tears, both from the vomiting and the horrible tidal wave of feelings crashing through her.

Genesis grabbed her by the shoulders, forcing her to make eye contact. "Stop letting that piece of shit ruin your life. She's gone.

And you don't need her. You don't need any of that anymore. You're better than this, Glass. Stop fucking around like you don't know that. You've got other, way more important, shit to figure out."

She made herself nod, not bothering to hide the tears that were landsliding from her eyes. "I just want to go home," Aubrey whispered.

"I'll take you home. But first you gotta tell me you're done."

Aubrey took as deep a breath as she could muster and let it out on a shaky exhale. "I'm done, Genesis. I'm done."

"You better be. I mean it, Glass. I will kick your ass if you keep up with this bullshit."

"I promise. I'm done."

Genesis looked like she wanted to keep going, but she took pity on Aubrey and released her. They began walking, Genesis leading the way. They made it four steps before Genesis relaunched her lecture, but Aubrey didn't care. She was going home.

CHAPTER TWENTY-THREE

"Try this one." Collins slid a full miniature glass of beer over to Emma, who inspected it without picking it up. The color was... interesting. Orange, which Emma was quickly learning was an acceptable color for beer. But the liquid looked almost milky. She was not a beer connoisseur by any stretch of the imagination, but she was pretty sure most beers didn't look so...thick.

"What is it?" she asked, glancing up at Collins.

"It's..." Collins looked down at the handwritten note on the table. "Hades's Haze." She giggled. "Wait, it has a subtitle. 'Taste the Underworld.' Catchy and a little creepy. I like it."

"Okay, I have a name and a subtitle, but you haven't told me what it *is*."

Collins rolled her perfectly mascara'd and lined eyes. With the makeup, she looked more like thirty than twenty-one, and Emma was again dizzied by the contrast between their appearances. Being around Collins made her feel like she had something to catch up to, but she couldn't figure out what it was.

"It's a hazy IPA. Just try it." Collins gestured toward the glass. "My brother said this place never goes wrong with their beers."

Emma took a tentative sip, swirling the liquid in her mouth. She raised her eyebrows and nodded. "Not bad. But it's kinda thick?"

Collins reached out for the beer, and Emma handed it to her. She waited for Collins to determine their next beer from the flight she'd ordered with startling authority, despite claiming she'd never before been to Harpy, the local craft beer bar dedicated to Greek mythology.

It was that kind of delineation between the two that continued to surprise Emma. Since she and Collins had reconnected, Emma had grown more comfortable with the reality that Collins hadn't changed at her core. Inside, she was the same teenager Emma had spent her high school years with. Externally, however, she was a whole ass adult—or at least looked like she was. Collins had always been more confident and self-assured than Emma, and now that gap between them felt like it stretched the length of the entire town.

Tonight, Emma had one goal for their bar outing: figure out how the hell Collins had so fully and unproblematically embraced her bisexuality.

"I love it here!" Collins exclaimed. "Isn't it such a cool little spot?"

Emma nodded, looking around. It was the epitome of cool, in a way that appealed to all legally drinking age groups. It was spacious but had cozy spots for more intimate conversations or gatherings. Volume was appropriately controlled with low music and whatever builders did to control the acoustics, and the lighting was at the level where everything was visible but nothing was blinding. Emma could see there was an outdoor area which was probably packed during the warmer months.

"Okay, spill it, Emmalynn."

She looked back at Collins, who was now leaning forward on the high-top table between them. "Spill what?"

"Whatever's on your mind. I can tell something's bothering you."

For a moment, Emma simply stared at her, wondering how to begin to explain the feeling of repeatedly fumbling the understanding of your identity to someone who had never faltered in her sense of self.

Before she could begin, Collins nodded knowingly. "It's school, isn't it? I told you, Emmalynn, Pennbrook should have stayed off-limits!"

"I actually really like Pennbrook," Emma said, reaching for the glass of Hades's Haze since Collins hadn't given her something new to try. "It's not what we imagined it to be. Not at all like thirteenth grade," she added with a crooked grin.

"Well, color me shocked." Collins winked dramatically before pulling her long hair over her shoulder and twirling her fingers through it. "By the way, I'm loving your haircut."

Emma, still a bit self-conscious about the drastic change, reached to touch the ends of her hair. "Yeah? I keep feeling like I shouldn't have cut it."

"No, no, not at all. You look all mature and shit. I love it."

Pleased, Emma smiled. The vision of Aubrey in the library, abruptly standing up when Emma approached her, glimmered in her mind. So too did the way Aubrey looked, eyes slightly hooded and expression intense, when she told Emma "You look very, very hot with your new haircut."

"You met someone." Collins's voice was firm, without question. Again, that confidence. Emma would kill for an ounce of it.

"I—what?" Emma shook her head, sending Aubrey careening into the sidelines. "What are you talking about?"

Collins lifted a finger and drew an invisible circle around Emma's face. "It's written all over you, babe. You've got the classic signs of infatuation."

Needing a way to stall the inevitable moment where she would have to come clean, she fixed her face in what she hoped was an annoyed expression. "And what, exactly, are those signs, Collins?"

"Casually disappearing in the middle of a conversation," she said easily, dark eyes glittering. "Slightly glassy eyes. A soft blush high on your cheeks, which is different from your usual full-face forest fire."

"Thanks for that," Emma grumbled before draining the small glass of Hades's Haze.

"And with your complexion, it makes you look like a heartsick little Victorian child who's coming down with the bubonic plague."

Emma rolled her eyes. "I think you mean scarlet fever."

Collins waved her hand in the air. "Whatever. The point is, Emmalynn, you've got the look."

Truly, Emma wasn't sure how she could have *the look*, since she hadn't spoken to Aubrey since their last meeting in the library, and that was almost four days ago. Emma scoffed, realizing the tiny amount of time that had passed, but the stronger point to her silent argument was that in all the days at work since then, she hadn't even glimpsed Aubrey.

She'd known she was there because of the music. That was all Aubrey, no doubt in Emma's mind. But Aubrey had slithered through the shelves and stacks in a way that had rendered her invisible for three whole days.

Which was fine. Perfectly fine! They were just friends, friends who didn't talk every day. Friends who wanted to kiss the air out of each other's lungs, but friends who could go three, seven, eighteen, however many days without so much as looking each other in the eye.

Emma shifted in her seat. Only since Aubrey Glass had come into her life had Emma realized how much she held inside. And it wasn't even just the "Surprise! You're attracted to women!" piece that Emma was still trying to neatly place in the right mental puzzle. It was *everything*.

Take Collins, for example. She had no issue with opening her mouth and letting anything come out. She had even less issue, it seemed, with acting on whatever her mind and heart told her she wanted.

Meanwhile, Emma couldn't recall a single deep conversation with Collins, or any of her other friends, throughout high school. She had never confided in anyone, never let her real thoughts out into the open. She kept it all locked tightly inside, figuring it would work itself out and she would get clear signs about how to proceed. And if it wasn't something she could figure out on her own, she compartmentalized it to death. (Sadly, she was finding out the hard way that she couldn't actually kill her own thoughts after all.)

Judging from the amount of dead ends she'd faced over the past three years, that method perhaps was not the best way to map out her life.

Emma bit the inside of her lip. Collins had gotten distracted by a guy who looked to be in his midthirties. She watched them interact, trying to figure out what was real flirting and what was simply playful conversation. Emma knew Collins was often all play, but other people didn't always understand that.

Sure enough, a few moments later, Collins spun around in her chair and eyed Emma. "Remember that jacket you wore the night you went out to that club with your work friends?"

Impossible to forget, but Collins didn't know that. At the memory of that night, Emma's cheeks set themselves aflame.

"Mmhmm," she said, reaching for the one glass of beer Collins hadn't finished.

"Can I borrow it?"

Emma shrugged. "Sure."

"Good. Let's go."

"Now?"

Collins gestured to the glass in Emma's hand. "Drink up. Let's go."

Hearing the weight behind the word, Emma threw back the last three sips of the beer—not as good as Hades's Haze, which Emma discovered she really liked even if its consistency was a far cry from the shitty water-beer she'd drank at parties in Philadelphia—and slid off her stool. Collins was a step behind her as they hurried out of the bar.

"Did you hear what he said to me?" Collins hissed as she linked her arm through Emma's and steered them toward Emma's car.

"That guy? No. What happened?"

Collins shivered, the frame of her body vibrating against Emma's. "He said, 'Your tits would look even more incredible with my dick between them.'"

Emma stopped short and Collins tripped, yanking Emma with her. "You're not serious."

"Oh, Emmalynn, I most certainly am." Collins shook her head and in the glow of the streetlight, Emma could see some of her usual vibrancy had faded. "If I could stop being bi and only be attracted to women, I would in a heartbeat."

Emma took that in, holding it close as they got into the car and, once they both made sure the locks were definitely engaged, waited for the heat to warm their chill. Collins had sunk into the passenger seat and pressed her hand over her eyes. Emma didn't want to disturb her, but she knew an opening when she heard one.

"So you can't?"

"Can't what?"

Emma gripped the steering wheel. "Just choose not to be attracted to guys anymore?"

"No. I mean, I don't think so." Collins dropped her hand and rolled her head on the headrest so she was looking at Emma. "Do you feel like you can choose who you're attracted to?"

Oh. Oh no. That wasn't the plan. Collins was supposed to provide all the answers Emma was seeking, *not* turn it right back to her.

Panicked, Emma shrugged. She drummed a chaotic beat on the steering wheel. The desire to turn on the radio as loud as possible was strong but she managed to fight it off. Instead, she began humming. Loudly.

"Hey," Collins said, pushing two fingers into Emma's upper arm. "You're giving me all the warning signs now. This is some forbidden love shit, isn't it?"

Emma stopped humming but kept up the drumming. She tilted her head in thought. "No. It's not forbidden."

"Thank God." Collins sighed heavily. "I was about to ask you if you're having an affair with one of your professors."

"No, absolutely not."

"Not that I wouldn't love to hear all the juicy details of that kind of entanglement." Collins wiggled her eyebrows. "But it usually ends in disaster. Okay, Emmalynn. Spill it. Who is she?"

The drumming ceased after one last off-tempo beat. Emma froze, unable to even blink.

"Oops," Collins said on a nervous laugh. "I meant they. Who are they?"

Slowly, Emma turned to look at Collins. She surprised herself by being able to maintain eye contact.

"Why," Emma began, her words paced with purpose, "did you say 'she'?"

"Oh, Emmalynn, come on." Collins apparently had no time or desire to pad Emma's feelings, but her tone was still on the compassionate side of the scale. "You really don't know?"

"Don't know what?"

"Shit. Okay. I thought you'd figured it out by now."

"Figured what out, Collins?" Her voice rose to a piercing level.

"That you're into girls!" Collins spread her hands out in front of her as though offering Emma a silver platter of sexuality. "Okay. Okay, okay, okay. I obviously came on too strong. I'm sorry. Seriously. I just really thought you knew and hadn't outright said it because you don't need to announce it. Not with me. Or anyone, honestly. You know?"

Emma struggled to find words. Finally, she sputtered, "How did you know before I did?"

Collins dropped her hands, which had continued to proffer that platter. "I...Sensed it?"

"*How?* And when?" Aghast, Emma brought a hand to her mouth. "Have I—have I hit on you and not realized it?"

"No! No, Emmalynn. I promise." Collins laughed a little. "Even if you did, I'd know you were joking because, no offense, but ew."

Emma nodded enthusiastically. "Total ew. No offense."

"Literally none taken." After an overly dramatic full body wiggle to rid herself of the horror of a potential attraction between them, Collins shot a smile at Emma. "You're just figuring it out, huh?"

Emma dropped her hand and blew out a breath that held all her frustration. "Yeah. And I'm doing a terrible job of it."

"Let me guess. You're overthinking it."

"Shut up."

"I knew it."

With a shrug, Emma looked at Collins, who was twisting her hair into a braid. "Turns out I don't know how to, like, just *be*."

"Yeah, that's going to be hard for you. Just remember there's no rush. Take your time and feel what you're gonna feel. You'll get to a place where you're comfortable. I'm sure of it."

Reassured but not exactly satisfied, Emma put the car into drive and backed out of the parking spot.

"Sorry for outing you to yourself." Collins cackled after she said it, but Emma knew the sentiment was true.

"Not one of your finer moments." Emma grinned, then felt one corner of her mouth drop. "Wait. What did you mean that you sensed it?"

Collins continued braiding the end of her hair. "A vibe. An energy. Gaydar. Whatever you want to call it."

"I give that off?"

"Quietly." Collins smiled when Emma glanced over. "Someone can only hear it if they listen closely, or if they know you well."

Emma's stomach twisted in a pleasant way, thinking again of that night outside of Lotus when Aubrey had kissed her. No signs, no warning.

She realized now she must have been the one giving off a sign. Emma pressed one hand against her stomach, which was swooping with renewed excitement and a fresh understanding.

"You're not the only one who noticed it," she said quietly, so much so that Collins, who was singing along with the song she'd cued up on Spotify moments ago, didn't hear her.

A few minutes later, Emma pulled up in front of Liam's house, her forehead wrinkling in confusion.

Collins, ever the voice to Emma's inner thoughts, said, "Whose car is that?"

"I think…" Emma trailed off. She had a good feeling she knew whose car that was, but couldn't imagine why that person's car would be at her brother's house at eight p.m. on a Saturday night.

"Let's find out." Collins got out of the car and bounded toward the house. She stopped on the front stoop to adjust her outfit.

"I thought you didn't want to find men attractive anymore," Emma said sardonically as she unlocked the door and ushered Collins inside.

"I will *always* find Liam Gallagher attractive," Collins yell-whispered, probably hoping Liam could hear her and would finally fall hopelessly in love with her.

Emma paused in the entryway to hang up her jacket. Collins, impatient as ever, skipped ahead toward the living room. At the precipice, she squeaked and darted a glance back to Emma before stepping into the room.

After that, Emma was almost certain she knew who was in the living room with Liam. She made her way down the hall, in no rush to have those eyes peer into her as they gently unwrapped all the gifts she had crowded around her heart, especially now that she knew she had a damn vibe. She'd have to ask Collins if there was a way to—

The thoughts of shielding something she had no control over disappeared the moment Emma stepped into the living room and made eye contact with Aubrey. There was no way around the attraction anymore, no delicate tricks to fool herself into thinking this whole thing was a fluke.

"Hey," Aubrey said, her voice clear and even. She looked different than she had the last time Emma had seen her. The miserable cloud that had dulled her features was gone. Her eyes were bright, keenly focused on Emma, and there was a trace of a shy smile on her lips. The baggy, faded olive crewneck sweatshirt she wore over equally baggy jeans made her look cozy and right at home in Liam's comfortable, homey living room.

"Hi," Emma said, waving a little. She avoided Collins's eyes, knowing she'd give it all away if they made eye contact.

"Let me get this clear, Emma," Liam said, not looking up from the TV where he was maneuvering a long-haired character through a maze in a jungle (that's what it looked like to Emma, anyway). "You guys went to Harpy and you didn't bring me a six-pack? What the hell kind of little sister are you?"

"A deeply, deeply negligent one." Collins was perched on the arm of the sofa, millimeters from Liam. If Emma didn't know in her gut Collins would never make a move on him, she'd be deeply, deeply annoyed. But this was just another example of Collins playing—and this time, it was safe.

"What are you guys doing?" Emma asked, immediately cringing. Her darling older brother shook his head, not bothering to address the obvious.

"I mean, what are you guys doing hanging around, playing video games on a Saturday night? Shouldn't you be, I don't know, out on the town or something?"

Collins's eyes nearly bugged out of her face. She mouthed, "Out on the town?" and shook her head, disappointed.

"Someone needed a chill night." Liam jerked his head toward Aubrey, who finally looked away from Emma and focused on the TV. She also kicked Liam.

"I've never seen this game before." Collins, giving up her ruse, moved to sit in the chair that was angled toward the TV. "Is there a point to it?"

Both Liam and Aubrey looked at her, disbelief mirrored on their faces. Liam launched into an explanation of *Divinity: Original Sin II*. Emma tuned him out immediately, both because she'd already heard this lecture and because she didn't want to focus on Liam.

Aubrey was sitting in the corner of the sofa, giving her a perfect line of vision that stretched between the TV and Emma. She continued the gameplay as Liam rambled on and on. Every couple of sentences, Aubrey looked over at Emma. Each time, her smile looked bigger. Idly, Emma wondered how strong of a girl-liking-girl energy she was giving off now that she knew she had it to give off.

"Emmalynn, can I get that jacket now?" Collins got up and patted Liam on the head as she walked over to Emma.

"Yeah, it's upstairs."

"Great." Collins grabbed Emma's hand and pulled her from the room, all the way upstairs and into Emma's room, where she closed the door and leaned against it with wild eyes.

"Emmalynn Gallagher," Collins said, her voice low but trembling with excitement. "When exactly were you planning on telling me that Aubrey Glass is madly in love with you?"

Emma felt her eyes bug out much like Collins's had not ten minutes ago. She opened and closed her mouth, shook her head, ran her fingers through her hair. That simply was not true. Love? *In* love? It wasn't—there was no way.

"It's not like that," Emma finally said, dropping both hands to her sides. "And even if it was, I keep fucking everything up."

"Wait, hold on, one moment. Pause." Collins pushed off the door and stood inches from Emma. "What is *everything*? There's something? There's an *everything*?"

Emma shrugged.

"Emmalynn!"

Emma walked backward till she felt the edge of her bed. She sat down and dropped her head into her hands. "She kissed me," she mumbled.

"I'm going to scream." Indeed, when Emma looked up, Collins was opening her mouth, her jaw stretching to a concerning degree.

"If you do, Collins, I swear, I will kill you."

"I'm about to kill you for not telling me sooner!" Collins bounded over to the bed and knelt on it, bouncing. "When? How? How long? How many times? What did it feel like? Oh my God, I seriously think I'm going to combust."

"Try kissing her," Emma said with a sly grin. "Then you'll really know what it feels like to think you're going to combust."

Collins groaned and flopped backward on the bed. "I want all the details, now. And don't skip a thing."

And so Emma unpacked the events of the past month: the kiss, the confusion, the discussion, the weak agreement. Slowly building a friendship only to have it knocked sideways after that second kiss.

Purposely, and out of respect for Aubrey, Emma skipped over the parts that were tenderly infused with whatever Aubrey was going through. As far as she could tell, the biggest roadblock to their moving past tutoring sessions and random kisses was Emma and her overly analytical brain.

"Wow," Collins said, blinking at her. "You and Aubrey Glass. Who would have predicted that?"

Emma held up her hand. "We're not together."

"I know. Heard that, loud and clear. But I also heard that you really like her." Collins grinned. "Emmalynn, you need to tell her that. Clear the air. And stop thinking so damn much." She squeezed Emma's shoulder. "You know it's okay to be attracted to her, right? And to explore what that means, even if it doesn't turn into a forever kind of thing."

Emma nodded, rubbing her hand across her forehead. She was tired of the thoughts sprinting nonstop through her mind, doing everything in their power to turn all the gray into black and white. She had to give it a rest and just feel. But she was so good at thinking.

"Walk me out."

"No! You have to stay! I need a buffer."

"No, you don't. And you know it." Collins got up. "Walk." She caught Emma's hand and gripped it. "Me." She pulled her to the door. "Out." And then they were at the stairs.

"I hate you," Emma hissed as they descended the stairs.

"Thank me later," Collins hissed back. "Bye, guys! Have fun video gaming!" she called loudly, then leaned in to kiss Emma on the cheek. "You better keep me updated, you bitch."

"I really do hate you."

Collins waved gaily as she walked down the front walk toward her car, which she'd left parked at Emma's before they went to Harpy.

With a sigh filled with buzzing bees, Emma looked down the hallway. She just didn't have it in her to socialize with Liam and

Aubrey at the same time. Realizing she was hungry, she made her way past the living room and into the kitchen.

Just as Emma was sitting down at the counter with a turkey sandwich (extra pickles, no cheese, a little oil and vinegar on a Kaiser roll), Aubrey walked into the kitchen. No, she didn't walk. She sauntered.

"Hey," Aubrey said, echoing her earlier greeting. "That looks good."

"Thanks," Emma mumbled around a mouthful. She swallowed before continuing, "I'd make you one, but I don't know how you like your sandwiches."

"I'm not picky."

Emma looked at Aubrey. She was about to offer her a sandwich when Aubrey continued.

"Listen, I'm sorry about earlier this week." Aubrey gazed toward the ceiling. "I'm sorry about a lot of things, actually."

Without knowing what all needed apologies in Aubrey's mind, Emma felt her heart dip and swell. While she was dying to say something, she'd learned enough about Aubrey to know when to stay quiet.

"I haven't been in a good place," Aubrey went on, keeping her stare on the toaster oven next to the refrigerator. "I've been quiet because of that." She looked over at Emma, but briefly, swinging her eyes back to the toaster. "I don't want you to think I've been avoiding you."

"But you have," Emma said bluntly.

Aubrey cracked a smile. "Yeah. I have. But not—" She looked at Emma again, holding her gaze there. "Not because you did anything that would make me want to avoid you. I need you to believe that, even if you can't understand it." She scratched the back of her neck. "For what it's worth, I've been avoiding everyone."

Emma swallowed another bite of her sandwich as she rooted through possible replies. She understood what Aubrey was saying, but she didn't like it very much. Plus, a silly little part of her wanted to be special—wanted to be the one person Aubrey didn't avoid. "I don't like being avoided. Especially by you."

The air softened between them, edges crackling with things neither of them were willing or ready to say. It was suddenly incredibly warm in the kitchen. Emma felt a single bead of sweat slide between her breasts and flushed at the feeling coupled with the desire for Aubrey's mouth to travel that same path.

How was she supposed to tell her that? That she wanted her, desired her, craved her? That she'd never known she could feel this way about a person—that she'd never imagined she could feel this way about a woman?

Emma took a steadying breath then realized Aubrey had said something. "Sorry. What did you say?"

"Collins calls you Emmalynn," Aubrey repeated, her eyes still steady on Emma. The pine green of her eyes was dark around the edges, glowing with a luminosity that sparked a deliciously dangerous feeling in Emma. "Do you…Would you rather be called that?"

The heat on Emma's cheeks increased with a hot rush. "You can call me whatever you want."

"See," Aubrey said, her voice barely audible above the booming sound coming from the living room. "Sometimes you do this thing where you—"

"Glass!"

Aubrey took a quick step back despite already being several feet away from Emma, and therefore a safe distance. Emma's heart was pounding, the single drop of sweat joined by several others.

"Yeah?" Aubrey called back to Liam, her stare never wavering.

"Grab me a beer while you're up?"

"Yeah, sure."

Emma placed the last bite of her sandwich into her mouth. She chewed as she watched Aubrey open the refrigerator and retrieve a beer. When Aubrey walked past her, she paused and leaned in so that her mouth was close to Emma's ear.

"I'll finish that thought another time," she whispered.

Emma froze. She was utterly without a witty or flirty comeback, but Aubrey left the room without waiting for a response, leaving Emma with a mouthful of turkey sandwich and a brain full of what-ifs.

CHAPTER TWENTY-FOUR

Aubrey tilted her head back and looked at the sky, wondering if it was going to snow. Again. Winter was having itself a blast this year, dropping bounties of snow and ice every chance it got. The roads were caked with layers of sludge and the sky was a perennial shade of silvery gray. Combined, it wasn't doing much to help Aubrey ease out of her desire to hibernate. She knew she was becoming too comfortable with hiding in her apartment, simultaneously stewing in and avoiding her feelings about everything she could think of. After nearly becoming one with her pile of blankets last week, she was trying to leave her apartment more, hence spending the previous evening playing video games with Liam.

"Glass, heads up."

She followed the command, though ironically, she had to put her head down to keep an eye out for the puck.

The skid of puck over ice halted at the end of Aubrey's stick. She bobbled the puck, moving her stick to the left side then the right. Then, with a grunt, she pushed off from her spot on the ice and skated forward.

When Liam had casually suggested that Aubrey join him and a few of his friends for hockey, she'd agreed. She hadn't thought it would actually happen, figuring he was throwing it out there as an option, not a requirement. He'd texted bright and early that morning with the location—the pond in Finch Park—and the time, along with a reminder to let him know her shoe size if she couldn't find her skates.

Aubrey had read the text and balked. Naively, she'd assumed he'd meant street hockey, or even indoor hockey at the rec center just outside of town. It hadn't crossed her mind that he could mean they'd be playing ice hockey on a frozen pond just two blocks from her apartment.

But, in her new effort to Stay Out of Her Apartment, Aubrey had responded that she'd be there. As for the skates…That had required a trip to her mother's house. Fortunately, it was Sunday, and the family was off at church, atoning for sins they hadn't committed while harboring secrets they'd never confess to.

Now, with the puck sliding along with her skates, Aubrey glanced around to see who was near her. She'd played ice hockey a handful of times when she was very young, during those blissful years when her dad was still alive, and in high school, she'd often crashed the games her male friends threw together on weekends. She hadn't touched the ice since then, but like every Chestnut Hill native with an athletic inclination, she always had a pair of skates at the ready.

"Glass, here."

She nodded and shot the puck to Liam's friend. He'd introduced the four of them to Aubrey when she'd arrived, but she hadn't been listening. She was more concerned with whether or not Emma was going to show up to cheer on her brother.

The night before, Aubrey had exercised the utmost self-control. The moment Emma said, "You can call me whatever you want," Aubrey felt the floor shift below her feet, like an earthquake sending a warning tremor. Had Liam not unknowingly broken the moment with his request for beer, Aubrey was certain she would have caved and moved swiftly across the kitchen to press her lips against Emma's. The attraction building between them was becoming a challenge, because she ached to act on it but wanted to be respectful toward Emma, who had yet to state what she wanted. Truthfully, she wanted Emma to kiss *her* for once. Aubrey knew the desire was there, but she also had a feeling Emma didn't even know how often her expression was scrawled with the words, "Kiss me, Aubrey."

Granted, kissing was just the tip of the iceberg of her desires.

The crack of someone's stick against the ice brought Aubrey out of her kissing (and then some) reverie. She located the puck flying past her and dug her skate into the ice, pushing off with some level of grace, hustling to catch up to the sliding black circle.

Once the group of six had tired themselves out—some sooner than others, considering two remarkable hangovers—the guys skated to the edge and clomped off the ice as Aubrey continued gliding around. She moved her stick as she skated and when she came back around to where Liam and his friends were standing, Liam tossed the puck onto the ice. Aubrey nodded her thanks, quickly scooping the puck with her stick and making her way around the pond.

She missed playing field hockey. It was a feeling that had swept through her for years, sometimes a breeze and sometimes a hurricane. The sport was in her bones, and it felt criminal to not be playing.

Aubrey bit down on her lip, almost hard enough to draw blood, as she began circling the pond, hitting the puck harder than was warranted. She could be playing professionally. She knew that deeply and with certainty. Had she not skipped out on her senior year to make someone else happy, she could be in Europe on a professional field hockey team, living her dream and building a life that felt complete and real.

She had no one to blame but herself. It was easy to blame Jamie, but Aubrey was the one who'd made the decisions that had stacked against her until she landed back in Chestnut Hill, here, working at Cornerstone and chasing a puck around a frozen pond. Amazing, how one broken dream could bring her right back to a place she couldn't bring herself to call home.

The voices on the edge of the pond rose and Aubrey looked up. It looked like someone's girlfriend had arrived. Casually, not wanting to bring attention to herself, Aubrey scanned the group again. Still no red hair in sight.

She sighed, making her way off the pond. After she'd delivered Liam's beer the previous night, Aubrey had doubled back to the kitchen to see if she could pick up the conversation with Emma. But Emma had disappeared, and when she hadn't reappeared two hours later, Aubrey had persuaded Liam to stop gaming for the night. A squishy emptiness had followed her home, a yearning to have done more than simply say goodnight.

"So," Liam said. He dropped down on the bench next to where she was unlacing her skates with frozen fingers. "What'd you think?"

"I liked it. Sorry if I sucked."

"Are you kidding, Glass? You got three goals."

Aubrey caught Liam's eyes and grinned when she saw his impressed expression. "Yeah, well. Beginner's luck."

"Says the top scorer of the great state of New Hampshire." Liam threw a powerless punch into Aubrey's shoulder. "You'll play again, right?"

A fissure broke open inside her. Yes, she would. Somehow. And ice hockey, too. "Yeah, definitely. I had fun."

"Good." Liam leaned back on the bench, aimlessly stomping his feet into the couple of inches of snow on the ground. "So. You and my sister, huh?"

Aubrey looked up at him, as much jarred by the switch in conversation as she was by the actual question. "What? No. That's not a thing."

"You sure?"

"Very." *Not at all.* Aubrey brought her hands to her mouth and blew on them, wishing she could untie her skates with her gloves on.

"I'm not blind, Glass. Emma might be." He laughed, shaking his head. "But I know you're not."

Aubrey didn't say anything. She didn't have the words to explain what she was feeling and all the fears and self-imposed complications that came with it. Instead, she settled for the simple truth. "I like your sister," she said carefully. "And for right now, there's all there is to it."

"Well, just so you know, my parents love you, so you've already got their blessing." He clapped Aubrey on the back and stood. "Speaking of," he said, grinning, "I'm headed there now. Wanna come?"

She did. Desperately, almost. But her mother had seen her on the cameras when she picked up her skates. A flurry of text messages later, Aubrey was obligated to return to their home and suffer through a "Sunday family lunch."

"I can't today." She stood up and put a hand on Liam's shoulder. "You're not...Is it okay?" Aubrey shook her head. "I don't even know what I'm saying."

"I trust you with her," he said, his voice quiet and serious. "Does that answer your question?"

Aubrey nodded. "Thanks, Liam. That means a lot to me."

"No problem. But don't fuck it up, Glass."

She tugged her beanie down lower over her ears, a smile hovering on her lips. "Wouldn't dream of it."

In a singular act of old teenage rebellion, Aubrey hadn't bothered to stop at home before heading to her mother's house. Sitting at the ornate dining room table with Pen and Trent's kids, all of whom were impeccably dressed from a long morning at church, she felt smug in her sweaty, unkempt, post-ice-hockey appearance. The old sweatshirt with holes in it was icing on the black sheep cake.

Her mother was less than thrilled.

"Honestly, Aubrey," she said in a low voice when Trent was out of the room. "You could have made an *effort*."

"I would have if you'd asked me to lunch *before* you saw me on your cameras and decided it was time to see me again." She popped a piece of bread in her mouth. "I told you I was going to play hockey and that I wouldn't have time to go home before coming here. Terribly sorry about that, Mother."

Trevor, the eight-year-old who didn't seem completely affected by his father's stiff, conservative personality, smothered a giggle behind his napkin. Aubrey winked at him.

"We're so glad you're here," Corrine said loudly, false enthusiasm sparkling like decades-old glitter in her voice. Trent, who was just coming back into the room, barely nodded as he sat down at the table. "It's been too long since you've visited, Aubrey."

"Weird, I don't think I've missed any invitations."

Silence skittered across the table, landing in Trent's lap. Everyone aside from Aubrey looked to see his reaction. When Trent did nothing more than pick up his utensils and begin slicing the pork roast on his plate, there were two sounds at the table: sighs of relief and sighs of exasperation.

Aubrey looked between Trent and her mother. Something was definitely amiss. They normally functioned like a tag-team demolition crew, one backing up the other until they achieved victory. Trent's silence was so far out of the ordinary that Aubrey actually felt a tiny flicker of compassion for her mother. Could it be she would soon be out seeking husband number four?

The thought didn't bring the kind of happiness Aubrey thought it might. Sure, Trent was an asshole, but he actually got along with Corrine, a feat that seemed impossible. He wasn't outwardly rude to Aubrey, even if he supported the opposite of everything she was.

Of course, Aubrey thought as she stabbed at the food on her plate, that could be a matter of yet.

The late lunch stretched on in silence. By the time Trent excused himself with, "Good to see you, Aubrey," she was fully convinced divorce was on the horizon. One by one, the younger kids left, each excusing themself with top tier manners.

Alone in the room with Corrine, Aubrey couldn't bring herself to look at her mother. She braced herself, knowing a storm was coming.

"What do you have to say for yourself?" Corrine's voice was clipped but with an underbelly of sadness.

Aubrey sighed internally. She'd been down this road many a time with Corrine; when she was hurt, Aubrey became her target. Over the span of Aubrey's lifetime, Corrine had perfected her aim, knocking the arrow straight into the bullseye with every comment.

"About what, Mother?"

"This." Corrine gestured to the empty table. "No one wants to be around you in your…your *state*."

"Oh, is that what it is?" Aubrey looked down at her outfit. It wasn't as offensive as Corrine wanted it to be. "It has nothing to do with them not wanting to be around you?"

The words shot from her mouth without a safeguard. Aubrey sat back in her chair, waiting. Considering she'd told her mother to fuck off numerous times in the past, that wasn't the harshest line she'd ever lobbed. Still, it had to have stung.

Mostly because it was true, and she and Corrine both knew it.

Her mother folded her napkin and set it next to her plate. "I've often wondered where I went wrong with you."

Aubrey balked. This was new territory.

"You were a spoiled child, Aubrey." *Ah, okay, back on track.* "When your father died, I wanted that to change. But Steven, oh, you had him fooled. He gave you everything you wanted, didn't he?"

Aubrey couldn't argue that. She'd give anything to have her dad back, but Steven had been a good stepfather. Too good for Corrine, though.

"And now look at you." Corrine's eyes glittered like a snake's settling on prey. "What a waste, Aubrey. All your talents and intelligence, tossed aside to work in a small-town bookstore."

A chill zipped down Aubrey's spine. She'd never questioned Trent about his "friend" who'd come into Cornerstone. She didn't think she had to. But now that encounter felt far more loaded than she'd realized at the time.

However, pressing the issue with her mother would get her nowhere. And after twenty-four years of trying to find a way to have a healthy, loving relationship—hell, Aubrey would even settle for accepting—with Corrine, she'd stopped looking for a way in.

"I'm leaving," Aubrey said, standing up. She tossed her napkin onto the plate of food she'd barely touched. "Thanks so much for another amazing family bonding session."

"There you go," Corrine said gaily, pushing her chair back so she could cross one leg over the other in her too-tight cream-colored pencil skirt. "Doing what you do best, running away."

Her words didn't hit with their desired impact. Instead, Aubrey laughed. She laughed so hard she had to steady herself with one hand on the archway leading to the hall.

"You don't know me at all, Mother." She looked at Corrine. "When I run, it's so I don't say or do something I'll regret. But I assure you, I rarely run. In fact, I stay. I stay too long. I stay and I put up with shit that no person should ever put up with. And you know who you can blame for that shitty character trait?" Aubrey pointed in the general area of Trent's study. "Your parade of husbands."

She didn't wait to see the reaction or lack thereof. Aubrey grabbed her jacket from the closet by the front door and left, shutting the door firmly behind her.

Several hours later, Aubrey was safely cocooned in her beloved blankets. After ice hockey (a positive) and family lunch (a perilous negative) she felt she owed herself some comfort. It had taken effort, but she'd settled on the sofa instead of in her bed, giving herself a fighting chance at doing something productive.

She'd avoided leaning into the comfort of getting high, too. It was tempting, sure, but she'd wanted to keep a clear mind as she rolled through the events of the day.

She knew nothing would ever change with her family dynamics. On the off chance Corrine found a husband who was kind and accepting, she'd steamroll him into something awful. Aubrey hoped Trent wouldn't give up quite yet. He wasn't Aubrey's favorite husband, but the older she got, the more she realized she could tolerate him—though she'd never tolerate his political stance.

As the night darkened outside her third-story windows, Aubrey left her cocoon to turn on the lamp. The poster hanging behind it suddenly glowed, drawing her attention. She studied it as she stood there.

That poster had been with Aubrey since her sophomore year of high school, the year she'd gotten into '90s music, particularly Tori Amos. With money her then-stepdad had given her for her report card (the last time for that grade bonus, as he'd left Corrine a few months later), Aubrey had gone to the mall and allowed herself a mini music-themed shopping spree. She'd spotted the Tori Amos poster and grabbed it, knowing it had to come home with her.

The poster featured a dark-blue background with a silver bird cage hanging from a tree branch. Across the bottom were the lyrics, "You're just an empty cage, girl, if you kill the bird." "Crucify" was one of Aubrey's favorite songs at the time. Then, that's all it was: a favorite song.

In the years since, it had become a sort of anthem for Aubrey. She didn't relate to the lyrics in the way they were written—however, and she smiled, thinking of Emma and Emily Dickinson, who was to say her interpretation was right or wrong?

The cage, though. The image and the word. Aubrey sat back down on the sofa, pulling the blankets around her, and she kept her eyes on the silver cage. It had faded over the years, but its bold power remained.

Idly, she wondered why the cage she'd kept herself in for—years? decades?—had remained just as bold, just as bright. Just as tightly locked.

And she knew she was the only person with a key.

"Oh, for fuck's sake," Aubrey said into the empty room, dropping her head back on the sofa. She wanted out. She was so bitterly tired of caging herself up. If only she could just pick up the damn key and put it in the lock. And then what? Fly? Or crash to the ground with yet another misdirected hope.

Memories and cast-off dreams surfaced. They were orderly, lined up, quiet. A thousand words crept through the darkened hallways of her mind, flashlights bobbing in sync with her heartbeat, but none stumbled toward the exit.

Wait.

Aubrey sat up. That. She could do that. It might not throw the door open with the gusto she desired, but it was a twist of the key in the lock. In the *right* direction, not the one that would jam the lock.

"Not gonna let my courage sell out now," she muttered, pulling her computer onto her lap.

CHAPTER TWENTY-FIVE

Bernard was having a rough morning. He seemed to have a cold—if inanimate machines could have a cold, that is. He was sputtering and making concerning choking sounds, like he wanted to cough but couldn't gasp enough air. Genesis had been freaking out all morning, leaving Emma to handle the steady stream of Thursday customers. Bernard was still producing, thankfully, but Genesis was convinced he was sending a message of imminent death.

"That's the wrong color," she muttered, eyeing the shot Emma had coaxed out. "It should be darker."

Emma held out the ceramic cup in her hand. "Do you want me to toss it?"

"No." Eyes wild, Genesis looked between the line of three customers and Bernard. "Make the drink. We just have to get through this rush."

After she poured the less-than-perfect shot of espresso into a to-go cup, Emma put the finishing touches on the winter white latte, a drink she'd created during a slow morning. The mixture of white chocolate and peppermint was a hit with their regulars.

Once the line was gone, Genesis informed Emma she was going to perform surgery on Bernard. She had a feeling, she explained, that the closing barista hadn't been thoroughly cleaning him. Emma had no idea what all that entailed, but she agreed to handle any customers who might request an espresso drink and kindly persuade them into a fancy regular coffee drink instead.

A series of steamy whistles and forceful huffs rang around the café. Through the noise, Emma caught the opening strains of one of her old favorite songs, "A Sorta Fairytale." She waited for her body's usual anxiety response, surprised when nothing flickered to life. Tori Amos had been the soundtrack of her recovery period after having her ankle shattered. The songs provided the perfect mix of melancholy and yearning, fringed with a fire line of anger. Emma had spent countless days under mental water, hearing nothing but Tori's voice and her fingers over piano keys.

She leaned against the counter, curious about the rest of the playlist. She could be patient and listen or she could hunt Aubrey down and ask her. It was well within the newest boundaries they'd wordlessly created after seeing each other in Liam's kitchen just shy of a week ago. To her credit, Aubrey was no longer avoiding her. But she was keeping a distance, probably some measure of safety from Emma's indecision. They hadn't met for a study session that week, and Emma had spent Tuesday feeling strangely empty.

If she were being honest with herself, she'd acknowledge that it was far more than the tutoring that she missed. Emma, tangled in a web of her own making, had never had to take the steps to move a flirty friendship into something bigger and better, something intensely more satisfying. She'd dated a couple of guys while she lived in Philadelphia, and they'd been in charge from the get-go. This, Aubrey, and women in general, was foreign territory, and Emma was terrified to move without a map.

She looked around the café. The people at the tables looked taken care of, and there was no one in line. Peering further into the store, Emma couldn't see anyone heading in the direction of the café. She nodded, clenched and unclenched her fists twice, and turned toward Genesis, figuring her next question was best asked while she was distracted by Bernard.

"Why did you invite me to Lotus?"

"Employee bonding." The fact that Genesis answered without hesitation or a "Why the hell are you asking me this now?" made

Emma smile. She'd been a little afraid of Genesis when she'd first started working at Cornerstone, but as the weeks went by, Emma began to see glimpses of the giant softie behind the gruff exterior.

Her smile drooped as she pushed out the next question. "Did you...Did you think I was gay?"

"Isn't everyone a little gay?"

Emma crossed her arms over her chest, immediately regretting the move because of the smeared chocolate sauce she'd forgotten to wipe off her apron. "Are you?" she shot back.

"I," Genesis said, stepping back from Bernard, who was quietly humming as he steamed, "am of the Dr. Renee Lawler sexuality spectrum. No notes."

"Okay, fine. But me, Genesis. What did you think about me?"

"Well, Just Emma, not everyone walks into a gay bar wearing a little white crop top with no bra. Does that answer your question?"

She huffed, remembering acutely the presence of her nipples that night. "I didn't know it was a gay bar."

"Oh, shit." Genesis threw back her head and laughed. "You're serious?"

"Yes!"

"So, wait. You go to all bars not wearing a bra?"

Emma furtively glanced around them, making sure no one was within earshot. Especially Aubrey, who probably would have thoroughly enjoyed their conversation. "No," she hissed. "My friend made me—you know what, that's not important. Just answer my question. Please."

"About your sexuality?" Genesis gave her an incredulous look.

"Yes! Just answer it!"

Genesis leaned her hip against the counter, regarding Emma carefully. It was the most serious Emma had ever seen her, and it made her knees feel weak.

"Respectfully, Just Emma, I could not give a fuck less about your sexuality. That's your business. It has no bearing on me. But," she said, her voice dropping, "what you decide to do with Glass does have a bearing on me, so figure that shit out stat. And yes, before you ask me, I told her the same damn thing."

Emma's jaw dropped. Selfishly, she had wanted Genesis to confirm her suspicions that she thought Emma was definitely on the gay spectrum. She hadn't imagined that she'd also get a miniature lecture on Aubrey, of all things.

"Close your mouth," Genesis ordered. "Yes, I've noticed. I see everything."

Emma did as told, then, through the corner of her mouth, asked, "Did she…Did Aubrey say something to you?"

"She doesn't have to. I just told you. I see everything." Genesis turned back to Bernard, who seemed to have settled down. "Now, I get that you're experiencing some classic Gay Panic, but you're a complete idiot if you let that keep you from Glass." She shot a look at Emma over her shoulder. "But if you fuck her up, I will have something to say about that. I'm not a violent person, Just Emma, but my mouth can cause harm harsher than my fists ever could."

The warning had the opposite effect and brought a smile to Emma's face. The idea of Genesis so much as killing a fruit fly was hard to imagine. Emma had no doubt, though, that she could yield quite the sword with her words.

"I'm not sure what to do," Emma said. "It feels like we're spinning in circles next to each other, and sometimes they collide, but not long enough to make a Venn diagram."

Genesis looked at her with muted disgust. "You're a nerd, Just Emma. Like, way more than I imagined."

"Yeah, I know." She grinned. "A nerd who has no idea what to do with things like feelings. Especially…" She trailed off, not wanting to imprint all her subconscious swirls onto Genesis.

"When you've never felt this way about a woman before?" Genesis shook her head. "No one thinks I pay attention, buddy." She put both hands on Bernard and bowed her head before him before continuing their confidential conversation. "When are they going to learn I know every damn thing that's going on around me? I hear it all, I see it all, even when they all think they're slick and hiding secrets. What a burden I carry."

Emma waited to make sure the intimate moment had passed before saying, "So, oh omnipotent one, any wisdom to pass on to me?"

Genesis released Bernard and buried her face in her hands. "Please, Just Emma, for the love of God. Take a class with Dr. Renee Lawler so you can learn how to use big words other than Venn diagram." She dropped her hands and grinned at Emma. "It's omniscient, and yes, I am, thank you for recognizing it."

"Fine, whatever. Focus." Emma clapped her hands once. "Guide me, Genesis. I'm begging you."

"Okay, here's a brilliant idea. How about you two idiots have a fucking conversation?"

Hadn't Emma tried that? She rolled through her interactions with Aubrey, her skin chilling as she realized they hadn't really *talked* about what they were doing. Or not doing. Or wanted to do. Both Genesis's and Collins's voices echoed in Emma's head, scribbling a cacophony of firm, self-assured fractions of sentences. The combined essay was a fragmented and overly energetic mess of advice and persuasion, causing Emma to giggle at the thought of having Collins and Genesis in the same room, and printed in bold. Emma had no choice but to read the twelve-point font flashing in her frontal lobe. She had to talk to Aubrey.

Well, no time like the present.

With a surge of misguided confidence, Emma stood up straight and ripped off her apron. "I'll be back," she said, not giving Genesis a chance to stop her before she skittered out of the café and headed toward the stockroom.

The moment she reached the door, her confidence wavered. Emma suddenly wished she'd kept her stupid chocolate-smeared apron on, just for another layer of protection. It's not that she thought Aubrey would be mean—she'd yet to show any sign of that potential—it's that Emma didn't yet know how fragile her own heart could be.

With a nod of resolution, she pushed open the door and was greeted with the image of Aubrey bent over a line of boxes. She was wearing dark green cargo pants and an off-white cardigan, along with those Boston clogs she loved so much. Impractical for the winter they were having, but Emma understood Aubrey placed comfort above practicality.

"Hi," Emma announced. She didn't wait for Aubrey to acknowledge her, preferring to speak to her expressionless back. "I want to talk to you. I mean, I want us to talk. We need to talk, Aubrey, so we can hash this out. Not like we're fighting, I mean, we just need to…Figure it out. Find common ground." Aubrey had stilled but hadn't turned around, so Emma kept going, dropping her gaze to the cement floor. "I feel like we're spinning in circles and the circles are right next to each other. Sometimes they touch and bounce apart, and I know sometimes I cause the bounce, but I think sometimes you do, too. I don't know why you're bouncing, but I know why I am. Well, mostly. Kind of?" Emma laughed nervously, running her hands through her hair. "I don't know what I'm doing, but I think you know that. You've learned it, I mean. Because you pay attention to me even when I think you're not, even when you're avoiding the world. I know you see me, Aubrey. And I know you know that I see you, even when you think you're invisible. You're never invisible to me. I don't know how it happened, but you've become the brightest star in my sky, the one that keeps me up at night because I want to reach out and grab it but I can't find the ladder that'll let me climb that high." Emma felt her shoulders sag. "And maybe I don't want to climb. Maybe I want you to fall, just a little bit, just close enough into my orbit so that I can wrap my fingers around one of your sharp corners." She smiled at the ground. "You're not as sharp as you think you are, Aubrey Glass. That's one of my favorite things about you." With a deep breath and a firm nod, Emma went on. "I think I could have a lot of favorite things about you. And I know I'm part of the prob—no, not the problem. We don't have a *problem*, we just have us. Two people bouncing into each other, knocking into doors and windows that are boarded up or never been opened. Those are mine, you know. The ones that have never been opened." Emma winced at her naked vulnerability, but she'd come this far and couldn't stop now. "I think I'd like you to open my doors and windows. Oh, God, okay, that sounded way better in my head." She looked up and, with disappointment and confusion, realized that Aubrey hadn't turned around. "Hey. Aubrey?"

Nothing. Emma put her hands on her hips, old coping mechanisms propelling her toward annoyance. "Aubrey," she said louder. "Hello?"

Still nothing. Aubrey just stood there before her line of boxes, head moving back and forth slightly, not with enough motion to be conceived as shaking her head. No, it was more like she was surveying the items before her.

Of all the potential outcomes of her impromptu speech, Emma had not prepared for being ignored. Her annoyance sliding into anger, she stomped forward and grabbed Aubrey's shoulder, pulling her around.

Aubrey jumped away, holding up both hands. Fear and alarm ran across her features until she recognized Emma. Then, with the casualness of a seasoned bartender pouring the tenth Long Island iced tea of the night, Aubrey reached up to both ears and pulled.

"Emma? What's up?"

Stunned, horrified, and mortified, Emma could only stare at the AirPods in Aubrey's hands. "You—what—no. Oh, God."

"Hey," Aubrey said, her voice a balm to Emma's growing panic. "Emma. What's wrong?"

"What's *wrong*?" she cried, taking a step back. "What's *wrong* is that I just—oh, my God. I just poured my whole stupid heart out to you and you—you—you didn't hear a single word of it."

Aubrey stuffed her AirPods in her pocket to hide the criminal activity. It didn't help Emma feel any better.

"You did what?" Aubrey shook her head. "How long were you in here?"

"You seriously heard nothing that I said?"

"No, I didn't. I'm sorry." And she did look genuinely so. "Can you...Can you say it again?"

"No!" Emma paused, trying to settle her racing emotions. "No, I can't. Not like I did."

"Okay." Aubrey's voice was so calm, so kind. Emma, despite her every urge to stay annoyed, felt herself falling right into it. "Could you maybe summarize it for me, then?" She locked eyes with Emma, holding their gaze, which only served to further melt Emma's emotions. "Please? I'd really like to know what your whole stupid heart has to say." She grinned. "Though, to be clear, I don't think your heart is stupid."

That did it. Every harried emotion swept right out of her, leaving nothing but that damn glowing, vaguely combustible feeling that came only when Aubrey was near. "I think I like you," she blurted.

The words hovered in the air between them, swaying in the nonexistent breeze. Aubrey, still but for the barely perceptible tilt of her head, waited several moments before saying, "You think?"

"No," Emma said, shaking her head. "I know I like you. I don't know everything about the feelings that come with that." She shut her eyes briefly, wishing for once in her life she could not ramble. "But I want to."

When Emma opened her eyes, Aubrey was looking at her in a way that was new, and not necessarily good. Emma knew immediately she should have skipped that weird comment about not knowing everything about the feeling. She understood Aubrey to be comfortable in her sexuality and Emma knew her own confusion wasn't exactly drawing Aubrey in.

"Emma." There was a gentle warning in her voice. "It seems like you're not certain about any of this."

Emma's heart sank with the truth of Aubrey's statement. She sorted around internally for an argument. "I don't know what I am. But I know how I feel when I'm around you," she settled on. It wasn't great, but it was at least true.

"I believe you do, but I'm not an experiment. I'm not a gateway drug." There was no malice in the words. Then, a flicker in her eyes. Emma nearly missed it. "Just…figure it out," she mumbled.

"I'm trying." A string of anger swung between Emma's ribs, wrapping around the bottom of her heart. "I literally just gave you an entire speech about how I'm trying and you didn't hear a word of it."

Aubrey nodded and looked at the ground. She scuffed her shoe in a circle. "I'm really sorry."

Emma laughed despite the tight squeeze that ribbon had on her heart. "If I could count the amount of times we've apologized to each other in the short time we've known each other, I'd…I don't know what I'd do. Or what I'd have, other than a shit-ton of I'm sorrys."

The room grew silent, the space between them still and solid. Emma felt worn around the edges, soft and tired. She shifted her gaze between Aubrey and the back wall of the stockroom. She could give up and walk away. After all, she'd used the best of her words and they'd fallen on deaf ears. Manufactured deafness thanks to whatever Aubrey had been listening to, but still.

"I don't know what to do with you." Aubrey's voice floated over to Emma, tendrils of vowels and consonants drifting against her ears.

The sentiment was not lost on Emma, but she still felt the tightness in her heart and was unwilling to give in so easily. "I'm not a thing you do something with," she said.

"I know, trust me." Aubrey finally looked up. Her dark-green eyes were wide and earnest. "It's just…Emma, you're not like everyone else."

That loosened the ribbon, allowing her to breathe easier. "Isn't that a good thing?"

"Yes," Aubrey said, but there was caution in her voice. "It's also a little scary for me."

Emma waited for Aubrey to go on, to explain something that would help her better understand the fear simmering beneath all the other feelings.

"I kissed someone else," Aubrey said instead.

The ribbon tightened to an excruciating degree. "You kissed someone else," Emma said flatly. "What, do you go around kissing people like it's your job?"

Aubrey's laugh was dark. "Hardly." She stopped laughing and stared at Emma. "I couldn't stop thinking about you, so I had to kiss someone else. It's stupid. Trust me, I know."

Emma took another step back. "You realize that makes zero sense."

"I do. Very much so." Aubrey hesitated, then, having made a decision Emma would likely never be privy to, went on. "It was when I was in a bad place. And that's not an excuse. It's not even something I can fully explain to you, and I wish I could." She stuffed her hands in her pockets. "When I kissed you that day in the library, I needed to feel something. And I wanted that feeling to come from you. It did. Believe me, Emma, it did. And then I freaked out, because I can't rely on you to…" She trailed off into a territory she didn't want to verbalize, shaking her head. "That's not something I can do to you."

"So your solution was to kiss someone else?"

"Kind of. Yeah. Stupid, I know."

"Very."

Aubrey nodded, toeing her foot in a circle again. "I wish I hadn't, but I did. And maybe this doesn't mean anything to you, but I want you to know I felt nothing when I kissed her. The whole thing—" She cut herself off with a sigh. "It was bad, all around. And I regret it."

"So you kissed me because you needed to feel something, and you did. Then you decided you had to kiss someone else to feel something, and you did, but you didn't. Is that right?"

Aubrey tilted her head from side to side. "More or less, yeah."

"And you also kissed someone else because you couldn't stop thinking about me. Right?"

"Yes."

Emma shook her head. "If you couldn't stop thinking about me, why didn't you just kiss *me* again? So you could feel whatever you wanted to feel? With me," she added quietly.

"Because, Emma." Her tone was serious again and Emma preemptively hated it. "Because you can't be the only thing that makes me feel something. And more importantly, because you don't know what you want. Or who you are. You're figuring it all out."

Emma fought the urge to stomp. "I'm twenty-one, *Aubrey*. Isn't that what I'm supposed to be doing?"

Her argument landed squarely. Aubrey, speechless in the aftershock of a truth bomb, shrugged.

"Maybe you had it all figured out at twenty-one, but I don't," Emma went on.

Aubrey smiled. "You know I didn't have it all figured out."

"No, actually, I don't, because you're like a locked suitcase when it comes to talking about yourself and your past. I know nothing."

Aubrey wrinkled her nose. "A locked suitcase?"

"Just go with it, okay? For the sake of the argument."

"Fine," Aubrey said. "I can carry a metaphor." She cleared her throat. "I have baggage. A whole set of luggage. And most of it is battered."

Emma rolled her eyes, hating that she'd handed Aubrey the perfect metaphor. "How? You're only twenty-four."

"Because I'm really good at making bad choices, okay?"

"Isn't that all part of growing up? Of figuring all of this out?" Emma did stomp then. "Aubrey! We're doing the same thing. Don't you see that?"

She blinked at Emma. "No. And I'm not trying to be an asshole by saying that. I really don't see it."

"Well, then, maybe *you're* the one who needs to figure that out."

"Touché." Aubrey lifted one shoulder. "But I do have to remind you—"

"God, yes, I get it." Emma couldn't help but roll her eyes again, though by now she was done with her anger and annoyance, and instead wrestling with that insatiable attraction. "You know you're a lesbian. Clap, clap, Aubrey Glass. So maybe I can't say that about myself yet, but, fuck, Aubrey. Isn't it enough for now that I know I want you to kiss me every time I see you?" Emma swallowed. *Say it*, she commanded herself. "And—and more than just kissing."

Aubrey's face lit up. The simple happiness setting her features aglow stirred a similar glow in Emma's chest. Was that all she'd had to say for this entire fucking time?

"Maybe *you* should try kissing *me* sometime," Aubrey said, smirking.

Emma crossed her arms, hoping the barrier would keep her a professional distance from the temptation standing (nay, slouching, with that perfect drop of the shoulders Aubrey had perfected) just two feet from her. "Maybe I will."

"Good."

"Great." Emma nodded. "Glad we got that settled."

The walkie Aubrey had attached to her back pocket crackled to life. Emma jumped, half-grateful for the interruption, half-disappointed that she'd missed her chance to close the distance and kiss Aubrey (though she knew she wouldn't have done it anyway, because she couldn't wrap herself around doing something that intimate while at work).

"Just Emma!" Genesis's voice rang loud and clear. "Now!"

"Duty calls," Emma said, wiping her hands on her jeans.

"Go before she starts yelling."

"Wait," Emma said. "Did she really tell you to figure your shit out? Like, in regard to me?"

Aubrey shook her head, her lips pressing inward. "You wouldn't even imagine the lecture she gave me the other night. I've tried to forget it, but yeah, she did. Amongst many other things."

Aubrey started walking toward the door and Emma followed, keeping a safe-ish distance between them. She failed at retaining it when they entered the bookstore, their arms brushing together.

"She knows way more than we think she does," Emma said quietly.

"Oh, Emma. You have no idea."

They paused by the café. A look passed between them, one Emma could happily sink into for hours. Aubrey lowered her glance to Emma's lips, then slowly dragged her eyes up to meet Emma's once again.

Emma's breath caught in her throat. Why did they have to be at work? She contemplated grabbing Aubrey's hand and dragging her back to the stockroom.

"You know I can't—I can't do what you suggested I do right now," Emma murmured.

"Oh, I'm well aware." Aubrey grinned, a full-face dazzle brightening her features.

"You frustrate the hell out of me," Emma grumbled.

Aubrey's grin widened and she gently bumped Emma before turning to walk to the front of the store. "Same, Emma. Same."

Emma wanted to stare after her, but she could feel Genesis burning the back of her head with a stare, so she turned and quickly jumped in to help on register.

Ten minutes later, the rush was gone, and Genesis turned accusingly to Emma.

"You did it, didn't you?" She leaned in closer. "You broke through the glass castle."

"I don't know what you're talking about," Emma said loftily. She busied herself with wiping up a milk spill.

"You don't need to confirm nor deny," Genesis responded. "I'm omnipotent, remember?"

Emma threw the milky rag at Genesis's retreating figure, but nothing could dull the tender surge of hope swooping through her heart.

CHAPTER TWENTY-SIX

The clock had yet to hit nine a.m. on Saturday morning and Aubrey had already accomplished a mountain of goals for the day. Okay, it was more like an anthill, but for her, it felt much bigger.

She'd been up by six thirty and, taking full advantage of winter's brief hiatus, jogged to the high school field with her equipment bag. She was certain she'd have a bruise on her hip from the repetitive smack of the bag. But the pain hadn't stopped her from lining up balls and taking shot after shot at the goal. The ground was crunchy and potholed with leftover snow, so the balls didn't fly with the zest she preferred, but the movement—familiar, repetitive, calming—kicked her pulse back to life.

On her jog home, she'd run through her conversation with Emma from two days prior. For as unresolved as their little flirty situation still was, Aubrey felt better about it all. She'd said things she'd been wanting to say. She'd listened to Emma and waited on a string of hope for her to say she'd figured everything out. There was a block there, something Aubrey couldn't move herself past. She'd been thinking about it since their conversation, and had yet to put her finger on it.

Also, Aubrey had yet to forgive herself for having her stupid AirPods on noise canceling mode when she'd been working in the stockroom. That was a mistake she wouldn't repeat.

After she got home from her solo field hockey workout, Aubrey had tackled her next task: cleaning. An hour later, her apartment wasn't the best it had ever looked, but it was a marked improvement from its disaster state of the past two months. She celebrated that win with a long, hot shower.

Satisfied with the cleaner environment and her clean self, Aubrey had settled at her desk and nervously checked her email. She'd been taking several leaps lately, ones she preferred to keep to herself in order to buffer potential explanations of rejection. As she skimmed her inbox, a pleasant burst of excitement rumbled through her. She opened Callie Lewes's response to her initial email and took a deep breath. Sadie had given her an exuberant go-ahead to initiate the conversation, but Aubrey had remained anxious about Callie's reply.

She nearly bounced in her chair as she reread the email. She read Callie's thoughtful lines a third time before opening a reply and attaching a document. She typed out what she hoped was a grateful and chill email, then hit send before she could overthink it. Toggling back to Callie's email, Aubrey studied the link she'd attached, then clicked on it. As she read over the website, an idea formed.

Now, as she gently shut the lid of her laptop, Aubrey kicked back in her chair and stared out the window. It really was becoming a beautiful day. Still cold, sure, because it was New England in the winter, but after endless weeks of snow, forty-five degrees and sunshine felt like summer. She couldn't use the weather as an excuse to hide from the world, nor could she use her mood, which was disturbingly good. Aubrey tapped her foot against the floor. She had no excuses, and more importantly, she didn't want any.

She reached for her phone and sent a text to Emma. She already knew Emma wasn't working. Beyond that, she didn't know if she was busy.

Aubrey's phone buzzed with a text. She laughed out loud when she saw Emma's reply.

No, Aubrey, I don't want a tutoring session on a Saturday. :)

Fair enough. That's what she deserved for sending a text that said nothing but, *Wanna do something today?*

Before she could fire back an equally sarcastic text, Emma texted again.

But if you had something else in mind, yes.

A warm, slippery sensation thawed any remaining ice in Aubrey's emotional ecosystem. There were many, many other things she had in mind when it came to Emmalynn Gallagher, but cautious forward movement sat stubbornly at the top of the list. There would be plenty of time for the constantly growing list. Of that, Aubrey was certain.

She'd meant every word she'd said to Emma during their last tilt-a-whirl discussion. Especially how Emma wasn't like everyone else. What Aubrey really meant was that Emma was like no one else she'd ever known, and certainly not like anyone she'd been involved with. It was equal parts thrilling and terrifying, something she didn't think Emma was ready to hear.

I do, Aubrey typed. *I know it's short notice but can you be ready to go in a half hour?*

She ran her hands through her still damp hair as she waited for Emma to reply. It was possible Aubrey had to stop protecting Emma from the truth of her feelings. Aubrey raised her hands over her head, interlocked her fingers behind her neck, and sighed. She just could not get past the fact that Emma was "figuring herself out." Aubrey didn't want to be a stepping stone, an experiment, a pair of pants to try on (or, really, take off if things went well). She wanted to be much, much more than that. And Emma—

Her phone buzzed. *Absolutely.*

Aubrey's face broke into a grin as she quickly typed back that she'd pick Emma up then. She pushed herself out of her desk chair and hurried to find an outfit that stated she was trying, but not trying too hard. That, it seemed, was the central story of Aubrey's life.

Aubrey pulled up to Liam's house right on time. She suffered a moment of angst over the intensely lived-in state of her car, especially when she glimpsed Emma's recently washed Mini Cooper.

"You are who you are," she muttered as she carefully shut the aging door of her car and strode up the path to the front door.

Liam swung open the door before Aubrey could knock. He gave her a rather shit-eating grin as he crossed his arms and attempted a look of intimidation.

"I'm not afraid of you," Aubrey said politely.

He dropped his arms and glared at her. "Not even a little?"

"No. But I appreciate you trying."

Liam leaned against the doorframe. "Emma won't tell me where you're taking her."

"That's because," Aubrey said with her own shit-eating grin, "I didn't tell her."

"Oh, I see. You've gone from denying that you've got something going on with my sister to planning a surprise date with her. That's quite a leap, Glass."

"It's not a—" The word "date" dissolved on Aubrey's tongue as Liam stepped aside to let Emma walk out the front door.

Aubrey had seen her in countless outfits: the mundane at work and the cute and classy during tutoring sessions, plus a few bonus "running off to class" outfits. But this was different.

Emma tugged at the bottom of the dark-brown blazer she wore over an off-white crewneck sweater. The high-waisted brown pants she wore had a thin mustard yellow plaid print and would have looked ridiculous on, say, Genesis, but they looked made for Emma. With dark-brown combat boots and her shorter hair grazing her shoulders, the overall look was quirky hot professor.

Aubrey swallowed. Not a date. Sure.

"Hi," Emma said brightly. "Let's please leave so my brother stops tormenting me, okay?"

Aubrey nodded, unable to get a word out. She waved to Liam, then flipped him off. The sound of his laughter trailed them to Aubrey's car.

"He's so annoying," Emma said as soon as she shut the passenger door. "Like, I get that's what brothers are supposed to do, but it's *you*. He knows you. You're literally friends with him."

"Do you think that makes it weird for him?"

"No, but if it does, he needs to get over it."

Aubrey smiled. There was a new confidence radiating off Emma. And it was intoxicating.

"So, no tutoring," Emma said, angling herself so she could see Aubrey.

"Nope."

"Are we going to sit in the café at Cornerstone and read magazines?" Emma asked, her tone dry and monotone.

Aubrey burst into laughter. "God, no. Why would you even guess that?"

"Because we've only been to those two places together. Pennbrook and work."

"Not true," Aubrey said lightly. "There's also Lotus."

Emma made a nondescript noise and Aubrey looked over in time to catch the flaming blush on her already pink cheeks.

"Well, I highly doubt you'd be taking me to Lotus on a Saturday morning," Emma finally said.

"I'm not." Aubrey tapped her steering wheel while they sat at a red light. "But we are leaving Chestnut Hill."

"Intriguing." Emma sat back in the seat, somewhat satisfied with the crumb of information.

"Have I told you my spring resolution?" Aubrey said, suddenly full of anxious energy.

"Your what?" Emma cocked her head. "Is that even a thing?"

"No, but who's to say I can't make it a thing?"

Emma laughed a little. "What is it?"

"To never again use the noise canceling feature on my AirPods while I'm at work."

Aubrey caught the flash of Emma's smile before she turned to look out the window.

"And why is that?"

"Because," Aubrey said, nervously reaching over to place her hand, palm up, on Emma's knee. "When I wear them and look down, I miss all the good stuff."

"And when you look up," Emma said, sliding her hand into Aubrey's, "do you trip over things?"

"Not if I'm riding alongside you."

Emma rolled her head against the headrest until she was staring at Aubrey's profile. "Did you just mix Tori and Ani in order to say something profound to me without really saying it at all?"

"Maybe." Aubrey grinned.

"You know, Aubrey, I feel like that's a compliment." Emma squeezed her hand. "Are you ever going to make a playlist for me?"

Aubrey squeezed back. "What makes you think you haven't already heard one?"

"Wait. Seriously?"

She looked over at Emma and willed herself to memorize her open look of wonder and lo—like. Just like. "Seriously."

A short drive later, Aubrey pulled into a parking space behind the library in Castlegreen, the small town that bordered Chestnut Hill to the south. She and Emma walked up the marble stairs and entered the quiet annex.

Emma started laughing. "Aubrey."

"Yeah?"

"Okay, just because I'm kinda starting to like my literature classes doesn't mean that I, like, *like* books. You get that, right?"

Aubrey placed her hand on the small of Emma's back and guided her up a flight of stairs. "Yes. And I'm not here to make you into a lover of books. But can you trust me on this one?"

"I don't think I have a choice," she stage-whispered as they walked into a large room.

Aubrey led them to a pair of open seats. "Something you've taught me in the short time that we've known each other," she began, "is that I don't always need to know what I'm doing. That it's okay for me to be in a space where I'm figuring things out." She ignored Emma's pointed look. "What's not okay is giving up. Not pursuing the things that make me happy, or things I think could make me happy." She rubbed the back of her neck. "Even when those things aren't exactly what I'd hoped they would be."

"Is now the time where I point out—"

"Nope," Aubrey said with a wide smile. "It is not."

Emma huffed and crossed her arms. "Fine, but you're a hypocrite."

"I know it sounds that way, but I'm really not." Aubrey moved in her seat so she could look Emma straight in the eye. "I'm scared, Emma. About more than just opening myself up to you. And I let my fear hold me back."

Before Emma could respond, a hush came over the crowd (a stretch, as there were probably only forty people in the room). Aubrey smiled before righting herself in her chair and looking toward the front of the room where the most adorably stereotypical of librarians stood behind a microphone.

"Hello, everyone, and thank you for joining us today. We're so pleased here at The Castlegreen Public Library to host this amazing author today. She has recently released her third book, titled *Why Give Up When You Can Give In?*, and is currently touring New England to speak about her own process of giving in. Please welcome Ana Bryant-Miller!"

A taller than average woman approached the librarian and shook her hand. When she turned to the audience, her smile revealed a tiny sparkling diamond in one tooth that caught the sunlight streaming in through the windows and nearly blinded Aubrey.

"Thank you so much, Janet. I'm so grateful that I'm able to be here with you all today." Ana Bryant-Miller clasped her hands together and sent another glimmering smile out into the audience. "Now, let's talk about passion."

"I can honestly say," Emma said as she and Aubrey walked through downtown Castlegreen, "that is not at all what I was expecting." She giggled. "I mean, when she opened up with that comment about passion, I got super worried we were about to sit through some kind of sex lecture in a library conference room with elderly people."

"Well, in that case, I'm extremely glad you were wrong."

"Me too." Emma shook her head, but it was in continued surprise, not borne of a negative emotion. "She was amazing. Everything she said resonated with me. That whole thing about attaching yourself to a dream and watching it dissolve in front of you? Got me right in the heart." She looked at Aubrey with a genuine smile. "Thank you so much for bringing me."

"You're welcome. I can't take full credit, though. Callie sent me the link."

"You...You talk to Callie?" She shook her head again. "That was weird, sorry. I didn't know you were friends."

Aubrey nodded toward the small restaurant they were about to pass. "Are you hungry?"

"Yes. Very."

Once they were seated in a cozy booth and had ordered brunch, Aubrey returned to their conversation.

"Callie and I aren't friends. She's somewhat of a mentor for me." Aubrey lifted one shoulder. "Or is becoming a mentor, I should say."

Emma raised her eyebrows. "Go on."

"I can't yet." Aubrey smiled. "And I'm not being an ass by saying that. I'm…figuring things out. And Callie is helping."

"You know," Emma said, and Aubrey did absolutely know. "It wasn't too long ago that you told me to figure things out, and then made it seem like I should already have all the things figured out."

Aubrey took a moment to spread her napkin over her lap before responding. "Yup. I did. And here's the thing, Emma." She leaned forward, piercing Emma with her stare. "I'm an idiot sometimes. An absolute huge asshole idiot who makes mistakes and says things the wrong way and forgets what it's like to be confused about feelings you've never had before." She inhaled slowly. "And I can be very impatient when I want something and the timing isn't right."

Emma blinked at her, round honey-brown eyes warm and concerned. "Is—are you talking about, um, us? Our timing?"

"Actually, not really." Aubrey picked up a fork and drew circles on the table with its butt end. "I'm beginning to realize our Venn diagram overlapped at exactly the right time. I am, however, impatient." She looked back up at Emma. "Because I really, really like you. In all the ways."

The blush that flurried across Emma's cheeks was both innocent and alluring. "Okay, wow. I thought I'd be super cool if and when you ever said that to me, but I feel like I'm about to melt over here."

"Please don't," Aubrey said with a smile. "I think Liam would murder me if I had to ladle you into a cup in order to drive you home."

"I'm solid, promise." Emma clasped her hands in front of her. Her cheeks were still bright red. "So you really, really like me. But you're scared."

Aubrey fought the urge to shut down the conversation right then and there. Ana Bryant-Miller's voice lingered in her brain, driving home one of her key talking points: If we don't embrace what we fear, we'll never achieve what we want.

"Not but. And," she said, hoping her voice was even. "I like you very much *and* I'm scared. And it's not just because of you—"

"Figuring things out," Emma finished.

"Right. I mean, that does scare me a little. However," Aubrey added before Emma could interject, "what scares me more is myself. Where I am in all of this." She was avoiding and she knew it, but she just could not give Emma the stone-cold truth. Yet. "I'm trying to find my way with life. In general. I don't want to…I don't want to ruin this good thing"—she gestured to the space between them, the air over the slightly sticky table—"while I'm doing all that."

"Okay, feel free to tell me I'm crazy, but…What if we figure things out together?"

It was the simplest of suggestions, and yet it threw Aubrey back into the cushion of the booth. She knew, as she'd belabored enough by then, that their "figuring out" was not the same. But if they were both in limbo, why couldn't they be in limbo together?

Because, Aubrey thought, her splash of happiness sinking to dark depths, Emma could wake up tomorrow and realize she wasn't into women and Aubrey would be left with half of her heart while the other half ran off into the sunset with Emma.

She looked up. Emma was waiting for her response, dark-red hair tucked behind her ears, hopeful expression on her beautiful face.

"I think," Aubrey said slowly, "we kind of already are?"

Emma took that in. After a moment, she nodded, but her blush had faded. Their food arrived and, saved by hunger, Aubrey settled in to eat, hoping they could avoid *that* conversation for the rest of the day.

"So you're telling me," Aubrey said as she began the drive back to Chestnut Hill, "that you never picked up a field hockey stick after your injury. Never."

"Never," Emma repeated. "I couldn't. I get kind of paralyzed even just thinking about it."

"And despite having been involved in a sport since you were five, you didn't even attempt to play a different sport after you healed?"

"I know," Emma said, shaking her head. "Crazy, right? But I couldn't do it. It's like that author said. When you give up on something, you have to mourn it. Believe me, I mourned the shit out of the death of my field hockey dream."

Aubrey was quiet for a moment. She hadn't mourned the death of her own field hockey dream, mostly because it hadn't been abruptly or painfully taken from her. She'd chosen to walk away from it.

"And then," Emma said, "my parents were like, you have to do something, some kind of extracurricular. Do you know what I chose?"

"No idea."

"The newspaper."

Aubrey laughed out loud. "You did not."

"I did. I figured," Emma said, twirling the ends of her hair, "it was as far as I could get from the whole athlete thing. I was wrong."

A memory flashed in Aubrey's mind, and she stole a quick look at Emma. "Wait a minute. You came to one of my games."

"You remember that?" Wonder sparkled in Emma's voice. "I actually went to a few."

"I remember seeing you at one." And she did, though the image was hazy. "You were interviewing players after the game."

"Yeah. Because the editor of the school newspaper knew I'd played field hockey, so they decided to have me write the sports column."

"So," Aubrey said through laughter, "let me get this straight. You hate writing, but you voluntarily wrote for the school paper. And you had major sports trauma and they made you the sports columnist. And you didn't ask for a different assignment?"

"I was kinda into torturing myself in those days."

"Apparently."

They were quiet for a while as the houses slipped past them. After brunch, they'd walked more of Castlegreen, finally deciding to head home when the temperature started to rapidly drop.

"Thank you again for taking me to listen to that author," Emma said quietly. "I feel like she kindly kicked me in the ass."

"I feel the same way."

"Do you think we'll figure it out, Aubrey?"

Aubrey nodded. "Yeah, Emma. I do."

"Since you're older and wiser, I'll trust you." Emma reached over and tucked Aubrey's hair behind her ear. The intimate action, one that seemed second nature to Emma, caused Aubrey's heart to swell. "Thank you for spending the day with me."

Aubrey put the car in park and turned to Emma. "Thank you for coming with me, even when I didn't tell you what I had planned."

"All in all, it was a pretty nice day."

"Right back where we started, I see." Aubrey made a mental note to include that Tori Amos song on her next Emma-inspired playlist.

"Not quite," Emma said softly. After the briefest of hesitations, she leaned over the center console and pressed her lips against Aubrey's.

A relief Aubrey had been waiting for exploded in her chest and she cupped Emma's face in her hands as she intensified the kiss. Their lips brushed together, tongues touching and retreating. Aubrey gently bit Emma's lower lip and smiled into the kiss when Emma practically climbed over the console to get closer.

"That," Emma said minutes later, her face millimeters from Aubrey's, "is so good."

"You finally kissed me," Aubrey whispered.

"Finally." Emma pressed her forehead against Aubrey's. "If you only knew how many times I've kissed you while I'm making lattes or sitting in class. So, so many times, Aubrey."

"You can do it just as many times in real life, you know."

Emma drew back a few inches. "You're sure?"

Aubrey nodded. She brushed her thumb over Emma's bottom lip. "We'll figure it out."

"Together?"

"Yes."

Emma's face glowed with happiness as she leaned in and kissed her again. Too soon, she pulled away with a sigh.

"I have an essay to write," she mumbled.

"It's okay. We've got time."

"Speaking of time," Emma said, sitting back and adjusting her blazer. "Do you have any tomorrow to go over this essay with me? I only have a paragraph written but I want to have it mostly done before I go to bed tonight."

"I work tomorrow. Do you have dinner with your family?"

"Yeah." Emma's shoulders slumped. "And it's due Monday."

"Do you want to come over after your family dinner?"

Emma furrowed her brow. "Not the library?"

Aubrey tried to suppress her smile, not wanting Emma to see how cute her innocence was. "Do you really want to sit in the library with me on a Sunday night?"

"That's where we always go…" After a moment, it hit her. "Oh. Okay. Yeah. Your place would be way better."

Aubrey saw the nerves flickering like fireflies in Emma's eyes. "To work on your essay," she clarified, but did so with a teasing smile.

"The essay." Emma nodded. "Of course."

"You know, to figure out if it…works."

"Okay, stop." Emma laughed. "I'm going inside now. Thank you again for today."

"You're very welcome." Aubrey leaned over and delivered a gentle kiss. "Now go write."

Emma saluted before leaving the car and making her way to the house. At the door, she turned to wave, and Aubrey waved back, waiting till the door was shut with Emma behind it before she pulled away and drove home.

When she pushed open the door to her apartment, her phone vibrated in her pocket. She pulled it out and squinted at the screen in the darkness.

I've got no illusions about you. I never did.

"Well played, Emma. Well played." She smiled as she took off her jacket, waiting no more than two minutes before replying with the line she'd kept tucked in her memory since the moment Emma had kissed her.

You (we) could taste heaven perfectly.

CHAPTER TWENTY-SEVEN

Yesterday's balmy weather had been a fool's ruse. As Emma walked up the pathway leading to the Victorian where both Sadie and Aubrey lived, she blew on her hands, regretting having forgotten her gloves. The temperature had plummeted overnight, and the clouds whispered a promise of more snow to come.

Emma, equal parts giddy and nervous about being alone with Aubrey in her apartment, squelched a giggle that bubbled in her throat. The thought of being snowed in with her was not terrible. No, not terrible at all.

A tiny bit terrifying at this juncture, but Emma was trying to keep her fear in check and focus more on what she wanted.

And what she wanted was right there looking back at her from the front door.

"Hey," Aubrey called. "Hurry up, it's freezing."

Emma hitched her backpack up as she closed the distance between them. "I forgot how endless winter is up here."

"Philly winters aren't as bad?" Aubrey shut the door behind Emma and gestured for her to follow her up the wide staircase.

"Oh, they're bad, just in a different way." Emma skimmed her frozen fingertips over the railing of the grand staircase. "This is beautiful."

"Yeah, Sadie showed me pictures of what the house was like before it was broken up into apartments. Very grand and all that."

Emma smiled as they ascended twists and turns, finally stopping before a closed door. Aubrey, once again sporting an expression that made Emma want to wrap her in her arms and usher away all her anxieties, kicked the door open and held out her arm.

"Welcome to my extremely humble abode."

As Emma entered Aubrey's space, she took a moment to appreciate Aubrey bringing her into said space. She had a feeling not many people crossed this boundary.

The apartment was small but inviting, aglow with light from several floor lamps. Emma bit back a smile. She knew that most people from their past would balk at this being the place where Aubrey Glass lived. There was absolutely nothing fancy about it. Nothing glamorous, nothing expensive. It was lived-in and comfortable. The furniture looked like it had been through several owners. Definitely not the vibe Aubrey had cultivated in high school—other than her beloved car, Emma remembered.

"I like it," Emma said, turning to face Aubrey. "It feels very you."

"Well, I spend a lot of time here, so…" Aubrey shrugged. She glanced at her watch. "We should probably check out your essay. We both have an early shift tomorrow."

Emma nodded as her heart drifted down. She had no desire to look at anything other than Aubrey, but she was right. There was an essay that needed her helping hand.

"Um." Aubrey was standing by a door that was ajar. "I thought we could work at my desk."

"Okay." Emma surreptitiously looked to her left. Yes, there was a small but very usable dining table with two chairs right there between the kitchen and living space. "Where's your desk?"

Aubrey nudged open the door. "In here."

Emma didn't see a desk. She saw a bed. Her pulse went into double time and she felt a heat rise over her neck and into her cheeks.

"Okay," she said simply, and walked into Aubrey's bedroom.

She was slightly disappointed to realize there was, in fact, a large desk there. And she'd cleared space for Emma's laptop.

"Oh," Emma said, holding out a foil-wrapped package. "I brought you this."

Aubrey wiggled her eyebrows. "Is it an Emma Gallagher special?"

"Do you really think I'd bring you something that wasn't?"

"Not for a second." Aubrey peeled back a corner of the foil and inhaled deeply. "Oh, God. What is this?"

"A cinnamon knot with coffee icing."

Aubrey held the package to her chest. "Thank you. This will make for a perfect breakfast." She stood and walked toward the kitchen.

With a satisfied smile, Emma set up her laptop on the desk and sat down in front of it. Aubrey returned from the kitchen and joined her, perching on the edge of her bed that was conveniently close to the desk, and within moments, it was as though they were back in the library. Except, of course, one of them was sitting on a queen-sized bed that was practically begging for Emma's company.

"I like what you did here," Aubrey said, pointing to the closing paragraph. "You do a really nice job of tying everything together but also leaving the reader wanting more."

"Is that okay to do?"

"Oh, definitely. You hit every good point about the qualities of *The Bluest Eye* that could make people want to ban it. Which is all stupid and ignorant, but you handled it with grace." Aubrey winked at her. "And you countered the points thoughtfully along with just enough research to back them up. So by the time I get to your conclusion, I know what you want me to think—but I also want to learn more."

Emma beamed. "You make it sound like I'm a good writer or something."

"Or something."

Emma glared at Aubrey, who laughed.

"In all seriousness, Emma." Aubrey waited till Emma looked at her before she continued, "You're a way better writer than you want to think you are."

"Thank you."

"You're welcome." Aubrey cleared her throat. "I don't think there's anything else we can do for your essay. I think Professor Frances will be thrilled with it."

Emma nodded as she closed her laptop. "I hope so. This one was a lot of work."

Once her laptop was secure in her backpack, Emma slowly spun in the desk chair so she was facing Aubrey. Inches separated their knees while a larger distance swayed between their mouths. Emma was just about to practice being bold and close that distance when Aubrey jumped up from the bed.

"It's snowing," she said, moving toward the window.

"Shocking," Emma mumbled. But she got up and joined Aubrey at the window anyway.

"Hang on." Aubrey walked toward the door to her bedroom and hit the light switch, throwing the room into a glowing darkness.

Emma looked up at the slanted ceiling. She hadn't noticed the strings of pale-yellow fairy lights until then. She smiled faintly, trying to connect what she knew of Aubrey with someone who liked fairy lights.

"Look that way," Aubrey said quietly, pointing into the distance. "Can you see the clock tower?"

Emma nodded. The snow was coming down quickly, smearing the brightness of Pennbrook's clock tower. Lights lined the streets and the treetops swayed beneath the bulk of new snow. The overall image was magical.

"When I moved back," Aubrey said, "I spent a lot of time looking out this window. I even moved my bed up against it for a while. I couldn't believe how beautiful this town is." She pressed one hand against the glass of the window. "Maybe leaving let me see it all through a different perspective. It's like sometimes you need a little distance and a little forgetting to be able to see something for how beautiful it truly is."

Emma's heart skipped. She reached over and took Aubrey's free hand in hers.

"Remember how I told you we have to return to the things that break us? Because they're part of what puts us back together?"

"Yes," Emma said slowly. "And I still don't love that theory."

Aubrey squeezed her hand. "I think maybe I was wrong about that." Aubrey moved them away from the window and pulled Emma with her to the bed. Aubrey flopped back, legs dangling off the side, eyes trained on the ceiling. Emma sat down, then laid down next to her.

The snowy silence from outside the window carried into the bedroom. Emma counted the seconds till she hit fifty-three, then tried to relax into the quiet calm. She stroked her fingers over the incredible softness of Aubrey's comforter. She blinked up at the fairy lights. She measured her breaths by length of inhale and exhale.

Emma wasn't someone who loved the quiet. Being alone with her thoughts wasn't something she craved. Her thoughts, much like her attempted life plan, were linear until they derailed due to an unforeseen—and unpredictable—break in the rails, like a painfully cute woman lying silently next to her on a bed that felt like a giant pillow.

"I need to tell you about—" Aubrey broke off and blew out a loud breath. "Okay. Emma."

"You can tell me anything." She was mostly just relieved to no longer be in silence; Emma would listen to whatever Aubrey might have to tell her in that moment.

More silence. Then, "Remember when you made that comment about our first kiss and how it didn't count because I was high?"

Emma cringed. All too well. "Yeah, but, Aubrey—"

"Wait. I need to say this." She linked their pinkies together. "First of all, I wasn't high. Was I when you first got to the club? Yeah. But I was pretty sober by the time we walked out of the bar."

"Okay—"

"Emma." Aubrey laughed a little. "I know you have tons of things to say, but if you want us to have a real chance at something, you have to let me talk right now. Okay?"

A real chance. Emma squeezed Aubrey's finger as a silent agreement.

"When I was in college, I had a relationship with one of my coaches."

Emma's stomach dropped, but she didn't say a word.

"It wasn't a fling. It went on for years. And yeah, I know it was wrong in so many ways. But, uh, she's also the reason I started smoking pot. And, she used to kiss me when she was high and blame it on the weed. So when you said that to me, it hit me hard." Aubrey paused. "When I kissed you in the library, I was completely sober. Just so you know."

Emma nodded, hoping Aubrey could see her in her peripheral vision.

"That relationship…It wasn't normal. She was so much older than I was and the whole thing was a big secret. I gave up"—Aubrey's voice cracked, and she cleared her throat to mask it—"a lot. A lot of my dreams. I have a lot of regrets from that time of my life, shit that still haunts me today. But that's a different conversation." She brought her free hand behind the back of her head. "My point is, Emma, I don't know how to do normal. Everything with my ex was hidden, or full of lies. And yeah, I dated women after that, but it…Nothing felt right. Everyone wanted something from me." She laughed darkly. "I've felt that way since high school. No one really wants me—they just want something from me. And the worst part was whatever I gave wasn't good enough, or it wasn't what they thought they'd get from me. Because of who they built me up to be in their heads."

"I'm not like them, Aubrey," Emma said softly. "I want you as is."

"Do you, though?" Aubrey let go of Emma's pinkie and propped herself up on her elbow, looking down at her. "Are you sure I'm not just a way for you to figure yourself out?"

"What do I need to do to prove to you that's not what this is?"

Aubrey gazed at her. In the glow of the lights from above, Aubrey's eyes hummed with a darkness that lured Emma closer.

"You don't need to prove anything to me," Aubrey said, her voice silken and soft as a caress. "And I don't ever want you to feel like you do."

"So you'll trust me?" Emma's stomach had filled with a hive of bees and she was pretty certain she was going to self-combust if Aubrey didn't kiss her soon. However, she knew this moment was bigger than the both of them, and any kissing that might happen needed to wait. "I won't break you," she added.

The corner of Aubrey's mouth lifted. "You can't promise that."

"We can't promise anything." Emma reached up and tucked Aubrey's hair behind her ear. "All we can do is try."

The other corner of her mouth hiked up. "You wanna try with me?"

"I swear to God, Aubrey, if you don't kiss me—"

The argument vanished the instant Aubrey dropped her lips to Emma's. Emma gasped, not from surprise but from the intensity of the contact. Each time she and Aubrey kissed, it felt bigger, better, and so, so much more powerful.

This was the kind of kissing that made people want to lose themselves for hours, for days. Emma reached up and slid her hand around the back of Aubrey's neck, holding her in place. The softness of Aubrey's lips felt impossible. She moved them with skill and exploration, capturing Emma's top lip then her bottom lip, then separating them with the tip of her tongue.

Emma tugged Aubrey closer. A noise—surprise mixed with passion—escaped her mouth as Aubrey settled her body on top of Emma's. Every nerve ending sped up into overdrive. Emma gripped Aubrey's hips. She wasn't sure if she was still breathing, but she quite honestly didn't care.

"Wait. Hang on." Aubrey pulled away. "I didn't invite you here so we could—do this," she said between breaths. "I don't want you to think I'm taking advantage—"

"Shut up," Emma said. Her body was thrumming with a need she'd never felt before. "And get it through your fucking head that I want you. All of you."

Grinning, Aubrey leaned in and reignited their kiss. Idly, Emma wondered if the bed would catch on fire from the sparks shooting from their connected mouths. She kissed Aubrey with every pent-up emotion, every set-aside desire she'd been collecting since the moment Aubrey had kissed her outside of Lotus. Finally, Emma had somewhere to go with them. Finally, her brain was moving in sync with her body.

Aubrey's fingers brushed the bottom of Emma's sweater, pausing when they connected with her skin. "Is this okay?" Aubrey whispered, tracing slow circles with her thumb.

"So okay," Emma managed to get out. "I'm yours."

Aubrey's hand stilled. Emma froze, flooding with worry that she'd lunged too far, too fast into this brand-new territory. She squeezed her eyes shut. So this was her true moment of Gay Panic. Maybe the snow would cause the roof to cave in and she could die peacefully, if coldly, right—

"Those are big words," Aubrey finally said.

"Quite aware of that."

"Emma." Her voice was part laughter, part sensuality. "Open your eyes."

She opened one, then the other. Aubrey was right there, smiling.

"You are nothing like my past, and I'm so thankful for that," she said softly. "You make me feel, Emma. I am so, so into you. I wasn't kidding when I told you I'm terrified."

Emma pulled Aubrey's hand up her torso and held it over her heart. "We'll figure it out. Together."

"You know," Aubrey said, eyes never leaving Emma's. "I'm pretty sure, considering the circumstances, I should be the one reassuring you."

Before Emma could argue, Aubrey's mouth was back on hers. Her hand slid back down Emma's torso, skirting the places Emma wanted it to land. But the moment Aubrey touched the sensitive skin below Emma's belly button, Emma realized *that* was exactly where she wanted her hand to land.

Aubrey kissed her way across Emma's cheek and jaw, nestling her lips below her ear. As her mouth moved, so, too, did her hand. Emma held her breath as Aubrey's hand slid over her skin, fingers stretching and caressing. She felt the brief hesitation when Aubrey's hand collided with her bra, and, not trusting words, Emma arched her back, hoping that would send the message.

The mouth-skin contact stopped as Aubrey sat up. Not taking her eyes away from Emma's, she reached down and lifted Emma's sweater over her head. The cold air of the room came as a shock, but not an unpleasant one. Between that and every movement of Aubrey's lips and hands, Emma's nipples were straining against her bra.

"You're sure about this?" Aubrey said quietly. She was still sitting up and her hand was stroking over Emma's ribs.

Emma sat up. Aubrey's hand dropped into her lap as Emma grabbed her shoulders and kissed her with every built-up flicker of intensity she had inside of her.

"Yes," Emma said when she pulled away. "I have never been more sure of anything."

Smiling, Aubrey reached around Emma's back and unsnapped her bra. Emma closed her eyes, languishing in the feeling of the satin straps gliding down her bare arms. Aubrey laid her back down on the bed. It wasn't until she lowered herself next to Emma and began a lazy trek upstream from Emma's stomach that something clicked.

"Wait."

Aubrey's hand stopped.

Emma rested her hand on top of Aubrey's. "Are *you* sure about this?"

"Very," Aubrey said, her voice deeper and hoarse with desire.

Holding that truth tightly in her heart, Emma moved Aubrey's hand back up her chest, placing it at the swell of her breast. "Then please, Aubrey, touch me."

And so she did. Emma's body tremored with heightened sensation every time Aubrey grazed her fingers over a previously untouched part of her skin. She cupped Emma's breasts and smoothed her thumbs over her nipples. When Aubrey broke their kiss, Emma groaned, then inhaled sharply as her mouth closed over a nipple. She writhed below Aubrey's mouth as she sucked and gently bit, her hand teasing Emma's other nipple.

Aubrey crashed her mouth back against Emma's. Her fingers skated down Emma's naked torso, gliding directly to their next destination. Emma, already riding an incredible high of being touched with so much desire, gasped when Aubrey unbuttoned her jeans.

"Yes," she said, certain another question of consent was coming her way.

Aubrey laughed softly, moving to pull off Emma's jeans. "Thank you."

Goose bumps prickled on her bare legs. Her hand drifted to her hip and she smiled, almost laughing, realizing that Aubrey had taken her underwear along with her jeans.

A nudge of fear, something more like intimidation, rocked in Emma's gut. She shut her eyes, willing the feeling away. Yes, Aubrey had experience, and no, she didn't. But she was here. With Aubrey. Who really, really seemed to want her right where she was, doing exactly what they were doing.

"You're beautiful, Emma," Aubrey whispered as she settled on top of Emma once again. Her knee nudged Emma's thighs apart and, feeling skin against her most sensitive parts, Emma bucked against her. Emma opened her eyes, split between warring emotions, and felt a trickle of relief to see Aubrey had only removed her jeans.

Emma pushed against Aubrey's thigh and was rewarded with a groan. She rocked several times, yearning for more friction, before rocking into air. Not a moment later, Aubrey's fingers moved across her upper thigh and dipped down, practiced and searching.

The moment Aubrey's mouth returned to her nipple, right as her fingers began circling Emma's clit, Emma was certain she was going to rip apart at the seams. She gripped the comforter with both hands, digging her heels into the bed. Seconds from what she thought would be a shattering release, Emma felt Aubrey's fingers slip down and push deep inside. Her gasp echoed around the room, followed shortly by cries she simply could not keep inside.

Too soon, her body clenched then burst. Emma sucked in breaths, trying to steady herself against the pleasure. Aubrey, likely sensing that attempt at control, moved down Emma's body and pressed her mouth between her thighs.

"Oh, fuck," Emma said. There would be no control tonight, she realized.

Aubrey's mouth, enticingly skillful at kissing, took it to a new level as she deftly moved her tongue over Emma's wetness. Emma's fingers strained from their hold on the comforter. She felt her legs begin to shake, though they were lying flat on the bed. In a moment, a breath, a rushing sensation coursed through her. Her mouth dropped open and she stilled, then bucked against Aubrey's mouth. The wave crashed over and over, and Emma, soundless, rode it till she dropped limply onto the bed.

She brought one hand to her mouth as she felt Aubrey lie down next to her. With her other hand, she grabbed Aubrey and pulled her close.

"You okay?"

Emma could only nod. Words were a long way away.

Aubrey draped her leg over Emma's. Slowly, as Emma dropped back into awareness, she became aware of the skin-to-skin contact. Thoughts and worries flurried through her mind, cleanly disrupting her postorgasmic—nay, her post-first-time-with-a-*woman*—bliss.

It was true: Aubrey had just shown her, rather well at that, what to do. But Emma knew this wasn't Aubrey's first time (obviously… after that…holy shit). And with that came expectations.

"We've got time," Aubrey said into Emma's hair.

She swallowed. "Um. Were you reading my mind?"

"No. But remember, I've been right where you are."

Not the greatest thing to think about after all *that*, but Emma appreciated it. She wasn't satisfied, though. Through all the shivering knots of nervousness and trepidation, she wanted to touch Aubrey. She wanted to make Aubrey feel something.

"Could you..." Emma twisted so she was looking directly at Aubrey. "I want to touch you."

"It's okay. You don't have to." Aubrey smiled and Emma could tell it was genuine, not meant to placate or hide something she was afraid to say. "We have time."

"I know." Emma reached over and took Aubrey's hand. She moved both of their hands to Aubrey's abs (of course she had incredible abs). "But for tonight, would you show me?"

The fire in Aubrey's eyes flickered with a wild heat. She gripped Emma's hand as she shimmied out of her underwear and laid flat on the bed.

"Actually," Aubrey said, moving so that she was kneeling over Emma's naked body, straddling her legs. "I like this."

Despite having entertained a wide array of fantasies, Emma was ill prepared for the sight of Aubrey hovering over her like that. She felt her body respond with urgency and wondered if Aubrey wouldn't mind repeating some of what she'd already done.

Those thoughts disappeared the moment Aubrey brought Emma's hand to the space between her thighs. There, arousal immediately coated Emma's fingers. Aubrey grunted and her hips dipped down, silently begging for more touch. She guided Emma's hand right to where she wanted it. They moved in sync, Emma quickly picking up the rhythm. Aubrey soon dropped her own hand down to steady herself.

"Quick learner," Aubrey mumbled, rocking against Emma's hand.

"Good teacher."

Aubrey cried out then grinned. "Yes. Just like that, Emma."

The closer Aubrey got, the less Emma felt like a novice. There was a freedom with Aubrey, a feeling that Emma could safely explore and peel apart. As Aubrey's hips picked up speed, Emma knew with certainty that this—the explosions of their combined desires—would only get better with time.

"God, Emma, yes." Aubrey gritted her teeth as she came. "Fuck. Shit. Okay. Wow."

Emma, bolstered by having brought *that* out of Aubrey, grinned as she pulled Aubrey's body flush against hers. "We're not done, are we?"

Aubrey laughed, then kissed Emma long and hard. "That depends. You still wanna be mine?"

"Yes," Emma whispered. "So much so."

"Then," Aubrey said, "we are far from done."

CHAPTER TWENTY-EIGHT

In the eleven days that had passed since Emma first spent the night with Aubrey, not twelve hours had gone by without them falling into bed together. The combination of a new relationship and a (for one of them) new sexuality to explore had brought everything else in their lives to a halt—except for the necessities, like working, going to class, and occasionally remembering to eat.

Aubrey was constantly amazed by Emma's thoughtfulness, by her curiosity and steadiness. She left no room for questions, no space for Aubrey to tuck into and worry. Even when she was deep in an awkward spell, Emma was the most up-front woman Aubrey had ever been involved with. While Aubrey still felt the stringy aftermath of her former busted love life, she was getting used to feeling safe with someone. That alone should have caused an increase of fear, and maybe would have with someone else. But Emma...Emma had a way with Aubrey that made everything feel easy.

It had been difficult to find time to write lately, what with fireworks constantly sparking between her and Emma, but she'd managed to carve some out before she found herself walking into the English department at Pennbrook for a much anticipated meeting.

"Thanks for meeting with me," Aubrey said, settling into a chair in Callie's office. "Especially since I'm not a student."

Callie held up one finger. "Not *yet*. Have you thought more about enrolling in the master's program?"

Aubrey's left leg started bouncing. She crossed her right ankle over her left knee to get it to stop. "Kind of."

"Kind of?" Callie smiled as she sat down next to Aubrey. "What's holding you back?"

"It's a big commitment," Aubrey said. "I guess I'm not sure if I'm ready to take that on. I want to," she added. "But I need to figure out if now is the right time."

"That's fair. I was talking about you with Kate, and she suggested you sit in on one of her graduate classes." Callie reached over to her desk and picked up a Post-it, the biggest one Aubrey had ever seen. "Here's her spring and summer schedule. And her email. She wanted to stop in and talk with you today, but she got roped into a meeting."

Aubrey took the Post-it and studied it. She wasn't reading the words so much as she was taking a moment to acknowledge how grateful she was to have these connections. Without Sadie, she wouldn't have reached out to Callie. And had she not reached out to Callie, she wouldn't be sitting there with a coveted invitation to observe one of Pennbrook's best professors teach a graduate course.

She was a long way from where she'd been the day she moved back to Chestnut Hill, bruised heart in her hand, hopelessness raging through her mind.

"This is awesome," Aubrey said. "Thank you."

"No problem. So"—Callie handed her a stapled packet of papers—"let's talk about this."

Aubrey gazed at the paper, tracing her finger over the typed words. *Her* words. The words she'd crafted and brought to life through anguish and elation alike. They were right there, staring up at her.

"Sorry." She laughed and shook her head, snapping back to the present. "I've never looked at something I've written if it hasn't been on a computer screen." Aubrey squinted. "Did that make sense?"

"It did, and you'll need to get used to that."

Aubrey's heart preemptively leapt, hoping she was understanding Callie's implication. "You think so?"

Callie nodded and tapped her pen against the packet. "We've got a little work to do, but once that's done, I want you to submit this to *Sapphisms.*"

Another heart-leap. "You're serious? You think they'll take it?"

Callie cracked a grin. "I mean, I know I'm biased because I have pull there. But there's not a doubt in my mind that the editor in chief will love your work." She tapped her pen again. "Are you ready?"

Surely she meant the editing and revisions they were about to go over. But Aubrey was somewhere else, toeing the precipice of a life she'd rarely let herself imagine she could enter.

"Very ready," she said.

And for the first time, she was.

Aubrey's long legs surpassed her usual speed as she trekked from Pennbrook's campus, down Finch Avenue, until she hit the corner of Finch and Main. She stood outside, looking up at the store that had held her so safely for the past three years. Aubrey couldn't help but wonder what her life would look like in that moment if she hadn't walked into Cornerstone looking for a job after she'd practically run away from her college graduation. Maybe she'd have a "real" job that she hated. Maybe she would have already gone back for her master's. She shuddered at that thought, knowing she would have had to move back in with her mother if she'd chosen that path.

It didn't matter what could have been. Not anymore. Aubrey had spent far too long in that headspace, rolling through endless possibilities until she created a maelstrom of panic and despair that she'd essentially existed in for several years. It felt good, if weird, to be breaking free from the whirlpool of her own making.

Aubrey stepped back on the sidewalk, trying to get a better glimpse at the café. She smiled when Emma came into view. She appeared to be in an animated argument with Genesis, who was repeatedly thumping her fist on the counter. Just seeing Emma, even from this distance with windows and tables and chairs and a bulky espresso machine between them, brought light into Aubrey's heart. It was a feeling she hoped would never dim, a feeling she would never take for granted.

A gentle breeze ruffled Aubrey's hair as she walked toward Cornerstone's main entrance. If she had to designate a place, this would be it: home. She walked into the store, the familiar sounds and scents covering her like a knitted blanket. Aubrey paused just inside the entryway. She really did love this store, and while she was excited about what was shifting in her life, she was sad that her time at Cornerstone would be affected by it. She wasn't leaving the store—she wasn't sure she'd ever be able to fully do that, anyway—but changes were coming, and fast.

"Hi, you."

Aubrey spun to face Emma, who had snuck through the magazine section.

"I saw you sneak in. I thought you were off today?"

They'd agreed to avoid affection while at work, but Aubrey couldn't resist reaching over and squeezing Emma's hand. She pulled it back quickly, though, wrinkling her nose.

"Do I want to know why your hand feels like you've been holding a bunch of half-eaten lollipops?"

Emma groaned. "No. You really don't."

"Then I won't ask. But I will ask that you wash them before you put this on." Aubrey handed her a backpack.

Confused, Emma stared at it. "What is this? What's happening?"

"Your shift is over, right?" Emma nodded. "Then please go wash your hands and change." Aubrey pointed to the backpack, which Emma was still holding as though it might contain a bomb. "Everything you'll need is in there."

When Emma hesitated, Aubrey took her by the shoulders and spun her around, facing her in the direction of the back of the store. "I'll be waiting for you at the Hub. Now go."

"How about a please?" Emma murmured over her shoulder.

Aubrey leaned in and lifted Emma's hair from her ear. "Please," she whispered, letting her lips brush Emma's earlobe.

The shiver that zipped through Emma's entire body vibrated into Aubrey's hands. She gave Emma a gentle push and watched her scurry to the bathroom.

"I knew it," Sadie said triumphantly as Aubrey approached the Hub. Her dark-green eyes, not far from Aubrey's own eye color, sparkled with mischief and knowing.

"You know nothing," Aubrey said happily. "There's nothing to know."

Sadie came around the Hub and threw her arm around Aubrey's shoulders. "Do you know how happy it makes me to see you happy?"

Aubrey wriggled out of her grasp. "I'm sure you and Penelope will be thrilled to share details with each other when you have dinner tonight."

"Oh, Aubrey." Sadie clasped her hands in front of her chest. "We're going to that new vegan restaurant in Castlegreen. I am *so* excited."

"You're not even vegan," Aubrey said, perplexed. "And neither is Pen."

"No, but we're *adventurous*." Sadie grinned, bouncing on her heels.

Aubrey rolled her eyes, but she'd come to terms with the friendship Pen and Sadie had formed. She wasn't entirely convinced there wasn't something else potentially brewing between them but tried her hardest not to think about that, especially after Pen had nonchalantly said a week ago, the morning after she and Sadie had dined at a trendy steakhouse, "You know, I never took the time to explore my sexuality."

Emma arrived at the Hub just in time to jar Aubrey out of that memory. She looked up and grinned. There was something incredibly satisfying about seeing Emma in her clothing, especially sweatpants and a hoodie.

"Are you trying to make me into Franklin Prescott's new mascot?" Emma asked, gesturing toward her high school branded outfit.

"Maybe. Ready to go?"

"Honestly?" Emma folded her arms over her chest, rumpling the image of the nighthawk that was screen printed in gold on the navy-blue hoodie. "I don't know what you're up to and it's making me nervous."

Aubrey had expected this. She just hadn't thought the nerves would come into play until they reached their destination. Eschewing their little antiaffection pact, Aubrey reached out and took Emma's hand. She watched the nervousness wash from Emma's features.

"Now are you ready?"

Emma nodded. "As I'll ever be."

"You two," Sadie said dreamily.

Aubrey tugged Emma away from the Hub, waving to Sadie as they made their way to the front of the store.

Once they were in Aubrey's car, which she'd parked at Cornerstone before her meeting with Callie, Aubrey turned to Emma and kissed her.

"I just have to stop at my place and change," Aubrey said, putting the car in drive.

"But you made me change here? That doesn't make any sense."

Aubrey side-eyed her. "And if we'd both gone to my place to change…"

Emma giggled. "Okay. So we wouldn't have left your apartment. What's so wrong with that?"

"Later. And," she said as the Victorian came into view, "you're staying here while I run inside."

"Aubrey," Emma said stubbornly. "I can control myself."

"Maybe I can't." She kissed Emma again before darting from the car.

Ten minutes later, they were sitting in the parking lot at Franklin Prescott High School. Aubrey knew this was where her plan would either flourish or fall apart.

"Why are we here?" Emma asked dully.

"Come on," Aubrey said, getting out of the car. Emma followed, though she did so petulantly. "Follow me."

Aubrey grabbed her equipment bag from the trunk and avoided the glower in Emma's eyes as they walked across the parking lot, making their way to the fields.

"I thought," Emma said, her voice dark, "we agreed not to go back to the things that broke us."

They were standing at the edge of the field used for field hockey. Considering it was mid-March, not field hockey season, and still quite wintry, the field was a hot mess. Swampy, even, but a cold swamp.

Aubrey felt her creative little plan fizzle. She'd wanted to create a special moment because without Emma in her life, she didn't think she'd even have this news to share. Maybe bringing her to the scene of her injury wasn't Aubrey's best idea, but…

"We did," Aubrey said, moving to stand in front of Emma. "But I don't think this broke you."

Emma reeled back, surprise and pain etched in her features. "How can you say that? You—you were there. You saw it happen."

She placed both hands on Emma's shoulders. "It was a dream, Emma. Not the injury," she added quickly. "Field hockey. For both of us. And in different ways, both of our dreams got crushed." She took a breath and steadied her anxious emotions. "I'm not letting that hold me back anymore, and I hope you'll be able to move into this next phase of my dream with me."

Emma shook her head, but she looked more confused than angry. "I don't—Aubrey, what are you talking about?"

"Maybe," Aubrey went on, "you'll even find a way to be a part of that dream again."

"I really have no idea what you're talking about."

Aubrey nodded. She took her hands from Emma's shoulders and, with one hand holding the hem of her T-shirt, pulled her sweatshirt up over her chest. She waited for Emma to read the front of her shirt.

"Okay," Emma said uncertainly. "So you kept your high school field hockey T-shirt."

"I did, but this one is new." Aubrey turned around and hiked her sweatshirt up to her neck.

"Coach?" Emma said, reading the back. "Wait. What?"

Aubrey turned back around, unable to hide her excited grin. "You're looking at Franklin Prescott's new assistant field hockey coach."

A range of emotions flashed in Emma's eyes. Aubrey waited her out, knowing this was still sensitive territory, but she hoped their connection was strong enough for—

"Aubrey," Emma breathed, a smile finally breaking over her lips. "Are you serious?"

"Completely."

Emma threw herself into Aubrey's arms. "I'm so proud of you. This is amazing."

Aubrey released her and put two fingers under Emma's chin, angling her face in a way she often did before kissing her. "I know field hockey is a sore subject for you, but if we're doing this together, I want you in every part of my life." She gestured to the field behind her. "And this is one of the most important parts of my life."

Emma wrapped her hand around Aubrey's. "You know, it's weird," she began. "When I started at Cornerstone, I was worried being around you would bring up all my bad field hockey memories. You know, from the extremely short season I played." Emma grinned. "But, I don't know, the opposite kind of happened. Like, I can be around you and think about playing and not feel like the world is ending."

"So you'll come to my games?"

Emma pulled Aubrey's face down and kissed her. "Every single one of 'em."

"Good." Aubrey bent down and unzipped her equipment bag. She stood up, holding two sticks. "Now for phase two."

"Nope." Emma shook her head. "*That's* not happening."

Nodding, Aubrey took Emma's hand and unclenched her fist, working the grip into her hand. "I think it is."

"Aubrey," Emma said, her voice firm but playful. "You can't make me play."

"Oh, I know." She grabbed a ball and walked away, dropping it and tapping it with her stick. "But I know you'll get bored watching me play, so come over here whenever you're ready."

Aubrey went through her usual solo "practice," whacking the ball down the field, chasing after it, driving it into the goal. Every so often she'd glance over at Emma, who, as the minutes ticked by, was looking more and more like she was going to explode if she didn't step onto the field and take a crack at a ball. Her eyes tracked every move Aubrey made, her lips moving as though predicting moves or creating a game scenario.

It took less than five minutes before she felt Emma come close, her stick moving in and whisking the ball away. She was off and running down the field, calling over her shoulder, "Your defense sucks!"

Aubrey stopped running and watched Emma advance toward the goal. She dodged and darted, a bit of caution showing in her movements, but plenty of determination coming through. Emma was lacking some of the grace and refined skill that she'd had as a confident freshman on the varsity team, but Aubrey could clearly see the innate talent coming through. She leaned on her stick. Not for the first time, Aubrey wondered what would have happened if Emma hadn't gotten injured, if they'd been teammates for longer than a couple of months.

"Get your head in the game, Glass," Emma called as she began her jog back to the center of the field where Aubrey had stopped. "There's no daydreaming in hockey."

Aubrey grabbed the bottom of Emma's sweatshirt and pulled her in close. "Not even if you're the one I'm daydreaming about?"

"Why," Emma said, her fingers already moving below Aubrey's T-shirt, "would you daydream about me when I'm right here?"

Their lips met, sticks dropping to the ground as they wrapped their arms around each other. Aubrey smiled into the kiss. Emma's confidence and comfort with her own sensuality was increasing by the day and it was so easy for Aubrey to melt into every kiss, every touch.

She had a feeling kissing Emma in high school would have been nothing like this.

"We need to keep playing before I take your clothes off right here on this field." Aubrey slid her hands down Emma's body, reaching around to grab her butt.

"What makes you think I'd stop you?"

"I feel like I've created a sex monster."

Emma grinned wickedly. "Not created. Unleashed."

"As long as I'm the only one who knows about it."

"Hey," Emma said, kissing Aubrey softly. "I'm yours. And only yours."

Aubrey hugged Emma tightly, pressing her head to her chest. She ran her fingers through Emma's hair.

"As much as I'd love to stay right here," Emma said, pulling away to look up at Aubrey, "I'm afraid you may have unleashed another monster. And that monster really wants to slam some balls into the goal while Franklin Prescott's newest assistant coach critiques me."

"As you wish." Aubrey kissed her forehead.

"Wait, one more thing." Emma pressed her hand against Aubrey's chest. "You're not going to sleep with any of your players, right?"

"Emma! God, no!" Aubrey shook her head, horrified at the thought. "Why would you—oh, for fuck's sake." She glared at Emma, who was smiling innocently. "Not funny."

"Just making sure I'm the only younger woman you're interested in," she said sweetly.

"You're the only woman I'm interested in, period."

"Good." Emma nodded. "Keep it that way."

And then she was off, sprinting down the field in search of a ball to dribble.

Aubrey watched her, the head full of dark-red hair bouncing with each step Emma took, her body nondescript beneath Aubrey's baggy sweats. There was a freedom in Emma's movements, an unburdened happiness as she darted around the field. She cheered for herself after she sunk the ball into the goal, then looked back at Aubrey, triumphantly raising the stick over her head with a grin that would melt any leftover fear or worry between them.

"I plan on it," Aubrey said into the breeze.

EPILOGUE

Five months later

A cloud of flour momentarily blinded Emma. She blinked, confused, then looked down at the stainless steel countertop. The cupcake batter she was working on—crème brûlée flavored, a custom order for a fortieth birthday—had its correct amount of flour and was whirring gently in the mixer. She hadn't added flour, didn't need to, so the flour bomb definitely hadn't come from her.

To her left, Viv was viciously punching flour into a circle of dough. Little puffs rose up, nothing like the blast that had pulled Emma from her daydreams.

"Head in the clouds again, I see," Viv teased. "Or, should I say, head in the glass?"

"Very funny. Where'd all the flour come from?"

Viv nodded to the space between them. Sure enough, a pile of flour sat on the counter. "Bag slipped from my hands."

She didn't need to say "again," though she could have. Viv's clumsiness was a standard feature of mornings at Dough Mama. Emma had been shocked by it at first, but grew accustomed to it quickly, since Viv couldn't get through a day without creating some kind of doughy disaster.

"I was thinking about using some of that edible gold leaf for the cupcakes," Emma said, eyeing the batter spinning away in the industrial mixer. After two and a half months, she wasn't yet used to the "bigness" of working at the bakery. When she baked at home, she followed regular recipes and ended up with servings for, at the most, twenty-four. But here, everything was extra. That cupcake order? It was for one hundred. Last week, Emma and Viv had tag-teamed a cake order that had requested four individual sheet cakes, each to serve thirty people.

"I like that idea. And I know you don't like the edible gold leaf, but I think it plays nicely with the flavoring of the cupcakes."

Emma sighed as she measured out cornstarch for the pastry cream that would be piped inside the cupcakes. "I just like simple decorations."

"And most of our customers do, too." Viv began cleaning up her flour mountain. "But part of what we do—"

"Is making others happy." Emma rolled her eyes playfully. "I know. You don't have to tell me that every day."

"Oh, but I do." Viv winked at her and walked through the swinging door into the front of the bakery.

After Emma's first semester at Pennbrook had come to a close, she'd made the difficult decision to cut her hours at Cornerstone and rediscover her passion for baking for people other than herself and her family and friends. She'd made the transition in late May, and spent the summer getting up at four a.m. to work for four hours at Dough Mama, then dashed the two blocks to Cornerstone, where she usually worked until one or two in the afternoon. Sadie and Genesis had been so happy Emma wasn't fully quitting that they were willing to do whatever they could with her schedule. So far, it wasn't the worst. Emma was tired by the time she finished work, but she had a perfect amount of afternoon time to sneak in a nap before meeting up with Aubrey in the evening.

And those evenings…Emma smiled, certain her face had that dreamy expression it took on whenever she thought about Aubrey.

Their relationship was nearly six months old and still held the excitement of their first night together. Simply put: Emma could not get enough of Aubrey. Lucky for her, Aubrey felt the same way. But it wasn't just their physical connection that kept them close. It was something much deeper and more involved, something neither of them yet dared name. Aubrey joked it was all because she was Emma's first, but Emma knew the joking was a deflection away from the intensity of her feelings—something Aubrey was still getting used to.

For Emma, showing Aubrey that she wanted her, adored her, and respected her was second nature. It was the easiest thing Emma had ever done, the least complicated journey her life had taken her on. While she preferred to spend all her time with Aubrey, Emma made sure they spent time apart with their own friends. Nevertheless, Emma couldn't remember the last time she'd slept in her room at Liam's house. Liam often joked that Emma should start paying Aubrey rent, since she spent more time there than at his house. "Then again," he'd said, "you never paid rent here."

Moving in together—officially, not just in the "we spend every night together" way that they'd been doing since the beginning of April—felt like a matter of when, not if. It was another topic they circled around.

There was no rush. Emma knew that.

She was just completely crazy about Aubrey Glass and sometimes still couldn't believe that Aubrey felt the same way about her.

"Emma," Viv said, sticking her head into the back room. "You have a visitor."

Emma glanced at the clock. Right on time. She dusted off her hands on her apron and flipped off the mixer before making her way out into the bakery proper.

There, in all her sweaty, post morning field hockey practice glory, stood Aubrey. She was grinning from ear to ear, her tanned face glowing with excitement.

"Hi," she said. Such a little word, but the voice, the tone, the promise: It was everything.

"Hey." Emma walked around the counter and gave her a quick kiss. "Hungry? How was practice?"

"Yes, and it was good." Aubrey wrinkled her nose. "Actually, a couple of the sophomores were extra annoying today."

Emma leaned over the counter and grabbed the bag she'd packed an hour ago. "Wanna sit outside and tell me about it?"

Aubrey's eyes lit up at the sight of the paper bag. "Cinnamon twists? God, I lo—"

Emma simply smiled, used to the way Aubrey cut herself off before letting her truth tumble out into the space between them. She didn't need to say it; Emma knew what love felt like, how it grew between the cracks other people had created, how it settled over your skin in the middle of the night and slipped into your lungs, burrowing next to your heart, when the sun rose.

Aubrey would say it when she was ready. That much, Emma knew for certain.

They sat on the bench outside of Dough Mama. It wasn't as hot as it had been over the last couple of days, and if the clouds had anything to say about it, there would definitely be a storm later. Emma felt the familiar dance of arousal deep within her. A thunderstorm and Aubrey—specifically, *naked* Aubrey—sounded like the perfect end to the day.

After Aubrey ate half of the cinnamon twist, she leaned over and kissed Emma. She tasted of everything—literally every single thing—Emma loved.

"I have news," Aubrey said, her eyes sparkling.

"More Pennbrook drama?" Emma wiggled her eyebrows. The professorial gossip circuit had been *lit* that summer, with Sadie feeding a constant stream of info to Aubrey, Emma, and Genesis. Emma couldn't wait for classes to start in a few weeks so she could get her boots on the ground and try to get some of the gossip firsthand.

"Not today." Aubrey leaned forward and rooted through the backpack at her feet. When she sat up, she handed Emma a glossy magazine.

"Aubrey," she said, excitement pouring through her voice. "Is this it?"

Aubrey nodded. "Page seventeen."

Emma wasted no time in flipping through *Sapphisms* until she landed on page seventeen. There, in black and white, was her girlfriend's name, typed beneath the title of her first published story: "Bold and Broken Desires."

Emma hopped off the bench, unable to prevent herself from jumping up and down in excitement. She held the magazine over her head like a trophy.

"This is absolutely amazing!"

"Emma," Aubrey said, laughing, "it's not that big of a deal."

She dropped back onto the bench. "It's a huge deal. This is—it's your dream, Aubrey. And you brought it back to life."

Aubrey nodded and looked away, but she took Emma's hand and held it tightly. Emma leaned in and rested her head on Aubrey's shoulder. Over the months, she'd come to learn more about the woman who had broken so much of Aubrey, so her emotional response made perfect sense. Here, on a weathered wooden bench on Ivy Avenue, wasn't the place for Aubrey to move through those feelings.

"Let's celebrate later," Emma said. "And don't argue with me. This—you—deserve to be celebrated."

"Months ago, I would have argued."

"Believe me, I know. Look how far you've come." Emma smiled. "Look how far *we've* come."

"You make everything better," Aubrey said quietly. "Thank you for being you."

Emma felt a tightness in her throat and willed it away. As much as she loved Aubrey Glass, she was not about to cry right then and there, no matter how deeply and warmly her words settled within.

"I'd love to sit here all day with you," Emma said, sitting up. "But I've got another hour to go and a massive batch of crème brûlée cupcakes to finish."

"And then you're heading to Cornerstone?"

"Yes, till one." Emma looked up at the sky. The storm, she hoped, would hold off until later.

"Perfect." Aubrey brushed a flyaway hair from Emma's cheek. "I'm meeting with Dr. Jory at noon. Come over when you're done with work?"

At the mention of Kate Jory, Emma's pride swelled up all over again. Aubrey had decided to begin her master's in literature—finally following her true passion—in the spring semester, wanting to wait until she had her first coaching season under her belt. Secretly, Emma loved the image of them holed up at the library, tucked into a corner, both deep in their studies.

"I wouldn't dream of being anywhere else," she said.

Aubrey's face lit up again as she grinned and leaned in to kiss Emma. Moments later, she was off, heading to her apartment to shower before making her way to Pennbrook.

Emma watched her walk away, feeling the full bloom of love spreading through her limbs.

All her dreams had come to life, those she'd known and those she'd barely imagined, in the shape of a woman named Aubrey Glass.

"Who knew it would be you?" Emma whispered. Satisfied with the promise of later, and of endless days to come, she walked back into Dough Mama.

More Titles from Bella Books

Hunter's Revenge – Gerri Hill
978-1-64247-447-3 | 276 pgs | paperback: $18.95 | eBook: $9.99
Tori Hunter is back! Don't miss this final chapter in the acclaimed Tori Hunter series.

Integrity – E. J. Noyes
978-1-64247-465-7 | 28 pgs | paperback: $19.95 | eBook: $9.99
It was supposed to be an ordinary workday...

The Order – TJ O'Shea
978-1-64247-378-0 | 396 pgs | paperback: $19.95 | eBook: $9.99
For two women the battle between new love and old loyalty may prove more dangerous than the war they're trying to survive.

Under the Stars with You – Jaime Clevenger
978-1-64247-439-8 | 302 pgs | paperback: $19.95 | eBook: $9.99
Sometimes believing in love is the first step. And sometimes it's all about trusting the stars.

The Missing Piece – Kat Jackson
978-1-64247-445-9 | 250 pgs | paperback: $18.95 | eBook: $9.99
Renee's world collides with possibility and the past, setting off a tidal wave of changes she could have never predicted.

An Acquired Taste – Cheri Ritz
978-1-64247-462-6 | 206 pgs | paperback: $17.95 | eBook: $9.99
Can Elle and Ashley stand the heat in the *Celebrity Cook Off* kitchen?

Printed in the USA
CPSIA information can be obtained
at www.ICGtesting.com
JSHW02135121052
63541JS00001B/2